NORTHWEST ANGLE

ALSO BY WILLIAM KENT KRUEGER

NORTHWEST ANGLE

A NOVEL

WILLIAM KENT KRUEGER

ATRIA BOOKS

New York   London   Toronto   Sydney   New Delhi

ATRIA BOOKS

A Division of Simon & Schuster, Inc.
1230 Avenue of the Americas
New York, NY 10020

First Atria Books hardcover edition August 2011

ATRIA BOOKS and colophon are trademarks of Simon & Schuster, Inc.

For information about special discounts for bulk purchases, please contact Simon & Schuster Special Sales at 1-866-506-1949 or business@simonandschuster.com.

The Simon & Schuster Speakers Bureau can bring authors to your live event. For more information or to book an event contact the Simon & Schuster Speakers Bureau at 1-866-248-3049 or visit our website at www.simonspeakers.com.

Designed by Davina Mock-Maniscalco

Manufactured in the United States of America

10 9 8 7 6 5 4 3 2 1

Library of Congress Cataloging-in-Publication Data

Krueger, William Kent.
 Northwest angle / William Kent Krueger. — 1st Atria Books hardcover ed.
  p. cm.
 1. O'Connor, Cork (Fictitious character)—Fiction. 2. Private investigators—Fiction. 3. Mystery fiction. gsafd 4. Suspense fiction. gsafd I. Title.
  PS3561.R766N67 2011
  813'.54—dc22   2011015331

ISBN 978-1-4391-5395-6
ISBN 978-1-4391-7216-2 (ebook)

For Morgan and Riley Buchholz,
two blessings who dropped from heaven into my heart.

ACKNOWLEDGMENTS

The Northwest Angle of Minnesota is an area remarkable in its geography, its beauty, and its people. I am indebted to those who live on the Angle, folks generous with their time, knowledge, and resources. I'm especially grateful to Debra Kellerman and Tony Wandersee, who own the Angle Inn Lodge on Oak Island. Better hosts or nicer people would be hard to find anywhere. I also extend a huge thanks to Tony Ebnet for an extraordinary day on Lake of the Woods that neither my wife nor I will ever forget. To those who live on the Northwest Angle or the Angle Islands, and to those who know the area well, I offer a caution when reading this novel, and a small apology. I have, of necessity, taken a few liberties with geography. Stump Island, for example, doesn't exist, but islands very like it do. I've tried to create the landscape necessary for the story without compromising the essential and marvelous reality of the Angle. I hope you understand.

A huge thanks to Erin Sullivan-Sutton of the Minnesota Department of Human Services, who gave me fine advice about adoption in Minnesota, and the ways in which a child's welfare, common sense, and bureaucratic requirements might work in harmony to achieve great good.

To the Powassin family of Windigo Island: Thank you for

inspiring Amos Powassin, a character who became very dear to my heart while I wrote this story.

To my agent, Danielle Egan-Miller, and her associates, Joanna MacKenzie, Lauren Olson, Shelbey Campbell, and Alec McDonald, my deepest thanks for helping to keep my worst tendencies as a storyteller in firm check, and for providing such sound direction in the revisions of this novel.

To the team at Atria—my editor, Sarah Branham, my publicist, David Brown, and the marvelous folks in the art department who create the stunning design of my books: I can never thank you enough for all that you do.

Finally, a tip of my hat to the Java Train, a lovely island of community, creativity, and occasional chaos, where I always find a warm welcome and a clean table for my work.

AUTHOR'S NOTE

On July 3, 1999, a cluster of thunderstorms developed in the Black Hills area of South Dakota and began to track to the northeast. On the morning of July 4, something phenomenal occurred with this storm system, something monstrous. At the edge of western Minnesota, the storm clouds gathered and exploded, creating what would become one of the most destructive derechos ever to sweep across this continent.

A derecho is a unique storm system, a bow-shaped formation of towering black clouds that generate straight-line winds of hurricane force. The derecho that formed on July 4 barreled across northern Minnesota. In the early afternoon of that Independence Day, its hellish winds, clocked at over a hundred miles an hour, struck the Boundary Waters Canoe Area Wilderness, a land so beautiful it's as near to heaven as you're likely to find anywhere on this earth. The storm damaged nearly half of the wilderness, toppling millions of trees, leaving whole hillsides barren of life. It killed one camper and trapped and injured dozens of others.

After it left Minnesota, the storm veered across the border into Ontario, Canada, and continued its destructive sweep to the east. It slammed into the state of New York and then into New England. It traveled out to sea, turned, and came at South

Carolina. The system, though weakened, continued its destruction until it finally fell apart over the Gulf of Mexico. By then, it had traveled nearly six thousand miles, the longest storm track of its kind ever recorded in North America.

I have always known that such a storm would play a part in one of my stories. This is the story.

PROLOGUE

He woke long before it was necessary, had wakened in this way for weeks, troubled and afraid. A dull illumination came through the houseboat window into the cabin he shared with his son. Not light exactly. More the promise of light. False dawn, Cork O'Connor knew.

He threw back the thin sheet, slipped quietly from his bunk, and stepped into the long central hallway of the houseboat. The air was still, which was odd on the vast lake where they lay anchored. No sound of birds either, no early morning chatter, and that, too, was strange. He walked down the hallway, past the room where his sister-in-law and her husband slept, past the rooms of his two daughters, onto the stern deck with its swim platform. He stood at the railing, looking across water as black as engine grease. The moon hadn't set yet but was so low and wan in the western sky that what light it gave was almost useless. There were stars, so many they felt like a weight pressing down on him. East, where dawn was still more dream than reality, he could see the dimmest outline of an island against a gray that ghosted along the horizon.

He lowered his head and stared at the water.

He should have been happy. He'd planned this vacation with happiness as the goal, and not his happiness alone. He'd conceived of this family gathering, bringing close to him everyone

he loved, in order to make them happy, too. They hadn't been together, all of them, in almost two years. Not since Jo had been
laid to rest in the cemetery in Aurora. In his imagining, the
gathering would be the ticket to finding happiness again—his
and theirs—and the houseboat would be the way. But like the
false dawn, the trip had promised something it had yet to deliver, and day after day, he found himself waking troubled and
restless.

The problem was simple. He'd always thought of his family
as if they were part of a tree he'd planted long ago. The tree had
grown and flourished, and just being in its shade had been such
a great joy. But it seemed to him that, with Jo's death, the leaves
had begun to fall away—his daughters gone to lives of their own
and his son soon to follow—and he was afraid that, no matter
what he did to save it, the tree would die. An irrational fear, he
knew, but there it was, pressing hard upon his heart, whispering
to him darkly in these lonely moments.

He heard a loud yawn behind him. Uncertain if his face
might give away his concern, he didn't turn.

"Dad?" his son asked from the houseboat doorway. "We're
going fishing, aren't we?"

"You betcha, Stephen."

"Good. I'll get dressed."

When he was alone again, Cork took a deep breath, pulled
himself together, and turned from the black water to meet
the day.

At his back, his fear went on whispering.

ONE

Later, when it no longer mattered, they learned that the horror that had come from the sky had a name: derecho.

At the time, all they knew was that the day had begun with deceptive calm. Rose was up early, though not as early as the men, who'd risen at first light and had taken the dinghy across the broad channel to fish. She made coffee and sat on the deck of the houseboat and said her daily prayers while a bright lemon sun rose above the lake and islands. She began with a prayer of thanksgiving for all she had—especially her husband and her family—then, as always, prayed mostly for the people who, in life, despaired. She prayed for those whom she knew personally and for the greater multitude she didn't. At last, she said her amen and gave herself over to the pure pleasure of the still morning.

Anne was up next and then Jenny, and the three women sat in deck chairs on the forward platform, sipping coffee, talking quietly, watching the sun crawl the sky, waiting for the men.

When she heard the dinghy's old outboard cutting through the morning calm, Rose got up and said, "I'll start the potatoes."

Anne stood up, too. "Let me give a hand, Aunt Rose."

"No," she said. "You and Jenny sit. Talk. It's what sisters should do. You almost never see each other these days."

She went to the galley to prepare breakfast. She planned to

roast potatoes with onions and red peppers and tomatoes. She thought she would scramble eggs with chives and cream cheese. She would slice melons and strawberries and toss them in a bowl with plenty of fat blueberries. And there would be, she was almost certain, fresh fish to fry.

She heard the men as they pulled alongside and tied up to the houseboat and clambered aboard. She heard Cork say, "Beer and pretzels," and she hoped he wasn't talking about breakfast.

Mal stepped into the galley, smiling hugely, and held up a stringer full of fat yellow perch. "The hunter home from the hill," he said.

"You shot them?" Rose replied. "Not very sporting."

Mal kissed her cheek and started toward the sink.

"Uh-uh," she said. "Those get cleaned on deck." She took him gently and turned him toward the door. "When you have them filleted, bring them in and I'll fry them up."

Stephen came in and went straight to the canister Rose had filled with chocolate chip cookies the day before. He took a handful and said, "Okay, Aunt Rose?"

"Don't spoil your breakfast."

"Are you kidding? I could eat a moose. Can I have some milk, too?"

He left with the cookies and a plastic tumbler filled to the brim. Moments later, Rose heard him talking with his sisters on deck and laughing.

The rented houseboat had a table large enough for all of them to gather around, and they ate amid the clatter of flatware against plates and the lively symphony of good conversation. Anne and Jenny offered to clean up, and they gave Stephen a hard time until he agreed to help. Mal showered, then Cork, and afterward both men settled down to a game of cribbage. The kids finished the dishes, put on their swimsuits, and dove into the lake. Rose set a deck chair in the shade under the forward awning of the houseboat. She sat down to read, but her mind quickly began to wander.

Nearly two years had passed since Jo had been lost in the Wyoming Rockies. Nearly two years dead. And Rose stilled missed her sister. Her deep grieving had ended, but there was a profound sense of something lacking in her life. She had taken to calling this the Great Empty. The kids—"kids" she thought them, though Jenny was twenty-four, Anne twenty-one, and Stephen almost fifteen—splashed and laughed in the water, yet she knew that they felt the Great Empty, too. Cork never talked about his own feelings, and Rose understood that the avoidance itself was probably a sign he was afflicted as well. She wished she knew how to help them all heal fully. In the days when he'd been a priest, Mal had often dealt with death and its aftermath, and he advised her that healing came in its own time and the best you could hope for was to help ease the pain along the way.

"And does everyone heal in the end?" she'd asked her husband.

"Not everyone," he'd said. "At least, not in my experience."

She watched the kids in the water and Cork at the table slapping down his cards, and she breathed in the pine-scented air above that distant, isolated lake, and she prayed, "Let us heal, Lord. Let us all be whole again."

In the early afternoon, Cork said, "It's time, Jenny."

She looked up from the table where she'd been writing, put the pencil in the crease between the pages, closed her notebook, and stood.

"How long will it take?" she asked.

"Less than an hour, if we go directly. But today we're going to make a little side trip."

"Where?"

"You'll see."

Her father liked mysteries, large and small. She understood it was part of what drew him through life, the need to find answers. In a way, it was also what drove her, but they went about it differently. He'd been a cop most of his life and now he was a PI. She, on the other hand, was a writer.

Stephen came from the galley, one hand filled with potato chips. "Can I go?"

"Not this time," his father said. "Jenny and I have things to discuss."

Things to discuss, she thought. *Oh, God.*

"Ah, come on," Stephen said.

Cork shook his head. "Oz has spoken. But if you want to help, go fill the motor on the dinghy with gas."

"I didn't say I wanted to help. I said I wanted to go."

"And now you're going to help," Cork said. He turned to Jenny. "Wear your swimsuit and bring your camera."

"Why?"

"You'll see."

Mysteries, she thought with a silent sigh. But maybe, if they were interesting enough, they would keep her father away from the things he wanted to discuss.

Early September. The air thick on the lake and the sky a weighty blue. The weather, he'd been told, was unusual for that time of year so far north. Hot beyond anyone's memory. Usually by the end of August fall was already solidly in the air. But not this year. The intense heat of the afternoon was bearable only because of the wind generated by the dinghy speeding over smooth water.

Though they were in Canada, Cork knew he could just about throw a stone onto U.S. territory. They were on the Lake of the Woods, a body of water roughly eighty miles long and sixty miles wide, containing over fourteen thousand islands. That's what he'd been told in Kenora, anyway. The lake straddled the U.S.-Canadian border. Border? Cork shook his head, thinking how easily that international marker was crossed on this lake. There was no line on the water to delineate one nation from the other. Kitchimanidoo, the Creator, had made the land a boundless whole. It was human beings who felt the need for arbitrary divisions and drew the lines. Too often, he thought, in human blood.

He held the tiller of the little Evinrude outboard, guiding the dinghy southwesterly across broad, open water toward a gathering of islands humped along the horizon. In the half hour since they'd left the houseboat, he hadn't exchanged a word with Jenny. Which, he strongly suspected, was just fine with her.

The lake was beautiful and, like so many things of beauty, deceptive. The water that day was like glass. The vast size of the lake suggested depth, but Cork knew that beneath the tranquil surface lay reefs and rocks that in the blink of an eye could slit a hull or chew the blades off a prop. He'd been using GPS to follow the main channel between the islands and had been keeping a good speed. But south of Big Narrows he swung the boat west out of the channel, slowed to a crawl, and entered an archipelago composed of dozens of islands, large and small. The shorelines were rocky, the interiors covered with tall pine and sturdy spruce and leafy poplar. Cork eased the boat patiently along, studying the screen of the Garmin GPS mounted to the dash, into which he'd downloaded a program for Lake of the Woods. The water was the color of weak green tea, and he told Jenny, who sat in the bow, to keep her eyes peeled for snags that the GPS couldn't possibly indicate. After fifteen minutes of careful navigation, he guided the dinghy up to the rocky edge of a small island. He eased the bow next to a boulder whose top rose from the water like the head of a bald man, and he cut the engine.

"Grab the bow line and jump ashore," he told Jenny.

She leaped to the boulder, rope in hand.

"Can you tie us off?"

She slid a few feet down the side of the boulder and leaped nimbly to shore, where she tied the boat to a section of rotting fallen timber.

Cork stepped to the bow, leaped to the boulder, then to shore. "Got your camera?" he asked.

Jenny patted her belt where her Canon hung in a nylon case.

"Okay," Cork said. "Let's take a hike."

The island was nearly bare of vegetation and was dominated by a rock formation that rose conelike at the center. Cork led the way along the rock slope, following the vague suggestion of a trail that gradually spiraled upward around the cone. All around them lay a gathering of islands so thick that no matter which way Cork looked they appeared to form a solid shoreline. Between the islands ran a confusing maze of narrow channels.

"Where are we?" Jenny asked.

"Someplace not many folks know about. Probably the only ones who do are Shinnob."

He used the word that was shorthand for the Anishinaabeg, the First People, who were also known as Ojibwe or Chippewa. Anishinaabe blood ran through Cork and, therefore, through his daughter Jenny.

"On a map, this island doesn't have a name," Cork said. "But Shinnobs call it Neejawnisug."

"What does it mean?"

"I'll tell you in a minute."

They reached the top, which was crowned by a great white stone that looked as if it had been cleaved by an ax. The southern side was rounded and pocked, but the north side was a solid face ten feet tall. It lay in full sunlight, golden, and when Jenny saw that glowing face of rock, her eyes went large.

"Pictographs," she said. "They're beautiful, Dad. Do you know what they mean?"

Cork studied the figures painted in ocher that covered the face of the stone.

"Henry Meloux told me they're a kind of invocation to Kitchimanidoo for safety. He said the Anishinaabeg who drew them were being pursued by Dakota and had come to hide. They left the children here, and that's why they call it Neejawnisug.

It means 'the children.' They left the women, too, and went off
to fight the enemy. They trusted this place because there are so
many islands and so many channels that it's almost impossible
to find your way here."

"You found it easily enough."

"When I was sixteen, Henry brought me. *Giigiwishimowin*," Cork said.

"Your vision quest," Jenny interpreted.

"By then it was no longer a common practice among the
Ojibwe," Cork said. "But Henry insisted."

"Why here?"

"He never told me."

"Did you receive your vision?"

"I did."

Jenny didn't ask about her father's dream vision, and if she
had, he probably wouldn't have told her.

"Have you been here since?"

"Never."

"How did you find it so easily? I mean, after so many years?"

"I spent a long afternoon coming here with Henry. He made
me memorize every twist and turn."

"That had to be forty years ago. A long time to remember."

"You mean for an old man."

"I couldn't find my way back here."

"If it was important, I bet you could."

Jenny snapped photos of the drawings on the stone and, for a
long time, was silent. "And did Kitchimanidoo hide the children
successfully?" she finally asked.

"I don't know. Nor did Henry."

He could see her mind working, and that was one of the reasons he'd brought her. Unanswered questions were part of what
drove her. He was uncertain how to broach the other reason he'd
asked her to come.

"God, it's hot," Jenny said, looking toward the sun, which
baked them. "Not even a breath of wind."

"Dog days."

"Not technically," she said.

"Technically?" He smiled. "So when are dog days? Technically."

"According to the *Farmers' Almanac,* the forty days from July third through August eleventh."

He shook his head. "You're way too precise in your thinking. Your mom, she was the same way."

Jenny brought her gaze to bear on her father. "She was a lawyer. She had to be precise. Legal strictures. I'm a journalist. Lots of the same strictures apply." She looked away, down at the water a hundred feet below. "Mind if I take a dip before we go on?"

"No. Mind if I join you?"

They descended the cone and retraced their path to the boulder where the boat was secured. They'd worn their bathing suits under their other clothing, and they quickly stripped. Jenny slipped into the water first and Cork followed.

The lake had been warming all summer, but even so it still held a chill that was a wonderful relief to the heat of the day.

"So?" Cork said, in clumsy opening.

His daughter turned her head to the sky and closed her eyes and lay on her back, so that her ears were below the surface and she could pretend not to hear him.

"I just want to know one thing. And I know you can hear me."

"It starts with one thing," she said with her eyes still closed. "It ends up everything. That's how you operate."

"Old dog, old trick," he said, waited a moment, then repeated, "So?"

She righted herself, treaded water, and gave in. "All right, what do you want to know?"

"Are you going to marry him?"

"That's a complicated question."

"I think the question is fairly simple."

"Well, I can't answer it."

"Because of you or him?"

"It's a decision we're both involved in."

"You'd tell your mother," he said.

"She wouldn't put me on the rack."

"Have I?"

"You will if you don't get an answer."

"I suppose you've talked to Aunt Rose."

She didn't reply, but her silence itself gave him his answer.

"But you won't talk to me."

"There are things women understand, Dad."

"There are things fathers should be let in on. Look, I don't know why you can't give me a straightforward answer, and that's what concerns me."

"There are issues we need to settle first."

"Children?"

"Ah, children," she said, as if she suddenly understood. "That's why you brought me here to show me those pictographs. This is all about children, isn't it?"

"Not completely. But you indicated there are issues," he said. "And I'm betting that's one. He doesn't want them, does he?"

"Maybe it's me who doesn't."

"Is it?" Again, her silence was his answer. "You've been down this road before, Jenny."

"See? Right there." She lifted her arm and pointed an accusing finger at him. Water dripped from the tip in crystal pearls. "That's why I don't talk to you."

"It was only an observation."

"It was a criticism, and you know it."

"I didn't mean—"

"I'm finished swimming. Let's go."

He'd blown it. In his imagining, the discussion had gone differently, had ended with them understanding each other, touching heart to heart in the way they used to when she was much younger. Instead he watched her breaststroke away from him to the dinghy, leaving him feeling stupid and treading water.

They threaded their way out of the convoluted gathering of islands. Jenny sat rigid in the bow, fiercely giving him her back. As soon as they hit the open water of the main channel, he headed the dinghy again toward the southwest.

When he saw the sky there, he was, for a moment, stunned breathless.

"Dad?" Jenny said from the bow. She'd seen it, too, and she turned back to him, fear huge in her eyes.

"Good God Almighty," he whispered.

TWO

Rose was in the middle of rolling a piecrust. She'd promised pie for dessert that night, and the kids had volunteered to hunt for blueberries. Though it was late in the season, weeks past the normal time for harvesting berries, at every place the houseboat had anchored so far, they'd had luck with their picking. It had to do with the unusual heat, Rose speculated.

Behind her, Mal came into the galley and encircled her waist with his arms.

"They're finally gone," he said.

"Let me wash my hands." Rose lifted them so that he could see they were covered with flour.

"No time. They'll be back before you know it." He turned her, kissed her long but delicately, and said, "And besides, the smell of piecrust is very sexy."

They made love in their cabin. Afterward, she lay cradled in the crook of Mal's outstretched arm.

The houseboat was lovely, but there was no privacy. It was a rare pleasure to have the boat to themselves. There was something about this untamed country that stirred the wild in Rose. She smiled, thinking how odd it was to her now that before Mal had come into her life she'd seriously considered joining an order. When she first met him, he'd been a priest, a cleric stumbling in his belief and assigned to a small parish in the great

North Woods of Minnesota. Rose had fallen in love with him; terrible events had followed, events not his doing or hers, nor was their love the cause, but in the end, Mal had chosen to leave the priesthood. He hadn't turned his back on the Church. He'd simply opened his heart to Rose. Something she thanked God for every day.

Mal kissed her shoulder. "They'll be coming back soon."

"They're such good kids," she said.

"The best."

"They're grown now."

"Not quite, but growing."

"I remember when they were small. Yesterday, it seems."

"Nature of the beast. We all grow up." He spoke softly into her ear. "Do you miss them being small and needing you? Are you thinking we should try again ourselves?"

She smiled. "We just did."

"You know what I mean."

She knew. The thermometers. The graphs. And the specialists.

"I'm forty-four years old," she said. "I think at this point it's a miracle I'm willing to leave in God's hands. They'll be coming back soon. We should get up."

She moved to rise, but Mal held her down for a moment, gently.

"I love you, Rose," he said. "I'll give you anything in the world that I can."

He looked so deeply, so seriously into her eyes that her heart melted all over again. "You've already given me the best thing, sweetheart." And she kissed him a very long time to let him know how much she appreciated the gift that was his heart.

She dressed and stepped out onto the platform of the bow, looking north across the little bay to the tip of the island where Anne and Stephen had swum to search for blueberries. She didn't see them. *Still hunting,* she thought. Her husband came to her side, and they stood together, and then she turned and looked to the southwest.

She gave a little cry and said breathlessly, "Oh, Mal."

He looked there, too, and uttered in disbelieving horror, "Sweet Jesus."

The formation stretched from horizon to horizon, a mountain of dark cloud. The leading edge was rounded, like a bow drawn taut. Or, Cork thought later in his recollections, like a great plateau in the sky, shaped by forces so enormous he couldn't even begin to imagine the scope of their power. The monster rose from the earth itself, straight up tens of thousands of feet in a sheer, curving wall the color of sooted stone. Behind it, there was no sky, only that great unstoppable body of storm. Lightning rippled along the top of the formation and struck deep inside in angry flashes that made the cloud, in moments of brilliance, seem almost translucent. The great plateau of the storm swept toward them with unbelievable speed. Before it, the lake was a swell of turbulent water. Cork understood that in only a few minutes all hell would hit them, hit them there in the open in their flimsy dinghy.

He swung the tiller, and the boat dug a deep, curling trough in the green water. Jenny gripped the bow and bent low as if to make herself more aerodynamic, although it could have been that she was simply cowering in the shadow of what was about to strike. Cork shot back toward the narrow channel where, only a minute before, they'd emerged from the gathering of islands. The outer islands were small and provided little protection. He hoped there was enough time to get well inside the archipelago. Full throttle, he cut along channels where the possibility of submerged rocks had, earlier, made him proceed so carefully. Desperately, he scanned the shorelines ahead, searching for some inlet that might offer the hope of shelter.

The beast struck before he could make them safe.

* * *

They were in one of the wider channels. Jenny was looking frantically forward. Ahead and to the left, she saw a small landing between two outthrusts of stone. Before she could turn to tell her father, the wind hit her as if someone had swung a telephone pole. She flew forward and smacked her head against the prow. She was stunned but still fully aware of the danger and held to the gunwales for dear life. She fought her way back onto her seat, but an instant later the dinghy swung sharply right, and again she was almost thrown overboard.

"Dad!" she cried, turning her face into the raging face of the wind.

Her father was no longer at the tiller. The stern of the boat was empty. Without any hand on the throttle, the little kicker engine was winding down, threatening to die. Jenny bent low into the gale and clawed her way to the back of the dinghy. She grasped the tiller of the outboard and gave the engine gas and tried to bring the boat about and find her father. A useless maneuver, she quickly discovered. There was no way she could put the boat crosswind and not be swamped by the waves, enormous even in that channel. And if the waves didn't get her, the wind was strong enough to lift her, boat and all, and throw her easily against the cliff face that loomed to her right.

Then the rain hit, a downpour pushed horizontal by the fury, threatening to drown her.

She had no time to think. She simply fought to survive. She gave the boat full throttle, shot from the channel, and curled into the lee of the starboard island. A great pine toppled almost directly in her path, and she swerved; the hull scraped wood and the props cut branches. She shot forward, the wind cupped her, and the boat tipped; she swung left, and the wind was again at her back, waves sloshing over the stern. Across the channel where she now found herself, she spotted a beach of small rocks at the base of a tall outcropping capped with cedars. The opening was only slighter wider than the dinghy was long, but she launched the boat straight for it and onto the rocks of the tiny inlet. She heard the rending of the hull and the grind and pop as the propeller blades were sheared off by stone.

She leaped from the boat, and the wind immediately knocked her over. On all fours, she crawled into the shelter of the out-cropping. The island was forested with pines bent by the force of the wind, their crowns pushed almost parallel to the ground. She heard an explosion like a shotgun blast very close. A second later, she watched the trunk of a hundred-foot-tall pine snap in two. Rain continued in horizontal sheets. Mixed with it were hailstones that hit the beach like rocks from a slingshot. Jenny pressed against the solid body of the outcropping, grateful for the little haven. Then she heard a deafening crack directly above. In the next instant, a cedar that had crowned the outcrop fell. It hit near her feet. The whipping of its branches lashed her, and she pressed still harder to the wall.

Through the mesh of the cedar boughs, she could see the dinghy. Each sweep of the waves forced it higher and higher onto the rocks and more and more into the rage of the wind. It was finally lifted off the ground, outboard and all, and thrown a dozen yards, where it slammed against a shattered pine trunk and lay in a crumpled mess.

Thunderclaps came one after another and with them the explosion of tree trunks, until the sound was like the discharge of batteries in a heated battle. Rain fell so thick that everything beyond the inlet became a blur. Water poured over her, not only out of the sky but also down the face of the rock, and she sat helpless in the deluge.

A quarter of an hour into the storm, she saw movement near the broken hull of the boat. Frantic motion. She thought it must be someone caught in the storm, and for a brief, almost joyful moment, she hoped it was her father. She rose almost fully upright and saw that it wasn't a human being at all but a gray wolf running round and round in blind terror. As she watched, a broken section of evergreen as large as a canoe fell from the sky and crushed the animal. Jenny crouched again and tried to hold to hope for her father's safety.

For nearly an hour, the world was in upheaval, then as suddenly as it had come the storm passed, the rain turned to drizzle, and the lake lay in a stillness like death.

Jenny stood slowly. The water had calmed. Far to the west, she saw blue sky.

She looked inland at the island where she was now stranded and gasped. The place was devastated, blasted, the forest that had covered it nearly obliterated. The great majority of the trees had been toppled and their trunks lay in jumbled masses on the ground. The ragged tops of stumps jutted up among them, the wood deep at their center exposed, white as bone.

Except in photos of war, Jenny had never seen such destruction. She edged her way from behind the fallen cedar and crossed the rocky beach of the inlet. The smashed boat was pinned beneath a long section of pine that she couldn't have budged even if she'd wanted to.

At her back, she heard a pitiful whining. And she remembered the wolf. She made her way to where she'd seen the animal go down and began pulling away evergreen branches. Near her hands came a sudden, vicious snarling, and she drew back. More carefully, she removed the remaining cover.

The gray wolf lay under the broken section of pine trunk that had plummeted from the sky. His eyes were milky red. His mouth, as he snapped at her, was a bloody foaming. His front legs fought for purchase, but his hindquarters were absolutely motionless.

Jenny guessed that the poor creature's back had been broken. Probably his insides were a mess. She knew what she should do but couldn't bring herself to do it.

"I'm sorry," she said and turned away.

She stared across the channel at the maze of islands and realized with a note of panic that she had no idea from which way she'd come. Everything looked the same, none of it familiar. In which channel had she lost her father? If she began to look for him, where would that be?

"Dad!" she screamed. "Dad, where are you?"

Behind her the wolf let out a groan that ended in a high-pitched cry. She could hear his painful, labored breathing.

"Dad!" she yelled again, so loud it threatened to tear her throat.

The only sound in return came from the suffering wolf at her back.

Tears welled up, of frustration, of fear. She wiped them away and turned around. She found a rock roughly the size and shape of a football, lifted it, and walked to where the wolf lay pinned.

All her life her father had pressed upon her the responsibility—any feeling person's responsibility—for a suffering animal. She looked down into the eyes of the wolf and saw clearly the terror and the agony. She said, "I'm sorry, *ma'iingan*," using, for some reason she couldn't have explained, the Ojibwe name for the animal.

When it was done, she threw the bloodied stone into the lake and washed her hands clean, then stood at the water's edge and stared at the confusion of islands. Out there somewhere was her father. And somewhere, too, were Anne and Stephen and Rose and Mal.

She spoke a prayer: "God, let them be all right. Let them all be alive."

THREE

The night before, they'd anchored the houseboat near an island in a huge area of open water north of French Portage. On the chart, the island was roughly crescent-shaped. They'd tied up off the northwestern tip so there would be nothing to block the cooling evening wind or their view of the sunset. The island was heavily wooded, with a steep ridge along its spine. At the other tip of the island, a quarter mile across the curve of a narrow bay, was a small beach where Anne and Stephen had swum in search of blueberries.

Mal had his field glasses out. He looked across a broad span of open water in the direction of the base of the blue-black wall of cloud sweeping toward them, gobbling sky as it came.

"The waves are at least eight feet high," he said. "The wind out there must be incredible. We've got to get into the shelter of the island, Rose."

"We've got to get the kids," she said.

"We'd never make it. Pull up the stern anchor," he ordered. "I'll loose the bow line."

He started away, but she grabbed his arm. "We can't just leave them out there, Mal."

"Rose, this boat is nothing more than a cigar box on a couple of aluminum cans. If we don't get into the lee of that ridge, we're dead. What help would we be to the kids then?"

"But Stephen and Annie," she protested.

"Pull up that anchor!"

She did as he told her, but her eyes seldom left the far tip of the island where the kids had gone. She was terrified, her throat closed so tightly she could barely swallow. Which didn't matter because her mouth was suddenly and absolutely parched. Without thinking, she prayed as she hauled in the anchor line, prayed desperately. Mal quickly finished drawing in the bow line and jumped to the control station in the main room. Rose joined him there. He kicked the two outboards into action and started the houseboat toward the shoreline that lay in the shadow of the island's ridge. The craft was ungainly on the water. It moved at a crawl across the lake surface, which had turned black with the shadow of what was looming.

Then Rose saw them. Stephen and Anne. They stood on the beach across the little bay, dressed only in their swimsuits, Stephen holding the nylon bag he'd taken for the blueberries they would pick. Rose knew they could see what was coming and could see that the houseboat was leaving them. She raced from the cabin onto the bow platform and stood at the rail and tried to call out to them, to explain and to warn them to seek their own shelter. But the monster wind was suddenly on her, all around her and over her, and her words were lost in the howling.

She was thrown against the railing. The force knocked the breath out of her and she fell. For a minute, she was stunned and felt only the great heave of the decking beneath her.

When she could think, she realized they were in the lee of the island, which had been Mal's intent. The ridge offered modest protection. Even though the wind was still fierce, she could now stand. She felt the pontoons scrape rock. Mal left the control station, and a moment later, Rose saw him at the stern, tossing the anchor. Then he ran through the houseboat and burst through the door to the forward deck, where she stood. Without a word, he grabbed the bow line and leaped into the shallow water. The houseboat had begun to swing sideways in the wind, moving away from the island. As Rose watched, the anchor line started to play out quickly. Mal splashed ashore and secured the bow rope to the horizontal trunk of a fallen tree. He dashed to the stern line, lifted the anchor, and dropped it between two rocks that jutted from the shore. Just as he finished, the lines played out fully and snapped taut. Mal leaped into the waves, waded to the steps of the swim platform located aft, and climbed aboard. He stumbled into the cabin, where Rose met him.

"Are you all right?" she said.

"Yes. You?"

"I'm fine." She looked toward the two rope lines pulled stiff and vibrating from the pressure. "Will they hold?"

"God, I hope so."

She turned to the windows that looked north toward the other end of the island. The little bay was a rage of tall white-caps, and the beach where Anne and Stephen had stood was flooded from the surge.

"Lord," she prayed aloud, "let them be all right."

The houseboat rocked and the lines jerked as if tied to wild bulls, but for the moment they held. Mal pulled out life jackets, and they put them on and huddled together in the cabin. Rain fell in sheets so thick that everything across the bay became obscured. Hail beat on the roof in a great din. Pines along the crest of the island's ridge bent as easily as prairie grass and began to snap. Soon their trunks littered the slope below.

After nearly an hour of battering, the wind finally won. The stern anchor line broke and the bow line followed. The houseboat began to drift rapidly into the bay.

"What now?" Rose said.

"Get to shore," Mal told her and pushed her toward the cabin door.

"But the boat—"

"Forget the boat, Rose! Get moving!"

They went out onto the bow platform. Twenty yards of angry water separated them from the shore, and the distance was rapidly increasing. Waves swept over the decking under their feet and rain peppered them hard as pebbles.

Inexplicably Mal stripped himself of his life jacket. "Take my hand!" he cried.

She did and they hit the water together. She was surprised to find that her feet touched the rocky lake bottom, but they didn't stay there long. The next wave lifted her and threatened to carry her out. Mal gripped her hand. Freed from the buoyancy of his own vest, he was able to hold himself against the waves, and he pulled her with him as he slogged to shore. They grabbed on to the pair of rocks where the stern anchor still sat wedged, and they watched the houseboat spin into the bay. A limb the size and thickness of an elephant's leg flew from the island and crashed through the window next to the helm station. In the next instant, with a sinking heart, Rose saw the houseboat suddenly rise up in the grip of the storm. The windward pontoon cleared the water, and the boat began to flip.

Then a miracle happened. Or what, afterward, Rose always thought of as a miracle. As quickly as it had come, the wind died. With a great splash, the lifted pontoon fell back onto the water, and the houseboat continued a placid drift into the lake.

In the quiet that followed, Mal said, "Rose, I'm hurt."

"Where?"

"My ankle. I turned it when we came in."

"Let me see."

She helped him lift his leg from the water. He wore shorts, and his feet, like hers, were bare. She saw the swelling immediately.

"Does it hurt much?"

"Like hell. But that's not important. You need to get the boat, and we need to find the kids."

She looked toward the open water. The houseboat was already a hundred yards distant and drifting farther as she watched.

"I'll be back," she said.

"I'm counting on it." He managed a brief smile.

She hated to leave him but knew he was right. She kissed him once, then began to swim.

FOUR

It had been a hard year and she'd needed this vacation. She'd been content to let her father and Mal control where they were and where they were going. Lake of the Woods? Fine. One of the largest lakes in North America? No problem. In the middle of fucking nowhere? Terrific. No, I don't want to know anything about the charts or the lake channels or the islands more numerous than the stars. I just want to relax.

Until now, Jenny thought, staring at the lumps of wilderness she could see from the rocky beach where she stood. Now she wished she'd listened and taken note.

Great journalist I am, she thought bitterly. *All that useful information, in one ear and out the other.*

She had no idea where she was on that vast lake. No idea which direction she'd been going with her father or from which direction they'd come. She'd been too deep in her own goddamn worries to let go and be a real part of the gathering.

And now she was lost. And her father was out there somewhere. Lost, too?

She almost thought, *Lost forever?* but wouldn't let herself go there. They weren't lost, none of them. Not her father or Anne or Stephen or Rose or Mal. They were somewhere out there, safe.

"But that's exactly what you thought about Mom, and she's dead."

She said this out loud, startled at the sound of her voice in all that numbed stillness. The effect was devastating. Her legs went weak, and she sat down on the little beach and didn't feel at all the sharpness of the stones beneath her. She stared dumbly at the water, which was calm now and choked with debris.

Yeah, she'd hoped along with everyone else—*believed* along with everyone else—that after her mother disappeared she would be found and she would be safe. But it hadn't been that way. All their hoping, all their praying, all their believing had been in vain. From almost the moment she'd vanished, her mother had been dead.

"Dad," she said hopelessly, speaking toward the devastation of the lake. "Annie. Stephen."

And then she began to cry, deep, racking sobs that went on and on.

In the end, she had no choice but to pull herself together. She wiped away her tears, forced her legs to lift her upward, beat her brain into thinking clearly. She had no idea how widespread the devastation of the storm might be, but judging from the islands around her, all of which looked like they'd been at the epicenter of a nuclear blast, the area was large. The lake water was full of uprooted trees and shattered trunks and sheared off limbs and strips of bark. A boat trying to get through that mess would have to move at a snail's pace. It would be a long time before anybody got to her, if anybody ever did.

"Dad!" she tried again, calling his name a dozen times as she turned in a complete circle. She got nothing in return.

"You're alone, kiddo," she said to herself. "You've got only you."

She walked to the place where the dinghy lay under a fallen pine. She worked her way through the mesh of branch and needle and groped beneath the crumpled seat in the bow of the wreckage. Her fingers found wet nylon. She gripped the material and pulled it with her as she eased herself free.

The knapsack was stained with pine resin and pungent with the scent of evergreen. She dug inside and pulled out packages of cheese and crackers and some trail mix and two bottled waters, completely smashed and emptied of their contents. She found her camera intact, then her cell phone, which was also undamaged.

"Hey, girl, finally a little bit of luck," she said, as if it was someone else speaking to her.

She powered up the phone, and the display came on and told her the device was searching. After a minute, it gave up. No signal.

"Shit," she said and was tempted to add the phone to all the other crap in the water. Instead, she slid it back into the knapsack. And then some journalistic instinct kicked in and she brought out her digital camera, turned it on, and shot a full panorama of the destruction around her.

"Great for the documentary when they find your desiccated body," she said.

She reviewed the photos she'd just taken and accidentally went one farther back, to an earlier shot. And there was Aaron.

From the beginning, she'd had a bad feeling about this trip. Her father had proposed it, a rare gathering of family at summer's end. He'd just finished working a case involving a decades-old serial killing that had ended in the suicide of a wealthy man. She could tell it had affected him deeply, for reasons he wouldn't go into, but he'd been almost desperate to have the whole family together again. Anne had come home from her mission in El Salvador, Stephen from a summer of cowboying on Hugh Parmer's ranch in Texas, Mal and Aunt Rose up from Evanston. And from Iowa City, she and Aaron. Except that Aaron couldn't come right away. He was committed to teaching a poetry workshop at a conference in the Black Hills and couldn't get free until three days into the trip. The plan had been to pick him up at Young's Bay Landing on the Northwest Angle that afternoon.

She'd been worried about him. They'd been a couple for almost a year and, in June, had moved in together. She didn't know what to call him exactly. Friend? He was way more than that. Boyfriend? Oh, God, how teenager was that? Lover? Way too explicit. Partner? For the moment, yes, but they hadn't talked much about what was beyond the moment. Significant other? He was significant, sure, but what a clumsy epithet. So she'd simply refrained from calling him anything except Aaron. This was going to be the first time the family would meet him, and she was concerned. Things between her and Aaron hadn't been exactly smooth lately.

She looked across the littered water and wondered if he'd made it safely to the Northwest Angle before the storm swept through. She wondered if he was all right. And if he was, was he worried about her?

Or, she thought in a sudden acid moment of honesty, was he relieved?

At last she dropped the camera back into the knapsack, shouldered the bag, and turned to explore the island onto which fate had cast her.

The nearly total destruction made it impossible to go inland, so Jenny began to walk the shoreline. The water was shallow, the bottom mostly rock, and she moved easily, though carefully, over the irregular stones. The sun was out, as bright as ever, and the sky was a soft blue, as if no storm had ever crossed its placid face. To one degree or another, all the islands, those she could see anyway, showed the devastation of the storm. All except for one across the channel, a small island that was composed mostly of a single tall rock outcropping with a cliff facing the direction from which the storm had come. All the trees that stood in the lee of that rock rise were undamaged. As Jenny watched, a small brown animal, something weasel-like, swam to the shore, climbed out of the water, shook itself, and scampered into the undergrowth and trees.

She walked nearly half a mile, calling out her father's name every few minutes like a kind of distress signal, before she rounded the far end of the island. She'd seen nothing helpful, destruction everywhere.

"Will anyone ever come by here?" she wondered aloud.

She pretty well knew the answer. The man who'd rented them the houseboat in Kenora had told them that it was possible to motor among the islands for days and never see another soul. When Jenny had asked if he knew the Lake of the Woods well, he'd answered cryptically, "Nobody really knows this lake."

If the others were all right, would they come searching for her? Of course they would, but it wouldn't matter. They would have no idea where to look. Her father had been circumspect about their excursion on the way to Young's Bay Landing to pick up Aaron. He'd told her he wanted it to be something special between the two of them. The children in the pictographs, she understood now. His not very subtle way of asking about her own intentions in that regard. Well, it had probably seemed like a good idea to him at the time.

She looked up and saw a couple of bald eagles circling, searching in vain, she speculated, for a nest that no longer existed.

The island was narrow—generally only a couple of hundred yards wide—and humped with two hillocks of smooth, white rock, one near either end. The shoreline was pocked with little coves and inlets, now clogged with fallen timbers.

She looked up at the blazing sun and said, "At least it's hot. I won't freeze. And I have plenty of clean water, if I'm willing to risk a little giardia."

She was speaking of the parasite that, she knew, sometimes inhabited the water of the North Country and that, if ingested, could play hell with her digestive tract. But it was infinitely preferable to dying of thirst.

Food was a different matter. She hoped she was rescued before that became an issue. She was glad she'd had both a hearty breakfast and lunch.

As she moved up the other side of the island, Jenny caught sight of something in the interior. She shaded her eyes against the brilliant sunlight and squinted. It was a small cabin amid the debris. Hope, a kind of spiritual adrenaline, ran through her. She turned quickly inland.

The going was far more difficult than she'd imagined. She worked her way laboriously over dozens of fallen trunks—pine, spruce, and poplar. Climbing and crouching and slithering, she took ten exhausting minutes to go only a hundred yards. She stood at last before a small structure built of logs and with a roof that was made of cedar shakes covered with birch bark. Each side ran maybe fifteen feet in length. Windows had been cut in each wall and were covered with soiled oilcloth. An enormous red pine had toppled in the storm and cleaved the roof, causing much of the back wall to tumble. It had come to rest on the top cross log of the front wall.

She'd seen such structures before, old trapper cabins or abandoned hunting camps in the woods of Tamarack County, north of Aurora. She walked to the door, lifted the latch, and entered.

It was a single room. The huge, fallen pine had invaded much of the area inside, creating a kind of labyrinth of sharply needled branches. The logs of the toppled back wall also cramped the room, and what open space was left felt tiny. Against the wall to her right, clear of the wreckage of the back wall and untouched by the pine boughs, was a bunk with bedding. Except for fallout from the damaged roof and the wetness from the rain that had come through, the bedding looked relatively clean. Toward the back, crushed under a couple of tumbled logs, was a rough-hewn table, with two broken chairs. In the center of the room stood a cast-iron potbellied stove. A long section of stovepipe had come down when the pine hit the roof, and it lay on the floor amid a shadowy splash of soot.

She ducked under the trunk of the protruding pine, and the far side of the cabin was revealed to her.

"Well, well," she said, pleased. "At least I won't starve."

Against the wall of the cabin, cardboard boxes stood stacked waist high. On the side of each box was printed the contents, which included canned peaches, canned lima beans, canned peas, canned Hormel chili, canned Spam, and half a dozen other edibles. A long, slender table had been shoved against the cabin wall next to the boxes. The tabletop was maple, planed smooth and cleanly varnished. On it sat a Coleman propane stove, open and ready for business. A little way down the table were neatly stacked cooking pots and two cigar boxes, one filled with utensils and the other with candles. There were kitchen matches in a sealed Ball jar. Near the end of the table lay a stack of folded towels. Arranged against the wall beneath the table were a dozen plastic, two-gallon jugs of distilled water.

At first, she considered that maybe this was a seasonal camp, but it looked as if someone had been there for a while and was planning to be there for a while longer. A semipermanent residence. There was only one bunk, and unless a couple of toothpicks slept in it, it was only large enough for a single body.

"Where did he go?" she said to herself and decided the cabin's resident had fled before the storm.

She spotted a cardboard box that was not stacked with the others but had been placed specially under the long maple table. The name on the box was familiar to her, and surprising. Similac.

"Baby formula?" she said to herself.

In the quiet of the moment that followed, from somewhere outside the cabin, came the whimper of what sounded very much like an infant.

FIVE

The wind was gentle, but the houseboat was large. Its broad side acted as a sail. Despite Rose's best and desperate efforts, the boat drifted farther and farther beyond her ability and her endurance. For what felt like hours, she swam through the debris the storm had littered on the surface of the water. She finally stopped, exhausted, and watched the boat scoot out of the little bay and into the great expanse of open water.

She kicked and pivoted so that she could see the shoreline where she'd been forced to abandon Mal. He sat against one of the big rocks. He appeared small and vulnerable, a consequence of the distance and his situation and Rose's love for him. She looked across the bay toward the beach where the kids had been. Still abysmally empty. She was exhausted. But for the life vest she wore, she would have had trouble staying afloat.

She laid her head back against the collar of the vest and stared up at the lie that was blue sky. It had promised calm that morning, promised heaven. It had delivered hell. Rose, who never swore, swore viciously, "God damn you!" Her anger was directed at the sky and the situation and herself for her helplessness. And some of it, she accepted, was directed at God.

Eventually she became aware of a distant cry: Mal calling to her. She peered at him and realized he was gesturing wildly toward the channel. Turning, she saw what he meant. The houseboat had stopped moving.

Rose looked up again. "Sorry, Lord."

And she began to crawl her way out of the bay.

It took another ten minutes of constant stroking. The whole time she feared the boat would begin to drift again, but it didn't. She reached the swim platform and climbed onto the aft deck. She bent over the railing and studied the clear water along the edge of the leeward pontoon. Rocks. The houseboat had come to rest against a submerged reef.

She headed to the control station in the cabin. She took the seat there and stared at the console, a dashboard that held a confusion of gauges and toggle switches. Whenever Mal and Cork had started the engines, she'd paid only vague attention. Because of the protruding key, she recognized the ignition. She also recognized the steering wheel, which Mal called the "helm." She knew about the throttle. But putting everything together in a process that would get the boat moving was another matter. After a few moments of hesitation, she turned the key to the On position. Nothing happened. She twisted the key to Start. To her great relief, the outboards fired and caught. She reached for the throttle handle and gently pulled it into reverse. The houseboat didn't move. She eased the throttle farther back, and a frightful scraping came from the pontoon wedged against the reef. She returned the throttle to the neutral position, left the station, ran out, and leaned over the bow railing. She could see that the wind had nudged the pontoon solidly onto the reef, which lay eighteen inches below the surface. Rose considered her options briefly, then hurried to the swim platform. She entered the water, swam to the shoal, and climbed onto the rock. She walked carefully to a spot that was roughly midship, where she spread her hands against the hull of the houseboat. She wedged her bare feet against the reef beneath her and pushed. Nothing happened. She tried again, harder this time. The houseboat would not budge. She realized that, once again, the wind, though gentle, was her enemy. She knew, too, that if she didn't get the damn boat off the damn rock, people she loved might be lost to her forever. She turned herself and squatted and this time laid her back against the hull. She put all her strength into the effort. Her legs quivered and her muscles burned. She saw black for a moment and then felt the boat slip into the clear.

She kept pushing until she lost her footing and fell into the lake. As quickly as she could, she made for the swim platform and climbed aboard. She raced to the helm, swung the wheel hard to bring the boat back toward the bay, and eased the throttle forward. The houseboat responded.

In a few minutes, Rose brought the boat carefully near the shoreline where Mal now stood, leaning against one of the tall rocks. He called to her, "Not too close! Don't hang her up on the bottom."

Rose throttled back, hit Reverse for a moment, and the forward motion ceased. Mal was less than ten yards away. On one leg, he hopped toward the houseboat until he was in water almost to his knees, then he crouched and began to swim. Rose met him at the platform and helped him aboard. She could see that his ankle was swelling badly.

"How does it feel?" she asked.

"Hurts like hell," he said. But he smiled and kissed her. "You did good. Now let's find the kids."

SIX

The whimpering came from under the trunk of a spruce that lay toppled by the storm. Jenny crouched and made her way into the tangle of branches. The little crying, which was like that of a small, hurt animal, guided her. She drew aside a sweep of bough and discovered a mat lying flat on the ground. The mat had been woven of reed and laced with brush to create a kind of blind. The whimper came from beneath it. She lifted the mat and found a deep basin dug into the earth. In the basin sat a dun-colored, oblong wicker basket. And in the basket, wrapped in a small, quilted blanket, lay a baby. The child looked to Jenny to be no more than a few weeks old and had thick black hair and a round face and dark little eyes. But what drew Jenny's attention, what would have drawn anyone's attention, was the misshapen mouth.

The child had an enormous cleft in its upper lip. It was as if some cruel hand had taken a pair of shears and snipped away a triangle of flesh. Through that cleft, a broad stretch of pink gum showed.

Jenny drew the basket from the basin, and the baby began to cry in earnest. Its little arms poked from beneath the blanket and flailed. Its face grew hot red. Jenny backed out from under the fallen spruce, lifted the child, and cradled it in her arms.

"Oh, little one," she said softly. "Where are your parents?"

She scanned the devastated island and answered her own question. "Caught outside in the storm." She looked down into the tiny red face with the gaping cleft in its upper lip. "Don't worry. We'll find them."

The child quieted for a moment, pressed against her, and turned its face into her body. She realized it was trying to suckle her breast through the flimsy cotton of her T-shirt.

"You must be starved," she whispered.

She laid the baby back down in the wicker, and the child began to scream again, though muted, as if it had already cried itself hoarse. Quickly, she returned to the cabin, set the basket on the bunk, and searched the maple tabletop on the far side of the room. Next to the stacked cooking pots, she found two clean glass baby bottles and several nipples.

Behind her, the baby's cries were growing ever more feverish.

"Hold tight, little one," she called. "I'll be right there."

She lifted the Ball jar, unscrewed the lid, and pulled a kitchen match from the supply inside. She pumped propane into the Coleman stove, something she'd done a zillion times with her father on camping trips, then opened the line to one of the burners and lit a flame. She took a quart-size cooking pot, filled it from the distilled water in one of the plastic jugs, and set the water over the burner to heat. From the opened carton under the table, she grabbed a canister of baby formula, popped the lid, and unsealed the contents. She measured formula into the bottle, filled it with distilled water, screwed on a cap and nipple, and shook it to mix. She set the bottle in the pan of water heating over the burner. Finally, she returned to the baby and took it in her arms. Immediately, its little face turned to her breast, and it tried again to feed.

"I wish I had something for you there," she said.

Now she smelled it. The baby needed changing. She remembered seeing a squat wicker hamper beside the bunk. When she lifted the lid, she found clean diapers inside, folded neatly, along with baby clothing. She took one of the diapers, spread it out on the damp mattress of the bunk, and set the squalling child on it.

"Ah," she said, when she'd unpinned the soiled diaper. "A boy. No wonder you scream so loud."

She could tell he hadn't been changed in a good long while, but fortunately no rash had developed. She grabbed another clean diaper, hurried to the jug of water, and soaked the cloth. At her back, the baby's screams grew more furious.

After she'd cleaned and rediapered him, all the time working around his flailing limbs, she carried him to the stove, where the bottle was heating.

She bent her face near his and said, as if he could understand, "Not long till dinnertime."

At last she removed the bottle and shook a few drops onto her wrist to test the temperature. It would do. She plugged the nipple into the baby's mouth, and instantly, he fell silent and tried to feed. He sucked loudly and then began to cry again in frustration. Jenny realized that the divide in his upper lip prevented him from forming a good vacuum. She gently pressed her finger over the cleft to seal it. The child sucked again, this time successfully.

"How long since you ate, little guy?" Jenny said, watching how furiously he worked at the nipple. She looked around her at the deserted cabin. If not for the damage from the storm, it would have been a clean, cozy place. "Where's your mother?"

While the child fed in her arms, Jenny stepped outside. She walked the perimeter of the cabin. She came across a wooden tub with a washboard inside. Strung between a couple of aspen saplings that had survived the storm was a fifteen-foot length of nylon cord. A clothesline. She ducked under the line and headed to a rocky rise that backed the cabin. But for the baby, she would have climbed immediately to have a look at her surroundings. *Later*, she decided.

By the time the baby had finished the bottle, his eyes were drifting closed. Jenny took a minute to burp him, then returned him to the wicker basket, where he fell instantly asleep. Hungry and exhausted from crying, she figured. How long had it been since someone had fed him, cared for him? Where was his mother?

She left the cabin again and this time climbed the rise behind the cabin. The crown of the hillock was bare and gave her a decent view of the island. She shielded her eyes against the low sun. She could see the rocky outcropping at the other end, where she'd sought shelter from the storm. What lay between that far place and where Jenny stood was total devastation: snapped trunks, uprooted trees, an enormous web of fallen timbers. She cupped her hands and hollered, "Hello! Can anybody hear me?"

No reply. She called again and again with the same result.

She deserted the rise. In front of the cabin, she found a trail that led toward the shoreline. The trail was blocked by fallen trees, but she followed it anyway, ducking and climbing, and, in a couple of minutes, stood at a little inlet littered with detritus from the storm. Around a ragged pine stump was a groove bare of bark, worn, Jenny guessed, as the result of a boat tying up there often. No boat was tied there now. She stared out from the inlet and saw only more destroyed islands across the channel. She was afraid for her father and for her family. She felt utterly alone and was tempted to give herself over completely to despair. But there was the baby to consider now.

She returned to the cabin, sat on the mattress beside the wicker basket, and studied the child. His skin was the color of sandstone. His hair was thick and black. When his eyes had been open, Jenny had seen their hard, almond color. *Ojibwe?* she wondered. She tried to sort through the whole strange situation of finding the baby in the basket hidden under the woven mat outside. One more odd circumstance in what was becoming a long line of circumstances that were not at all right.

"I've been thinking," she said quietly to the sleeping child. "Maybe I'll build a bonfire on top of the rise out there, keep feeding it until someone sees the smoke and comes."

But will anyone come? said the voice of reason inside her head.

"It may take a while, but yes," she replied aloud. She looked toward the stacks of cardboard boxes on the other side of the cabin, beyond the fallen pine. "If we have to, we can wait a long time."

Yeah, as long as there's propane for the stove, reason pointed out.

"Let me see what we can find," Jenny said.

She hadn't seen another propane tank near the stove, so she began to clear away debris where the fall of the pine tree had toppled the back wall. She pulled away broken branches and put her back into moving one of the logs enough to create a gap for her to slide through so that she could explore the corner of the cabin where the crushed table and chairs lay. She made her way into a tiny open space behind the logs and stopped. A woman lay on the cabin floor, facedown, her cheek in a puddle of coagulated blood. She was utterly naked.

Light came into the cabin through the shattered roof and fell across the body in a swath of bright yellow-orange that was like a satin ribbon. Jenny stood a moment, absolutely stunned. Slowly, and with great reluctance, she knelt and checked the woman's neck for a pulse. Nothing, and the skin was cold to her touch. She drew her hand away, then reached out again and carefully rolled the woman onto her back. Young, Jenny saw. No more than seventeen or eighteen. Her hair was long and black and done in a braid. Her skin was the same color as the child's, faded sandstone. Her cheekbones were high and proud. She was clearly Indian. Jenny knew that in this area it meant she was probably Ojibwe or Odawa or maybe Cree. The side of her face that had been pressed against the floor was covered with clotted blood. The other side was a mottle of deep bruising. There were burns on her breasts, little singes dark and round as old pennies. And there was also a bullet hole dead center in her forehead.

Jenny turned away. She rose and stumbled back, scrambled

through the gap she'd created in the tumbled logs and stood shaking. She wished her father was there. Her father would know what to do.

But he wasn't. There was no one but her.

Whoever did this may be back, said the voice inside her head.

"They've already killed her," she said aloud. "Why would they come back?"

Do you want to take that chance?

She knew then that there would be no bonfire. Although it might bring rescue, it might also bring back a murderer. She looked the damaged cabin over carefully, forcing herself to think clearly. She knew she had to leave that place, find shelter somewhere else. She said aloud but quietly, "I'll take the stove, a pan, some formula, and a few canned goods."

They might see that some things are missing, the voice told her.

"Can't be helped." She took the damp blanket from the bunk, spread it on the floor, and threw in a few canned goods, the canister of formula, some utensils, a can opener, the pan she'd used to boil water, a couple of candles, and the Ball jar of kitchen matches.

"Clean diapers," she reminded herself.

She grabbed a handful of diapers and tossed them onto the blanket with the other items. She brought the four corners of the blanket together and tied them.

Water, she thought, grabbed one of the unopened jugs of distilled water, and put it beside the blanket. She went to the propane stove, closed the lid and flipped the latch. As she drew the stove off the long, hand-hewn table, she spotted a knife. It was a clip point hunting knife with a five-inch fixed blade and black rubber handle, a good utilitarian knife that might have been used to cut meat for cooking. She grasped it and slipped it into her knapsack with her useless phone and camera. A final time, she scanned the room.

Then she looked at the sleeping baby. He'd been well cared for, she understood. The dead woman, his mother, had loved him, it was clear.

"I'll find somewhere to hide us, somewhere safe, and I'll be back for you, little man," she promised.

The voice said, *Is there anywhere safe on this island?*

For that one, Jenny didn't have an answer.

SEVEN

Mal piloted the houseboat while Rose tried in vain to raise someone on the radio. The dismal scratch of static was all she got, and finally Mal said, "Give it up, sweetheart. I think the beating from that storm did it in. We're lucky our GPS still works." He tapped the unit on the console.

"What about your cell phone?" Rose asked.

"I haven't been able to get a signal on that thing since we left Kenora."

They'd motored out of the bay and come around the end of the island where Anne and Stephen had disappeared. Rose looked at the destruction, and she thought hell couldn't look any worse. Trees lay cleaved as if with a battleax. Those few that had somehow managed to survive upright were stripped bare. The houseboat pushed through flotsam thrown off the island by the angry hand of the wind—bark and branch and brush. Fifty yards to the left of the boat and a little behind them, two shapes floated, dark and indistinct in the blue of the reflected sky. Something about them suggested to Rose that they had not come from a tree.

"Mal," she said, almost breathless, and she pointed him back.

He spun the wheel, and the houseboat came about and nosed toward the floating shapes, which were different from the stiff detritus of tree parts around them, riding the gentle undulations from the wake of the houseboat like things made of flesh and bone.

Oh, God, Rose prayed silently, *please, God, no.*

She ran to the bow platform, wanting to be certain and at the same time terrified by what she might discover. At the rail, she gave a little cry.

"What is it?" her husband called.

"Oh, Mal," she said, her voice choked. "It's a doe and a fawn. They're dead, poor things."

"Let's find the living, Rose," Mal said and swung the boat back toward the island.

They eased along the shoreline, moving through the eerie calm, looking west into the sun, shielding their eyes, straining to see movement of any kind. Rose remembered the field glasses she'd brought for birding and hurried to her cabin. Everything in the houseboat had been thrown into disarray, and her small cabin looked as if it had been ransacked by vandals. She finally found the glasses under the bunk amid the clutter of clothing and paperbacks, and she raced back to the control station. She scanned the island as they circled, she and Mal hardly speaking.

They came around at last to the bay where they'd begun.

Rose had always prided herself on being a woman of profound and indomitable hope, but at the moment, she could barely hold back tears.

"I didn't see a thing," she whispered.

"We'll go around again, Rose. We'll go around until we find them."

She looked into his eyes, green eyes, like spring grass. "We will find them, won't we, Mal?"

"God will have to answer to you if we don't," he said. "And I know he doesn't want that." He smiled gently and touched her arm, then looked past her and said, "Well I'll be damned. Look, sweetheart."

She turned where he pointed. Inside the bay, at the very rocks on the shore where Mal had tried to safely anchor, Anne and Stephen stood, waving their arms.

"O ye of little faith," Rose said to herself. And she kissed the top of her husband's head.

Mal guided the boat to within a dozen feet of the shore. Anne and Stephen waded out to meet them and climbed aboard using the ladder of the swim platform. Rose hugged them both and said, "Are you all right?"

"Yeah," Stephen said. He had several long scratches across his bare chest, as if a cat had raked him with its claws. "As soon as a couple of trees went down, we kind of wedged underneath them and they protected us."

"We were more worried about you and Mal, out there in the houseboat," Anne said. Her red hair was blown wild and filled with dust and twigs, but there seemed no real damage.

"What about Dad and Jenny?" Stephen said.

Mal had left the control station and, favoring his injured ankle, had limped aft to where the others stood. He said, "The radio's out, so we don't have any way to get word to or from anyone. I think we should head to the Northwest Angle and see if your dad and Jenny made it there safely."

"If?" Anne said.

"Confirm they made it safely," Mal corrected himself. "Anybody have a better idea?"

No one spoke, and Mal hobbled back to the control station with the others following.

"How long do you think it will take us to get there?" Anne asked.

Mal kicked the engines into action and began to back away from the island. "I don't know," he said. "With all this crap in the water, we'll have to move slowly. Several hours, at least. Well after dark."

They motored out of the bay and into the broad open water, and Mal headed the houseboat southwest.

Rose stood at the railing of the bow with Stephen and Anne,

and they all looked toward the vast horizon spotted with islands destroyed in the storm, rising out of the lake like carbuncles festering in the afternoon sun. There was not a human thing in sight, and Rose recalled the words of the man who'd rented them the houseboat.

"Lake of the Woods is a place you can get well and truly lost if you're not careful. You can go for days among all those islands and never see another soul."

They would be careful, Rose knew. With the GPS, they would not get lost among the thousands of islands. And she prayed that there were at least two other souls they would yet see.

EIGHT

It took Jenny three trips to bring all the materials—blanket, knapsack, and water jug—and carry the baby to the place she hoped would be sanctuary. She'd chosen a spot at the other end of the island, as far from the cabin as she could get. The baby, no longer starved but still exhausted, continued to sleep.

She spent an hour building a blind from all the waste of branches sheered off by the horrific wind. She constructed it around an uprooted pine on the far side of the rock outcropping that had protected her during the storm. The pine lay a fair distance from the wreckage of the boat, which she also tried to hide, and completely out of the line of sight from the cabin. She didn't know if the girl's killer or killers would be back, and she didn't know if they would look the island over, but she didn't want to take any chances. Against a firearm, she was almost powerless. When she finished, she created a little shelter in the lee of the fallen pine, whose roots were like a great claw spread toward the south. She wove a kind of roof of evergreen boughs overhead to provide shade from the sun. Finally, she spread boughs across the ground to give some softness there and overlaid them with the blanket she'd taken from the dead woman's bunk. Inside this makeshift shelter, there was just room enough for her and the baby and the things she'd brought.

She understood that most of this she was able to do because

of her father. Even before she could walk, he'd taken her camping in the great woods north of Aurora, the Boundary Waters Canoe Area Wilderness. Growing up, she'd learned how to survive. In her office in Iowa City, these skills had seemed distant and useless. Now she was grateful.

But Iowa City had given her other skills that were important at the moment. During all her years of college, because her scholarships didn't completely cover her costs, she'd worked in the nursery of a day-care center at the university.

Her father had once told her that life was always preparing you for what lay around some corner in the future; smart people paid attention. She hoped that she was smart enough, because God only knew what lay around the curve just ahead.

By the time Jenny had done all she could, the sun was low in the sky. She sat, very tired, and watched the sleeping child. Neglect was sometimes the inevitable result of teen pregnancy, she knew, but this child had obviously been loved and well cared for. She wondered how anyone could do the things someone had done to the child's mother. It could have been cruelty, pure and simple. The sad reality was that some men fed on that. Or, she considered, it could have been that they wanted something from her she wouldn't or couldn't give them.

"Like what?" she asked aloud.

Even to begin to speculate on that one she would probably have to go back to the cabin and have a really good look around. And she had no intention of doing so.

The evergreen boughs cast a shadow over the baby, but not completely. There were places where the needles didn't quite mesh, and waning sunlight came through and fell on his face in soft tangerine splashes.

"She was so young, your mother," Jenny whispered to him, and she heard in her voice the imbroglio of sadness and anger. The young, she knew, were often the victims of the worst cruelties.

Because the girl had been naked, Jenny wondered if she'd

been raped. And that possibility sent more ice into her blood. She didn't want to be anywhere near whoever had been there, whoever might return.

The baby began to stir. Jenny took the cooking pot to the shoreline only a few yards distant and filled it with lake water. She lit a burner and set the pan on the stove. She made up a bottle of formula and set it in the heating water. By that time, the baby was fully awake and fussing.

She picked him up, sat herself on the blanket, and cradled him. He was, despite his cleft lip, a lovely child, with fat cheeks and a broad little nose. He looked up into her face, and his dark eyes seemed to be searching for understanding. *He's wondering who I am, this stranger who smells nothing like his mother,* Jenny thought. He lay quiet in her arms. She felt his breath break upward against her neck, and his heart beat against her own heart. He reached up a tiny hand and touched her chin.

Jenny wondered how long the girl had been dead. How long had the child gone without food, without touch?

She cooed to him. "There, there, little one. Don't be afraid. I'm here for you. I'm here for you. No one will hurt you, I promise."

After the baby fed, he slept again. Jenny was hungry, starved in fact, and she opened a can of Spam and a can of pineapple slices. She diced them together in the same pan she'd used to heat the baby bottle, and she fried the concoction over the burner of the Coleman. The result was outrageously delicious.

In the middle of cleaning up afterward, she stopped suddenly and listened. The wind had returned, but gently so, and the lake water shushed against the shoreline so that she wasn't certain she'd really heard anything. She checked the baby, then left the little shelter and climbed to the top of the rock outcropping, where a few of the cedars, though ragged, still miraculously stood. The sun was just setting, and the islands to the west wore peach-colored halos; their faces were going dark. In the shadows, the water was silver-black. The lake surface rolled in the breeze, and all that floated there—trees and parts of trees and God alone knew what else—lifted and fell as if on the chest of a breathing thing. In the dimming light, it all seemed to be part of one living organism, one great, wounded creature. She listened again and heard only the water and the soft sigh of the wind among what remained of the cedar branches.

She looked toward the far end of the island, where she could see the damaged cabin amid the rubble. Behind it rose the small, bare hillock where she'd stood that afternoon and had called in vain for the baby's mother, a young woman who could not answer and was past caring. She was tired, and that moment seemed long ago now.

She was about to leave the outcropping and return to the shelter when she took a last look at the lake, and she froze. There was movement in the water, movement out of sync with the easy rise and fall of the swells. Something, she couldn't tell exactly what, was approaching. It came purposefully, propelled by a mechanism that, at the moment, she couldn't discern. It was long and dark in the water, with a wide splay of what might have been antlers at the head. *A buck?* she wondered. But the body seemed much too long, so perhaps a moose. The creature pressed on, and as it neared the island, she realized with a sickening jolt what exactly she was looking at: a section of shattered tree, and the antlers were branches, and what propelled it was a man.

She dropped to the ground and lay on the hard cap of the outcropping, watching the figure swim the log toward shore. In her mind flashed the horrible image of the naked girl who'd died so brutally less than a quarter of a mile from where she lay. She was dreadfully afraid for the baby. And she felt her own maddening helplessness in the face of all the terrible possibility ahead.

The man let go of the log and slogged ashore. In one hand, he held a long, thin object that Jenny was certain had to be a rifle. He was a good hundred yards from where she lay, and because of the distance and the dim light, she couldn't make out any detail except for the firearm he carried. She waited, barely breathing.

He stood a long moment, as if catching his breath, then began to walk the shoreline in the direction of the cabin.

From below and behind Jenny came the sudden bawling of the baby.

The man stopped and turned.

NINE

Any fear Jenny had ever felt before was now dwarfed by her panic. She slid from the top of the outcropping and frantically descended. She slipped into the shelter and lifted the baby in her arms. He quieted almost immediately, but Jenny was certain it was too late. Her eyes shot toward all the items she'd brought from the cabin and settled quickly on the hunting knife that lay next to the Coleman stove. She grasped the black hard-rubber handle, brought the blade up, and readied herself. She wished it were a magnum handgun she held, but the five inches of razor-sharp steel would have to do.

She waited a long time. Finally, with a measure of blessed relief, she began to think that maybe he'd changed his mind, though why in God's name he would do that she couldn't have said. Just as she was about to let herself relax, she heard the brittle crush of underbrush outside the shelter. Her heart became a hammering fist. She held the baby against her chest, thrust the blade in front of her, and tried to steady her shaking hand. She would do whatever was necessary to protect the child and herself. She knew it without a whisper of doubt. She would kill this man.

Through the mesh of the drooping pine boughs, she saw the tall shape approaching. He came from behind the outcropping, from the darkening of the eastern horizon at dusk. She heard the squish of his boots still soaked with lake water and the draw of his breath from the effort of climbing through the debris. She caught a glimpse of the long black barrel of the rifle gripped in his right hand. She saw his left hand reach forward and pull aside a low-hanging bough. She crouched half a dozen feet away ready to spring at him.

He bent and entered.

Later, Cork would recount how his daughter had nearly killed him. How, when the bawling child had led him to her, she'd been like a tigress. How the blade of that marvelous Cutco knife was poised to carve out his heart. And how, at the last moment, she'd recognized him and had melted in tears of relief.

The child, however, had screamed bloody murder.

"I thought you were— I don't know," Jenny cried when she was finally able to speak. "I thought you had a rifle and were going to kill us."

"A rifle? You mean this?" He held up the staff in his hand, a thin, sturdy maple limb. "I've been using this to shove away debris when I swim. And I've been swimming most of the afternoon looking for you."

He spoke in a rasp that was barely above a whisper, and Jenny asked, "What happened to your voice?"

"I think I strained my vocal cords calling for you all afternoon. I'd've yelled when I came ashore here, but I don't have much voice left."

"How did you find us?"

"Us?" Cork shook his head in disbelief at the screaming baby clutched to her breast. "How did you become 'us'?"

"It's a long story, Dad, and a horrible one."

Seeing the great weariness in her face, he laid his maple staff on the blanket and said, "Tell me."

"First let me take care of this little guy."

Amazed, he watched her prepare a bottle from the astonishing array of supplies in her little makeshift shelter. Of course, he saw the baby's upper lip, the wide cleft. But what was there to say about that? He said nothing.

When the bottle was prepared and the baby feeding, she told him the story.

Though he couldn't see the cabin, he stared east where it stood. "I think I need to take a look."

"Wait," she said. "How did you find us?"

"Like I said," he rasped, "I've been swimming from island to island all afternoon, hoping like crazy you and the boat made it somewhere safe."

"What happened to you? I looked back, and you were gone."

"The wind knocked me right out of the boat. Felt like a semi plowed into my back. Next thing I know I'm in the water, and the waves are all over me, and I'm thinking I'm a goner. And you, too, kiddo. I finally washed up on one of the islands and hunkered down until it was all over, then I came looking for you."

"Just luck you found us?"

He shrugged. "I could've sworn I smelled something cooking."

"Spam," she said and laughed. "I'll fix you some."

"Later." He stood up from where he'd been sitting on the blanket. "First I want to have a look at that cabin."

"I'd rather you stayed, Dad. I feel safer with you here."

"Safer?" He looked around him. "Kiddo, you've been doing just fine without me. I won't be gone long, promise. Just keep that boy quiet if you can. He's got a set of lungs on him, and until we understand what's going on, I'd just as soon nobody knows we're here."

"All right," she said, but he could hear her reluctance.

He followed her directions and found the cabin without difficulty. The destroyed tree cover made the small structure easy to see once he knew where to look. He could tell that before the storm the cabin would have been invisible from the lake. Probably a good place to hide, if that's what you were hoping for.

In the blue light of dusk, he entered. The place was just as Jenny had described it. He spent a few moments taking stock of the layout, then went to the tumbled logs from the damaged rear wall and slipped through the gap his daughter had created earlier. The girl lay just as Jenny said she'd left her, on her back with her dead eyes to the twilight sky visible through the rend in the cabin roof.

Though he was absolutely certain he'd find no pulse, he pressed her neck, the carotid artery there. Her skin was cold. He examined the bruises and the burns Jenny had described. The girl had suffered before she died. There were a couple of short lengths of nylon cord on the floor nearby, and Cork checked her wrists and ankles. He found bruising and figured she'd been bound, maybe to the chair that lay tipped over near her body. In the end, she'd been killed with a single bullet to her brain. Entry wound in her forehead, no exit wound. Small caliber. A .22 probably, chosen for the execution because the bullet wouldn't penetrate the back of the head and would ricochet several times inside the girl's skull, making Swiss cheese of her brain in the process. It was sometimes the way people who killed for a living operated.

He rolled her onto her stomach, which was how she'd been positioned when Jenny found her. He retreated from the body and tried to return the fallen logs to the way they'd probably been before Jenny had disturbed them. He looked the cabin over and knew there was no way to disguise the fact that someone had been there and had taken things.

But it was what it was.

He left the cabin and scoured the area outside for anything additional that might be important. He found a washtub and a clothesline, and finally an old wooden outhouse destroyed in the storm. At last, he headed through the twilight back toward the shelter, where Jenny and the child were hiding.

* * *

She was changing the baby when her father returned.

"So?" she said.

"Someone wanted something from her." He sat down against the fallen pine log that ran along one side of the shelter. "I don't know if they got it before they killed her. Whatever it was, they didn't think it was in the cabin."

Jenny was wiping the baby's bottom. He endured her ministrations without complaint. "Why do you say that?"

"They didn't toss the place. Except for the damage from the storm, everything was pretty orderly."

"Were they looking for the baby, maybe?"

"Possible, I suppose."

"It's also possible that they weren't looking for anything. Maybe they just did it to her out of pure psychotic cruelty," she said bitterly.

"That's possible, too," he said. "Except that the killing itself looked professional, like a hit."

"Who would want to execute a teenage girl? And why?"

"I've got no answers, Jenny. But the whole reason she was there was to keep her hidden."

"How do you know?"

"There was a perfectly good woodstove in the cabin, but it hadn't been used in forever. Why? My guess is so that there wouldn't be any smoke rising up to give away the cabin's location. Only one bunk in the room, and that just large enough for one body, so she lived there alone. But it's clear that someone's been keeping her supplied. They could've been helping her stay hidden. Or," he added, "they could have been keeping her prisoner."

"No bars that I saw," Jenny said.

"The confusion of this lake itself is probably enough to keep someone trapped here, especially if there's a baby to consider and no boat available to get you safely away." Her father shook his head, clearly troubled, then went on. "There's another thing. It looked like her breasts were full of milk. Out here, breast-feeding would make the most sense. So why all the baby formula?"

"Maybe he was allergic to her milk," Jenny offered. "It happens sometimes."

"I thought about that," he said. "But there's another possibility. It could be that whoever kept her here needed a way to feed the child after she was dead."

"They planned on killing her but leaving him alive? Why?"

"Why any of this? Your guess is as good as mine." He sounded angry. He rubbed his eyes a moment, seemed to gather himself, then spoke more evenly. "I'd say she's been dead a day, more or less."

"Which means this little guy didn't eat for a long time. No wonder he's been so ravenous."

She'd finished the changing and took the baby in her arms, where he nestled easily against her breast.

Her father watched her and nodded. "You have a way with kids. Your mother did, too. She could take a crying baby, anybody's baby, in her arms, and within a minute, that kid was all gurgles and smiles." He thought a moment and added with a laugh, "She could take opposing counsel apart pretty ruthlessly in about the same amount of time."

Jenny glanced from the baby to her father. The darkness in the shelter was growing deeper with the approach of night, and he was darkening with it. "How long?" she asked. "Until someone comes?"

"I don't know. I just hope, when they show up, they're the good guys."

"What if they aren't?"

He turned his face in the direction of the damaged cabin, invisible on the other side of the outcropping. "You'll need to be able to keep the baby quiet."

"Babies are unpredictable, Dad."

"The kinds of men who do the kinds of things done back there in that cabin aren't. They hear that baby, they'll come for us all."

"Maybe they won't be back."

"Maybe," he said.

He stood, though not fully because of the low pine bough canopy.

"Where are you going?" she asked.

"To the top of the outcropping here. If someone comes, I want to know it."

"Are you kidding? It's so quiet you can hear the dark sliding down the sky. If anybody comes, you'll know it, Dad."

"Just want to be sure. Need anything before I go up top? Bottle cleaned or a diaper rinsed out? I did a lot of that when you were a baby."

"We'll be fine," she said.

He picked up the hunting knife that Jenny had brought from the cabin and had almost plunged into his chest. "Keep this very close to you," he said.

Although he wasn't a tall man, he had to bend low as he left, and even then the needles of the boughs overhead scraped his shoulders. She watched him begin to climb the gray outcropping that had sheltered her in one way before and was now sheltering her in another. Her father wore khaki shorts and a dun-colored T-shirt with BOUNDARY WATERS printed in black across the chest. His hair was a dark red-brown and in need of cutting. He was an athletic man, a runner, a hunter from childhood, a fisherman. He was also, at least in her own experience, gentle. But she knew he'd killed men. And because he never talked about that and because she could not see it in his face or feel it in his touch or hear it in his voice, she didn't quite know where to fit that truth into the puzzle that was her father. All she really knew at the moment was that she was grateful he was there.

TEN

Though ragged, a few cedars atop the outcropping had miraculously survived the fury of the storm. Cork stood among them and scanned the archipelago around him. The whole area had suffered tremendous damage. The only decent stand of trees was on a tiny island two hundred yards across the channel to the north. A long spine of upthrust rock seemed to have protected the pine copse. He figured that, if they were forced to desert the island, he might be able to construct some kind of raft, and they could float themselves and the baby over to the cover of those trees. At the moment, he had no idea what might be necessary.

Just before hard dark descended, he found out.

The sky was deep amethyst when the man came. In the quiet that was a natural part of evening and yet, in all the destruction of that day, still felt unnaturally profound, Cork heard the growl of a powerful engine. The maze of islands hid everything. A long few minutes passed before he spotted the craft. It was a sleek cigarette boat. Though capable of extraordinary speed, it moved at a snail's pace, the result, Cork understood, of having to make its way through all the floating debris. The boat came slowly around an island to the south and up the channel in front of where Cork lay on his belly, glued to the top of the outcropping. He saw two big engines, a dark blue hull. The man at the wheel wore a ball cap that shielded his face. In the weak light of the waning evening, that was all Cork could see. The craft followed the shoreline, then the motors cut out, and the sleek vessel eased into a little cove near the cabin. Cork could barely make out the boat's pilot as he jumped to shore and quickly disappeared among the tangle of debris. Cork spotted him once more just outside the cabin, then the man was gone.

He slid down the outcropping and went back to Jenny in the shelter. She held the baby in her arms. Even in the dark, he could see the fear in her eyes, and he knew she'd heard the boat.

"Are we rescued?" she asked.

Cork said, "I don't know. Keep him quiet if you can."

He quickly returned to his post atop the outcropping.

A few minutes later, the man emerged from the cabin. Again, he was lost from sight for a while, then Cork spotted him, searching the cabin's perimeter. Next, he clambered up a rise that stood back of the cabin and had been balded by the storm. At the top, he became a silhouette, lean and black against the threadbare blue of the eastern evening sky. He turned in a circle, scanning the island. Finally, he raised a dark, silhouetted arm. Almost immediately the crack of three gunshots shattered the stillness that lay over the island. Cork figured those shots shattered as well his hope that this new arrival might mean rescue.

The man descended and reentered the cabin. He was inside a good while. The light in the sky faded, died, and Cork could no longer see anything. A glow blistered on the eastern horizon. The moon. It would be up within the hour. Cork stayed on top of the outcropping, watching. Eventually, the beam of a flashlight began to sweep the area near the cabin and then move steadily toward the cove, where it was lost from Cork's sight. A couple of minutes later, the big engines kicked in. Cork thought the speedboat would head away. Not so. A powerful searchlight snapped on. The engines growled like a couple of hungry predators, and the boat crept along the channel, the searchlight sweeping the shoreline of the island. As the vessel neared the tiny cove where Jenny said the dinghy lay crushed, it slowed. Cork hoped that his daughter had done a good job in hiding the wreckage.

He held his breath and watched the crawl of the searchlight.

Jenny had heard the shots but had no idea what they meant. She'd hoped her father would come down from his observation post and say they were rescued, but he didn't. A while later, she heard the boat returning and waited, and still her father didn't come. The baby had gone back to sleep in his basket. If it was true, as her father had said, that the woman in the cabin had been dead a day, then the baby had probably cried himself out several times over the course of all those hours during which he had been so cruelly abandoned. Tired, hungry, thirsty, wrapped in a soiled diaper, his mother dead within a stone's throw. In her head, Jenny knew that the baby had no concept of what had taken place in that cabin, but her heart broke for him nonetheless. She wondered if the child had been awake during any of it, had made the noises babies make, had drawn attention to himself. If so, whoever had killed his mother hadn't cared. Had left the child to the elements, left him to die of dehydration or starvation, as cruel in its way as the death of the young mother. Jenny listened to the sound of the boat drawing nearer on the other side of the outcropping and wondered what kind of monster had visited that cabin.

She heard the engines slow and thought that the boat must be passing the cove where she'd taken shelter. It was one of the few landing places along the channel. She waited to hear the sound of her father hailing whoever was at the wheel, but he remained silent. Not a good sign.

The baby began suddenly to stir and fuss, as if disturbed by a bad dream. She lifted him, and he turned his head immediately toward her breast. She tried to offer her pinkie as a pacifier, but he shook her little finger off and pressed his face adamantly to her breast.

The boat continued around the tip of the island. A beam of light suddenly appeared, sweeping along the shoreline. It illuminated the clawlike roots of the fallen pine where she'd built her blind and her shelter. The baby furiously nuzzled the thin cotton of her T-shirt, and she could tell that he was about to cry out in frustration. With desperate speed, she lifted her T-shirt, fumbled her breast free from the halter of her swimsuit, and pressed him to her. He took her nipple into his little mouth and was quiet.

Her hand shot to the hunting knife that lay beside the propane stove, and she grasped the handle, ready to defend with her life the life of the baby in her arms.

At that same moment, the light died. The engines kicked in powerfully, and the boat growled away into the distance.

A crackle of branch came at her back, and she spun, thrusting the knife threateningly before her.

"Whoa," her father said. "Just me."

She saw the astonishment on his face when he spied the baby sucking at her breast. She said, "He was about to cry, and I don't have a pacifier." She turned her back to him discreetly. "Would you fix me a bottle? There are some matches and a couple of candles mixed in with the canned stuff I brought from the cabin. You can use one of the candles for light to see by."

Her father groped among the items she'd piled into the blanket, and a minute later, a candle flame illuminated the shelter.

"Who was it?" she asked.

"No idea." She could hear the exhaustion in his croaky voice. Hell, she was beat, too.

"He knew about the cabin, though," her father said. "If he didn't know about the body before, he knows now."

"I heard shots."

"I'm not sure what that meant. Maybe a signal to someone else out there on the lake. Maybe some kind of threat or warning, I don't know. But once it was clear that he had a gun, I didn't want to take any chances."

"Will he come back?"

He didn't reply immediately, and Jenny wondered if it was because it hurt him to talk, or if he was simply reluctant to answer. "If I were him, and I wanted to be sure of the situation here, I'd come back at first light, when I could see everything better."

"What do we do?"

He spoke as if the answer was obvious. "We make sure we're not here."

ELEVEN

Mal navigated by moonlight. They were moving along a corridor he said was called Tranquil Channel. Fortunately, the running lights still worked. The storm had littered the lake with all kinds of debris, and Rose was posted forward with Stephen and Anne to watch for anything that might damage the bow at waterline. They all had flashlights, and the beams crisscrossed the tea-colored water ahead.

Stars lay on the sky like sugar tossed on an onyx plate. The moon, frost-colored and nearly full, was at their backs. The islands rose black all around them, their outlines visible from the way they blotted out the stars.

They'd been intent on their responsibilities, on keeping all eyes toward the lake in front of them, and for a long time they had not spoken. Rose was tired, tired physically and mentally, tired of considering all the tragic possibilities they might have to face. She'd lapsed into a long, silent prayer.

"I keep trying to figure that storm," Stephen finally said, without looking away from the broad yellow oval where his flashlight beam met water. "I never saw anything like it before. Like a tornado except it was everywhere."

"Straight-line winds," Anne said. "We had a storm like that once at St. Ansgar. A bunch of trees on campus blew down. A lot of damage in town, too."

"I wonder how far the damage goes here," Stephen said. "All the way to the Northwest Angle, do you think? And back to Kenora?"

"That's something we probably won't know until we dock," Anne said.

The progress of the houseboat, though measured, created a small breeze that felt cool against Rose's face. Her eyes hurt from the intensity with which she scoured the lake and the darkness ahead. Mal had said that, as soon as they hit open water, he'd try to give the houseboat more throttle. Until then, it was best to proceed with utmost caution.

"Do you think they're okay, Aunt Rose?" Anne asked.

Anne stood to her left. Rose tried to remember what that side of the boat was called. Starboard? Port?

"I really think that, yes," Rose replied, trying to keep the exhaustion out of her voice.

Stephen stood to her right. He turned his face toward her sharply. In the moonlight at his back, half his features were brilliant, the other half in shadow. "Why?" he challenged.

"It's simply what I choose to believe."

"What if they were caught in open water?" he threw at her. "They'd never make it."

"Then they weren't caught in open water," she said calmly. "They made it somewhere safe before the storm hit. Until I'm proven wrong, I'll believe the best."

"You actually think that way?" His tone suggested that she was more than a little foolish.

He had good reason to be skeptical of her philosophy. Almost two years earlier, when his mother had disappeared on a charter flight over the Rockies during a horrific snowstorm, they'd all held to an impossible hope that she would be found alive. It had been Stephen's father who'd pursued the truth and brought it, like a slaughtered animal, home. All of them, Rose thought, in their own ways, were still reeling. And now this. This pushing through the dark again.

"Stephen," Anne said, "it will be all right."

Her voice was gentle, but the strength in it was undeniable, something annealed in the fire of her heart. Several years earlier, when she was eighteen, she'd stood toe-to-toe with death during the rampage of a high school shooting. Bloodied, she had cradled the dying in her arms, had walked out of that hell a different person, had followed a road many would have called pointless. She was preparing to be a nun.

"Okay," Stephen said, though he didn't sound fully convinced. "But say they didn't make it all the way to the Northwest Angle. Where would they have put in?"

"There are probably a thousand islands they could choose," Anne replied.

"How would we know which one?"

"A signal fire?" Rose suggested.

"Maybe they simply waited it out and then went on to the Angle," Anne said.

"No," Stephen said. "They'd have come back to check on us after the storm passed."

He was right, Rose knew. But nothing of the dinghy had been seen or heard since Cork and Jenny motored away hours ago.

"So, they took shelter on an island," Rose said, "and they're stranded, and the boat's damaged. Okay?" She looked toward Stephen.

This seemed to be a scenario he could accept. He nodded. "The fire would be difficult," he said, thinking it through. "Everything's wet. Did they take matches?"

None of them knew.

"He's got gasoline in the outboard," Stephen went on, as much to himself as to the others. "He could soak a bunch of the wood and all he would need would be a spark to get it going. Once he did that, he would just have to keep feeding it." He looked north toward a long island that was like a black caterpillar on the shimmering surface of the lake. "We could probably see it a long way off."

"Or someone could," Anne said.

"What do you mean someone?"

"I'm sure there are folks out searching for people lost in the storm. The Coast Guard, the sheriff's office, the provincial police."

"And locals giving a hand," Rose threw in.

Stephen scanned the empty horizon. "Why haven't we seen anyone?"

"It's a big lake," Rose said. "But they're out there, I'm sure."

She realized that her words weren't just for Stephen. They helped her hold to her own hope.

They were all quiet again. Again, for a long time.

From the east came a sound like a buzz saw working through wood. All their heads turned in that direction, and six eyes scanned the liquid silver that was the lake.

"A boat?" Anne asked.

"Yeah," Stephen said. "Powerful. Look, there it is!"

He poked a finger into the wall of night, pointing directly toward the moon, where a broad avenue of silver lay across the water, and where, for a few moments, the black silhouette of a boat was visible.

"A cigarette boat!" Stephen cried.

"What's a cigarette boat?" Rose asked.

"A long, fast powerboat," he replied. "They're called cigarette boats because they've been used a lot to smuggle cigarettes into Canada. They were designed to outrun the boats the Coast Guard and customs people have."

"How can you tell it's a cigarette boat?"

"Gordy Hudacek's father has one. I ride in it all the time on Iron Lake. They have a different look and sound to them, and, man, can they fly."

The boat was gone in almost the same instant she'd seen it.

"I can't tell which way it's going," Rose said.

Stephen listened. "North," he said. "It's headed away from us."

"I don't see running lights," Anne said. "Aren't you supposed to use running lights at night?"

"Not if you're smuggling," Stephen said.

"But it's going so fast in all this . . . this garbage," Rose said, indicating with a sweep of her hand the debris they were slogging their own way through.

Stephen shrugged. "Desperate, maybe."

Desperation, Rose thought. That was something they all knew about. She listened to the sound of the boat growing distant. It was good to know that they were not alone on the lake. She said a little prayer for whomever it was so desperate that they risked speeding across treacherous water, prayed for their safety.

Then she prayed once again for Cork and Jenny.

TWELVE

Jenny said, "Where are you going?"

The moon had been up for an hour, and the island was like a charcoal etching, black shapes against white light.

"Back to the cabin," Cork replied.

"Jesus, what for, Dad?"

Cork stood bent at the edge of the little shelter, peering out at the blasted landscape. In the moonlight, it seemed to him to be an island made of bone. He spoke in a whisper in order not to disturb the baby.

"If I'm going to build a raft to get us off this island, I'll need some things I don't have now."

"Like what?"

"Rope, for starters. I saw a clothesline at the cabin." He stepped outside into the clear night and brought himself upright.

Jenny moved away from the where the baby lay on the blanket, left the shelter, and stood beside her father. "Isn't there something else we could use? Tear strips from our clothing or something."

"Rope's better," he said.

"What else?"

He was looking at the lake now, at the tall islands around him, black as char. The powerboat had gone away, far enough that the sound of the engines had faded to nothing. Cork hoped that somewhere in the hard dark he might see a light—a camp-fire or lantern or flashlight—something that would indicate they weren't completely alone, though he knew in his heart that was exactly what they were.

"What do you mean 'what else'?" he said.

"You said 'for starters.' "

"Oh. Maybe a flashlight."

"Or maybe a gun," Jenny said, nailing his real thought. "You told me you'd never touch a gun again."

He faced her. In daylight, her hair was so blond it was nearly white. When she was a little girl, there were times that her wind-blown hair had reminded him of the silky fibers of milkweed. Her mother's hair had been the same color and texture. Jenny was like her mother in many ways, Cork thought. Lovely, smart, perceptive. But her mother was dead, and Jenny was very much alive, and Cork meant to keep her that way, whatever it took.

"I told you I'd never fire a gun again at a human being," he said.

"When you were sheriff, you told me, and I quote, 'Never aim a firearm at someone without being fully prepared to use it.' End quote."

"Journalists," he said. Then he said, "Yes, I'd prefer to be in possession of a firearm at this moment."

"I'd prefer that, too," she said. She looked deeply and sadly into her father's eyes. "I'm sorry, Dad."

"Not your fault," he replied. "I'll be back, and then we'll throw something together to float ourselves off this island."

She unscrewed the cap on the Ball jar, took a handful of matches, and gave them to him. "There are more candles in the cabin, in a cigar box," she told him. She also handed him the knife. "You'll need this to cut the clothesline."

He kissed the top of her head, threw a glance at the child, and left. He began to make his way to the other side of the out-cropping, where he intended to follow the shoreline until he reached the cove near the cabin.

The moon had risen to a point roughly forty-five degrees above the horizon, so bright that he could see much of the detail, if not the color, of those island features within a few dozen yards of his position. Whenever he glanced back toward the outcropping to gauge his progress, he found his shadow floating behind him on the water, a familiar companion in all that was so strange.

He did something dangerous as he slogged along. He thought. Not about his current situation, which he'd already spent enough time considering that he had a working plan. He was thinking about Jenny and how startled he'd been when he saw her with the baby sucking at her breast. He'd stood paralyzed for a moment, but it wasn't because of the odd circumstance. What shocked him was that for a brief instant it wasn't Jenny he'd seen. In the dark, with her white-blond hair and her slender body and her protective pose, it had been Jo, Jenny's mother, holding the baby in her arms. And now Cork couldn't shake the confusion of emotions that vision had brought with it. Paramount among them was a relapse into grief, which he thought he'd put behind him.

Grieving wasn't only useless, it was dangerous, especially now, when he needed to focus. From grief he slid easily into anger, all directed at himself. What had he been thinking, bringing everyone he loved here, isolating them at the end of the earth, putting them in such great danger? This was his fault, all of it. And all because he wanted his family to be happy. Christ, how stupid, how selfish was that?

He tried to shake off his black mood with some useful thinking. He considered Anne and Stephen and Rose and Mal, imagining what their situation might be. He thought about the anchorage of the houseboat when he and Jenny had left. He visualized its orientation with regard to the approach of the storm. He decided that someone on the boat would have seen the monster front sweeping across the lake, and they would have steered into the bay of the little island and tied up somewhere in the lee of the ridge. And if they were even only a little bit lucky, they would have emerged from the fury in good shape.

That's what he wanted to believe, decided to believe.

And if that were true, then they would probably try to get Jenny on her cell phone, and when that didn't work, they'd radio Young's Bay Landing on the Northwest Angle to find out if he and Jenny had arrived safely to pick up Aaron. When they had their answer, they would begin motoring toward Young's Bay, keeping an eye out along the way, maybe in conjunction with a search mounted from the Angle itself.

And if all this were true, then a signal fire would be the best way for him and Jenny to be found. But a signal fire could alert the wrong people. The man in the cigarette boat, if he was responsible for the young woman's death, or if not him, then whoever it was who'd inflicted the cruelties.

A gun, Cork thought. *If only I had a gun.*

Which was a thought of enormous and uncomfortable weight, because Jenny was right: Cork had taken a vow never again to raise a firearm against another human being. In too many ways, his history was written in blood. The blood not only of enemies but more especially of those he loved. He'd lost his wife to a bullet. He'd lost his father that way as well, and also Sam Winter Moon, the man who'd taken the place of his father in so many ways. He'd lost friends and allies. He'd seen the carnage of mindless, brutal killing in the streets of South Side Chicago and in school hallways and in what should have been the heaven of the great north wilderness he called home, violent death that, even when it was perpetrated in the name of things sacred, ended the same pointless way.

And so, he'd given up his firearms and promised himself that his part in the killing, which would doubtless continue in the world just fine without him, was over.

How very strange, he thought now, his mood still bleak, that circumstance kept bringing him back to the place where his hand ached for the grip of a gun. The destinies of some men and women, he'd decided long ago, were bound to the sulfur stink of cordite and the iron odor of blood. He'd tried his best not to be one of them. Yet here he was again.

At the cove, he turned inland and, with the help of moonlight, made his way through the web of branch and timber to the damaged cabin. The door stood open. Inside, moonbeams shot through the shattered roof and gave definition to what would otherwise have been utter dark. He carefully navigated the labyrinth of the boughs thrust down from the fallen pine. At the tumble of logs from the destroyed back wall, he peered through the opening where he'd first spotted the dead girl in a pool of blood. A splash of bleached-white light illuminated the area. He saw clearly the pooling of dried blood, but the woman's body was no longer in it.

He found the cigar box with the candles and lit one with a kitchen match. He searched the cabin thoroughly, looking for the firearm he hoped like hell he might find. When he'd satisfied himself that the woman had none, or if she had it had been taken, he blew out the candle and headed back outside. In the moonlight, he located again the clothesline he'd discovered when he first explored the area. He cut the nylon where it was knotted around the aspen saplings, coiled it, and started back toward the shelter to rejoin Jenny and the baby.

Before he reached the little cove, he turned and took a last look at the ruined cabin. He felt tired beyond belief, heartsick with an aching weariness that came from the understanding that he was deep into another chapter of his life that would probably be inked in blood.

Half an hour after her father walked away, Jenny left the baby sleeping in the shelter and climbed the outcropping, where she sat among the ragged, twisted cedars that remained. Tough little trees, she marveled. They'd wedged their roots into the crevices and held tenaciously to what seemed solid rock. They reminded her of Manidoo Gihiiganze, what many white people called the Witch Tree, a gnarled cedar that had been growing for centuries out of the bare stone above Lake Superior near Grand Portage and was sacred to the Ojibwe, sacred in part because of the impossibility of its location. Many things existed where they should not, she thought, and she considered the baby's mother, alone on this island. How long had she been here and why had she come? Was this place refuge or prison? Had the man in the powerboat been friend or keeper?

Anishinaabe blood ran in Jenny's veins. Her great-grandmother had been true-blood Iron Lake Ojibwe. Her father was a man of very mixed heritage, with strong ties to both the Anishinaabe and white communities in Tamarack County, where he'd lived almost his entire life. Jenny, however, had been raised with a decidedly Anglo sensibility. She never denied the Ojibwe part of her ancestry, but neither did she much celebrate it. She'd been to powwows, but they remained exotic to her. She was more at home with a folk festival or a poetry slam. She had friends from childhood who were Ojibwe, but with her they'd usually shared their lives on other, more general levels. Still, alone atop that rock, bathed in moonlight, she closed her eyes and tried to imagine herself as the young woman in the cabin, focusing not just on the slender thread of Ojibwe blood that precariously bound them but also on the more common grounding of their gender.

She experienced two incredible emotions. First was an overwhelming, almost consummate joy that came from the company of the child. She recalled the feeling when the baby had sucked at her breast, how unifying it seemed and how she'd never experienced anything quite like it before. And second, she felt a deep isolation, a loneliness whose origin she couldn't explain.

She opened her eyes and saw a small, flickering light in the cabin. Her father, she figured, searching for a gun. In the dark of that isolated island, even a small light made a great impression. She turned her eyes toward the southwest. The stars there came right down to where sky met earth.

As she stood watching, she realized that some of the stars were moving. A boat. Not the powerboat, which had run without lights and had moved with reckless speed. Maybe a houseboat? Oh, God, if she could just signal it. She thought frantically but came up with nothing. If only they'd prepared wood for a fire, something she could set a match to.

And then what, Jenny? Use a blanket to send smoke signals? And what if the man in the powerboat came instead?

She heard the rational voice in her head speaking words her father might have spoken, and she watched the lights vanish behind the blind of other islands.

She returned to the shelter, fighting the urge toward discouragement, a fight made easier whenever she saw the baby. He was awake, but not crying. He lay caught in a netting of moonlight that fell through the cracks in the evergreen boughs above. He looked at her silently as she knelt beside him, his dark little eyes intense. She reached out and took his small hand. He gripped her thumb with a strength that surprised her.

She'd almost had a baby once. And when she didn't, she'd worked very hard at not imagining what that might have been like. She'd struggled to close the wound in her heart.

"Don't you worry, little guy," she said gently. "I won't let anyone hurt you. I promise."

She took him in her arms and carried him out of the shelter and stood looking down at the little white moon of his face, and she couldn't help but smile. She heard a cricket chirping somewhere near, the first sound of life from the island since the storm.

"See?" she said to the child. "Everything will be just fine, don't you worry."

She heard underbrush and branch breaking not far away. She turned, knowing it was too late to hide, and she waited. Her father appeared and seemed surprised to see her in the open with the baby.

"How's he doing?" he asked.

"Just fine," she replied. "We both are."

"Wonderful," her father said. "Now let's get the hell out of here."

THIRTEEN

Cork searched the shoreline until he found two snapped trees suitable to his purpose. They were poplar, the broken sections eight inches in diameter. One was roughly ten feet long, the other six. He'd have preferred them to be more or less the same length but knew he had to make do. He hauled the trunks to the rocky cove in the lee of the outcropping and worked by the light of the moon. Using the hunting knife, he cut away as many of the branches as he could and put the trunks side by side. The fit was far from perfect, but it would have to do. He cut the fifteen feet of clothesline cord he'd taken from the cabin into two equal sections and lashed the broken trees together. The result was a long raft just barely wide enough for the baby and some of the items from the shelter. He dragged his construct into the water and was satisfied with its buoyancy. When he was finished, he returned to the shelter.

Jenny had prepared things there. The stove was closed and latched. The blanket was tied in a bundle with the most necessary things inside—diapers, formula, bottle, some canned goods.

"Ready?" Cork asked.

"Do we really need to do this?"

"Maybe not, but I don't want to take any chances. Do you?" He pointedly eyed the baby she held.

"No," she agreed.

"Bring the little guy. I'll get the other things."

The moon was directly above them, and they walked in puddles of their own shadows. Crickets chirped all around now, a hopeful sound, Cork thought, as he led the way to the cove.

When Jenny saw the raft he'd built, she said, "That's it?"

"That's it."

"Dad, that won't hold us."

"Not us, but it will hold him and the other things. You and I are going to swim." He pointed across the channel to the little island with the stand of trees still intact. "I figure it's maybe a couple of hundred yards, that's all."

He made it sound like no big deal, though he knew there was great potential for danger. If the baby got fussy or restless and kicked around a lot and ended up in the lake. If another storm whipped up out of the blue and caught them in open water. If the cigarette boat returned while they were making their passage.

Jenny said, "And if he falls in? Or if that guy comes back in the boat while we're crossing?"

He laughed, despite himself and their precarious situation, because Jenny, in her own thinking, was right there with him, neck and neck.

"All right," he said. "I admit it's got its risks, but I don't have a better offering at the moment. Are you game, or do we stay here and wait it out and hope cigarette boat man doesn't come back looking for us? You have an equal vote in this."

She rocked back and forth as she held the baby. He'd fallen asleep again, cradled in her arms. Cork was a little disturbed at how natural it seemed to see them both this way.

"Okay," she finally said. "But we swim on either side of him. Everything else can go to the bottom of the lake, but we make sure he's safe."

"Of course," Cork said. "Give me the basket."

He'd left a few branches in the center of the raft as a kind of cradle. He placed the wicker basket there. Ahead of it, he put the stove and Jenny's knapsack and, behind it, the blanket bundle and the jug of distilled water. He stripped to his swimsuit and laid his dry clothes on top of the blanket. He held the baby while Jenny did the same, then handed the little guy back. She took him, waded into the lake, and carefully laid him down in the basket. He didn't wake.

"You ready?" Cork asked.

"Let's go," she answered.

They shoved off, carefully guiding the raft between them. The lake was cool but calm. Each held to the makeshift float with one hand and with the other pulled through the water. As they swam, they pushed away the debris that clogged the channel. Their movements created a profound disturbance. Undulations crawled away in all directions, and the surface of the water became mercurial in the moonlight, silver along the crests and black in the troughs.

Cork had grown up on Iron Lake, the crown jewel of Tamarack County, and he'd been a swimmer all his life. He'd taught his children to swim almost before they could walk. So he didn't worry about Jenny. A couple of hundred yards was nothing. Unless the baby gave them trouble. But the child was quiet, riding comfortably as young Moses might have in his basket of woven reeds. Cork wondered just a little at the child's apparent complacency, which all things considered, seemed unusual, maybe even a little unnatural. His own children, as he recalled, had all been light sleepers, and he and Jo had spent long hours at night walking them. On the other hand, his children, when they were babies, had never been left alone for a full day without food or liquid, had never cried hour after hour until sleep came only with complete exhaustion. Which was how he imagined it had been for this baby boy. The child was still recovering, still bone weary, Cork decided. When he regained his strength, maybe he wouldn't be so placid.

They were a little over halfway across when Cork heard the distant sound of powerful outboards.

Jenny heard it, too. "Dad," she said quietly, but with a trace of panic.

"Just keep moving."

"Maybe it's not him," she said.

"It's him."

They kept stroking, kept the same measured pace, which helped maintain the stability of the thrown-together raft and avoided jostling the sleeping baby too dramatically. Cork was concerned that very soon it wouldn't be the motion of the raft that would waken the infant but the sound of the big outboards as the cigarette boat made its way through the debris of the channel. He tried to formulate a plan, some way of heading off the disaster that was approaching. When the boat swept past, the roar of the engines might be loud enough to drown out any noise the child would make. But once the engines cut out, it would be a different story. The baby's crying would carry forever in the calm of that night. Cork thought that if he were the man in the cigarette boat, he'd come back slowly, perplexed by the child's presence in the middle of the channel. He'd use his searchlight to sweep the water. And what would happen then?

Cork decided, and he knew he was getting a little desperate here, that when the light snapped on, he and Jenny would loose their hold and go under and swim away. They would resurface at a distance, perhaps using some of the debris as a shield, and maybe, just maybe, when the boat eased up to the raft, Cork could somehow surprise the man at the wheel.

All this thinking took place in the course of less than a minute. It wasn't much, but it was something.

Jenny whispered from the other side of the raft, "If he comes, you swim away. I'll try to keep him focused on me and the baby, and maybe if he's distracted you'll have a chance of surprising him."

Which, except for the obvious danger in which it put his daughter, wasn't a bad idea. Better, probably, than his own. Because if Jenny stayed with the raft, she would make sure that the baby, in his flailing, didn't tumble into the lake.

He said, "All right."

They both kept swimming.

The boat didn't come, not then anyway. Cork heard it veer southwest, somewhere beyond the little island toward which he and Jenny were swimming. In another minute, the engines died. He wondered if maybe he'd been wrong. Maybe it wasn't the man in the cigarette boat, although all his sensibilities told him otherwise. And it was safest, he knew absolutely, to proceed as if it was that man and he was someone to be avoided.

As they approached the island they hoped would provided sanctuary, Cork's feet touched rock. He found footing, and he and Jenny eased the raft to shore.

"I'll hold," Cork whispered. "You take the baby."

Jenny grasped the wicker basket and lifted it. Cork watched for the small eyes to blink open, but they didn't. He grabbed the stove and the bundled blanket and led the way into the trees.

Moonlight fell between the boughs and lay on the ground in bright, shattered pieces. In this helpful glow, Cork picked his way carefully through the underbrush. He went until he reached the place where the trees met the protective rise of rock. He found a fold in the formation, a kind of alcove where the underbrush gave way to coarse grass and was walled by rock on either side. The baby had awakened and begun to make fussing noises, turning his mouth toward Jenny's breast. Cork quickly set up the stove, unbundled the blanket, and pulled out a bottle Jenny had prepared earlier. He grabbed the pan and said, "I'll be right back."

At the lake, he dipped water and heard clearly the hungry baby beginning to cry. Cork wondered just how far such a sound would carry, and he was angry with the child. An irrational anger, he knew. The baby was just being a baby, but he was putting them all in danger. He hurried back and set the pan on the stove and the bottle in the pan. Jenny had laid out the blanket on the wild grass and was doing her best to soothe the infant, to no avail. Cork slipped his knife from his belt and held it up near the baby's face. The polished blade caught the moonlight, and Cork played the silvery reflection across the baby's face. The child stopped fussing, captured by the sudden glittering. He reached for the blade, curious and intent. Cork moved it away, then near, then away again in a kind of game. In this manner, he kept the baby quiet until the bottle was warm enough to feed him.

Jenny settled herself on the ground with her back against rock and the baby in her arms, sucking greedily. "Thanks," she whispered.

Cork turned away, still angry and ashamed at his anger, and he said, "I'm going to the top of this rise, see what I can see."

"The boat didn't come this way. What does that mean?"

"Maybe I can find out."

Under the moon, the rocky rise lay mostly white, though it was cut by long fractures that were dark, like poisoned veins. The outcropping was bare, no cedars or any other growth offering cover. Cork recalled how clearly the man in the cigarette boat had stood out in silhouette on the rise back of the cabin, and he was careful to keep himself low as he approached the top, which was only slightly higher than the crowns of the trees it protected. He found an isolated boulder and sat in its shadow while he studied the other islands to the southwest. There were so many that they seemed to merge into one inseparable mass. He focused and tried so hard to see detail that his eyes began to hurt and his vision blurred a little.

He closed his eyes. Images came to him, unbidden, of the body in the cabin.

During his life as a cop, he'd seen cruelty in so many forms. What he'd found in the cabin topped them all. She wasn't much more than a child. There was something about her face, something he couldn't quite put his finger on, that was disturbing. Not the bruises that had resulted from beatings—though these were horrific enough—but something in the structure itself that nagged at him. Her body was small and lean, the weight she had to have put on during her pregnancy nowhere evident. Was it possible she wasn't the baby's mother? No, he decided. There were stretch marks. And her breasts were full, as with milk. The hard life alone on the island could have rid her quickly of extra fat. Which made him wonder how long she'd been there. Since winter? But how would she have kept warm? She couldn't have built a fire in the stove if hiding out was the point of her being there; eventually the smoke would have given her away. So probably, she'd come after the thaw. Had she delivered the baby there, in that primitive place? Or had she come afterward?

Cork rolled around in his head the question Jenny had considered: Was there evidence of rape or some other form of sexual violation? He tried to recall the locations of the bruises and if he'd seen a pattern. There'd been discoloring across her left cheek and around the left eye. She'd been hit repeatedly from the right. Bruising also across the left side of her torso. Bruising as well where she'd been bound about the wrists and ankles. But no bruising of the insides of her upper thighs, which he would have expected had she been sexually molested.

He was not terribly shocked at his ability to recall all these horrific details. A lifetime of training, he understood. What really bothered him was that he couldn't help seeing Jenny in that young woman's place. As soon as his mind started to go there, his gut drew taut and his eyes blinked open.

And he saw it. A small flicker of light. Maybe only a match struck for a cigarette. But there it was. For a few long moments. Then gone. Although the dark made it difficult for him to judge distance accurately, Cork made a rough guess that the light had come from three or four hundred yards away.

Why had the man in the cigarette boat stopped there? Simply to wait at a safe distance until it was light enough to check the island where the woman had been murdered? Or was there something particular about the place he'd tied up?

Questions, only questions. Cork would have given his right arm to know who was out there and what they were after. His right arm to know what he would be facing when he finally took his stand.

FOURTEEN

At eighteen, she'd been in love. Desperately in love. The way you can be in love only once and only when you're very young. His name was Sean Pflugleman. He was a poet and the son of a pharmacist. She was a writer of—well, everything then. They'd begun dating when he was seventeen and she sixteen. They'd talked of going to Paris together after graduation, of becoming the new Lost Generation, of embracing the bohemian, of throwing convention to the wind and living simply to discover life and all the experiences that the world offered. Sex was, of course, a part of that discovery. And although they were careful—condoms—in the summer after she finished high school, Jenny O'Connor had become pregnant.

And that had changed everything.

Sean, so eager in his lovemaking and gallant in his poetry, bridled at the idea of becoming a father. He became sullen and accusatory, and when his parents strongly suggested that he "do the right thing," he blamed Jenny for ruining his life. It was odd, she'd thought then, how quickly that kind of love could die. She wasn't necessarily thinking of Sean's love for her; when she saw what he'd become, she'd wanted nothing to do with tying her life to his, or his to the child they'd conceived, and her love for him had shriveled to almost nothing. She'd been determined to have the baby, and her mother and father had pledged their full support in helping her raise their grandchild.

Near the end of her first trimester, she'd miscarried. She was counseled not to think of it as losing a child, but how could she not? Life had been inside her, connected to her, dependent on her. Her blood had flowed through the baby and the baby's blood through her. She'd felt it every day, a connection more powerful than anything she'd ever known, including her passion for Sean. Once she'd accepted her situation and had made her decision to keep the baby, she'd embraced her new life with joyful expectation. A baby. Her baby. She would wake sometimes, alone in her bed in the house where she'd grown up on Gooseberry Lane in Aurora, Minnesota, and feel tears of happiness as she imagined what her new life would be like. Not easy, she clearly understood. A single mother. It would mean a shift in all her plans. She'd been accepted to the University of Iowa, with the idea that someday she might become part of the famous writers' program there. But that wouldn't be. The child would come first. Maybe she would attend Aurora Community College. Maybe she would take over management of Sam's Place, the burger stand her father owned on Iron Lake. It didn't matter. What she did would be done for her child, and whatever was required of her, she would do it with love.

The miscarriage had changed everything again.

She'd gone to Iowa City, graduated with honors, been accepted in the writers' program. She'd met Aaron Houseman, a poet-farmer who lived in the area. He was older than she by several years, but he was a good man and shared with her a love of language and an understanding of the power of words. Last June, they'd moved in together, his place, an old farmhouse on acreage that straddled a little creek a few miles outside Iowa City. He hadn't grown up farming, but land was part of his inspiration and poetic vision, and he dabbled at planting and harvesting, though his real money came from a trust fund. He'd built a shack on the stream, where he would disappear for long hours to write. She had a job at the *Press-Citizen*, the Iowa City newspaper. In the evenings, she worked on a novel.

It was a good life. But there was a complication. Aaron

wanted to marry; she did not. The reason for her reluctance was the whole question of children. She wanted them; Aaron didn't. In a way, he was like Sean. He had his work and he had Jenny and he was happy with that. It wasn't that she didn't understand. To be an artist required so much focus, so much energy. But she believed that this kind of creation was only a part of a life. And in its way, Aaron's refusal to have children was a refusal to participate fully in the panoply of existence, and wasn't that really the responsibility of an artist? To experience life in all its aspects?

When she was honest with herself, she knew that her arguments were intellectual justification for a desire that ran deeper than the mind, that grew from her own knowledge of what it was to have life inside her, real life, not imagined in typed lines or on scribbled pages. She wanted life in her that way again. She wanted to produce life. She wanted, and God help her it sounded so mundane, to be a mother.

Her father had climbed the rock rise and been gone a long time when the baby began to fuss. She sniffed his diaper and understood. She laid him on the blanket in the moonlight and took care of cleaning and changing him. His face was round and luminous, as if the man in the moon himself lay on the ground before her. His eyes, dark and beetle-shell shiny, watched her face intently.

"Oh, little one," she cooed and lifted him into her arms.

He reached up. His fingers, tiny as caterpillars, crawled her face.

A soft scraping came from above her on the rise, and she spotted the shape of her father, gray against the white rock and black veins, making his way down. When he stepped away from the formation, she asked, "What about our friend in the cigarette boat?"

"He's landed on an island a few hundred yards south," her father replied. "As nearly as I can tell, he's just waiting."

"For dawn?"

"That would be my guess. Probably being cautious. If he didn't kill the girl, he may be figuring that, if whoever did is still on the island, they're armed, and dark isn't a good time to come calling. If he's the one who killed her, he may be coming back because he saw that things had been taken from the cabin, and he needs to check it out further. Same issue with the dark."

Jenny rocked back and forth, and the baby sighed in her arms.

"If I were him and I'd killed the girl," she said, "know what I'd do?"

"What?"

"Burn the cabin. You told me he took the body, so he's probably already dumped it somewhere it will never be found. Now he should get rid of any evidence he left behind that might link him to the crime."

Cork looked at her. "Where do you come up with this stuff?"

"I'm just thinking," she said.

"It's good thinking. Come dawn, I guess we'll find out. In the meantime, why don't we try to get a little sleep? Me, I'm bushed." He eyed the baby. "Will he sleep now?"

"I'll put him down and see. I could use some sleep, too."

She covered the baby with the blanket from the wicker basket, lay down next to him, and rolled to her side so that she could watch him. She thought of the horror of what had occurred inside the old cabin. She was afraid, but not for herself.

I swear to God, little guy, she promised silently, *I won't let anything bad happen to you.*

He smiled in his sleep, as if he'd heard.

Ever, she promised.

FIFTEEN

Rose was dreaming. Dreaming about the attic bedroom Cork had created for her in the house on Gooseberry Lane in Aurora, where she'd lived for many years before Mal had come into her life. But dreaming it in ways different from how it had been. In the dream, it was a place of secret passages that led nowhere. Of steps that threatened to collapse under her weight. Of ornate fireplaces and red velvet curtains with brocade. A place of sanctuary, certainly, but also of menace. Welcoming and at the same time disturbing. Her sister, Jo, was still alive somewhere below her. Impossibly, wonderfully alive. And the house was full of activity. She needed to get downstairs to help with things. That was her purpose, to help, and she was desperate, but because of the labyrinth of passages, she couldn't find the way.

Stephen's cry from the deck above woke her: "Lights!"

She came awake fully, sitting on a canvas chair, slumped against the railing on the bow of the houseboat. It was still dark, the moon still high in the sky. She saw pinpoints of light along the southern horizon. She got up, wincing at the deep soreness in her shoulders, the result of her long swim to catch the houseboat, she thought. And probably from the worry as well.

"I see them," Anne cried. She stood near Rose, her flashlight in hand, still scanning the water for debris. "There," she said and pointed toward a couple of points of light far ahead.

Rose went to the open window near the helm station and spoke to Mal, who was still at the wheel.

"Young's Bay?" she asked.

"Not if the GPS is correct. We still have several miles to go."

"How's your ankle?"

"Big as a cantaloupe and purple as a plum."

"Does it hurt much?"

He smiled, looking tired. "Only when I laugh, sweetheart."

Stephen came down the ladder from the upper deck, where he'd gone once the houseboat had cleared Tranquil Channel and entered more open water. He'd stationed himself there to watch for lights, or a signal fire from his father and sister, or anything that might be helpful or hopeful. Anne had stayed below with Rose to continue to watch for debris. Both kids had managed to keep their eyes open, while Rose, though she'd tried valiantly not to, had fallen asleep. They were remarkable, these children who were hers and not really hers.

"The Northwest Angle, Mal?" Anne asked.

"Nope, not yet."

They both looked tired, Stephen and Anne, but in the light that fell on the deck from the cabin, Rose could see hope bright in their faces.

"The lights are moving," Stephen said. "Probably running lights. And they're headed this way. Maybe it's Dad and Jenny coming back to us?"

He looked to his aunt for an answer, looked to her for hope, which was something he and the other O'Connor children had done from the time they were born.

Most of her life, Rose had taken care of others. First her mother, an alcoholic army nurse, who at fifty, had suffered a severe stroke and needed constant attention. It hadn't been a difficult decision for Rose, giving up her own life to make her mother's life easier. She'd never thought of herself as an attractive woman. Boys—and, later, men—had always had eyes for Jo, who was brilliant and beautiful and wild. Rose was devout, and so her life had become the Church and taking care of her mother.

After her mother died, Rose still had the Church to hold to, and she seriously considered entering an order. Then Jo, who'd married a Chicago cop named O'Connor, had given birth to her first child, a baby girl. Though it was a joyful event, it was difficult in a way. Jo was a lawyer with a career on the rise. A baby, no matter how welcome, presented great hardship. It was Rose who'd suggested that perhaps she could help. The situation wasn't one that any of them had foreseen as long-term, but once she joined the O'Connor household, Rose had become an integral part of it. She'd seen the other two children born and helped raise them and thought of them, in a way, as her own.

The Church had continued to be her rock. Somewhere in the back of her mind still lurked the idea that someday, when the children were grown and gone, she would give herself over fully to the service of God. But when she lay alone at night in her cozy attic bedroom, a little voice of truth would sometimes speak to her. It would whisper to her that becoming a bride of Christ was a blessed calling, yes, but for her it was an escape. It was a way not to have to face a terrible reality, which was that Rose wanted desperately to be loved. Not by the Holy Spirit, although that was fine in its way. The truth was that she longed to hear a man whisper he loved her, and she longed to whisper the same words in return. She suffered terrible, lustful desire, and sometimes wondered bitterly why she was being tested in this way.

When she was nearing forty and beginning to lose hope of ever finding love, Father Mal Thorne had been assigned to St. Agnes in Aurora, a remote parish buried deep in the North Woods. He'd been sent, ostensibly, to help the aging priest there. In truth, he was sent into exile, because he was a priest on the edge of falling completely away from the grace of the Church, a priest full of question, full of doubt, and too often, full of alcohol.

Looking back on it, Rose saw God's hand at work. Two people desperately in need of a connection more human than ethereal had been given each other and, in this unlikely union, had found their way back to the divine.

God, Rose believed fervently, worked in mysterious ways.

So when she peered toward the lights across the moonlit water of Lake of the Woods, she believed that, no matter how blind she and the others might be to the ultimate purpose of events, there was a great and compassionate heart at work. And her answer to Stephen's question—did the lights mean his father and sister were safe and returning—was deceptively simple but deeply felt: "God willing."

It was, indeed, a boat, a big power launch. It came straight for them, moving slowly across the water, and when it was near enough, a searchlight played over the houseboat, and a man hailed them.

"Hullo! You folks okay?"

"Yes," Anne called back.

"Why don't you cut your engine, and I'll pull alongside?"

At the helm, Mal eased back on the throttle, and the engine idled. The big launch drew up alongside. The shape of the man at the wheel, large as a bear, was visible in the moonlight. The ambient light from the GPS screen on the dash of the helm gave his broad, bearded face a ghostly look. As the bow neared the houseboat, he cut his own engines, leaped forward, and grabbed the bow line.

"Catch this, son, and tie me up," he called to Stephen and tossed the line. Then he stood next to the gunwale, meaty hands fisted on his hips, grinning up at Rose and the O'Connors.

"First folks I've run into out here," he said. "I was beginning to be afraid nobody'd made it. Glad to see you're all right. Were you caught in the blow?"

"The blow?" Stephen said.

"The storm," the man replied. "It's played hell across the lake from Baudette to Kenora." The man eyed the shattered window at the helm station. "Looks like you got some damage."

Mal limped out and came to the railing. "We lost the radio and got shook up a bit, but we're okay. But we're missing two of our party. They headed to the Northwest Angle this afternoon, but since we lost the radio we haven't been able to check to see if they made it."

"Let's find out," the man in the launch said. "What are their names?"

"Cork and Jenny O'Connor."

The big man returned to the wheel, lifted a radio mike, and raised someone at Young's Bay Landing. The answer from whomever he spoke to was that nobody by those names had come in that afternoon, either before or after the storm. But someone was there waiting for the O'Connors and worried as hell.

"Aaron?" Rose asked.

"Is the guy named Aaron?" the man relayed over the mike.

"That's a roger, Seth," came the reply.

"Tell him I've got some of his party here with me. We'll be coming in."

"Will do."

The man in the launch said, "My name's Seth Bascombe. Tell you what, folks. There's an old Indian fishing camp just ahead. What say you tie up to the dock there and come on with me to Young's Bay Landing. You can see about this Aaron, and we can figure what to do about your missing parties."

"Can we go back out looking tonight?" Stephen asked.

Bascombe stroked his beard as if considering, then shook his head. "Son, the truth is it would be best to wait until morning for that. Mine's one of the last boats still out searching, and I count myself lucky to still be afloat in all this damn debris. It may be that your missing parties made it to one of the inhabited islands, and we'll be hearing from them before too long anyway. And to be honest, I'm pooped. Need some shut-eye. We'll head back out at first light. Ought to be a flotilla along with us then. You all onboard with that?"

Their reluctance was obvious to Rose, but Bascombe's wisdom was hard to argue with, and so they all agreed.

They crossed the international border in the dark. Once they'd left the area the storm had devastated, Bascombe made good time across what seemed, under the face of the moon, to be a lake of liquid silver.

"Young's Bay Landing," he called out, pointing toward a cluster of lights looming ahead.

He throttled back, and they entered a narrow passage and motored to a brightly lit dock where several people stood waiting. Bascombe eased the boat against the dock and asked Stephen to toss the bow line. One of the men caught it and looped it around a piling, and someone else tied the stern line to a cleat. Lots of hands helped Rose and the others from the launch.

"Everyone all right here?" The question came from a woman who scrutinized them with what appeared to Rose to be a trained eye.

"No," Rose said. "My husband's hurt. A broken ankle, maybe."

"Let's get him inside so I can take a look."

Two men flanked Mal and gave him their shoulders for support, and he hobbled between them toward a long, lighted building that stood a dozen yards back from the dock.

The others followed, except for a tall, lanky young man who hung back. Rose hung back with him.

"Hello, Aaron," she said.

She knew him from pictures Jenny had sent, knew him from the talks she'd had with her niece, the kinds of talks Jenny would have had with her mother if Jo were still alive. Jenny had told her Aaron was twenty-nine, but Rose saw something in his face, pinched and critical, that made him seem much older. For Jenny's sake, she wanted to like him, and, instead of a handshake, she gave him a hug.

"You must be Rose," he said. "Jenny's told me all about you." He looked toward the building where everyone had gone. "She's told me about all of you."

They stood together under the light on the deserted dock. Night insects flew about them. From inside the building came the hubbub of voices, and Rose heard the kids and Mal telling their story.

"You must be worried sick," she said.

His hair was the color of wet sand and unkempt. His eyes were deep green and heavy with fatigue and concern. "They never showed up," he said. "We could see the storm from here. It looked like some kind of monster barreling across the lake. Folks said it was headed straight up through something called the Narrows and God help anyone caught in it there."

"She's with her father," Rose said, taking his arm. "If anyone could keep them safe, it's Cork."

She walked him into the building, which turned out to be a general store and café. Mal was at the center of the gathering inside, his injured ankle cradled in the lap of the woman who'd met them on the dock. With her fingertips, she felt carefully around the bruised area and finally pronounced, "I don't think it's a break, just a really bad sprain. Ice," she said to no one in particular. "We need ice. And a towel."

"Are you a doctor?" Rose asked.

"No, but around here you see everything," the woman replied. "Fishhooks through the thumb, fingers nearly sliced off by some drunk trying to fillet a walleye, heart attacks, you name it."

"Lynn here is the closest thing we got on the Angle to Florence Nightingale," Bascombe said.

"Lynn Belgea," the woman said and offered her hand to Mal. She was perhaps fifty, small, with a plain face honest as the day was long. "I'm a nurse practitioner. We probably ought to get you to Warroad and have that ankle X-rayed, just to be on the safe side."

"I can drive him, Lynn," one of the men offered. "Got my truck outside."

Mal waved off the offer. "Ice and ibuprofen'll be fine. We have some folks still out there on the lake who need finding."

"Those two Seth called about?" Belgea asked.

"Yes," Stephen replied. "My dad and my sister."

Bascombe said, "I explained to them we'd best wait until morning."

Belgea nodded. "Seth's right. Morning's safest and will come soon enough. We got lots of folks still unaccounted for. Don't need to add any more to that number by sending boats out in the dark. Where you folks staying?"

"Our accommodations are somewhere out there," Mal said, waving toward the lake. "We docked our houseboat."

"Look, folks," Bascombe said, his eyes drifting over Mal and Stephen and Anne, and finally Rose. "I have a little resort on Oak Island. Got some empty cabins. Be glad to put you up while we look for your family."

"That's awfully nice of you, Mr. Bascombe," Rose said.

"It's Seth. And anybody here'd do the same. On the Angle, folks help each other out. There's a lot of territory between us and the rest of the world."

Belgea, who looked as tired as everyone else, smiled wanly and said, "Sometimes up here, I get the feeling there is no 'rest of the world.' "

SIXTEEN

Bascombe said, "You folks hungry?"

They'd landed at an unlit dock on the far side of Oak Island, a fifteen-minute boat ride from the mainland. Bascombe had shown them to their cabins, small and rustic and with only the very basic amenities inside: two bunks in each, a table with a single lamp, a sink with a mirror, and a small bathroom/shower. No bedding on the bunks, no towels hanging on the bathroom racks. Bascombe had apologized for the austerity.

"I don't rent them out anymore, and when I did, it was to fishermen who didn't particularly care about their comfort. They came to catch walleye. I've got bedding and towels and such at the lodge, if you want to come up and snag them."

Rose and Mal had taken one cabin, Stephen and Aaron another, and Anne had been given a cabin to herself. They were all ready to get their sheets and blankets and turn in, but Bascombe's question about food seemed to stir the realization in them all that they hadn't eaten since lunch.

Stephen leaped at the offer. "You bet," he said.

"We don't want to put you out any more than we already have," Rose told their host.

They stood in front of the open door to the cabin Rose and Mal had been given, in a drizzle of light that came from the table lamp inside. Bascombe held a big flashlight, which he swung toward the largest of the buildings in the resort.

"Up here, it's a long trip to the grocery store, so I keep the lodge pretty well stocked. And the kitchen's in good shape. I'm not much of a cook, but I can rustle you up something."

"Aunt Rose is the best cook in Minnesota," Stephen offered eagerly.

"That so?" A broad smile spread across Bascombe's long, broad face. "You want to give me a hand, Rose or, hell, give me instructions, I'd be fine with that."

"No, that's quite all right—" Rose began.

Mal cut her off. "Ah, go on. Give him a hand, sweetheart. He's pooped, too. And your cooking might be a small down payment for his hospitality."

"These days, I only cook for myself," Bascombe said. "Mostly I'm a connoisseur of the lumpy, the soggy, and the burned. Be nice to eat a decent meal for a change."

"All right, Seth. If you're sure."

"If I didn't want your help, Rose, I'd say so. On the Angle, we all pretty much speak our minds. Follow me."

The lodge turned out to be an amiable place, far less austere than the cabins. It had a small dining area with four tables and chairs. The knotty pine walls were hung with maps of the Lake of the Woods and photographs of fishermen holding up prize catches, and a couple of stuffed muskies, huge and with vicious-looking teeth, mounted on polished plaques. There was a long glass counter with a display, dusty now, of lures and fishing knives and bug repellent and pamphlets about U.S. and Canadian regulations. Set into one of the walls was an open fireplace with a fieldstone hearth, and everything in the lodge had the distant, pleasant scent of woodsmoke. Mal, who was hobbling around on a pair of wooden crutches that Lynn Belgea had scrounged from somewhere back at Young's Bay Landing, sat at a table, and the others, except Rose and Bascombe, joined him. Rose followed the big man into the kitchen and was pleasantly surprised to see that it was quite modern, with a large refrigerator and commercial stove, both stainless steel. There was a pantry, modestly stocked at the moment, but it could have held supplies for an army. The stainless-steel sinks were broad and deep.

"Back in the days when this place was still a moneymaking operation, I had me a fine cook," Bascombe said. His big shoulders slumped a little, and there was a mist of sadness over his words. "Renee McGuire. That woman could do things with walleye should've been illegal."

"What happened to Renee McGuire?" Rose asked, because she had a strong sense there was a good deal to the story.

"In the end, I guess, both me and this place proved to be disappointments to her. She found herself better prospects down in Warroad."

Rose looked at the man, who was bearded, bear-big, wildhaired, and from the musky smell coming off him, a good day or two overdue for a shower, and she understood what a challenge he would present to any woman.

Bascombe waved off his dour mood. "But that's water under the bridge. Tell me what you need, and I'll see what I can find."

Rose made frittatas with diced ham and onion and melted cheese. She fried potatoes as an accompaniment, and Bascombe toasted bread. When they brought everything to the table, along with a pitcher of orange juice, the eyes of the others grew big with anticipation.

"Thanks, Aunt Rose," Anne said.

Aaron, who'd been mostly quiet since their meeting at Young's Bay Landing, said graciously, "Thank you, Rose. This looks incredible."

"This barely scratches the surface of what our Rose can do." Mal gave her an appreciative wink.

They ate without much talk at first, but as their appetites were satisfied, they turned eventually to a discussion of the situation on the lake.

Bascombe said, "Heard someone at the landing say that the storm ripped through Kenora, then turned east and was looking to tear a path all the way to Quebec."

"A derecho," Aaron said.

"A what?" Bascombe gave him a look of incomprehension.

"I heard on the radio that the weather service called it a derecho. They said it was a storm made up of straight-line winds of hurricane force. Gusts in Baudette in excess of a hundred miles an hour. They're rare, apparently, but when they hit . . ." He stopped and eyed the lake outside, which was full of islands as numerous as flies on a carcass. "When they hit," he went on, "they tear up everything in their path."

"Jenny's all right," Rose said to him. "They're both all right."

He accepted her assurance with a nod and nothing more.

"Okay," Bascombe said. "Let's see what we can pin down. When they left, did they say anything to you about where they were going?"

Anne said, "Just to the Angle to pick up Aaron."

"Where were you anchored?"

"In a bay up above Tranquil Channel," Mal replied.

"Okay," Bascombe said. He stood and went to the nearest wall, where a huge map of the lake hung. He pointed to a wide area of relatively empty water. "To get to the Angle there would be three main routes. Anybody who knows the lake knows that you have to stay with the main routes, otherwise you're very likely to hit one of the rocks or reefs hidden just under the surface. Did they have GPS?"

"Yes," Mal said. "Loaded with a program specifically for Lake of the Woods."

"So he would have been able to follow the main routes, known where the shallows and reefs are. Okay. This Cork, is he a pretty responsible guy?"

"Most definitely," Stephen replied without hesitation.

Bascombe looked to Rose for confirmation of the son's confidence in his father, and she nodded.

Their host went on. "What time did they leave?"

"A little before two," Stephen said.

"What time were they supposed to pick you up?" he asked Aaron.

"We set it up for three-thirty," Aaron replied.

"An hour and a half to get to the Angle." Bascombe scratched his beard and studied the map and seemed disturbed. "What were they in?"

"A small dinghy," Mal said.

"What kind of engine?"

"Evinrude. Don't know the model. Not much horsepower, though."

"Hmmmm." Bascombe thought and shook his head. "Even with a small outboard, an hour and a half is way too much time. The storm swept through a few minutes before three. They should have been at Young's Bay Landing easily by then."

Silence settled over the room, then Stephen said, "Wait. I think Dad said something about making a stop along the way."

"Oh? Where?" Bascombe asked. "Do you remember?"

"I don't think he said exactly. I think it was going to be kind of a surprise or something for Jenny."

"Think, Stephen," Mal urged. "Anything you remember might be helpful."

Stephen squinted, as if trying to picture the past, and then spoke carefully. "He told her to make sure she took her camera. I don't know what that was about, though."

"Some interesting sight he wanted her to see?" Rose speculated.

"That could be any number of places," Bascombe said. "There's nowhere on earth that's quite like Lake of the Woods."

"Something Ojibwe," Anne said suddenly.

Bascombe looked to her. "What do you mean?"

"This morning—yesterday morning," she corrected herself, "Dad said something kind of enigmatic. He said he was going to give Jenny an Ojibwe lesson about children."

"Children?" Bascombe said.

Rose glanced at Aaron, who sat tall and, at the moment, stiff in his chair. She and Jenny had talked at length about the issue of children, something divisive in Jenny's relationship with Aaron.

"Not much help probably," Anne said.

Bascombe gave her a hopeful smile. "You never know." He turned back to the map. "Like I said, there are basically three routes through the maze of islands to the Angle. The south track and two branches of the main track." He followed each route quickly with his index finger. "The central track would be the most logical, unless Anne's right and he made some kind of excursion to see something special. But for the moment, let's stick with considering this track. It would have taken them through Tranquil Channel—"

"We were there," Stephen burst in. "A little while before we ran into you."

"That's right." Bascombe gave him a patient smile and went on. "That would have taken them past Royal Island, Lily Island, between Falcon and Windfall." He stepped back, studied the map, and spoke to himself. "What's interesting along there? Interesting and has to do with children?" He shook his head. "I'm coming up with nothing. So let's try assuming they took another route. The south track would have taken them through French Portage and the Tug Channel." Bascombe's thick index finger touched the map and he traced the route. "Mostly they'd have been traveling between the Aulneau Peninsula and Falcon Island. It's a beautiful route, but not much there, at least along the shoreline. Inland, God only knows what you'll find. But maybe . . ." He stopped and thoughtfully stroked his beard.

"Maybe what?" Anne said.

"Maybe he was thinking of taking her to Massacre Island."

"That doesn't sound good," Stephen asked.

Bascombe laughed. "Nothing particularly ominous about it now, but back in the real early days, the French had a fort up near Angle Inlet. Fort St. Charles. Pretty important in the fur trade. The Sioux threatened it, and a party set out for Mackinac

Island to rustle up some help, but they didn't get far. They were ambushed and massacred their first night out."

"Bummer," Stephen said.

"I hope your Cork wasn't planning on going out any farther than that," Bascombe said.

Rose didn't like the sound of that. "Why?" she said.

"The big water begins just beyond it."

"Big water?"

"It's what we call that end of the lake. Almost forty miles of open water between the islands here and the mainland, War-road and Baudette. Nowhere to find shelter if they were caught out there in the blow that came through today. That—what did you call it?"

"Derecho," Aaron said.

"Yeah, that."

Mal said evenly, "So let's assume that's not the way they went."

"Then they could have split off here." Once again Bascombe touched his index finger to the map. "And followed the north branch of the main track. Would take them closer to Windigo Is-land, which is where a lot of the Indians in this area live."

"Ojibwe?" Anne asked.

"Yes. The Reserve Thirty-seven band."

"Maybe Cork was going to take her to visit somebody there," Rose said.

Bascombe nodded, as if the idea appealed to him. "Sounds like as good a place as any to start looking. Tell you what, first thing tomorrow we'll head over and see if anybody there can help us." He let out a tired sigh and rubbed the back of his neck, then cocked his head, as if listening. "Wind's up again."

Stephen stood and walked to the window. "The sky's clear. There couldn't be another storm moving in, right?"

"Don't worry, son. From what I understand, we should have clear skies for the next couple of days at least," Bascombe re-plied. "And it's supposed to stay hot, and in this kind of situa-tion, that's a good thing."

Stephen put his face near the window screen. "They wouldn't be trying to get here in the dark, would they?"

"Did they have a spotlight on that dinghy?" Bascombe asked. "Or a good powerful flashlight?"

"No spotlight," Mal said. "And I don't recall that they took a flashlight either. Why would they? They expected to be back well before dark."

Their host shook his head. "Nobody with any brains would try running on this lake at night without both GPS and a good light."

Stephen turned back to him. "We saw a boat out there tonight, running without any lights. A cigarette boat."

"Cigarette boat?" Bascombe scowled. "Running without lights? How could you have seen it?"

"It crossed through moonlight, and I saw it for like a second."

"Running without lights." Bascombe looked as if he was either puzzled or disbelieving.

"A smuggler maybe," Stephen said with authority.

Rose thought Bascombe might laugh, but he didn't. He walked to Stephen. "Any idea where this was, son?"

"No. It was all dark and we were pretty lost."

"Somewhere this side of Tranquil Channel," Mal said.

Bascombe stood beside Stephen and stared out at the darkness. He put his hand protectively across Stephen's shoulder.

"I know for a fact that there are men greedy enough and stupid enough and desperate enough to run that risk. They're not the kind of people I'd want to encounter alone out there at night. If that's who it was, I think you folks are lucky that you just heard them."

"What if Dad and Jenny ran into them?" Stephen said.

That prospect seemed to kill all discussion, until Rose spoke up. "Let's pray they didn't."

SEVENTEEN

She woke herself from a nightmare set among ruins and discovered that her father was gone. The night was blessedly warm. The wind was up again, though nothing like the storm that had stranded them. The breeze ran among the leaves of the poplars and needles of the spruce in the stand that served as sanctuary, and Jenny lay still, listening to that restless sound. At last, she pushed herself up. Her body was stiff from the hard ground, and probably from the tension of the worry that hadn't left her even in her sleep. She found a bottle of formula prepared and sitting beside the Coleman stove. There was water in the pan over the unlit burner. On a flat surface of the rock sat an empty can of peaches. She looked up the rock rise, stark white under the moon, and although she didn't see him, she figured that her father must have gone back to the top to watch for the man in the cigarette boat.

She was hungry. From the supply of goods they'd brought, she took a can of pineapple rings and used the opener. She drank the juice first, then one by one, lifted out the rings and ate greedily. As she was finishing, the baby began to stir. She lit the burner, put the bottle in the pan to warm, then sat beside the child, watching him wake. His face was drawn into tight lines, and his tiny hands were clenched into fists. She wondered, with a stab of sorrow, if somewhere in his little brain would be stored forever the memory of what had happened on that devastated island. No one remembered that far back in their lives, did they? Oh, God, she hoped not.

His eyes finally opened, and her face was the first thing he saw. To her great surprise, he smiled. She picked him up and cradled him.

"What's your name, little guy?" She nuzzled his nose with her own, and a small cry escaped his mouth. She put a finger to her lips and whispered, "Shhhhh."

When the bottle was warmed, she fed him and burped him. As she was changing his diaper, she heard the powerful engines kick in beyond the rise.

A few minutes later, her father came down the face of the rock. He looked tired and he looked grim.

"He's on his way?" she said as she walked the baby.

"Yes."

"It sounds like he's circling to the east. Why?"

Although she knew he couldn't see the boat, she watched her father's eyes follow the deep growl of the engines.

"Probably thinking of coming in with the sun at his back," he said. "That way, if someone's on the island and planning on taking a bead on him, the sun will be in the shooter's eyes."

"But if it's that dangerous, why would he come back?"

"Maybe to look for the baby. Or, like you said before, to remove all evidence that might tie him to what he did there. Which would include us."

"He doesn't know about us, Dad."

"I'm sure he knows someone was in the cabin."

"For all he knows, we could have left."

He nodded faintly, his eyes still tracking the course of the boat from the sound of the engines. "So maybe he's not back for the baby. Maybe he's looking for something else that he knew he couldn't find in the dark. I'm just guessing."

She looked at the sloping rock her father had just descended. "What if we went to the other side of this rise?"

He shook his head. "Two problems with that. One, there's no cover on the ridge. Two, when you get to the top, it's a sheer drop to the water. For better or worse, this is where we make our stand."

"Our stand?"

"Sorry. Bad choice of words. This is where we hunker down and wait it out."

"Until he's gone? Then what?"

"Let's figure that out when the time comes. This little guy's the big question mark now. Think you can keep him quiet?"

"I'll do my best, Dad," she promised. She smiled at the baby in her arms. "He will, too."

They listened as the boat continued circling, then the engines cut, and all they could hear was the sound of the wind in the trees.

Her father turned back to the rise. "I'm going to see what he's up to now."

He climbed the sloping rock wall and cleared the top of the trees. The moon had long ago passed its zenith, and the island across the channel was a tapestry of silver and black. Off the eastern tip lay a little islet barely more than a round cone of bald rock the size of a two-story house. He tried to reckon where the cigarette boat might be anchored now, and figured that the far side of that islet was a good bet. When morning came and the boat made a run for the island—if, in fact, that was the plan—the launch would be coming directly out of the glare of the rising sun. The man at the wheel would land without incident. And then he would begin his hunt.

But hunting what? Cork wondered. Jenny and him? The baby? Something else entirely? Impossible to know.

Cork tried to put himself inside that man's brain, to stay ahead of his thinking.

If the mystery man believed someone was still on the island, he would probably work his way carefully from one end to the other, keeping to the cover of the downed trees. It would be hard to move quickly or quietly, so what would his advantage be? Cork figured if it were him, he'd make sure that he had firepower on his side. He'd have brought a good rifle with a powerful scope. He'd have brought field glasses. Maybe he'd even have dressed in camouflage, or at least clothing that would blend easily into the underbrush. If he was as cruel as the torture of the young woman in the cabin indicated, he'd shoot to maim, to disable, and in that way try to ensure an opportunity for interrogation, the kind of sadistic interrogation the young woman must have endured.

But to what end? What was the purpose of what had occurred in that isolated place? Inflicting pain for pain's sake? There were people capable of such inhumanity, but this felt different to Cork. The woman's isolated situation felt purposeful, a hiding. If the storm hadn't destroyed the tree cover, the cabin would be difficult, if not impossible, to spot from the water. It was a rustic structure but had been comfortably accommodated. Until the fallen pine had breached the roof, it was sturdy. The cooking had been done on the Coleman, so no fire in the stove and no smoke to give away the location. All in all, not a bad place to hide. But why and from whom? The man in the cigarette boat, what had he been to the dead girl? Protector or prison guard? Keeper or killer? And what was he now to those he hunted?

The baby was yet another unanswered question. Clearly, he'd been hidden, and the place of his hiding had been prepared long in advance. The dead girl must have known they were in danger. She'd done her best to save the child, maybe even sacrificed herself. But why? What was the importance of the baby to anyone but her? And was the baby the reason she died?

And then he wondered, with a bitter edge that shamed him, would this child be responsible for the death of another woman?

Because he knew without a doubt that Jenny was prepared to sacrifice herself, if it came to that.

Cork was exhausted; his brain was going in dizzy circles, and he couldn't think clearly. It didn't much matter. In a little while, when the sun rose, all his questions would be answered, one way or another.

EIGHTEEN

Rose couldn't sleep. She was tired through and through, but her brain kept working, wouldn't give in to exhaustion, circled and circled, always coming back to the same place: Everything was in God's hands. It was always a question of submitting to his will. Wasn't it?

But what did that say about God when his will seemed to be visiting one affliction after another on the people she loved? What could possibly be his purpose?

In his bunk on the other side of the small cabin, Mal slept dead as stone. Rose finally slipped out of her own bunk and went to the window. In the east, she saw a thin vermilion line, the approach of dawn. She also saw Aaron, standing alone on the dock, hands deep in the pockets of his jeans, staring where the day would break. Quietly, she dressed in the clothes she'd worn the day before, put on her canvas boat shoes, and eased herself out the door.

The birds were calling to one another. She realized that, after the terrible storm, everything had been stilled, even the sound of the birds. Had they fled to safety somewhere and now returned? The air was cool and moist, the wind steady and fresh against her skin. She smelled the scent of wet earth and evergreen coming from the woods at her back.

"Can't sleep?" she asked as she approached Aaron. She'd softened her voice in order not to startle him.

He turned his head, showing the strong profile of his face. She didn't know much about him, but she could clearly see one of the reasons Jenny had been attracted to him. With all that tousled hair and those haunting green eyes and the brooding aspect of a poet, he was beautiful.

"Can't stop worrying," he said. "Can't stop wondering where she is out there, if she's okay, if she's hurt, if she's scared, if she's—" He stopped himself.

"If she's even alive," Rose finished for him. She stepped to his side and stood near enough that she could feel the warmth of his bare arm. "I've been praying all night that they're safe."

He stared at the bloodred line in the sky. "I don't believe in prayer. But right now I wish I did."

"I wish you did, too. I find that, when I have no control over something, it's a comfort to let go and put my trust in a prayer."

Aaron said, "Did you pray for Jenny's mom?"

"Yes."

"Excuse me for reminding you, but it didn't do much good."

"Not for my sister, no."

Somewhere far out on the lake, in water that was still the color of night, a loon called. It seemed an utterly sad sound.

"I'm sorry," Aaron said. "That was unkind of me."

"Maybe, but it was the truth of how you feel. It helps me know you better."

"This," he said, lifting his hands in quiet frustration, "wasn't how you were supposed to get to know me."

"Nor you us. It is what it is." The vermilion line in the east was growing wider and more diffuse, and the surface of the lake had picked up a hint of color, which was the hue of old blood. "She was worried about you."

"Why?"

"Only one of you, lots of us. And the O'Connors can be clannish."

"Show me a family that isn't. But I'm guessing that's not what was really worrying her." He turned to her fully, and even in the dim illumination that was a long distance from daylight, she could discern the intensity in his eyes. "She's talked to you, I know. Things haven't been exactly easy between us lately. I wasn't even sure I should come. Now I look out across this lake and I think to hell with the small squabbles. I just want her to be with me and be safe."

"I understand."

He studied her and nodded. "She's told me a lot about you, about everyone. She's pretty high on her family."

Rose smiled. "We're all pretty fond of her, too."

Jenny hadn't said much about Aaron's family, and what little she did wasn't encouraging. They lived somewhere in Virginia, near D.C. They had money, from banking, she thought. Aaron was their only child, which to Rose meant that they should dote on him. But Jenny said there was something not right in his relationship with his parents, something festering, something that Aaron wouldn't talk about but that kept him at a distance. He hadn't been home in several years, and if his parents wanted to see him, they had to come to Iowa. They almost never did. She had yet to meet them.

"You really heard a smuggler out there?" Aaron asked.

"We heard a boat running through the dark. From what Seth said, the circumstance seemed consistent with the action of a smuggler."

He thought about that, then his gaze made a long sweep of the lake. "A big place, this. Probably not much chance of them running into that kind of trouble, don't you think?"

What she thought was that she didn't know the Lake of the Woods and so had no idea what might be possible. What she said was "I'm sure you're right."

"I guess we should try to get some sleep," he said.

"Do you think you can?"

"Maybe I'll try saying a little prayer before I lie down."

He didn't look at her or smile, and she had no idea if it was meant as a joke.

She hoped it wasn't.

NINETEEN

The cigarette boat roared out of the glare of the rising sun, just as Cork had predicted. He shielded his eyes and squinted and watched it race over water that reflected morning sunlight with painful brilliance. It swung to the far side of the island, where he lost it behind the bald rise that backed the old, damaged cabin. The engines cut out suddenly, and Cork suspected that the boat had entered one of the many inlets along the island's shoreline, where it would anchor.

He slid toward a small formation of rock that was like a lifted shoulder, slipped into the long trough of morning shadow that it cast, and tried to be still as the stone where he lay. He scanned the island across the channel for any sign of the man who'd come hunting. The birds had returned, and he saw white pelicans roosting along rocks that shot up from the waterline like a row of molars. An eagle rode the wind, circled the island, and finally landed in the crown of one of the few ragged spruce trees that had survived upright. It was an hour before he saw movement of a larger creature near the center of the island, scuttling over a long outcrop of flat-topped rock. Cork wouldn't have seen him except that the rock was pale as ice and the mottled green of the man's camouflage fatigues stood out for a few moments in sharp contrast. The figure quickly crossed the rock and vanished amid the debris on the other side. He was too distant and too soon gone for Cork to make out how heavily armed he might be. From the man's position, Cork was fairly certain that he was, in fact, working his way down the length of the island.

Cork had been right in much of his thinking so far. Not that it pleased him. During the night, as he'd kept his lonely vigil atop the rock, he'd allowed himself to hope that he might be wrong about everything. That the man had fled the island in order to alert the authorities and let them deal with the girl's murder, and that with the morning light they would come, and he and Jenny would be rescued. Of course, there was the fact that the man had already returned once and carried away the girl's body, but maybe there was a reasonable explanation for that, too, one that, because he was tired and battered, Cork simply wasn't seeing.

Now, as he watched for the lone figure to reappear, he was pretty certain the man had taken the body to dispose of it. No corpus delecti, no proof of a crime. This time the killer had returned to be certain that, if there were witnesses, they, too, would disappear.

Now Cork speculated that the man in camouflage would reconnoiter the island and probably find the smashed dinghy and the little shelter Jenny had built and understand that someone had been there after the storm but was no longer. He would realize that in this place visited by no one, someone had come, thrown there by providence and the storm. They'd found the murdered girl, and maybe the baby, and then what? Been rescued? Probably not, or at least not yet, since the island was so remote. So what, then? Gone somewhere else would be the most obvious answer, slipped off the island seeking a better hiding place. And where would that be? The hunter's gaze would swing across the narrow channel to the only stand of trees in sight that was still upright and offered shelter.

Cork began planning for what he knew would come then.

*   *   *

She'd heard the engines kick in and had listened as they whisked the man to the island where the girl had been murdered, and then she'd waited, which was hard to do. She wanted desperately to be up on the rock with her father, observing the man's movements, knowing the way things stood. But the baby couldn't be left alone, and she knew that one more body above the trees would be one more object the man who hunted them might spot. Better, she understood, to stay below, to see to the baby, and to trust that her father would be her eyes.

But she could still use her brain.

She was thinking: What if the man checked the whole of that devastated island? And what if he found the shelter she'd built but didn't find her? What would he think? What would he do?

She paced, cradling the baby, who was sound asleep in her arms. Dragonflies darted through the shafts of sunlight, and bees hovered around what might have been the only wildflowers for miles. She barely noticed these things, because her mind was so focused on trying to anticipate the thinking of the man who hunted them.

He would, she decided, wonder first if they'd been rescued, but the evidence—the smashed dinghy, the shelter itself, and the fact that they were in a terribly remote area of the lake—would tell him no. If he was smart, he would understand that they'd fled, looking for a safer hiding place. And where would that be? The only stand of undamaged trees anywhere in sight. He would eye those trees like a hawk might eye a patch of tall grass where it understood a mouse could hide. And then he would come for them.

They had to be prepared. They needed a plan.

That was as far as she'd gotten when she heard the slither of her father down the sloping face of rock. He was sweating when he finally stood before her. He looked grimly at the baby.

"He sleeps like a log, thank God," he said.

Jenny asked, "What about our hunter?"

"He's working his way down the island, looking for us."

"Where is he now?"

"Halfway. We've got maybe forty-five minutes before he reaches your shelter."

"I've been thinking," she said. "He'll know we're here. It's the most logical place."

"I agree. Unless we divert him."

She could see that he was ahead of her in his thinking, but as soon as he spoke those two sentences, she was right there with him.

"No, Dad."

"It's the only way," he said.

"Make you the target, right?"

"As unappealing as that is to me, yes."

"There's got to be another way."

"I'd like to hear it."

He waited, but they both knew he was right. Maybe if they had hours to think, to plan, to prepare, but they had only minutes.

"Where?" she said.

"The island just to the south. It's larger than this one, so more area to hide in."

"But no cover. Everything's blown down."

"This is how I figure it. There's a bluff at this end."

"I remember it," Jenny said. "It's got a cliff face that drops straight down forty or fifty feet to the waterline."

"That's the one. I'll swim to the island and haul ass up the back of the bluff and make myself visible. I'm thinking our hunter friend, when he stumbles across your shelter and finds you gone, will climb that outcropping with the cedars on top. It's got the best view of the whole area. He'll look back at where he's been, and then he'll look around at other possibilities."

"And that's when he sees these trees."

"Yeah. So I have to make sure that he sees me, too. Best if he sees me instead."

"You said if you were him you'd come well armed. So he'll probably have a good rifle."

"Probably," her father agreed.

"Dad, that bluff you're talking about is only a couple of hundred yards from those cedars. Even a bad shot could pick you off easily, and I'm thinking this guy's probably pretty good."

"I'll do my best not to give him much of a target. And I need to stay alive so he'll come for me there and not give any thought to you here."

"I don't like this."

"I don't either. But we don't have much time, so I guess we're stuck with it."

"What if . . ." She couldn't bring herself to say it.

"If he gets to me? Good question. And I've got an answer. After he's seen me, I'm going to make myself scarce. He'll beat cleats back to that launch of his and come hunting me. As soon as he leaves those cedars, you put everything on the raft I made and . . ."

"And what?"

He looked at the baby, looked at him not with love but with a kind of regret. She was afraid that he was going to suggest that she leave the child behind, and if he did that, she would hate him.

"You take the baby back to the shelter," he went on. "If our hunter gets past me, that'll be the last place he'll look for you. But, Jenny, you've got to leave no trace that we were ever here. I mean nothing, do you understand?"

"Yeah, Dad."

"Okay."

He took a deep breath, and then he hugged her, with the body of the sleeping baby between them. She understood that, if things went bad, it might be the last time they ever touched this way. She felt herself on the edge of despair and knew that she couldn't allow herself to go there.

"Dad, take the knife." She nodded toward the blade that lay next to the Coleman stove.

"No, you keep it."

She shook her head. "If he gets through you, the knife won't do me any good. That's the truth, and we both know it."

His face went hard. He took the knife and slid the blade into his belt. He kissed the top of her head as he passed, then ran for the lake.

Jenny laid the baby carefully in the wicker basket and turned to her own duty.

TWENTY

First thing in the morning, Bascombe spoke with the mainland and learned that, in addition to the missing O'Connors, half a dozen other people were still unaccounted for, all visiting fishermen staying at lodges in the area. A search effort by local volunteers was being organized. Neither Lake of the Woods County authorities nor the Coast Guard station in Warroad could send help; with the devastation that the derecho had wreaked on the communities along the lake's southern shoreline, they already had their own hands full.

"Like always," Bascombe said, scratching at his beard, "we're on our own up here. But don't worry. We know what we're doing."

The O'Connors were happy to believe him.

Bascombe's boat was large enough to accommodate only three passengers comfortably, and he called a friend to lend a hand, a guy named Tony Ebnet, who was a guide at Angle Inn Lodge, a resort half a mile distant. Ebnet motored up to Bascombe's, where he picked up Anne and Aaron and took off to search the Tug Channel and north through French Portage. Bascombe took the others in his launch. They stopped at an unmanned customs station on Cyclone Island, where he phoned in and explained the situation to both the Canadian and U.S. officials, who were, he reported, understanding. Then they continued to Windigo Island.

Over the noisy splash of the boat through the swells that rose with the wind, Bascombe explained about Windigo Island and the Reserve 37 Ojibwe.

"There are two bands of First Nations Indians in this area," he said. "The Reserve Thirty-three Ojibwe live north of Angle Inlet. The Reserve Thirty-seven are broken into two groups. The largest bunch are way over on the northeastern side of the lake, on Regina Bay, but the administration for the band is handled by the folks here on Windigo and Little Windigo. Good people, although sometimes the men, especially the young ones, are prone to get a little drunk or a little high and get out of line. No real trouble though. Like I say, good people. We're going to talk to a woman named Cherri Allen. I called to let her know we're coming. She's from the States, somewhere in Michigan. Married into the Powassin family on the island, and handles a lot of visitor issues. Canadian fishing permits, arranging for Indian guides, that kind of thing. She'll be a good place to start."

They motored to a long dock and tied up. A trail led from the dock into some trees through which a white clapboard house was visible. The island was well west of the track the storm had followed, and the tree cover was undamaged. As they disembarked, a woman appeared on the trail, walking out of the shadows of a stand of paper birch, smiling warmly.

"*Boozhoo!*" Bascombe cried, offering the familiar Ojibwe greeting.

"*Boozhoo*, Seth," the woman called back.

She looked to Rose to be in her early fifties. Attractive, with blond hair blown a little askew by the wind. She wore loose jeans and a plaid flannel shirt with the sleeves rolled well above the elbows. Her eyes were blue and every bit as friendly as her smile.

"*Anin,*" Stephen said, in formal Ojibwe greeting, and the woman was clearly pleased.

"*Anin,*" she replied. "Are you Indian?"

"Mixed blood," Anne said. "Our great-grandmother was true-blood Iron Lake Ojibwe."

"Near Aurora, Minnesota," the woman said, beaming. "I know

that area well. There's a wonderful elder who lives there, a Mide."

"Henry Meloux," Stephen said with amazement.

"Yes, you know him?"

Stephen laughed. "He's practically part of our family. My great-grandmother nearly married him."

"Then welcome you are," the woman said. "Would you like to come up to the house? I have fresh coffee brewing."

"We're on a kind of pressing mission, Cherri," Bascombe said. "We're hoping the questions we have'll be easy to answer."

Cherri opened her arms, and in the morning sunlight, her shadow was like a dark bird preparing to fly. "Ask away."

Rose said, "Some of our party went missing in the storm yesterday. My brother-in-law and my niece. They were headed to Young's Bay Landing but never made it."

"I'm sorry," Cherri said. "Where were they coming from?"

"Above Tranquil Channel," Mal told her.

"In a launch?"

"A dinghy with an old outboard." Mal explained the time frame of departure and expected arrival at the landing.

Cherri frowned. "There should have been plenty of time for them to reach the mainland before that horrible storm blew through."

"There was something on the way that my dad wanted my sister to see, something Ojibwe," Stephen said.

"And what was that?"

"We don't know," he confessed with a shrug. "But we think it has something to do with children."

Cherri gave it long thought while the wind pulled at her hair and the birch leaves quivered restlessly at her back. Finally she shook her head. "I honestly don't know what it could be."

"Is there anyone who might?" Anne said.

"Maybe Amos Powassin."

"Who's that?"

"One of our elders. Quite old, but he knows more about this lake and its Ojibwe history than anyone I can think of."

"Where do we find him?" Bascombe asked.

"If you've got room for me in your boat, Seth, I'll guide you there myself."

Amos Powassin sat in an Adirondack chair on a dock empty of boats a dozen yards from his small house. He was fishing. A young girl, maybe seven or eight, was with him, sitting cross-legged near his feet, tending a bait bucket. She wore yellow shorts and a T-shirt with an image of the Frog Princess on the front. Her feet were bare.

Stephen leaped to the dock, and Mal threw him a line. When they were tied up, they all disembarked and walked toward the old man, who slowly reeled in his line. He didn't look at them as they came.

"*Boozhoo*, grandfather," Cherri Allen said.

"The way this dock's shakin', feels like you brought an army with you, Cherri," the old man said.

"Visitors, grandfather. They need information."

"Thought that was something you gave out," he said. "Part of your job." He lifted his line, swung it clear of the water, and laid it on the dock beside his chair. He bent and whispered something to the little girl, who smiled and nodded, then got to her feet and ran toward the house.

"The question these people have I can't answer, grandfather."

He finally turned to them. His hair was long and white and spilled down from a broad-brimmed canvas hat. His wrinkled face was in shadow, and from the way his eyes didn't focus on anyone, Rose understood that he was blind. He reached out, found the walking stick that leaned against his chair, and used the stick to help himself rise. Rose saw that the top of the stick was carefully carved in the shape of a wolf's head.

Stephen must have seen it, too, because he said, *"Ma'iingan,* grandfather."

The old man leaned on the stick and addressed the direction of Stephen's voice. "Keep talking, boy."

"On your cane," Stephen said. "We're *Ma'iingan,* grandfather. Our clan."

"You Indian, then?"

"I have the blood of The People in me," Stephen said. "Iron Lake Ojibwe."

"You got a name, boy?"

"Makadewagosh."

Rose knew that this was Stephen's Ojibwe name. It meant "Silver Fox."

The old man considered the name and nodded. "Sleek and cunning. I got a sense whoever named you knew what they were doing."

"I was named by a wise man, grandfather. Henry Meloux."

A broad grin stretched across the old man's face, putting dozens of extra wrinkles into his cheeks. "Now that's a name I know. Christ, been a long time since we smoked together. How is my old friend?"

"He's well, grandfather," Stephen said. "When we go home, I'll tell him *boozhoo* for you."

"You do that, Makadewagosh. I'd be grateful. Now, what is it a blind old fart can do for you folks?"

Stephen, who'd clearly connected with the old man, explained for them. Powassin listened without emotion and, when Stephen had finished, was thoughtfully silent for a very long while. Rose knew that Ojibwe time was different, and knew that, even though their mission was pressing, great patience was required.

"That storm was a real bastard," the old man finally said. "Didn't even feel it comin', which is pretty strange. I don't see worth beans anymore, but I can usually tell about weather. Especially lousy weather. My bunions give me hell." He lifted a hand spotted as an old banana and pointed north. "There's a place many miles from here, an island that the Anishinaabeg once used to hide their children from our ancient enemy, the Dakota. It's not easy to find. The water's full of hidden rocks, and the shoreline's pretty unfriendly. Probably why our ancestors chose it in the first place. They painted pictures on the rocks there, pictures of children. Our people used to paint on rocks quite a bit, I guess, and most of those paintings are well known around this lake. They've been visited and sometimes violated, but not these. Only a very few know about these paintings. Maybe, Makade-wagosh, that's what your father was going to show your sister. Are children an issue of some kind?"

No one spoke. Finally Rose said, "Yes, grandfather."

"Then I'd look there. It's a place to start anyway."

"How do we find it?" Bascombe asked.

Powassin smiled. "You don't. Unless you take me along. I think I'd enjoy a boat ride today."

TWENTY-ONE

Cork swam hard for the island with the high bluff. The wind had been up all morning, and the debris that had choked the channel the night before had washed against the shorelines. He had a clear passage, but he swam against the wind and wasn't making the crossing as quickly as he would have liked. He knew that he had to reach the island and climb the bluff before the man who hunted them found Jenny's shelter. How much time he actually had he didn't know. All he really knew was that every second was precious.

He'd discarded his pants and hidden them in a thicket. He'd removed his shirt and had rolled his sneakers in it, along with the knife, and had tied the bundle around his waist. The distance to the island was roughly three hundred yards. Cork was a runner, a man with several marathons to his credit, but swimming was a different ball game, especially battling waves and carrying the ballast around his midsection. He tired faster than he'd imagined. With still a hundred yards to go, he was breathing in gasps, and his arms and legs were burning with fatigue. As much as he hated having to do it, he stopped for a couple of minutes and floated on his back to keep from completely exhausting himself. He stared up at the sky, which was remarkably clear and breathtakingly blue. He watched a pelican glide effortlessly along the current of the wind, and he wished he, too, could fly. He wished he'd never brought his family to this place. He wished he'd never shown Jenny the rock paintings. He wished he'd never tried to interfere in her life. He wished, as he sometimes did in the dark of his own regrets, that he was a different man, a wiser man, a better man. Or at least, he thought now, a better swimmer.

He rolled onto his stomach and began again to stroke hard for the island, battling once more the relentless wind and endless waves.

Jenny's heart was a wild horse galloping. After her father left, she realized how much his presence had meant to her, and for a short while, she stood absolutely paralyzed by the enormity of the threat they faced, frozen in the little sanctuary they'd found among the trees, wishing desperately that she and her father and the child could simply hole up there and be safe. She gazed down where her baby boy lay asleep, blessedly oblivious to all the danger around him.

Her baby boy. In less than a day, that's how she'd begun to think of him. Irrational, she knew. The child had relatives, people who had legal claim. But had they risked their lives for him? Had they sweated bullets worrying about him? Wasn't that what made people belong to each other, what they risked and what they sacrificed and what they shared?

"Won't matter one way or the other, girl, if you don't get moving," she finally whispered and forced herself to act.

She gathered the items they'd brought, set them in the blanket, and tied the ends together. She carried the blanket to the edge of the trees a few yards from where the narrow raft her father had constructed the night before lay drawn up on the shore. She set the blanket bundle down in the tree cover. Before she moved into the open, she carefully studied the island on the far side of the channel for any sign of the hunter. Nothing moved there, and finally she risked a dash to the raft and eased it almost completely into the water so that it would shove off easily when she was ready to evacuate. Back among the shadows of the trees, she lingered a moment, looking south toward the bluff island, trying to spot her father, but she didn't see him. Should that concern her? She had no idea.

She made three trips between the shoreline and the small area of grass and wildflowers at the base of the rock wall where they'd spent the night. Each trip, she followed a slightly different route so that she wouldn't wear a visible trail. All that was left at the end was the wicker basket and the baby. She looked at the flowers and grass, much of it flattened where their bodies had lain. A good hunter would know that something had bedded there recently. But it was the kind of place deer might lie down, and with all evidence of their presence gone, Jenny hoped that was exactly what the hunter would assume.

She lifted the basket, and the baby opened his eyes and blinked and stared at her. There was such concentration on his little face that he looked as if he was thinking deeply. But what could a child so young think about?

"Are you wondering where she is, little guy? Your mother?" she asked gently. "Are you wondering who I am and will I leave you, too?" Jenny put her hand to his warm cheek. "The answer is no. I absolutely won't leave you. And whoever he is out there, I won't let him hurt you."

She spoke more for herself than for the child, but, God, it felt good and right for it to be said.

She turned and carried the basket through the trees toward the shoreline, where she waited in the shadows for her father to play decoy. Waited for him to put himself in the crosshairs.

He made the island and staggered ashore on the back side of the bluff, where he fell to his hands and knees and struggled to catch his breath. He looked up at the height still ahead to be climbed and tried to calculate how much time he might have before the hunter found the shelter, mounted the cedar-capped promontory, and had a good look around. He hauled himself up, untied the bundle of his shirt, put on his sneakers, and started the long slog to the top of the bluff.

Most of the trees on the south slope had been toppled, and Cork fought his way through one tangle of branches after another. He dragged himself over horizontal trunks or slithered under them. His wet clothing caught on snags that seemed determined to keep him from his goal, but he tore loose again and again until nothing remained of his shirt but a few strips of rag. He was scratched and bleeding, and blackflies had begun to land on his wounds and add their own torment. His whole body was in rebellion. But he kept thinking how much depended on him, how much Jenny and the baby needed this from him, and he kept on going.

And then he was at the top. He dropped to a crouch and cautiously made his way to the edge of the bluff, which dropped straight down into the murky green of the lake water fifty feet below. He shielded his eyes and looked across the channel to the island and to its outcrop topped with cedars. He saw no sign of the hunter. He swung his gaze northwest, to the island where Jenny, he hoped, was prepared to return to her shelter. He had only a general idea of how long it had taken him to reach the place where he now stood, and he hoped he'd arrived in time to do what he'd come there for.

To his right lay the snapped trunk of an aspen. He hunkered down behind it and watched the cedars across the channel, praying he'd guessed right about everything.

She saw her father on the bluff three hundred yards away, but only for a moment before he dropped from her sight. He'd done his part. Now she waited to do hers. The baby had begun to fuss. He squirmed and made little noises. Jenny had put a prepared bottle in his basket, and she took it out and fed him. She was proud of herself for this forethought. She was doing all she could to make this plan, which she and her father had formulated together, work.

While she sat idle just inside the blind of trees, blackflies and mosquitoes had begun to gather and to land on her and the baby. She shooed them away, but they became more and more persistent and greater in number. She hadn't remembered them being this bad the day before in the shelter, but maybe, like every other living thing, they'd been temporarily disoriented by the storm. If so, they weren't disoriented any longer.

She walked and burped the baby, then set him in the wicker basket and covered the whole thing with a blanket to protect him from the insects. He began to whimper immediately, as if he didn't like not seeing her, or didn't like not being in her arms. The insects had become a swarm, a shifting cloud of tiny mosquitoes and large blackflies, and Jenny waved her arms wildly trying to disperse them. It did no good. She needed to move away, but if she did, would she miss the hunter and the exchange, whatever it turned out to be, between him and her father? Would she jeopardize the only chance she might have of escape?

The insects crawled her arms and legs and face and were in her hair. En masse, they crawled over the blanket that shielded the baby. Jenny reached for the basket and would have grabbed it and turned and run, but she saw the hunter.

He hadn't climbed the outcrop as her father had predicted. He'd come along the base of the rock to the small inlet where Jenny had beached the dinghy. He held a rifle in his hands, and she could see that it was mounted with a powerful scope. He moved cautiously, and she understood that he was, indeed, a man who knew how to hunt. He paused and used the barrel of his rifle to move aside some debris. Jenny realized he'd found the wolf that, out of mercy, she'd killed. The hunter's head turned, and his eyes swung to the island where she stood in the shadows, besieged and tortured but struggling to remain still. His gaze hung there an eternity while her skin crawled. Then he moved again, this time to where the dinghy lay crushed. He studied the obliterated hull, then turned and went to where the base of the outcropping met water. He waded into the lake until he could see the island where her father had taken a position atop the bluff. The hunter looked there, looked to his right across the channel toward Jenny's island, and finally to his left beyond the outcrop at something Jenny couldn't see. For a few moments, he was like the rock he stood next to. He lifted the rifle, fitted the stock to his shoulder, sighted through the powerful scope, and swung the barrel in a slow, purposeful arc. He didn't have field glasses, Jenny guessed, and was using the scope for that purpose.

He carefully scanned the island where her father was atop the bluff, scoped another island farther south, and finally directed his eye to the island where Jenny hid. She flattened herself on the ground with her arm wrapped protectively around the wicker basket crawling with flies. Inside, the baby's fussing was becoming more pronounced. She prayed he wouldn't begin to cry. They were shielded by a very porous wall of underbrush. Jenny could see the hunter and knew that, with his magnified vision, he could see her, and any movement at all might be her undoing. The scope swung gradually until it held directly on the spot where she lay. She stared, and the black eye of the rifle barrel stared back. The baby squirmed, his little arms batting at the blanket that covered the basket. Jenny began to sing in a whisper, "Hush, little baby, don't say a word. Papa's going to buy you a mockingbird." The man lifted his face from where he'd laid his cheek against the rifle stock and studied the island with his naked eye. Had he seen the raft? If he came for her and the baby, what would she do? Her mind began to search desperately for a fallback plan.

The hunter put his cheek to the stock again and continued

his scan of the area. Finally he lowered the rifle, turned, and disappeared into the devastation at the base of the outcrop, heading in the direction of the makeshift shelter.

As soon as he was gone, Jenny grabbed the basket and bolted for another hiding place, fleeing the swarm of insects threatening to drive her mad. In her haste, she caught her foot on a snag and went sprawling. The basket flew from her hand. The baby spilled out onto the ground. He lay a moment, staring up at the sun as if dazed; then he let out a wail that could have been heard in Greenland.

Jenny shot a look toward the island across the channel. The hunter broke from the cover of the fallen timber, eyes on the place where the baby lay. He lifted his rifle, and he sighted.

TWENTY-TWO

Fourteen thousand islands," Mal said. "Who owns them all?"

"Some of them belong to our people," Amos Powassin replied.

"And most of the others are what's called Crown Land," Bascombe said. "They belong, technically speaking, to the monarchy of England. But they're overseen by the provincial governments, who set them aside for preservation. That's why most are uninhabited. Pretty much, you can't build on them. Which is a good thing, I think. To my mind, this whole area ought to remain wild forever."

They'd returned Cherri Allen to her home on Windigo Island. Those remaining in the boat—Rose, Mal, Stephen, Bascombe, and Amos Powassin—had headed north and were now in the devastated area, weaving among islands where trees lay fallen like blades of mown grass. It was a terrible sight, and although he was blind, Powassin seemed to sense it.

"I can feel the change here," he said sadly. "Something magnificent has been wounded."

"It all looks dead," Stephen said.

"No." Powassin shook his head, then repeated, "Wounded. The energy of life is still everywhere. I can feel that, too."

"I don't understand, grandfather," Stephen said.

"Don't understand what?"

"Why Kitchimanidoo would do this kind of thing to a place so beautiful."

"And who is Kitchimanidoo?" the old man asked.

Stephen seemed surprised by the question. "The Creator, grandfather. The Great Mystery."

"Sometimes us Shinnobs get lazy in our thinking, Makade-wagosh, and we think of Kitchimanidoo like a human being, some kind of powerful old man, maybe. An old fart shoots sparks and magic out of his fingers, like one of them wizards in a Harry Potter movie." The old man laughed at the image he'd created for himself. "Know what I think? I think Kitchimanidoo is not the Creator but the possibility of creation, all creation, good and bad. You understand?"

"I'm not sure," Stephen said.

"In all good is the possibility of evil, and in all evil the possibility of good."

"So," Stephen said, mulling it over carefully, "a thing that seems good at first might be bad in the end?"

"Or the other way around," the old man offered.

"So there's the possibility of something good in all this destruction?"

"That's exactly what I'm saying. Who knows what Kitchimanidoo is capable of? You, me, we're just humans. In the big picture, we don't see nothin'. And Kitchimanidoo is the big picture."

Stephen was quiet after that. They all were. And for a long time the only sounds came from the engine grind and the propeller churning water.

"If I'm correct in my judgment of distance," the old man finally said, "we should be approaching Bishop Point Island."

"You nailed 'er, Amos," Bascombe said.

"Point the bow of this tub west," the blind man said.

"Toward Outer Bay?"

"For a bit, then we're turning north again."

"You're the captain," Bascombe said. He consulted his GPS and carefully swung the launch left.

"Long time since I visited Neejawnisug," the old man said. "In the old days, it was a place our young men often went for *giigiwishimowin*."

"Their vision quest," Stephen said.

The blind man seemed surprised. "You know about this old Shinnob ritual?"

"A little over a year ago, after my mother died, Henry Meloux guided me on my vision quest."

The old man nodded. "No wonder you're so sensible. Wish I could convince more of our young men here to give the old way a try. They think ownin' a gun or maybe a fast boat is what makes 'em a man. I think it's about time we headed north. You ought to see an island with a cliff face white as pigeon shit."

Bascombe laughed. "I do."

"Run along the left side. Real careful. Lots of hidden rocks. And with that storm, maybe some snags, too."

"Roger," Bascombe said.

He cut the engine, and the launch cruised slowly between the island with the pigeon-shit cliff and another island just to the south. When they came out of that passage, all Rose could see was island after island with a labyrinth of channels running between them.

"How does anyone keep from getting lost here?" she asked.

"In the old days, they didn't," Powassin said. "That's why our people were able to hide the children here."

"But you know the way, and you're blind," Stephen pointed out.

"I learned the way early, and in those early days I came here often. It's a special place. A powerful place."

"Where now?" Bascombe said.

He'd no sooner spoken the words than they heard a sound like a firecracker exploding.

"What was that?" Rose said.

"Sounded like a gunshot," Bascombe said.

"A rifle," Powassin said. "A big rifle. In that direction." The old man pointed ahead and to the left.

"Cork?" Rose said.

Mal shook his head. "I don't think he took any kind of fire-arm with him."

"Hunters?" Stephen said.

"Nothin' in season," Powassin replied. "Then again, maybe what's being hunted hasn't got a season."

Bascombe said, "I think we should have a look-see."

And he eased the throttle forward.

TWENTY-THREE

Atop the bluff, Cork had hunkered behind a blind created by the trunk and branches of the fallen aspen. He'd waited patiently for the hunter to appear on the outcropping where the few ragged cedars still stood. His clothes had begun to dry, and his muscles had begun to cramp, and when the hunter didn't show, he'd begun to believe he'd been miserably off target, miscalculated completely. All his predictions about the man's behavior had been wrong. He was afraid that being wrong could lead too easily to being dead.

He should continue to wait, he knew, to be patient, to trust his instincts. That's what his years as a hunter had taught him. But things were different when the life of his daughter and an innocent child were at stake. Where he hid, he had a view of only the upper half of the cedar-topped outcropping. If the man chose not to climb that promontory, Cork realized he might not even see the hunter. He battled with himself over the urge to get up and stand at the edge of the bluff for a clear view all the way to the waterline. What held him back was the stubborn certainty that the hunter, when he reached the end of the island, would climb the height for the view it would give him. That's exactly what, in his place, Cork would have done.

Then he heard the baby scream.

He leaped up and looked north. At three hundred yards, he

couldn't see much. He dashed to the edge of the bluff, where he had a clear view of the base of the outcropping and the little beach on which the dinghy lay crushed. He saw the hunter standing there, sighting his rifle. He followed the line of the barrel and spied the distant image of Jenny scrambling madly at the edge of the trees. He realized the hunter was probably drawing a bead. He gave a shrill whistle, earsplitting, waved his arms wildly, and screamed, "Up here, you son of a bitch!"

The hunter turned his head. Quicker than Cork had ever seen a man move, he swung the rifle, and the scope was dead on Cork.

Cork hit the ground and heard the shot in the same instant. The bullet snipped the branches of the fallen aspen behind him. He rolled left and lifted his head, risking a glance to see where Jenny and the baby might be. On that far little island, he saw nothing. He threw a look toward the base of the outcropping. The hunter, too, had vanished.

Cork wasted no time. He knew where the man was headed: back to the cigarette boat, which would shoot him across the channel to Jenny and the baby. Cork turned and stumbled through the devastation that littered the back of the bluff, desperate to reach the lake, knowing he was in a race he had almost no hope of winning.

Jenny swept the baby into her arms and, without a glance back, bounded deeper into the trees. She heard the distant crack of the rifle and tensed for the impact of the bullet, but nothing happened. She kept running while the baby screamed into her breast and his little arms flailed madly.

But where to go?

She reached the tiny clearing where they'd bedded for the night. God, how long ago that seemed, those hours of quiet, of sanctuary. She looked up the rock wall her father had scaled several times in the night to keep his vigil. Where was he now? She wished they'd never formed this plan of separation. What had they been thinking? Didn't they have a better chance together than separated? Alone with the baby, she was helpless against a hunter and his rifle.

For the briefest of moments, she had a deep, gut-wrenching temptation: Leave the baby. Without the baby, she could run. She could swim to another island. She could hide herself. The screaming baby would become a decoy while she escaped. What was this child to her, after all? A foundling, nothing more. She had no responsibility for him. If she hadn't stumbled on him, he would have been dead by now anyway. Leave him. Leave him to the thread the fates had already spun for him.

But, with almost no effort at all, she put that temptation behind her. She knew that, whatever the outcome, the thread of her own fate was now bound up with the child's. They would both live or they would both die together.

With a fiery strength of purpose, she hit the rock wall and began to climb, clutching the baby to her with one hand and clawing her way toward the top with the other. She had no idea what she would do when she got there, but she knew that the hunter, if he wanted his prey, would have to climb, too. At the very least, she would buy time, and at the moment, time seemed to be the only hope she had.

As Cork descended the back side of the bluff, he discarded his shirt and sneakers and even the knife, anything that might hold him back in the water. When he hit the lake, he was down to his black Lands' End swim trunks. He made a long, arcing dive into the green-tea-colored water and began stroking as if hellhounds were nipping at his bare feet.

The wind was with him on this crossing. The swells as they swept forward carried him on their crests. It didn't matter. Jenny and the baby were alone on that island, and if he'd had to swim through a lake of hellfire to get to them, that's what he would have done. Each time he tipped his head to breathe, he listened a fraction of a second for the sound of the cigarette boat's powerful twin engines.

As he swam, his brain went swiftly over the elements of the situation. The island where the girl had died was a quarter mile long. It was an impossible landscape to cross quickly. Even if the hunter kept to the shallows and skirted the devastation on the island itself, the shoreline offered its own obstacles. The man with the scoped rifle would not have an easy time returning to his launch.

Cork stroked hard and decided to believe that he had a good chance of making it to Jenny first.

He was three-quarters of the way there when he heard the engines. He didn't hear them on the air. It was the lake that carried the sound to him when his whole head was submerged. The dull, unmistakable drone of propellers churning water. He didn't pause for even an instant but kept digging at the lake with his cupped hands, shoving distance behind him. His breath came in gasps, and his lungs were ablaze. His legs were made of hot lead. Yet he drove himself harder.

He felt the wet, velvety touch of lake weed on his chest and, looking up, saw that he was only a dozen yards from shore. He glanced north, just in time to see the cigarette boat swing into the channel. With five more strokes, Cork was ashore and running for cover. The cigarette boat was still a hundred yards out, closing fast.

He didn't know for sure where Jenny was, but he knew where they'd spent the night, and he made for that tiny clearing. If she wasn't there, he hoped she would be above it, seeking high ground, which in his own thinking was now the only possibility of an advantage they might have. If the hunter had to come up after them, maybe they could find a way to keep him at bay. It was the thinnest of hopes, but it was something.

* * *

She'd rocked the baby, sung to him, and soothed him until at last his crying had subsided into little hiccups.

"It's all right, little guy," she cooed. "Everything's all right."

Though it wasn't.

She lay against the only cover the top of the stone wall offered, a rock that stuck up like a solitary molar three feet above the rest of the formation. She'd heard the cigarette boat enter the channel, and she tried desperately to figure what to do next. She scanned the top of the wall and saw loose stones, fractured by the melt and thaw of countless winters. Reaching out carefully so that she wouldn't startle the baby, she gathered as many of these stones as she could, piling them into a small arsenal within easy reach.

She whispered, "If he comes, we'll stone him. If that doesn't work"—she eyed the precipice a few feet away—"we jump and take our chances. What do you say, little guy?"

She smiled, and to her great surprise, the baby responded with a beautiful, gapped smile of his own.

The powerful engines cut out, and she knew the hunter had landed. It was only a question of time now before he found them. She took deep breaths and tried to prepare herself.

The sound of rocks being dislodged on the slope of the wall below brought her rigid. *Too soon,* she thought. How could he have found her hiding so quickly? She reached out and took the largest of the stones she'd gathered. She laid the baby down carefully and crouched. The sound was very near now, almost to the top of the wall.

One chance, she thought. *I'll have one chance. Please, God, let me hit my mark.*

She heard labored breathing on the far side of the rock that shielded her. She took one final breath, stood, and prepared to fling the stone.

"Dad!" she cried.

"Down," he said, motioning frantically with his hand. "Get back down."

Jenny dropped into the shadow of the rock, and her father joined her there. He looked at the baby.

"What happened?" he asked.

"I tried to run and tripped. He went flying. I'm sorry."

"It's all right." He saw the pile of stones she'd prepared. "Good work," he said.

"They won't stop him."

"With only one rock, David stopped Goliath."

"When did you become such an optimist?" She smiled, then she glanced past him and looked horrified.

"What is it?" He turned where she looked. "Shit," he said.

There was no way to miss it. A trail of bloody footprints up the rock, leading right to the place where they lay hidden.

"Your poor feet," Jenny said.

He studied the torn flesh of his soles and shook his head. "I didn't feel a thing. Adrenaline." He eyed the bloody prints he'd left. "Well, that's bound to make it a whole lot easier for our mystery man to find us."

"Any suggestions what we do now?"

Her father crawled on his belly to where the wall dropped to the lake, thirty feet below. He spent a moment in thought and looked back over his shoulder.

"Think you can swim with that little guy in tow?"

"Yes, but how do we get down there?"

"Not we. You two. Take your T-shirt off and tie the tail in a knot so that you've closed up that end. Take the belt off your shorts and slip it through the arms of your T-shirt. Put the baby into the shirt, and loop the belt over your shoulder, with the baby against your side. It'll be like a knapsack, and it'll leave your arms free to climb down this wall with the little guy. There are enough handholds that it shouldn't be that difficult."

"What about you?"

Her father crawled back and picked up a stone from the pile

she'd created. "I'm going to do my best to keep our mystery man occupied."

"Dad—"

"Do you have a better idea?"

She tried to think, but came up empty.

"All right, then," he said. "Get that shirt off."

She did as he'd instructed, and when she'd created the little carrier, she eased the baby inside. Cork helped her loop the belt over her shoulder so that the baby rode against her side loosely but securely.

Her father held her briefly, then said, "Go."

And once again, she left him to his own fate while she tried to save the child.

Cork watched her descend the wall. She moved slowly, carefully. When it was clear to him that she would make it, he returned to the rock where Jenny had hidden, and he began gathering more loose stones, the only weapons he had against the man with the scoped rifle.

"David and Goliath," he said quietly and shook his head. "Right."

He flattened himself against the top of the ridge with a view of the trees and the tiny clearing directly below. He couldn't yet see the hunter, but he knew the man was coming. And he was pretty certain of the outcome of their meeting.

How many times in his life had he counted himself dead only to have God or Kitchimanidoo or the fates intervene?

"It ain't over till it's over," he said quietly.

And the man appeared.

He didn't rush into the clearing. He stood at the edge of the trees, his body shielded by the trunk of a spruce. He studied the clearing, then slowly his gaze rose, following, Cork guessed, the line of bloody footprints up the sloping face of the rock wall. The hunter raised his rifle and scanned the top of the wall with the scope. Like a turtle, Cork drew back his head into the shadow of the rock that hid him. He waited and listened. A moment later, he heard the sound of boots scraping rock.

He risked a peek. The hunter was climbing, the sling of the rifle hung over his shoulder. He was thirty yards below. Cork considered letting him come closer so that he would present an easier target for the stones. But unless Cork got the granddaddy of all lucky throws, the stones wouldn't stop the man. Best, he decided, to keep him from climbing in the first place.

Cork stood up and threw the first stone. It landed wide by a foot. At the sound of it hitting, the hunter pressed himself to the wall and, in a frighteningly fluid motion, slipped the rifle from his shoulder, laid his cheek against the stock, and fired. If Cork hadn't reacted with great instinct, his head would have exploded like a melon. He spun into the protection of the rock and filled his empty hand with another stone. He heard the skittle of the hunter scrambling across the face of the wall, trying to put himself out of range of Cork's throwing arm. Cork stood again and got off another stone. This one caught the hunter in the ribs. The man grunted in pain, and a small thrill of victory ran through Cork.

The hunter quickly maneuvered to fire again, but in the quiet of that moment before his finger squeezed the trigger, the baby cried out from the wall where Jenny had descended. The hunter's eyes shifted from Cork in the direction of the baby's crying. It made Cork think of a hawk that had spotted a field mouse. He flung another stone and it bounced off the hunter's shoulder, but the hunter was no longer interested in the man throwing stones. He slung his rifle and reached up a hand to climb to the top of the wall.

Cork figured it was now or never, and he tensed himself for a suicide dash at the hunter.

But another sound caused both men to go still again: the engine whine of a powerboat approaching. Cork saw a launch swing into the channel from the south. It was dark against the sparkle of the sunlit water and hard to see clearly. Even so, he could make out several passengers, both male and female. Whoever they were, they were a godsend. They must have spotted him, because they came straight for the little island. As soon as the launch came into view, the hunter scrambled down the wall and sprinted into the forest. Cork watched until he saw the cigarette boat shoot north and he was sure the hunter had fled.

The baby was still crying. Cork hobbled to where the wall fell straight down to the water. In the lake, Jenny was holding the child and stroking as best she could for another island several hundred yards distant.

Cork shouted, "Jenny, come back! He's gone!"

She paused and cried above the baby's wails, "What?"

Cork kept it simple. He called out, "We're saved."

TWENTY-FOUR

They returned Amos Powassin to his home on Windigo Island. Once Jenny and Cork had told their story, the blind man had been mostly silent. On his weathered wooden dock, before Cork and the others left for Young's Bay Landing, Powassin offered some parting advice, directed mostly at Stephen.

"Remember what I told you. In all that's good, the possibility of evil. And in evil, the possibility of good. There's gonna be a lot of people try to tell you otherwise, Makadewagosh. Don't you listen to 'em."

"I won't, grandfather," Stephen promised.

Then the old man's sightless eyes swung in Cork's direction. "Goes for you, too."

"*Migwech*," Cork said, thanking the old man in Ojibwe.

To Jenny, Powassin said, "A bird sheds a little feather, that feather comes to rest where Kitchimanidoo always meant for it to be. Nothing in all creation happens by accident. Granddaughter, you take care of this little feather that's come to rest in your hands."

"I will, grandfather."

The old man stood on the dock a long time, and although he could not see them, his face turned as if watching them until they rounded a point on Windigo Island and were lost to him.

Deputy Sheriff Tom Kretsch awaited them at Young's Bay

Landing, along with a small gathering of other residents of the Angle. Bascombe had radioed ahead, reporting the gist of the situation. When Bascombe's launch pulled up to the dock, Kretsch helped everyone out and took a good look at the baby, who lay awake but quiet in the wicker basket.

"This is him, eh?" The deputy wore no uniform. He was dressed in jeans and a rugby shirt. He glanced at Jenny, who held the basket. "You the one who found him?"

"Yes."

"Seth radioed that you found a dead girl, too."

"That's right."

"Murdered you think, is that correct?" Kretsch didn't try to hide his skepticism.

Cork stood behind Jenny and the baby. He said, "What was done to her she didn't do to herself, Deputy."

Which earned Cork a long look of appraisal from the man.

Kretsch could have been fifty-five or thirty-five. He had one of those boyish faces that would never age. He was just under six feet tall, handsome, with a thick shock of wavy brown hair and blue eyes that had an enviably uncomplicated look about them. There was a leanness to his body and a firmness and definition to his muscles that suggested he'd always been athletic. Bascombe had told Cork that Kretsch was the only official law enforcement on the Angle, and he was pretty much part-time.

"You're O'Connor?" Kretsch asked.

"Yes. Cork O'Connor."

"And you saw this dead girl, too?"

"I did."

"And you're sure it wasn't the storm that killed her?"

Cork said, "Tom, is it?"

Kretsch said, "Tom'll do."

"Tom, I was a deputy and a sheriff for nearly twenty years. I know a murder victim when I see one. I can tell you without a doubt it wasn't the storm that put a bullet through that girl's forehead."

Kretsch chewed on that piece of information and seemed willing to swallow it. He said, "This was on one of the islands out there on the Canadian side?"

"That's right."

"Out of my jurisdiction, but I think we ought to have a look before I alert the provincial police in Kenora. Can you find this island again?"

"I'm sure I can." Cork nodded toward the deputy's empty belt. "When you go, you ought to take a sidearm at the very least. A good rifle would be better."

"Why's that?"

"There's a man out there with a scoped rifle that looked to me to be a Weatherby. Could be he killed the girl. In any case, judging by his reaction to our presence on that island, he won't take kindly to us coming back."

Kretsch looked at the baby in the basket in Jenny's hands, and in his uncomplicated eyes was the very simple presence of great compassion. "Tough way to start a life." Then he said to Jenny, "I've let Lynn Belgea know what's up. I think you should take this little fella to her place and have her look him over. When your father and I get back from checking out this dead girl, we'll figure what to do with him. Probably have to talk to county social services down in Baudette. In the meantime, are you okay taking care of him?"

"Yes," Jenny said.

"Babs," he said to a woman standing near him, "can you get these folks over to Lynn's place?"

"No problem, Tom." She lifted her hand and said by way of introduction, "Babs Larson."

Kretsch turned back to Cork. "You got something more than that swimsuit to put on?"

"Not at the moment."

"You look about my size. I suppose I can rustle up something for you. How about shoes?"

Cork shook his head, then showed Kretsch his wounded soles.

Kretsch whistled. "Let's go to my office and tend to those feet. I probably can spare you a pair of sneakers, if you can tolerate wearing something. Then we'll have a good long talk. Seth, you mind coming along?"

"Fine by me," Bascombe replied.

Cork turned to Stephen and Mal. "Why don't you two wait here, at that grill across the road. When Tony Ebnet comes in with Annie and Aaron, get him whatever he wants to eat, and yourselves, too, then order something to go for everybody else, okay?"

Stephen seemed uneasy about deserting the others, but Mal clapped him on the shoulder and said, "Remember, son, an army moves on its stomach."

That was all the encouragement Stephen needed. "I'm starved," he said. "Let's go."

Kretsch had a small place near Young's Bay Landing, a little square of a house painted green. There wasn't much furniture, and the clutter made it clear that this was the home of a bachelor. Kretsch had Cork and Bascombe wait in the living room, then he disappeared for a few minutes. He returned with a pair of baggy khakis, an old green Henley shirt, white socks that could have used a good soak in bleach, a pair of oil-stained canvas boat shoes, and a battered canvas hat. He also had some gauze pads, a roll of adhesive tape, and a tube of Bacitracin ointment.

While Cork tended to his feet, Kretsch said, "That'll keep those cuts from getting infected until we can get you looked at professionally."

"The cuts are nothing. I'm more interested in getting some answers," Cork told him.

When Cork was dressed and had slipped on the socks and boat shoes and succesfully tested his ability to walk, Kretsch said, "Let's go into my office."

Which turned out to be a small, fishing-gear-filled room off the kitchen. His desk was cluttered with lures. His walls were hung with stuffed and mounted muskies and northerns. Kretsch sat in the chair behind his desk and indicated that Cork should take the chair opposite him. Cork lifted a multibarbed Rapala Husky Jerk from the chair seat and set it on Kretsch's desk.

"Sorry," the deputy said. "I don't get a lot of visitors here."

Cork nodded toward the lure and said, "Don't think you'll catch many with that."

Bascombe laughed and leaned against the wall, near enough to the open mouth of a mounted muskie that it looked as if the big fish was going to feed on his head. He said, "They have any luck locating the other folks missing in that storm?"

"All accounted for," Kretsch said and filled them in. Boats had been damaged or destroyed, and some of the fishermen had sustained minor injuries, but all things considered, they'd been pretty lucky.

"Now, down on the south shore of the big water, that whole area between Warroad and Baudette's been pretty well torn apart. I spoke with the sheriff this morning, and he's got his hands full. Anything happens up here right now, we're on our own."

"What about the Canadian authorities?" Cork said.

"Basically in the same situation as our people. Kenora was dead center in that storm's path, and I'm sure they're scrambling, trying to keep things civil and ordered. That's why I'd like to have a look at the island myself before they have to pull people off other duties to come all the way out here to the boondocks to investigate."

It made sense to Cork. And the truth was that he wanted another chance to look the scene over himself without having to talk his way across a line of yellow crime scene tape.

"First, tell me about this girl," Kretsch said. "And then we'll get to the guy with the Weatherby. Can you give me a good description of her?"

Cork said, "Somewhere between sixteen and twenty years

old. Long black hair. Not tall, maybe five-three or five-four. A hundred and twenty pounds. Pretty. Ojibwe."

Bascombe crossed his meaty arms and said to Kretsch, "Lily Smalldog."

"Don't go jumping to conclusions, Seth," Kretsch said. "That description would fit a lot of First Nations girls."

"Sure, but how many First Nations girls who fit that description have been missing for four months?"

Cork cocked an eyebrow at Kretsch. "The girl's been missing?"

"*A* girl's been missing," Kretsch clarified.

"What happened?" Cork asked.

Kretsch ran a hand through his thick brown hair, and his boyish face took on a slightly troubled look, as if debating whether to offer Cork the details. Finally he said, "Four months ago, Lily Smalldog disappeared. She'd been working for some religious folks who own a camp on Stump Island, which is way the hell out there, south of Garden Island. One morning those folks woke up and Lily was gone. Just like that."

"Somebody took her off the island?"

"That was certainly one of the possibilities. None of the camp's boats were missing, so Lily didn't take off by herself."

"One of the possibilities?"

"There was some speculation that she might have thrown herself in the lake and drowned. They found a sweater of hers floating on the water, but we never did find a body to go along with it."

"Any reason to think she might have killed herself?"

"According to the folks at the camp, she'd become pretty despondent."

"Because she was pregnant?"

"They didn't know that. That speculation began only recently. A few days ago somebody spotted Sonny Chickaway loading a big box full of baby formula onto his boat."

"Who's Chickaway?"

"A friend of hers. Bachelor. Lives alone. Because of all that formula, folks started putting two and two together."

"There's something else about Lily. She's kind of a special case," Bascombe added.

"Special in what way?" Cork asked.

Bascombe said, "I think these days we call those folks 'challenged.' "

"Mentally retarded?"

"Mildly retarded," Kretsch said. "Sweet as they come, that kid. Someone took advantage of her."

"Any speculations?"

"Oh, yeah."

It was clear from the way Bascombe spoke that this was the kind of scandal a small community chewed on with delight.

"Seth," Kretsch cautioned.

Bascombe pushed away from the wall. "Now, Tom, you know there's good reason for what folks are saying."

"Christ, just tell me," Cork said.

"Her brother, for one," Bascombe blurted.

Cork looked to Kretsch for confirmation, and the deputy reluctantly nodded. "His name's Noah. Noah Smalldog. He's kind of infamous in these parts."

"Infamous how?"

"Shady. Elusive. Hates whites with a passion. Back in the days when Indians were into scalp taking, Noah Smalldog would've had enough to sew himself a winter coat."

"Criminal record?"

"Nothing serious and nothing recent. Too smart. But most folks are pretty sure he's big into smuggling. He's got himself a cigarette boat that can outrun anything on Lake of the Woods."

"As I understand it, going too fast on that water can be disastrous."

"Smalldog grew up on this lake," Kretsch said. "His father was one of the best guides in these parts, and Smalldog did a lot of guiding himself when he was younger. I'm not sure there's anyone knows Lake of the Woods better."

Bascombe said, "I heard that when he smuggles he runs at night without lights or GPS."

"This guy sounds a little mythic," Cork said. "Like Paul Bunyan."

"Yeah, if Bunyan had been a son of a bitch."

"Smalldog got into trouble in his late teens," the deputy went on. "D and D mostly, that kind of thing."

"Just that, drunk and disorderly?" Cork said.

Kretsch shook his head. "Other things, too, but like I said, nothing really serious. It was clear that he had anger issues, and if he kept going in that direction he was looking at the possibility of jail time down the road. I guess the First Nations elders gave him the option of channeling his anger or getting run off the rez. So he joined the army and went to war. From what we heard, he was pretty good at it. Fought with the Canucks in Afghanistan. Came back a couple years ago, and pretty much disappeared in Lake of the Woods. We get Smalldog sightings all the time. Like Elvis, you know."

"But he had this sister, Lily," Cork said.

"Half sister, really," Bascombe said. "Same mother, different fathers."

"He must have had some contact with her," Cork said. "He must have come out of hiding enough to justify the speculation that he fathered her child."

"The folks at the camp filed complaints alleging that Smalldog sometimes trespassed at night to visit his sister."

"Alleging?"

"They never caught him, but somebody was there. Left her little gifts," Kretsch said.

"Gifts?"

"The camp folks figured they were bribes or payments for letting him have sexual relations with her."

"Did they ever have her examined by a doctor after one of these visits?"

"Not as far as I know. But from what you found on that island out there, it's clear something of a sexual nature went on."

Kretsch picked up the Rapala lure and idly touched the hook, as if thoughtlessly checking the sharpness of the barb. "So, what did this guy with the Weatherby look like?"

"My height," Cork said. "Probably about my weight, one eighty. Long black hair in a ponytail. He had on a tan ball cap that shaded his face, so I didn't get a good look at his features. But Indian, I'd say."

"How old?"

"Hard to tell. A lot younger than me, but that seems like everybody these days."

"Could be Smalldog," Bascombe said.

"Or any number of First Nations men." Kretsch put the lure down. "I think it's time I had a look at that island."

TWENTY-FIVE

Lynn Belgea stood at the open door to her home, which was nestled among a stand of tall red pine on Angle Inlet, a small community a couple of miles north of Young's Bay Landing. She watched Rose and Jenny and Babs Larson pile out of Larson's truck and start up the dirt path through the patch of wild grass and flowers that was her yard. At her feet stood a brown and black dog, a standard poodle, who barked at their approach and eagerly wagged his tail.

"Hush, Teddy," Belgea said. "You'll wake the baby. Come on in, folks. I've been expecting you."

They entered her home, a modest little cabin nicely furnished with pine furniture and braided rugs, and immaculately clean. The dog danced along beside them, jumping up on his hind legs to get a look inside the basket.

"Sit, Ted," Belgea said, and the dog obeyed. "I haven't had him long," she apologized, "but he's learning. I've found that peanut butter works wonders with him. This way."

She led them to a small examining room with a view of the pines in back.

"Let's have a look at this little man," she said.

Jenny took the baby from the basket and handed him to Belgea, who didn't blink an eye at his misformed upper lip. The woman laid him on the examining table and looked him over carefully while Jenny explained the circumstances in which she'd found him.

"I'd say he's between eight and ten weeks old," Belgea said. "His weight seems good, despite his ordeal. He's been well cared for."

"What about his lip?" Jenny asked.

Belgea's capable hands cradled his little head, and she looked closely at his mouth. "Not all that unusual. Native Americans have the highest rate of children born with cleft lips and palates."

Rose said, "Why would that be?"

"Some of it's genetic. Babies inherit a gene that either causes the cleft directly or is part of a syndrome that includes clefting as one of its symptoms. Sometimes it's simply a gene that makes a child more susceptible, and an environmental issue actually triggers the clefting."

"Environmental issue?"

"Smoking or drinking or drugs during pregnancy. Sadly, that's a real problem for a lot of young Indian mothers. And this guy has another strike against him. Male babies are twice as likely as females to have clefting."

"What can be done about it?"

"He's young enough that the cleft can be easily closed surgically. In a few years, all that will show is a bit of a scar that most people won't even notice."

Jenny said, "You're from the Angle. Do you have any idea who he is?"

Belgea and Babs Larson exchanged a brief but knowing look.

"Go ahead, Lynn," Babs said. "She's bound to hear the whole story eventually, so it might as well come from you."

Belgea handed the baby back to Jenny. The grating call of a blue jay from outside drew her attention. She stared beyond the window screen where the pines isolated her home, spent a moment gathering her thoughts, then told what she knew.

* * *

It began with Vivian Smalldog, a woman of mixed heritage and mixed nationality, who'd grown up on the Angle. Her father was a logger and a drunkard, her mother a First Nations Ojibwe from Reserve 37, a weak, battered woman. Growing up, Vivian never had much of a chance. She was wild and pretty and got into trouble early on. When she was seventeen, she met an Ojibwe from Sioux Narrows on the north end of the lake, an older man named Leon Smalldog, who saw the pretty in her and ignored the rest. They got married and had a child, a boy they named Noah. Leon Smalldog was a well-known guide, a settled man, who soon wised up to the fact that the woman he'd married was not the marrying kind. He remained in the marriage for nearly a decade before his wife's drinking and infidelities drove him to separate from her. As far as Belgea knew, the couple never officially divorced. Smalldog moved back to Sioux Narrows and took Noah with him.

Soon after, Vivian left the Angle. For good, she swore. Occasionally word came back. She was in Bemidji; she was in Brainerd; she was living in the Heart of the Earth community in Minneapolis. Bits of news here and there, scraps torn from the whole fabric of a life folks on the Angle didn't really give a damn about. After a dozen years, she came back, a hollow-looking woman by then, as if the world had taken a knife and filleted her, left her with no spirit and no bone. She brought a child with her, a pretty little girl named Lily, who said almost nothing and wouldn't look at you directly, and folks, when they talked about her, called her "slow." Vivian's mother was dead by then, a suicide drowning. Her father, a raging alcoholic, had moved away. Gone to Fargo, was the word, though no one could say for sure.

Vivian went to work as a housekeeper for a Baptist church camp on Stump Island that operated a year-round program. She had her own little cabin, where she and Lily lived. The camp folks were good to them. Lily attended the one-room schoolhouse in Angle Inlet, where they didn't really have the resources to help a challenged girl, although they did their best. Mostly Vivian and her daughter stayed on the island, happy from all accounts, though it was common knowledge that Vivian was given to bouts of severe depression and every once in a while found solace with a friend named Jack Daniel's. The camp folks nursed her through these periods, and life went on.

Three years ago, the Baptist group, who'd run the camp for forty years, sold it to another religious organization called the Church of the Seven Trumpets, with the stipulation that Vivian and Lily be allowed to remain on the island, living in the cabin they'd come to call home. It looked like everything would be fine.

But two years ago, Vivian went missing. They found her three days later, floating in the lake. The autopsy, done by the Lake of the Woods County medical examiner, revealed that death was, indeed, the result of drowning. At the time she died, Vivian's blood alcohol content was three times the legal limit for driving. The official determination was that she'd become intoxicated, had fallen into the lake, and had drowned. Folks on the Angle, who knew how Vivian's mother had died, figured it was no accident.

The Seven Trumpets people were more than happy to allow Lily to stay on as before, living in the cabin she'd shared with her mother, earning her keep doing housekeeping and cooking.

And that's when reports of Noah Smalldog began to surface.

"We all heard that he'd come home," Belgea said.

"Home from where?" Rose asked.

"Afghanistan. He'd been serving with the Canadian army as part of the Coalition forces there. From all accounts, he'd come home angry as hell."

"Why?"

Belgea shrugged. "He was an angry kid, and when he came back, he was an angry man. And way mysterious. Nobody ever sees him."

"What does that have to do with Lily?"

"Apparently, on his return, Smalldog began visiting his half sister. The folks out there on Stump Island reported that they'd had trouble with him trespassing."

"He's family. What's the harm?"

Belgea considered her words carefully. "There's been a good deal of speculation that Noah Smalldog hasn't been treating his sister in a strictly brotherly way."

Jenny said, "Abusing her sexually?"

"Yes."

"Did Lily ever make that complaint?"

"As I understand it, Lily remained absolutely silent on the whole situation. Out of fear or confused love, I don't know."

"It sounds like you believe that what they say about Noah Smalldog abusing her is true."

Belgea said, "I didn't believe it. Until I saw this child. You see, Noah Smalldog was born with a cleft lip, too."

The child began to fuss, and Jenny said, "I brought some formula and his bottle back with me. They're in the basket. Aunt Rose, would you mind?"

"I'd be happy to, honey."

"Water and a pan in the kitchen," Belgea said.

"I'll show her," Babs said. "I know my way around your place, Lynn. And, honey," she said to Jenny, "you're probably hungry, too. What if I made a sandwich?"

"That would great, Babs. Thanks." Jenny picked up the baby and held her nose to his diaper. "He needs changing. I didn't bring anything for that."

Belgea said, "Not to worry. I always keep a few disposables

on hand. Up here, I try to keep a little of everything available."
She opened the cupboard beneath the sink in the examining
room and brought out a box of Pampers. She took a disposable
diaper and brought it to Jenny, but before she handed it over,
she eyed the baby and then Jenny with obvious concern. "That
baby's taken to you."

Jenny was pleased that the bond was so obvious.

"Just a word of caution," Belgea went on. "This baby belongs
to someone else. Eventually, you'll have to give him up."

"I know. But in the meantime, he needs someone, and here
I am."

"That's abundantly clear. And he's lucky. But when the time
comes, it may break your heart." She spoke with great compassion, as if it were her own heart on the line.

Jenny looked down into the baby's dark, gentle eyes. "It's
been broken before," she said. "And I survived."

Ted got up from where he lay, trotted to the front door, and
began to bark. A moment later there was a knock at the screen,
and a man's voice called out, "Jenny?"

"That's Aaron," Jenny said.

She heard Rose's voice from the front room. "Come in.
They're in the examining room. This way."

A moment later, Aaron and Anne walked in. Aaron came to
her directly and looked as if he would have given her a big hug
but for the baby she held. As it was, he leaned over the child and
kissed her.

"Oh, God, Jen, I've been so worried."

"We're safe now."

The baby's face was turned against Jenny's T-shirt, as if seeking her breast. Aaron glanced down at him, obviously discon-
certed, and stepped awkwardly back.

Anne moved in and gave her sister a hug. "They told us
everything at Young's Bay Landing. Are you all right?"

"Fine," Jenny said.

Anne smiled down at the squirming child. "This is
him, huh?"

"Yep."

"I'll give you folks some privacy," Belgea said. "When the bottle's ready, we'll bring it in."

"Thanks," Jenny said.

Belgea left, and the room was uncomfortably quiet. Then Aaron asked, "What are they going to do with him?"

"I don't know," Jenny replied. "For the moment, I'm in charge of his well-being."

The hungry baby finally cried out and turned his head away from Jenny's body. Aaron and Anne got their first good look at his face.

"Jesus," Aaron said.

"He has a cleft lip," Jenny explained tersely. "It can be repaired surgically."

"God, I hope so. For his sake."

A little flame ignited in Jenny, and she snapped, "He's beautiful, Aaron. Even if that lip never got fixed, he'd still be beautiful."

To that, Aaron had no reply.

"You found his mother, we heard," Anne said. "Dead."

"Yeah."

"And we heard something about a psycho with a rifle," Aaron added.

"You heard right."

"But you're okay?" he said. "For sure?"

Jenny looked down at the child in her arms. "If it hadn't been for this little guy, I might not be. I think I would have freaked, except I had to keep myself together for him. In a way, we saved each other."

Aaron eyed the baby, and Jenny went hard inside, because it was clear to her that he wasn't at all certain that was necessarily a good thing.

TWENTY-SIX

The soles of Cork's feet hurt like hell, but he tried to ignore his discomfort. He had more important things to worry about.

Bascombe was at the helm. Beside him was a Marlin 336, lever action, which the tall man had picked up at his lodge on the way from Young's Bay Landing. Kretsch sat opposite Cork. The deputy was packing, too. He'd put on a gun belt, and holstered there was a Smith & Wesson .38 revolver, the same kind of handgun Cork had carried when he was sheriff. Kretsch had also brought a scoped bolt-action Remington 700, his deer rifle, and a box of cartridges. He'd offered Cork the rifle, and Cork had accepted, but with reluctance. On the island, with Jenny and the baby in jeopardy, he would have snatched up the weapon and used it without a second thought. But he was on a different mission now, and as the launch took them deeper into Canadian waters and nearer the island, he weighed seriously the vow he'd made several years earlier never again to raise a firearm against another human being. He was uncomfortable carrying; yet if the man they were after fired on them, Cork didn't want the responsibility for what happened afterward to rest on the shoulders of the others. Bascombe and Kretsch were there mostly because of Cork and his family, and it seemed to him that at the moment he owed these two men a debt that superseded his own moral misgivings. As they bounced over the swells and veered toward the archipelago where the island lay, he opened the box of cartridges and fed the Remington's magazine.

"Cork?" Bascombe called over his shoulder.

"Yeah?"

"That island of yours, it'd be to the northwest, right?"

"That's right."

Bascombe pointed. "Take a look."

Deep in the archipelago, a thick column of black smoke rose straight up a few hundred feet into the air, where the wind kicked in and spread it like an oil slick across the blue sky.

Bascombe approached the island from the south, motoring slowly up the channel. Cork had the Remington across his lap, and Kretsch had unsnapped the hammer guard of his revolver so that he could easily draw and fire. The men didn't speak as they neared the inlet close to the burning cabin.

Bascombe cut the engine to idle, and they drifted and stared at where the flames and smoke roiled up among the destroyed trees.

"What do you want to do?" Bascombe finally asked.

"Not much point in going ashore," Kretsch said. "That cabin'll burn for a long time, and for a long time after that, it'll be too hot to sift the rubble."

Cork said, "My daughter told me if she was our man she'd burn the cabin, burn all the evidence."

"Smart girl," Bascombe said.

"I don't think our time'll be wisely spent here," Kretsch said. "I think we ought to find Noah Smalldog."

"Do you know where he lives?" Cork asked.

Bascombe laughed. "Nobody knows where Smalldog lives. He understands this lake better than anybody, and he's probably got himself squirreled away somewhere you couldn't see even if you were three feet from it."

Cork said, "How do we find him then?"

Bascombe glanced at Kretsch, and both men seemed to be in unspoken agreement. "Sonny Chickaway," he said.

"Chickaway? The guy with all that baby formula in his boat?"

"He's a Red Lake Ojibwe lives on Oak Island," Kretsch explained. "He and Smalldog are pretty good buds. And him we know where to find."

"All right," Cork said. "Let's go talk to this Chickaway."

They headed back under a clear sky, and wherever there were bare rocks above water, Cork saw white pelicans roosting. Crows circled the islands, and gulls rode the swells, and despite the destruction, Cork sensed a strong spirit in the Lake of the Woods, something that felt indomitable.

Except for the canned peaches that morning well before sunrise, he hadn't eaten, and he was hungry.

As if he'd read Cork's thoughts, Bascombe said, "Got sandwiches in my cooler. I threw 'em together this morning when I wasn't sure how long we might be out looking for you today, Cork. If you guys are hungry, you're welcome to them. And pull one out for me while you're at it."

The cooler was in the back of the boat, and Cork wasted no time taking Bascombe up on his offer. The sandwiches were bologna and cheese, and there were apples, too, and bottled water. Cork handed out the food, then settled down to eat. Christ, it felt like a feast.

"Tell me more about Chickaway," he said.

Kretsch washed down a bite of sandwich with water. "Some people believe he's involved in Smalldog's smuggling activities. You're ATF, Seth. What do you think about that?"

"ATF?" Cork said.

"Former ATF," Bascombe clarified. "Before I retired, I spent almost thirty years as a field agent, working mostly in the Pacific Northwest, out of the Seattle division. I thought moving to the Angle would be a relaxing change," he said with a horsey laugh.

"What about Chickaway?" Cork said.

Bascombe shrugged. "It's possible he used to be involved in smuggling with Smalldog. But I don't think they're such good friends anymore."

"Why?"

"How about you tell him, Tom? You know what folks say about Lily and Sonny Chickaway."

"Folks say a lot of things that aren't worth the breath it takes to say 'em," Kretsch replied.

Cork swallowed a mouthful of sandwich. "What do folks say?"

Neither man replied. In the absence of conversation, there was only the sound of the wind and the grind of the engine, and the bang of the hull against water.

Finally Kretsch said, "Hell, you might as well go ahead and tell him, Seth."

Bascombe kept his eye on the GPS and spoke loud so that Cork could hear over the other noises. "Like we told you before, Sonny Chickaway is Red Lake Ojibwe. Him and Noah Smalldog used to be good buddies, and Chickaway's always looked out for Lily. Kind of like an older brother. Except some folks think Chickaway's interest in Lily was more than just brotherly. That maybe it wasn't only Smalldog who trespassed on Stump Island to visit her."

"Chickaway might have been taking advantage of her, too?"

Kretsch said, "I don't believe it. Chickaway, well, he's a good man. And if he visited Lily, there was good reason, and it wasn't just to be taking advantage of her. Maybe he's involved in the smuggling, I don't know. Hell, what if he is? That's an enterprise got a lot of white men rich over the years."

"Whoa," Bascombe said. "Didn't mean to push a button, Tom."

"It's just that it's easy to criticize the Ojibwe for things white folks are guilty of, too. White men get drunk. White men break the law. And nobody says it's because they're white. But an

Indian does the same thing and the first reason people come up with is that he's Indian."

Cork was liking Kretsch more and more all the time.

"Okay, judgments aside," Bascombe said, "I'm just going to point out here that it was Chickaway who loaded all that baby formula on his boat. And if what folks on Stump Island say is true and both men had a similar and unsavory interest in Lily Smalldog, in my experience, there's nothing that can come between friends faster than a woman."

"Why did everyone have to trespass to visit Lily Smalldog?" Cork asked. "These religious folks don't let people on the island?"

"A pretty reclusive bunch," Kretsch said. "Kind of a sect, I guess. They don't really interact with folks on the Angle, but they never give us any trouble either."

Bascombe said, "I run into 'em from time to time. They're decent enough. I understand they do mission work in places like Africa. Even though they kind of inherited her, they've done their best to look out for Lily Smalldog." He cut back on the throttle and said, "There's Chickaway's cabin."

The sun was hot, and Cork was grateful for the old canvas hat Kretsch had loaned him. He stared from the shadow of the brim toward the long wooded peninsula on Oak Island that Bascombe had indicated. Built all along the shoreline of the peninsula were some grand lake homes, million-dollar affairs, Cork figured. But, at the very end of the point, he saw a wooden dock and, among the oak trees, a rustic-looking little cabin greatly at odds with the stately homes that were its neighbors.

Cork said, "How'd Chickaway manage to wedge himself in there with the rich folk?"

Bascombe said, "Land holdings up here are kind of odd. Sometimes the Ojibwe hold a whole island in trust, and sometimes only a part. Most of Oak Island, for example, is privately owned, but that little point belongs to the Red Lake Ojibwe. Nobody except Sonny Chickaway has ever lived there. Not a real popular resident on the island."

"We're in luck," Kretsch said. "His boat's there. Means he's probably at home. Pull on up, Seth, and let's have a talk with Sonny."

Bascombe brought them in, and they tied up on the opposite side of the dock from where Chickaway's boat was moored. It was a new-looking Monza with two Evinrude V4 engines, a combination that made for a good, fast craft. But it wasn't a cigarette boat. They walked the path twenty yards into the shade of the oaks, where the little cabin stood. Kretsch opened the screen door and knocked on the closed inner door. Nobody answered, and he knocked again. He tried to look through the door's glass panes, but they were curtained. Bascombe moved left to one of the front windows.

"Curtain's been torn off this one," he said. He pressed his nose to the glass. "Jesus Christ. Looks like that storm blew through here, too. Come take a gander."

Cork and Kretsch joined him and eyed the inside of the cabin. Bascombe was right. The place had been destroyed.

Kretsch said, "I think I better take a look."

They followed him to the front door. He tried the knob, and it turned; the door opened onto a scene of utter devastation. But Sonny Chickaway was not there.

"Wasn't a storm blew through," Kretsch said. "Looks more like a pissed-off grizzly bear got turned loose in here."

Bascombe said, "Yeah, and he must've eaten Sonny Chickaway." He pointed toward a huge dark pooling beneath an overturned chair.

Cork walked to the chair and knelt and touched the pool with the tip of his finger.

"Is it?" Bascombe said.

Cork looked back to where the others stood near the door.

"It is," he said.

TWENTY-SEVEN

Kretsch sat at his desk in his office, a telephone pressed to his right ear. The features of his lean, boyish face were drawn taut, as if he were battling a bad headache.

"No, sir, there wasn't a body."

He listened and picked up a lure from his desktop and dug the hook into the wood.

"Yes, Chickaway sometimes drinks, and he's been in fights before, and I suppose that could explain why his place was torn up and maybe even the blood, but—"

Cut off, he dropped the lure, sat back, took a deep breath, and listened some more.

"No, nobody's reported anything. But, hell, that storm yesterday's got everything and everyone tied up. I mean—"

He nodded and pinched the bridge of his nose.

"Yes, sir, I called several of the Ojibwe on Windigo and Little Windigo to see if Chickaway might have shown up there looking for medical assistance. No one's seen him. And that's my point. If he was hurt—"

He balled his hand into a bloodless fist.

"Okay, so even forgetting about Chickaway, what about the baby and Lily Smalldog?"

Kretsch's face, as he listened, grew redder and redder.

"I know it's out of our jurisdiction," he finally exploded,

"and I do intend to talk to the provincial police in Kenora, but, sir, we have a baby on our hands and a mother who, as nearly as I can tell, was tortured to death, and it seems to me we ought to be beating the bushes for Noah Smalldog, and, honest to God, I can't do that by myself."

He shut up, and the red drained from his face, and he relaxed.

"You're right, sir. We don't have a body there either. And now that the cabin has burned, no evidence of a crime and no way of knowing if Smalldog was involved. I understand. I'll inform our Canadian counterparts and let them handle things."

He was just about to hang up when something more came through the receiver of the phone, and he jammed it once more to his ear.

"No, I understand your situation, sir. I can appreciate that you have your hands full down there."

He hung up and stared at Cork and Bascombe. Then he looked out the window at the big lake, which was all waves in the strong afternoon wind.

"Did you know, Cork, that the Angle tried to secede from the United States?"

"No," Cork replied.

"Was a few years ago. Angle folks were all pissed off because Canada wouldn't let the guests in our resorts take fish from their waters, and our resorts were suffering. We complained, but nobody gave a shit about us. Which is the way it's always been. So we decided maybe we'd see about joining Manitoba. We finally convinced our U.S. congressman to introduce a constitutional amendment that would have allowed us to vote to secede."

"Didn't go anywhere," Bascombe reminded him.

Kretsch shook his head. "Nobody took us seriously." He gave the phone a dour look, then lifted his eyes to Cork. "You told me you were a county sheriff."

"Nearly a decade. A deputy for six years before that. And before that I was with Chicago PD."

"You ever work a murder investigation?"

"Several."

Kretsch turned his blue eyes on Bascombe. "What about you, Mr. ATF? You ever work a homicide?"

"I saw the aftermath of a couple while I was an agent," Bascombe replied. "Never worked the investigations, but I've got all the instincts, Tom."

Kretsch was quiet a moment, then hit the desk with his fist and said, "Fuck 'em. We're getting to the bottom of things."

And he stood up.

They tracked down the others at Lynn Belgea's, and found Mal and Stephen and Tony Ebnet at Jerry's Restaurant across the road from Young's Bay Resort, where each had finished off a monster of a burger that Stephen swore was the best he'd ever tasted. They had a sack of burgers and lots of fries. They divided themselves between the two launches, Bascombe's and Ebnet's, and headed back to Oak Island, with Tom Kretsch along. Ebnet left them at Bascombe's dock, saying he was always available if needed, then boated away.

They gathered in the small dining area of Bascombe's lodge. The big man pulled out beer for those who wanted it and Coke for the others. Cork split up the burgers and fries among those who still hadn't eaten. The baby was sleeping in his basket, which Jenny had set on the floor near her chair. They all looked to Kretsch, who shrugged and looked at Cork and said, "Where do we begin?"

Cork laid out the facts as they knew them, then spent a minute thinking, slowly turning his beer bottle on the table as he considered the elements of the situation. "Okay, let's assume that Chickaway's been murdered and, like the girl's, his body's been disposed of somewhere else. What connects these two people in a way that would get them both killed?"

"Noah Smalldog," Kretsch said.

"That's one possibility," Cork agreed. "But did he kill them?"

"Why would he?" Anne asked. "His own sister?"

"And a guy who's supposed to be his good friend," Mal put in.

"I don't know Smalldog, except from what people have told me," Cork said. "Is he the kind of man capable of these things?" He glanced at Bascombe, then Kretsch.

Bascombe spoke first. "He's a hard one to figure, but I'd say, given the right motivation, it's something he might do."

Kretsch shook his head. "I don't think so. I don't pretend to know him—I don't think anybody on the Angle does—but it would take someone more cold-blooded than anything I've heard about or seen from Smalldog to do what's been done here in the last couple of days."

"Who around here might be capable of such things?"

"Christ, nobody in their right mind," Kretsch said.

"I don't think we're dealing with a psychotic killer, Tom," Cork said. "There's a reason behind the murders and why they were so gruesome."

"You think Chickaway was tortured, too?" Bascombe asked.

"There was an overturned chair and some rope in the middle of the pool of blood in Chickaway's cabin. Same thing was true when we found Lily Smalldog. So let's assume for the moment that he was tortured and killed in the same way she was. Why would someone do that to both of them?"

"Someone wanted to know where the baby was," Jenny said.

"Why?" Cork asked.

Jenny looked clueless and shrugged.

Quiet followed, then Anne said, "Who took her from Stump Island and put her in that isolated cabin, and why?"

"It seems obvious to me it was because of the kid," Bascombe said.

Anne frowned. "Why not leave her on Stump Island, where she and the child had a better chance of good care? And was she taken before or after she gave birth?"

Rose said, "Does it matter?"

"I don't know," Anne replied. "I'm just asking."

"My vote is for before," Bascombe said. "Noah Smalldog's the father, or maybe Chickaway, and neither of them wanted her delivering the baby among white people. They snatched her, one or both of them, and took her to the cabin on that island. She delivered like Indians have been delivering for hundreds of years."

Cork said, "So why is she dead now and why Chickaway?"

Jenny looked down at the child asleep in the basket. "It all comes back to the baby."

"Did folks on the Angle know she was pregnant, Tom?"

"Once we all heard about Chickaway and all that baby formula he loaded on his boat, word got around pretty fast. Speculation about the father has been a popular topic since then. But I don't think anybody knew anything before that."

"The people on Stump Island had to know, right?" Cork said.

"If they did, they never mentioned it."

"Who reported the girl missing?"

"Gabriel Hornett. He's the head of the camp," Kretsch replied.

"Did you investigate?"

"Sure. Well, as much as I could."

"Did you talk to her brother?"

"Couldn't find him."

"What about Chickaway?"

Kretsch nodded. "Claimed he didn't know anything. I asked all around the Angle and the islands and came up with zip. Then the Seven Trumpets people found a sweater that belonged to her washed up on the shore of Stump Island. Honestly, I figured that sooner or later we'd find her floating in the lake, like her mother."

"Maybe we should have another talk with the folks on Stump Island," Cork suggested. "They were the last to see her before she disappeared."

"I'm game," Kretsch said.

"Can I go?" Stephen asked.

Cork looked around the table. "Anybody else?"

Mal said, "My ankle's killing me. I'll stay back."

"Seth," Rose said, "if you'll give me free rein in your kitchen, I'll see about having some dinner ready when you come back. And maybe Annie would be willing to give me a hand."

Bascombe grinned hugely and waved in the direction of the kitchen. "Be my guest."

"I'm staying here with the baby," Jenny said.

Aaron said, "And I'm staying with you."

Cork eyed the baby asleep in the basket, then he eyed Jenny. "As soon as we can, we turn this child over to the authorities. For his safety and ours." He waited for her to object, but she said nothing. "All right." He tapped the tabletop, as if adjourning a meeting. "Let's see what the folks on Stump Island have to say."

TWENTY-EIGHT

When her father and the others had left, Jenny took the basket with the sleeping baby and went outside. Aaron went with her. They walked to the end of Bascombe's old wooden dock, where there was a bench, and they sat down. Across the channel lay Birch Island, a broad, unbroken shoreline of birch and aspen, yellow-green in the late afternoon sun. Forty miles north lay Kenora. Somewhere between here and there, Jenny knew, was the place where the child's mother had suffered horribly and died. Died, she was certain, without saying a word about where her beloved little baby was hidden. Jenny felt a weight on her shoulders and understood that it was a sense of responsibility, not just to the child but to the mother.

She stared down into the basket, and her heart melted. "Look at him, Aaron. He's so vulnerable."

Aaron glanced, then looked away. "All babies are vulnerable, Jenny."

"Not like him. His mother's dead. Nobody seems to know who his father is. From everything we do know, he doesn't have a family or anyone who cares about him."

"The truth is that we don't know much at all about him, Jenny. When we do, maybe we'll know about things like family." He eyed the child again. "And whether there's hope for that face of his."

Something inside her shriveled into a hard little ball. "That's all you see?"

"It's tough to get past."

"What if he had a normal face?"

"What do you mean?"

"Would that make a difference in how you felt about him?"

"I don't feel anything about him, Jenny. He's not my child."

"Maybe he could be."

Aaron stood up, and the whole dock seemed to shiver. "I know where you're headed here. But, Jenny, you're going to have to give him over to the authorities at some point. He'll become the responsibility of the county or the state or someone."

"I mean, Aaron," she said, trying to keep her voice even, "suppose we had a child and the child wasn't perfect."

"Let's cross that bridge when we come to it."

"I think it would be too late then."

"Jesus, Jenny." He threw his hands up, as if scattering something—crumbs, maybe—across the lake. "I love you. I want to marry you. And I've been thinking about this whole issue of children. Okay, I admit it scares me. It's not something I've wanted in the same way as you. But I do want you, and if children will make you happy, then I'm fine with that."

She gave him a curt little clap of her hands. "Bravo, Aaron. So rational. But I don't want it to be something that comes from your head. I want it to come from here." She reached out and thumped his chest over his heart.

"What I feel for you does."

They were quiet after that, painfully so. A flight of white pelicans cut along the channel, so near the crests of the waves that Jenny was afraid their wings would catch and they would crash into the lake. She watched them curl to the west and glide smoothly to rest in the calmer water of a little bay.

"I just . . . I wasn't expecting this," Aaron said at last. "We're apart two weeks, and when I see you next, you have a baby practically stuck to your breast."

"I didn't plan it. But I believe it's like Amos Powassin said. He's come to rest where he's supposed to be."

Aaron eyed the baby with what Jenny perceived as distaste and said, "Listen to me. You can't keep this kid."

"I know that."

"Do you? Because anyone who sees the way you look at him would believe he's yours."

"I don't think I want to have this discussion with you now."

"Fine. But we'll have to have it at some point."

"Will we? I'd like to be alone with him right now."

"Perfect," Aaron said.

He walked away, and in the quiet after his leaving, she could hear the soothing spill of waves against the shore and the soft breathing of the baby asleep at her feet.

"I don't think it's going well," Anne said from the window of the lodge, where she'd been watching the exchange at the end of the dock.

Mal said, "What do you think of him?"

Anne crossed her arms and gave the question a good long think. "He's smart. He's handsome. He loves Jenny. He seems very nice. What's not to like?"

Mal bent and gently touched his injured ankle. "That sounds rhetorical."

Rose came from the kitchen, holding a big package of frozen hamburger. "Not the best of circumstances under which to meet the O'Connors, you have to admit. What about meat loaf for dinner? And I can do up some garlic mashed potatoes, and there's a big bag of peas in the freezer. Nothing for a salad, unfortunately."

"You know," Mal said, "I keep thinking about that girl and her situation and who might have been cruel enough or angry enough to do what was done to her. And this other one, too. This Chickaway."

"Thinking what?" Rose said. She sat down at the table with her husband.

"I had a man in confession once who told me he had horrible thoughts about killing his girlfriend."

"Are you allowed to tell us this?"

"I won't tell you who he was, sweetheart. And it was a long time ago. He and God have already had a face-to-face on this issue."

"He's dead?"

"Yes."

"Go on," Rose said.

"He was inclined to kill her because she'd betrayed him, slept with another man. Sent my guy into a murderous rage. He was going to kill her, and then he was going to kill the guy she'd slept with."

"But you talked him out of it?"

"I didn't say that."

"Did he?"

"You mean did he kill her? No. He killed himself instead."

Anne said, "And the point is?"

"Maybe Chickaway fathered the child and took Lily Small-dog off Stump Island before she began to show and anyone would know. He hid her on that remote island and was keeping her safe there."

"Safe from Smalldog?"

"That's what I'm thinking. Because he knows Smalldog and what he's capable of."

"But Smalldog gets wind of it because of all that formula, tortures Chickaway until he tells where Lily is, then kills him, hauls the body off, and goes after Lily. Is that it? A murderous rage? I don't know, Mal," Anne said.

Mal shrugged. "I'm just thinking out loud."

"But the baby has a cleft lip," Rose pointed out. "Lynn Belgea said Noah Smalldog was also born with a cleft lip. So wouldn't the baby be Smalldog's?"

Mal considered the possibility, then offered, "You told me

she also said that Indians have a much higher rate of cleft lip than other ethnic groups, so maybe it's just chance."

Anne said, "He's leaving her."

Rose and Mal swung their attention to Anne, who was still looking out the window.

"What? For good?" Mal asked.

"I mean right now. She's staying on the dock with the baby. He's heading back here."

"I guess we can't talk about him behind his back then," Mal said.

"You make it sound awful," Rose said. "It's just a family discussion."

"If you say so." Mal let out a small groan.

"Oh, sweetheart, I'm worried about that ankle."

Mal laughed. "With everything else we have to worry about, this ankle's nothing, Rose. What kind of Catholic would I be if I couldn't take a little suffering?"

Anne said, "I'm going out to be with Jenny for a while."

"Go on," Rose said. "She could use family about now, I bet. And, Mal, would you mind having a little talk with Aaron while I make myself scarce?"

"A little talk? About what?"

"Whatever he wants to discuss," Rose said.

"If it's women, I won't be much help," Mal said.

Aaron opened the screen door and stepped in. It was clear he was deep in thought, and when he looked up, he seemed surprised to find them there.

Anne said, "I'll be back," and she slipped past him and out the door.

Rose said, "I'd better get to that meat loaf."

She went into the kitchen, but not so far away that she couldn't hear what passed between the two men in the other room.

Mal said, "You look like a guy who could use a beer."

"Thanks."

"Rose, you mind bringing a couple of those beers out here?" Mal called.

She went to the big refrigerator in Bascombe's kitchen and pulled out two bottles. When she took them in, she found Aaron sitting at the table with Mal. The look on his face reminded her of the thousand-yard stare she'd heard about in men suffering from shell shock. She set the beer in front of him.

"Thank you," he said and looked at her with those vacant eyes.

"Thanks, sweetheart," Mal said.

She returned to the kitchen and began to prepare the meat loaf. All the while she kept an ear tuned to the conversation between Mal and Aaron.

"This beer's Capital," she heard Mal say. "Sounds like an endorsement, but it's the name of the brewery. Out of Middleton, Wisconsin. You like it?"

"It's fine, I guess."

"One of my personal favorites. Speaks well of Bascombe's taste that he keeps it stocked even out here in the middle of nowhere." They were quiet in a way that made Rose uncomfortable. "Tough circumstances for meeting the family," Mal finally said.

"Tell me about it."

"We've heard a lot about you, Aaron. All good."

"I'm not so sure you'd get the same report now."

"People under stress sometimes say things they regret later."

"But that doesn't mean it's not how they feel."

"Maybe only how they feel in the moment," Mal said. "We change, moment to moment, circumstance to circumstance. That's what forgiveness is about."

"Jenny said you used to be a priest, right?"

"That's right."

"Forgiveness was pretty big in your line of work, I imagine." Rose heard the cynical undertone.

"I like to think it still is," Mal replied.

For another long minute there was only a huge, looming silence from the other room. Rose peeked through the doorway and saw the two men on opposite sides of the table sipping their beer. She wasn't sure it had been such a good idea to leave Mal alone with this responsibility.

But she could see her husband's face, and she didn't see any alarm or discomfort or unpleasantness there. He simply looked as if he was waiting.

And she remembered something Cork had told her about interviewing suspects, how silence was a pretty good way to get someone with something on his mind to talk.

And then Aaron said, "It's the baby."

"What about the baby?"

"Jenny wants to keep him. She's been with him like two days, and she's already thinking about him as if he's her own. How crazy is that?"

"They've been through a lot together. She risked her life for that little guy, and is probably the reason he's still alive. There are cultures that believe that kind of relationship binds people forever."

"The deal is this, Mal. I didn't go through any of that. I have no emotional attachment to this kid at all. And what kind of kid is he? Let's be honest, he's got a lot of strikes against him. Hell, I'm not even ready to take on the challenge of a normal kid. That baby—and how Jenny feels about him—scares me to death. Christ, and I thought the toughest thing I was going to face was meeting the incredible O'Connors."

"Incredible?"

"That's how Jenny talks about her family."

"She loves them."

"Well, bully for her." The room plunged again into awkward silence. "I'm sorry. I didn't mean that."

"I know."

"Mal, can Jenny forgive me, do you think?"

"Forgive what exactly?"

"Who I am?" Aaron said. "Or maybe who I can't be."

"I think that's a question only Jenny can answer. Your beer's getting warm."

Jenny said, "He's a selfish idiot."

"Maybe. To me, he just seems really confused, Jenny. Who wouldn't be?"

"I'm not."

"What if you have to give this baby up?"

"I know I'm going to have to give this baby up."

"Really? Because that's not the sense I get from you at all."

Jenny looked down at the child, who lay in the basket at her feet, awake now and staring up intently at her face. She said sadly, "Who's going to take him?"

"I don't know. I imagine a decision like that gets made by people with authority."

"According to rules," Jenny said bitterly.

"The rules are there to protect the children. You know that."

She did, but it didn't matter. Suddenly she was crying. It came over her in an unexpected flood, as if some flimsy dam had finally burst inside her. She leaned to her sister, who held her.

"I know it's crazy," she confessed. "Don't you think I know that? But I can't help it. The moment I saw him, I knew. It was like I was meant to find him."

"It's okay," Anne said and smoothed her sister's hair. "I understand."

"I was so scared out there. Scared for him and Dad and me. I didn't know if we were going to make it. All I could think about was that poor girl in the cabin and what had been done to her, and would they do the same to me, and, God, what would they do to him?" She drew away from Anne and reached down, pulled the baby from the basket, held him and went on crying.

"It's all right," Anne said. "It's over, Jenny."

"Is it? We don't know who that man out there was or why he wanted the baby. Because it was the baby he was after. That much I'm sure of."

"Okay. But we're all here to help protect him. He's safe now."

"Then why am I so afraid?" She ran her hand along the baby's soft cheek, then gave her sister a desperate look and spoke words that came out of some dark place of knowing deep inside her. "Can't you feel it, Annie?"

"Feel what?"

Jenny clutched the child as if some terrible force were trying to wrench him from her. "It's not over yet," she said. "The worst is still to come."

TWENTY-NINE

How far to Stump Island?" Cork asked.

"Another five miles," Kretsch said. "It's the last of the islands before you hit the big water, so it's pretty far out there."

The wind was against them, and Bascombe, at the helm, gripped the wheel and seemed tense as they bounced through the chop of the waves. They'd passed to the west of Massacre Island, which lay on the other side of the boundary line with Canada, and then Little Oak Island, and finally Garden Island, where the lake had opened up in front of them. On the horizon far to the south, Cork could see nothing. The big water, he knew. There was something about that vast expanse of looming emptiness that was a little frightening. He much preferred the sense of intricacy created by the tangle of islands behind them. Or better yet, the intimacy of the small, clear lakes of home, Tamarack County.

"What do you know about the folks who run the camp?" he asked Kretsch.

The deputy squinted against the wind, and lines cracked the suntanned skin of his face. "Not much. Not quite as accessible as the Baptists used to be. Keep pretty much to themselves, but no trouble. They have money, apparently. They bought the island outright with cash."

"What denomination are they?"

"I'm not entirely sure."

"No particular denomination," Bascombe said to them over his shoulder. "They call themselves the Church of the Seven Trumpets."

"Never heard of them," Cork said.

"Pretty fundamentalist, I understand. Holy Rollers or something," Bascombe said. "But like Tom was saying, no trouble. Me, I think religion is for the faint of heart."

"What do you mean?" Kretsch asked, a little edge of irritation to his voice.

"I know you're a good Catholic boy, Tom. But it seems to me religion mostly offers false comfort to folks afraid of dying."

Stephen had seemed intent on studying the islands as they passed, but now he turned to Bascombe. "You're not afraid of dying?"

"Sure I am. But when I'm standing at that door, I don't want some pasty-faced young minister telling me things are going to be better on the other side. Hell, how would he know? You man up to things in life, and I figure death's no different. That's all I'm saying."

Stephen looked off toward a small gathering of bare rocks surrounded by angry water and seemed to think about Bascombe's comments. Finally he said, "Mr. Bascombe, I respect your opinion, but for me, my religion's about a way of living, not dying."

Kretsch's clear blue eyes sparkled with approval, and the deputy gave Stephen a broad grin. "I've never heard it said better."

Bascombe glanced back and said affably, "Call me Seth, son."

Stephen looked again at the great water across which they bounded. Cork was proud of his son. Stephen, in his short life, had suffered great blows. He'd been kidnapped when he was very young. He'd seen his father shot—nearly fatally—right in front of him. He'd lost his mother. Yet his faith was strong. And Cork knew it wasn't the result alone of his Catholic upbringing, nor was it strictly Christian. Of all his children, Stephen was the one in whom the blood of the Anishinaabeg ran most powerfully, and his spirituality came as much from the teaching of men like Henry Meloux, the old Ojibwe Mide, as it did from the text of the New Testament.

"There it is," Bascombe hollered over the wind and the slap of waves. "Stump Island."

He pointed south, where a long gray-green worm seemed to sit on the sun-stained water. As they drew nearer, it grew into a flat, heavily wooded island. Cork could see nothing beyond it but the blue horizon. It felt to him as if he was looking at the last outpost in a great liquid desert.

"Anybody else on the island besides the camp folks?" he asked Kretsch.

"Nope. They've got the whole place to themselves. Don't need outside help. For their electricity and heat, they've got solar panels and that big wind generator." He pointed toward a white wind turbine that stood high above everything else on the island. "Propane for backup. They filter their own water, grow a lot of their own food. Pretty much self-sustaining."

The island was easily a half a mile long, flat and heavily wooded, and the shoreline looked to be all rock. Bascombe guided the launch around the west end, where a gathering of cabins and other buildings came suddenly into view, spread out along the finger of a broad peninsula. The cabins were clapboard painted cedar red. Two structures stood out: the tall wind generator, bone white, and the dark metal spider webbing of another tower currently under construction. The tower looked as if it might, when finished, be used for radio broadcasting. Bascombe guided them toward a long dock, where a couple of big powerboats were moored. Near the dock stood a large boathouse. As they approached, two men came from the boathouse to meet them. The first was tall, blue-eyed, black-haired, gothic looking in the angular cut of his jaw and the long slope of his nose. He wore a denim shirt with sleeves rolled back and clean, faded jeans. The other man was younger, slender, willowy, handsome in a brooding way. He had the same black hair and blue eyes as the other man, and even without having been introduced, Cork figured they were family. They both cradled rifles.

"What's with the hardware, Gabe?" Bascombe called as they motored up.

The taller, older man let the rifle hang in one hand, barrel toward the ground, unthreatening. "Just making sure that I knew you and that you're friendly, Seth. We had someone trespassing last night, someone with a firearm. Took a couple of shots at us."

"Anybody hurt?" Kretsch asked.

"No, thank God."

"You see who it was?"

"Didn't, Tom. But it was someone in a cigarette boat, I can tell you that much. Took off fast once we came after him."

Bascombe said, "Noah Smalldog?"

The man named Gabriel nodded. "That's what I figured. There's a soul bound for hell as surely as I'm standing here."

They tied up, and when they'd all disembarked and stood together on the dock, Cork asked, "Why would Noah Smalldog come here in the middle of the night?"

Cork placed the tall man in his early forties. His hair, wild in the wind that blew across the big water, gave him a restless, almost manic look. He had eyes so blue-white they seemed made of crystal, and those eyes were looking at Cork pretty sharply.

"I don't know you," he said.

"My name's Cork O'Connor. And I think this Smalldog may have taken a potshot at me, too."

"Well, I guess that puts us in the same boat." The man shook Cork's hand. "I'm Gabriel Hornett."

"This is my son, Stephen," Cork said.

"Stephen, eh? Fine Christian name, that. A brave Christian martyr."

"Yes, sir," Stephen said with a brief, courteous smile. "Is that Hornet, like the insect?"

"Two *t*'s at the end, son. Makes my sting twice as dangerous."

Hornett laughed, and Cork could tell it was a line he used often and was fond of. "This is my brother, Joshua." He indicated the willowy man with brooding good looks who stood at his side. The younger Hornett gave a silent nod in acknowledgment. Cork placed Joshua in his mid-twenties, a good fifteen years younger than his brother.

"What does Smalldog have against you?" Hornett asked.

"Long story," Cork replied.

"And part of the reason we're here," Kretsch said. "Can we go somewhere out of this wind and talk?"

"Sure thing. Let's go to the community hall. This way."

Hornett turned and led them away from the shore. His brother brought up the rear, following a few steps behind the others. Hornett took them into the heart of the church camp, a clean and pleasant place. The cabins and buildings, all sturdy-looking structures, had been recently painted and were in good repair. In addition to the metal tower under construction, there was another major project under way: a long wooden skeleton, a two-story framework of studs that appeared as if it might become a dormitory, or maybe even a barracks. The grounds were immaculate, and the paths through the trees were of crushed limestone, beautifully white against the green of the grass and the trees. There were a number of people about, all busy with the various constructions as well as the normal work of a camp—repairing steps on a cabin or raking leaves or collecting garbage. No one seemed to take any particular notice of Cork and the others.

"Quite a place you have here," Cork said.

"The Lord has guided us well," Hornett replied. "We call it the Citadel."

"And your church is the Church of the Seven Trumpets, is that correct?"

"Yes, sir, it is."

"Interesting name. Where does it come from?"

"Read your Revelation, Cork. The Apocalypse is coming,

make no mistake. We're preparing ourselves and our souls here."
He gave Cork and Stephen a sidelong glance and added, "We
open our arms to anyone wanting to accept Jesus before it's too
late."

"You're talking End Times?" Cork said.

"You say that with a smirk, sir, which I'm sorry to see."

Cork thought the man was way too sensitive, but in his experience, a lot of deeply religious people were. In his own mind,
there was often a profound difference between those who
thought of themselves as religious people and those who preferred to think of themselves as spiritual. Given a choice, he'd go
with the latter every time.

The community hall was a new structure, large and simple,
a great room with high ceilings and thick rafters of dark wood.
Half the area inside was taken up with tables. The other half
held chairs arranged in rows that faced a simple altar. The wall
behind the altar was dominated by an enormous banner that
held the image of a man with black hair and a black beard and
crystal-blue eyes that, no matter where you stood in the great
hall, seemed to follow you.

"One of the prophets?" Cork asked.

"In a way. The Reverend Jerusalem Hornett, founder of the
Church of the Seven Trumpets."

"Any relation?"

"My father," Hornett said.

Because of the severe blue eyes in both men, Cork wasn't
surprised in the least.

"The hall serves two purposes," Hornett explained. "We
gather here for our communal meals, and this is where we wor-
ship together. We think of it like the upper room of the Last
Supper, a place where we nourish both our bodies and our souls."

"I don't know what you're having for dinner tonight," Bascombe said, "but it smells like heaven."

"Esther's in charge of that. My wife," he said for the benefit
of Cork and Stephen. "Why don't we all sit down so that we can
talk?"

Gabriel Hornett leaned his rifle against the wall next to the front door, walked to one of the dining tables, pulled out a chair, and sat down. The others joined him, all except his younger brother, who stayed near the door, rifle still in hand, as if on guard duty. Gabriel Hornett folded his arms on the table, leaned toward Cork, and said, "Tell me about your trouble with Smalldog."

Cork recounted the story of the ordeal on the remote island. Hornett listened without comment but clearly looked disturbed. At the end, Cork said, "Seth and Tom think the dead girl might have been Lily Smalldog and the man who shot at me her brother, Noah."

"No," the younger Hornett said from the door. "That couldn't be Lily."

Cork had paid no attention to Joshua Hornett when telling his story, but now he saw how stricken the young man looked at the news.

"Why?" Cork asked.

"Lily drowned," he insisted.

"Or," the elder Hornett said, "someone made it look that way, Josh. And my guess would be Noah Smalldog." He frowned and shook his head. "That poor girl, that poor tortured soul. Dear Lord." Then he eyed Cork and Stephen and Kretsch, each in turn, with a look of profound solemnity. "This barbarism is just further proof. End Times, gentlemen. You understand now why we see so clearly that the Apocalypse is upon us. Everywhere we look, the signs are there."

"The signs?" Stephen said.

"Eighteen signs, Stephen," Hornett replied with evangelistic fervor. "Five given by our Lord Jesus Christ himself to indicate his coming and the end of the age." He lifted his right hand and began counting off on his fingers.

"One, Matthew twenty-four, eleven: 'And many false prophets will arise and will mislead many.' Think about it for a moment, Stephen. Jim Jones, David Koresh, Osama bin Laden, the Dalai Lama. All falsely using the name of God to lead masses away from the true path shown to us by our Lord Jesus Christ.

"Two, Matthew twenty-four, six: 'And you will be hearing of wars and rumors of wars.' Stephen, when was the last time you turned on your television or radio or connected to your Internet and didn't see some report of war somewhere in this world? The death toll rises daily, and everywhere nations are preparing weapons of mass destruction.

"Three, Matthew twenty-four, seven: 'For nation will rise against nation, and kingdom against kingdom, and in various places there will be famines and earthquakes.' When we were in Zimbabwe, Stephen, we saw the good Christian farmers there being driven out and replaced by godless men growing poppies that supply twenty-five percent of the world's drug trade. Now Africa hungers. There's famine in Pakistan and India and China, and mark my words, very soon there will even be famine here in America as the climate begins to change because of God's wrathful hand. As for earthquakes, there have been more recorded in the past one hundred years than in all history before that. Soon the whole earth will shake so badly that people will tremble for fear it's falling apart.

"Four, Matthew twenty-four, nine: 'Then they will deliver you to tribulation, and will kill you, and you will be hated by all nations because of My name.' Christians are scorned today, Stephen, under attack around the world. The Muslim nations would love nothing better than to wipe Christianity from the face of the earth. It has been bad, but it will get far worse.

"And the last sign, Stephen, Matthew twenty-four, fourteen: 'And this gospel of the kingdom shall be preached in the whole world as a testimony to all the nations, and then the end will come.' You saw the tower we're building out there? That's a radio tower and will have a powerful signal. When we're finished, we'll be able to broadcast the word of God for a thousand miles. We already have an Internet site, and every year here we train men and women to travel to the darkest places imaginable to preach the holy word. Make no mistake, Stephen, the end is almost upon us. And those who haven't accepted Jesus

Christ as their savior will suffer torment you can't even begin to imagine."

When he'd finished, Hornett looked hard at Stephen, as if trying to melt the young man's flesh with the fire in his eyes.

Stephen didn't reply for a moment. Then he said, "Do you have a bathroom?"

"A bathroom?" Hornett seemed caught by surprise.

"Yes, sir. I have to pee."

A flicker of irritation crossed the man's face, and he pointed toward a door at the far end of the great hall. "Over there."

"Thank you."

Stephen left the table, and Hornett followed him with a cold, disappointed stare.

"Long boat ride," Cork said. "You told me Noah Smalldog trespassed last night and did some shooting. What time?"

"Shortly after midnight," Hornett replied. "Everyone was sleeping."

"What woke you up to his presence? Did he shoot first?"

"I happened to be up. Some nights I can't sleep, and so I come here to pray. I was on my way to the hall when I spotted him."

"Where exactly?"

Hornett looked at Cork with the same irritation Stephen seemed to have engendered. "Does all this really matter?"

"Cork's got a long background in law enforcement, Gabe," Kretsch said. "Just where did you spot Smalldog?"

"Sneaking around Josh and Mary's cabin."

"Mary?"

"Joshua's wife."

Cork glanced toward the door where the younger Hornett stood. The man stared at the floor, frowning, lost in deep, unhappy thought. He didn't appear to have heard his wife's name mentioned.

"Did Josh or Mary see him?"

"No, they were sleeping."

"Is that where he fired at you?"

"Yes."

"And you returned fire?"

"I did."

"With that?" Cork nodded toward the rifle Hornett had left near the door.

"No, with my handgun."

"What kind?"

"A Colt Commander."

"You always take the Commander with you when you go to pray?"

"I started wearing it when we first began having trouble with Smalldog trespassing."

"After you exchanged fire, that's when he ran?"

Hornett nodded. "To the dock, and then he shot off in his cigarette boat."

Kretsch asked, "Any idea why he was here, Gabe?"

"I don't pretend to understand how evil thinks."

A door on one side of the big room opened, and a woman entered. She was stocky, with a single braid of gold hair down her back. She wore khakis and a dark green T-shirt and hiking boots. She reminded Cork of the stout Swedish immigrant women who'd helped their men carve farms out of the wild Minnesota prairie in the 1800s.

"I thought your guests might be hungry, Gabriel," she said and brought to the table a plate filled with slices of dark bread.

"My wife, Esther," Hornett said and introduced Cork and the others.

"Abigail is coming with tea," Esther said.

As if on cue, the door opened again and a second woman appeared. She was older, maybe late fifties, hair gone gray. She was lean and fit like Hornett and with many of the same sharp features in her face. She wore jeans and a short-sleeved denim shirt and sneakers. There was a fluidity to her movement that made Cork think of an athlete. She carried a tray that held a white ceramic pot and several mugs. She swept across the hall toward the table.

"The tea, Gabriel."

"Thank you, Abigail," Hornett replied.

The woman slid the tray from her hand. "Hello, Seth, Tom." She turned a gracious smile on Cork. "And hello to you. Welcome to Stump Island."

"Cork O'Connor," Bascombe said in introduction. "This is Abigail Hornett."

Cork wouldn't have needed to know she had the same last name as Gabriel and Joshua. It was clear all three shared the same genes.

"How do you do?" Cork stood up and offered his hand. Her palm and the pads of her fingers were callused. A woman used to hard physical labor, Cork thought. There was something in her face as well, something hard and solid, that spoke of an acceptance of travail and an abundance of grit to face it.

"You would be Gabriel and Josh's mother?"

"I am. I hope you gentlemen are okay with tea. It's herbal, my own creation, a little sweet. I think you'll find it energizing. Most folks do." She glanced around the great hall. "I thought there was a young man with you."

"My son," Cork said. "He's using your restroom."

"Ah," she said with a smile, as if she understood perfectly.

The door opened yet again, and a third woman appeared and shuffled toward the table. She was bent, as if from age, though Cork thought she couldn't have been more than a few years past twenty. She had mouse brown hair cut very short and wore a plain yellow dress and white sandals. If there'd been any life in her face, she might have been pretty.

"Mary," Abigail said with a little surprise and a lot of irritation.

The shuffling woman looked up and seemed astonished to see them all there.

"They killed my son," she said.

The hall fell silent. Cork heard the high whine of a saw cutting metal outside. It came from the direction of the radio tower and reminded him of the sound of cicadas.

"Joshua," Abigail snapped. "Come and take care of your wife."

Before the younger Hornett could move, his wife said again, "They killed my son."

"Yes, we know, Mary," Gabriel Hornett said gently. "They crucified him. But remember, he died for our sins. Josh?"

The younger Hornett leaned his rifle against the wall and walked stiffly to Mary. Without a word, he turned her roughly and, with a firm grip on her arm, urged her back into the kitchen.

Abigail said to the men, "Will you excuse us? Esther, we still have work to do. Come along."

The two women vanished into the kitchen, where Mary and her husband had gone.

A moment later, Joshua Hornett returned, drifted back to his place near the front door, and took up his rifle again.

Stephen came from using the restroom and sat down and looked at the bread and tea on the table, which had appeared in his absence.

"You should try some of Esther's date nut bread," Gabriel Hornett said. "She's rather well known for it." He picked up a slice for himself, took a bite, then spoke to Cork and Kretsch. "Josh's wife has suffered for years from the delusion that she's the Virgin Mary. We tolerate her delusion and pray daily for her to be cured. In the meantime, we all help Josh care for her."

Cork said, "You took in Lily Smalldog and took care of her, too, is that right?"

"We tried. She was really a sweet girl. But we couldn't watch her every minute of every day, and her brother and that other Indian, they . . ." He paused and shook his head as if he couldn't find exactly the right words for what the two men had done.

"Took advantage of her?"

Hornett looked at Stephen and seemed to decide that Cork's delicate characterization was appropriate. "Exactly."

"Did you ever actually see them?"

"We caught sight of them on occasion, but we never actually caught them."

"They sneaked onto the island?"

"It's a big island, Cork. We can't watch every inch."

"Why did they have to sneak onto the island? Didn't you allow Lily visitors?"

"This isn't a prison. She wasn't a prisoner. At first, we welcomed Smalldog and Chickaway. But when we found out what they were doing to that poor, sweet thing, we banned them absolutely from coming here."

"How did you find out what they were doing?"

"Lily told us."

"She just came right out with it?"

"Not in so many words. She didn't really understand what they were doing, what sexual relations were about. They brought her little gifts and filled her head with stories, and she told us the stories. It wasn't hard to understand what the visits from those two men were really about."

"How old was Lily?"

"She'd just turned eighteen when she disappeared."

"So she was a minor, or at least a vulnerable adult, when these men were abusing her. Did you call Tom?"

"We complained, of course."

"Tom, did you investigate?"

"I talked to Lily, but she wouldn't say anything to me," Kretsch said.

"And nobody had her examined to confirm that she'd been abused?"

"We knew," Hornett said. "We didn't need to have her examined."

"What I'm saying here, Gabriel," Cork said evenly, "is that if you could substantiate a claim of sexual abuse of a minor or a vulnerable adult, a warrant could have been sworn out for the two men. The law could have stopped them."

"The law would have had to catch them first," Hornett replied. "Not an easy thing."

"All right," Cork said, "let's move on. When Lily Smalldog disappeared, did you know that she was pregnant?"

"We didn't suspect it at all. She said nothing to us, and she wore such loose-fitting clothing all the time. Only after we heard about the boxes of formula that Chickaway had carted off across the lake did we put two and two together."

"When she disappeared, you notified Tom immediately?"

"Of course."

"What did you think had happened to her?"

"She didn't leave the island on her own, we knew that much. We've got only two launches here, so they're easy to monitor. We figured one of the Indians had come and taken her. Then, when we found her sweater, we thought she'd gone into the lake, same as her mother. Both women suffered from periods of darkness you can't imagine."

"Depression?"

"I'm no doctor, so I couldn't really diagnose it."

"Were they being treated?"

"We treated them with prayer, Cork. It's our way."

"I understand Lily and her mother had their own cabin."

"Yes."

"Could we see it?"

"Now?"

"As good a time as any," Cork said.

Hornett stood up and led them to the door. "You stay here, Josh. And mind Mary," he said with a note of chastisement.

His younger brother glared at him but said nothing and obeyed.

The cabin was several hundred yards east of the peninsula where the other buildings of the camp stood. They reached it by walking a narrow path, almost overgrown now, that ran among the birches along the shoreline. It was a small, isolated little structure built of logs, without electricity and with an outhouse off to one side. The great restless blue of the big water was visible through a wide break in the trees at its back. In the wind off the lake, the sound of the birch leaves rustling was like fast-running water. Cork thought it was a lovely spot.

"It's pretty rustic, but Vivian and Lily seemed to be just fine with what they had," Hornett said as they approached the place. "We were planning at some point to run electricity out here and put in indoor plumbing, but all our efforts for quite a while have been focused on our larger projects."

The door was padlocked, but Hornett brought out a set of keys, undid the lock, and shoved the door open. He stepped inside, and the others followed.

The windows were closed and clouded with dust. Judging from the stuffiness of the room, they hadn't been opened in a great while. There was a table, and there were two chairs and two small bunks. There was a cast-iron stove for heating. That was all. Nothing personal remained in the cabin, nothing that would have spoken to the nature of the two women, mother and daughter, who'd lived there.

"What happened to Lily's belongings?" Cork asked.

"We've got them boxed and stored up at the camp, should anyone ever want to claim them. There's nothing much, though. Clothing, a few pictures. Vivian and Lily lived a pretty simple existence. Took their food with the rest of us, washed their clothes in our laundry, bathed in our showers. They didn't need much here."

Cork recalled the cabin on the isolated island where Jenny had found the body of Lily Smalldog. It was a simple affair, too. Lily had been used to isolation, to making do by herself. As far as Cork could see, she hadn't had much in her life, but what little she did have was apparently enough.

"Dad," Stephen said.

He'd wandered away from the men and stood looking at the wall of the cabin above one of the bunks. Cork joined him and saw what he'd found.

"What is it?" Hornett asked.

"A word carved into the wood," Cork said.

Hornett came and looked, too. "I can't make it out. Looks like gibberish. But Lily wasn't good with reading or spelling."

"It's an Ojibwe word," Stephen said. *"Gizaagin."*

"What does it mean?"

"I love you."

Stephen stepped closer and looked down, then slid the bunk out a foot and pulled a folded paper from where it had been caught between the bunk frame and the wall. He unfolded it, studied it, then handed it to his father.

It was a drawing, simple pen and ink but really quite lovely, of a deer and fawn in a meadow. It was signed "Sonny."

Cork handed it to Tom Kretsch. Bascombe and Hornett looked at it over his shoulder.

Hornett said, "One of those little gifts I was telling you about. It didn't take much to get that poor girl to spread her legs."

Not much, Cork thought. *Just love.*

THIRTY

He stared up at Jenny with an intensity that would have been unnerving in someone grown, but he was only a baby and understood nothing except the nearness of her face, the scent of her body, the beat of her heart, the comfort of her presence, the electricity of her love. What had his mother been to him but these same things? Did he understand that, although Jenny offered him all of this, she was not his mother?

His left hand, so tiny, reached for her mouth, took her lower lip between his fingers, squeezed. He was strong, and it must have hurt her, but she made no move to stop him.

"Do you know what love is?" Rose asked.

They sat together in the dining room of Bascombe's lodge. Lynn Belgea had come with Babs Larson and had offered to take someone back to the houseboat to get suitcases so that everyone would have clean clothing. Mal and Aaron and Anne had gone with them, and Rose and Jenny were left alone. The lodge smelled of the baking meat loaf, of herbs and hot meat juices.

Jenny carefully removed the baby's fingers from her lip. "I used to think I did."

"I believe it's a life tied to another life in a way that feels inseparable. We care about a lot of people, but we choose to love a very few."

"Choose?" Jenny looked down at the baby. "I didn't choose this."

"Ask your sister, and she might tell you that God chose for you. Are you unhappy with the choice?"

"Aunt Rose, do you believe, really believe, that I could love this baby? I've only known him for a little more than a day."

"I believe what I see. And, Jenny, all I see in your face when you look at him is love."

"Aaron thinks I'm crazy."

"I think he's just afraid."

"Of what?"

"Of what's in your face when you look at this child. Because it's not what's in your face when you look at him."

"What I feel for Aaron is different."

"I don't think he understands that."

"Come on, Aunt Rose. He's a grown man. This is a baby."

"A baby you've fallen in love with in just one day. How long did it take you to fall in love with Aaron?" When Jenny didn't answer, Rose asked, "Are you in love with him?"

"I thought so. I don't know now."

Rose smiled gently. "And you wonder why he's afraid?"

She ran her hand down her niece's hair, smoothing wild strands in the way Jenny's mother might have had she been alive and a part of this conversation.

"Are you afraid?" Rose asked.

"Of what?"

"Losing him." She nodded at the little face staring up at Jenny. "He has family somewhere who have a legal right to him."

"I know."

The words sounded like acceptance, but what Rose heard in her niece's voice was something more like a faint trumpet of defiance.

The baby was asleep again when they heard the cut of an engine over the sound of the wind outside. Rose went to the window and saw Babs Larson's boat drawing up to Bascombe's dock. Everyone piled out and walked to the lodge. They were talking in loud voices as they approached.

Rose stepped to the door and put a finger to her lips. "The baby's asleep," she told them.

"We'll just stay out here then," Larson said. "Everyone give a hand, and we'll get these things to the cabins."

The others headed away carrying duffel bags, but Lynn Belgea came in. Her dog was with her. He went to the basket and sniffed at the baby.

"Careful, Teddy," Belgea said.

The dog backed away and lay down in an alert pose.

"He looks like a watchdog," Rose said.

"He's a good boy." Belgea petted him fondly. "I just stepped in to check on the baby. How's he doing?"

"He's fine," Jenny answered. "I wish I knew his name, though. It's getting awkward always calling him 'the baby' or just 'him.' "

"Maybe he doesn't have a name yet," Belgea said. "Did I tell you how Ted got his name?"

Jenny and Rose both shook their heads.

"I'd been alone for quite a while, and everyone on the Angle knew I was thinking of getting a dog. It was a pretty popular topic of conversation. Everyone began referring to the pet I'd get as The Eventual Dog. TED. I got so used to thinking of him that way that, when I finally brought him home, that was his name."

Jenny said, "Wouldn't work for this little guy. Two days ago, I had no idea I'd have a baby on my hands."

Belgea looked at her and at the child, and she smiled gently and said, "Could have fooled me. If there's anything you need for him or for yourself, you be sure to let me know."

"I will."

Outside the others returned. Belgea said good-bye, and the good women of the Angle went back to Larson's boat and headed away.

"Clean duds," Anne said, as she came into the lodge. She held up a folded stack of clothing for Jenny.

Jenny still wore the things she'd had on when the storm threw her onto the island. The idea of cleaning herself up was wonderful. She said, "Would someone watch him while I shower and change?"

Rose and Anne replied almost in unison, "We'd be happy to."

"You'll let me know if he cries or if he needs me."

"Go," Rose said. "He'll be fine with us."

Jenny took her clothing and started to leave but at the door turned back and glanced at the basket with concern.

"Go!" Anne ordered.

Jenny left.

Mal, when he'd come in, had sat at the table, and now he gingerly rubbed his damaged ankle. "If she has trouble leaving him for a few minutes, it's going to be hell on her when she has to give him up for good."

They all looked at the baby, and then at the empty doorway through which Jenny had disappeared, and no one had a thing to say.

When Cork and the others returned, the sun was behind the trees on Oak Island, and Bascombe's lodge lay deep in the shadows of evening. As they approached the lodge, Cork's mouth began to water at the aromas drifting outside. When they stepped in, he saw that the table was set, and he could hear the clatter of activity in the kitchen.

"We're back," he called.

Anne came out and said, "Wash up. I'll call the others."

Over the best meat loaf Cork swore he'd ever tasted, he recounted the events on Stump Island.

"What did you think of them?" Rose asked.

"They were friendly enough," Cork replied.

"But?"

"I got a hinky feel from the place."

Bascombe shrugged and said, "Religious folks always give me the willies. I figure they're okay, just a little lopsided in their view of human nature."

Cork looked at his brother-in-law. "Mal, you ever hear of a group called the Church of the Seven Trumpets?"

"Can't say I have." Mal worked his tongue over something stuck in a back tooth. "But if it's a biblical reference, it probably refers to the seven trumpets in the Book of Revelation."

"Mr. Hornett told us to read Revelation," Stephen said. "What did he mean?"

Mal said, "Basically, Revelation states that at the end of the world angels will blow seven trumpets. The first six will bring devastation and death to the earth with a lot of fire and bloodletting and plagues and things falling from the heavens and eventual darkness. The seventh will signal the second coming of Christ, and the defeat of Satan's armies and the Antichrist, and the final judgment."

"They're certainly firm believers in the Apocalypse," Kretsch said. "Rumor is that they're stockpiling supplies on the island in preparation."

"Hornett called their camp the Citadel," Cork said. "Which sounds sort of like siege mentality, but I didn't see any evidence of huge stockpiles."

"Stump Island's a big place," Kretsch said. "You could hide an army there."

Bascombe said, "I don't see what that has to do with the Smalldog girl."

Cork shook his head. "I don't know either. Except that everything Hornett said rang wrong. I don't like to go on hunches, but I've got a hunch they weren't being exactly forthcoming with us."

"That may have nothing at all to do with Smalldog or Jenny's baby," Bascombe pointed out.

Jenny's baby. Cork realized it was the first time anybody had used that term, had spoken it, anyway. It didn't please him. The child wasn't Jenny's responsibility, wasn't the responsibility of any of them. Though it wasn't the baby's fault, he was dangerous. Death shadowed him, and that shadow had fallen across Cork's family. Cork was determined, as soon as was humanly possible, to get the baby into the hands of the proper authorities. But he tabled that issue for the moment and returned to the matter at hand.

He said, "If you're looking at one thing that's amiss and you stumble onto another, in my experience, it pays to look for connections."

Kretsch said, "I agree. But how do we take a closer look?"

"Do you have access to the Internet here, Seth?"

"Yep," Bascombe said, "but it won't do you any good. My computer crashed a while back, and I haven't had any reason to get it fixed. I kind of like not being connected with all the craziness of the world outside the Angle."

Cork swung his gaze to the window. Beyond, the lake was growing pale in the dying light. A few stars were already twinkling in the eastern sky. He thought for a moment about asking Bascombe to take him to the mainland, where he might find what he wanted. But the wind was still blowing strong, and waves galloped across the water like wild horses. And he was dead tired. They were all tired, he could see.

"Why don't we get a good night's sleep," he suggested. "We can tackle all this again in the morning. And maybe we can figure the best way to get the child to where he ought to be."

He glanced at Jenny, expecting an objection, but all he got from her was a stone-hard stare.

Bascombe said to Kretsch, "You probably want to get back to the mainland, Tom."

Kretsch must have heard the weariness in the other man's voice. "If you've got an extra bunk, Seth, I'd be fine sleeping here tonight. That way we can get an early start tomorrow."

"You can have the last cabin," Bascombe said and sounded relieved. "I'll get some bedding."

"If you've got a sleeping bag I could throw on the bunk, that'll do."

"I have, but it smells of woodsmoke."

"I'm so beat it could smell of skunk and I wouldn't care."

They all laughed and, quiet and tired, rose from the table to get ready for the night.

THIRTY-ONE

Jenny couldn't sleep. Her body vibrated. From exhaustion, probably, but also from something else, something that felt to her like vigilance. It was much the same feeling she'd had the night before, stranded on that island. But she was safe here, wasn't she?

She lay in her bunk listening to Anne's soft, steady breathing from the other side of the small cabin, listening to the great breath of the wind outside. Before lying down that night, she'd drawn aside the curtains over the eastern windows so that the moon would light the room and she could see the baby. He lay in the wicker basket on the floor within easy reach of her hand.

Aaron slept in another cabin with Stephen. It was odd, having him so near but not sharing her bed. Odd but not unpleasant. The moment she'd seen the look of horror on his face at the sight of the child's cleft lip, something had changed in her. Something, she knew, had died. It wasn't a whole thing but an essential. As if her love for Aaron had lost its heart. She couldn't hide it from him. He'd gone to the cabin with Stephen walking like a man to a prison cell.

The baby began to fuss. Jenny had already prepared a bottle, and Bascombe had insisted she take a hot plate and saucepan to her cabin so that she could heat the formula easily in the night. She got up and, in her preparations, woke her sister.

"Go back to sleep. I'm just seeing to the baby."

"You're a good mom," Anne said drowsily, and she rolled over and faced the wall. In only a moment, she was breathing deeply and steadily again.

Jenny took the bottle and the wicker basket with the baby inside and left the cabin. Moonlight silvered the island and the lake, and she had no trouble making her way to the end of the dock, where she sat on the bench. She lifted the baby and gave him the bottle. She gently pressed her finger to the cleft in his lip, and still mostly asleep, he began to feed.

She loved this aloneness with the child, this sense that, for the moment, the whole world was just the two of them, and the only thing that was important was seeing to his safety and his need. How blessedly simple her life could be, she thought.

Except this baby wasn't hers. Maybe as soon as the next morning, she would have to give him up. She tried to accept the idea, but everything inside her went rigid in protest. She was angry, and her anger was directed mostly at her father, who seemed not to care in the least and whose only concern was how quickly he could get the child off their hands. She couldn't understand him and didn't want to. If it were possible, she'd have fled the Lake of the Woods herself and taken the baby with her.

The wind made the night restless. The lake surged and retreated against the dock pilings. The leaves of the poplars along the shoreline shook with a sound like a thousand rattlesnakes. The moon was nearly full and cast the island in a sharp contrast of silver light and black shadows that shifted in the wind.

And among those shadows Jenny saw something move.

At first she thought it was only a trick of the changing patterns of light and dark. Then she realized the motion was independent of the erratic way the wind made the trees sway. It was steady and directed toward the cabin she'd left only a few minutes before. She thought at first it might be Aaron, coming to check on her, and she felt a sad kind of gratitude. But when they came fully into the apron of moonlight in front of the cabin, she realized there were two figures and one of them held a rifle.

As the figure in front neared the cabin door and reached for the handle, Jenny let out a bloodcurdling scream. The figures at the cabin turned and fled toward the woods that backed the cabins and disappeared.

Jenny leaped to her feet. Lights went on in the cabins and in Bascombe's lodge, and everyone spilled outside into the night.

"Jenny!" Anne called.

"Here!" she cried back.

They ran to the end of the dock and huddled around her and the child, who seemed oblivious to all the activity.

"Christ, Jenny, are you all right?" Aaron asked.

"Yes."

Her father said, "What happened?"

"The baby was hungry. I came out here to feed him. I saw someone creep out of the woods and go to my cabin. There were two of them, Dad, and one of them had a rifle."

Bascombe stood at the edge of the gathering. He gripped a rifle in his hands. "Was it you, Seth?"

"Not me. I just grabbed this on my way out."

"Where's Tom?" Mal said, because Kretsch wasn't among them.

"Maybe he's still sleeping," Rose offered.

"Through this?" Bascombe said. "I don't think so."

"I'll check his cabin," Stephen said.

But just as he started away, a figure came from the woods, entered the light in front of the cabins, and walked toward the dock. He carried a rifle, too.

Cork nodded at the Remington in his hand. "What's with the rifle, Tom?"

"I heard a scream and someone ran past my cabin. I grabbed this and tried to follow them. Whoever it was, they got away."

From beyond a little wooded point to the north came the sound of powerful boat engines. A moment later, they saw a sleek launch shooting across the channel toward Birch Island. They watched it leap along the tops of the waves and curl to the north, leaving behind it a wake bone white in the moonlight.

"Cigarette boat," Stephen observed.

Bascombe nodded. "Smalldog."

"He wasn't alone," Cork said. "He had help."

"They were after the baby," Jenny said. "But why?"

Bascombe gave a shrug. "If you believe what some folks say about that child's parentage, Smalldog was probably just coming for his son."

They looked at the baby, his face aglow in the moonlight, unperturbed by the chaos that had erupted around him. He smiled up at Jenny. The divide of his upper lip parted easily, and the shape of his mouth was like a boat with a little sail.

Cork and Mal sat on the dock bench, facing Jenny's cabin, their turn on watch. Cork cradled Bascombe's Marlin on his lap. In the moonlight, the lake had become a great gray luminescence where whitecaps rose and fell.

"This Smalldog, he's something else," Mal said. "I'd like to see him."

"I have," Cork said. "We locked eyes when he was hunting us on the island."

"Did you see the devil there?"

"I saw a man I knew absolutely was capable of killing us."

"I've always believed that, even in the worst of men, there's still some humanity alive. But I don't know about Smalldog. If what Seth Bascombe says about him abusing his own sister is true, he's a piece of work. It would be interesting to talk to him, find out his truth."

"You can't save every soul, Mal. It's not even your business anymore."

"I'm just talking about understanding someone, Cork. I think it's the business of us all. Now soul saving, that's something else."

Cork stared at the angry lake and tried to make sense of Noah Smalldog.

The blood of the Anishinaabeg ran through Cork's veins. He had an Ojibwe name, Mikiinak, which meant "Snapping Turtle." The name had been given to him by the old Mide Henry Meloux, who'd seen the tenacity in him even when Cork was a small child. He loved the Ojibwe people, *his* people. But he knew the reality, which was that years of poverty on reservations and neglect by the agencies charged with helping them and misconceptions and prejudices deeply believed and perpetuated by whites had resulted in the misshaping of the spirits of far too many Indians. They drank to excess. They abused their women and their children. They abandoned their families. There was reason for their behavior, certainly, but that didn't excuse their actions.

Smalldog, Cork decided, was a misshapen spirit. He wondered what Henry Meloux, in all his patient wisdom, might say about the man. Would he, like Mal, believe that even the most grotesque of spirits could be reshaped and brought into harmony? Did Meloux have a ceremony powerful enough to redeem Smalldog?

Maybe it wouldn't matter, Cork thought, gripping the Marlin tightly. Because if Smalldog tried anything again, threatened Jenny or any of his family, Cork would shoot him down, shoot him down without a moment of hesitation or a measure of regret.

"What about the baby?" Mal said.

It was as if Cork's conscience had spoken. In thinking about the safety of his family, Cork had excluded the baby.

"As soon as possible, we deliver him wherever it is he should be."

"And where's that?"

"I don't know. The county authorities down in Baudette probably."

"We get rid of him," Mal said.

"That's not how it will be."

"That's how Jenny'll see it."

"She'll understand."

Mal shrugged. "If you say so."

"Look, Mal." Cork spoke with an intensity that bordered on anger. "A very bad man is out there in the dark somewhere, and he's threatening my family. Why? As nearly as I can tell, it's because of that baby. If the baby's gone, my family's safe. It's as simple as that."

"Simple doesn't necessarily translate into right."

"You think I'm wrong? You think Jenny should keep that child? You think Jenny *could* keep that child?"

"I don't know what might be possible, Cork. I just know that everything that threatens this family right now isn't necessarily out there in the dark."

Cork rose to his feet and glared down at his brother-in-law. "When you have a family of your own to worry about, Mal, then you can start offering me advice on how to take care of mine, okay?"

"Okay," Mal said without rancor.

"I'm going to check the cabins."

"I'll hold down the fort here," Mal said.

As Cork left, the old dock groaned under his weight. The wind gusted around him, and the lake surged at his back. Wrapped up in his own fury, a rage of uncertainty and worry, Cork was numb to it all.

THIRTY-TWO

Rose had coffee going when Bascombe came into the kitchen. He walked awkwardly, still stiff from sleep. His hair was unbrushed and stuck out in tufts of black and gray. He closed his eyes and stood a moment, his nose raised, as if sniffing the wind.

"Been a long time since I woke to the good smell of strong coffee made by a woman."

"I've pulled out some eggs and cheese and onion for breakfast," Rose said, setting a wooden cutting board onto one of the counters. "I hope you don't mind."

"Mind?" Bascombe laughed. "If you weren't already taken, Rose, I'd get down on my knees and propose."

"Hold on there," Mal said, coming in at his back. "I'm a reasonable man, but there are limits."

"I'll arm-wrestle you for her," Bascombe suggested.

"Tell you what," Rose said. "Whoever's willing to make pancakes, I'm all yours."

"Done," Mal said and got to work.

The others began to drift into the lodge. Bascombe poured them coffee while Rose and Mal prepared the meal. Jenny was the last to arrive, with the baby in his wicker basket.

"How's the baby this morning?" Cork asked. To Rose, his concern sounded clinical.

"Doing just fine," Jenny replied curtly.

"Coffee?" Rose offered.

"Thanks, Aunt Rose."

Aaron sat at the table, silently observing Jenny and the attention focused on her and the baby. He didn't attempt to greet her in any special way, Rose noticed, just sipped his coffee without apparent emotion. Rose wondered if it was exhaustion or if he was steeling himself against caring or if it was a cover for all the confusion he might be feeling.

When they were settled around the table, Rose and Anne served breakfast, and they ate and planned.

"So where do we go today?" Stephen said.

"I'd like to have a better look at Stump Island," his father replied. "See if I can figure out what it is those folks don't want to talk about."

"It might not have anything to do with Lily Smalldog," Bascombe pointed out.

"Maybe. But it's still a question I'd like answered."

Kretsch said, "I think we need to track down her brother."

"Got a suggestion how we do that?"

The deputy shrugged. "Talk to some more Ojibwe over on Windigo Island."

"You've dealt with the Ojibwe before?" Cork asked.

"Sure."

"And as a police officer, do you find them particularly forthcoming?"

"Not especially," Kretsch admitted.

"So they'd be more inclined to talk now because?"

Kretsch didn't have an answer.

"How about we talk to Amos Powassin?" Stephen suggested. "He knows us. And if he can't tell us anything, maybe he could introduce us to someone who can."

Cork was quiet a moment, thinking. "That's not a bad idea, Stephen. Mr. Powassin seemed to take to you. Maybe you should do the talking."

"Who goes?" Anne asked and glanced in the direction of the baby.

Rose understood the reason for the question. Jenny and the

baby needed protection. Someone willing to use a rifle had to stay back on Oak Island. That probably wasn't her or Anne, though Jenny might be willing.

"Seth's got to take us in his boat," Cork said. "Tom should come. It would be best to have an official legal presence. Stephen, because Amos Powassin might be more willing to talk to him. And I'll go. Mal, Aaron, you guys willing to stay and stand post?"

"Sure," Mal said.

"You'll need to keep a rifle."

"I won't promise to shoot, but I can hold the damn thing in plain sight. A deterrent, I suppose."

"Aaron?" Cork said.

"I've only shot pheasants."

"You're one up on me," Mal said.

"Okay," Cork said. "We'll leave the rifles. Probably best if you all stay together. When we get back, we'll talk about the baby and where to take him."

This was directed at Jenny, whose face was stone and who didn't reply.

Cork took one last sip of his coffee and stood up.

Rose said, "Vaya con Dios."

And Mal said, "Amen."

The ride to Windigo Island was a rough one. The wind hadn't let up at all. Ragged white clouds tumbled across the blue of the sky, and under the hull of Bascombe's launch, the lake bucked and kicked like a thing alive and wild.

They rounded the southeast end of Windigo, and Amos Powassin's small dock came into view. It was crowded with boats. As they approached, a group of men came from Powassin's house. They carried rifles and went to their boats, and one by one they motored away, so that the dock, when Bascombe pulled up, was empty save for one small motorboat. They tied up, and as they disembarked, Cherri Allen, who'd brought them to Powassin the day before, stepped onto the narrow front porch of the blind man's plain little house, shaded her eyes against the sun, and watched them come.

"Morning, Cherri," Kretsch said in jovial greeting. "That looked like a posse leaving."

Cherri didn't reply but said darkly, "I suppose you came to see Amos."

"Yes," Kretsch said. "Could we talk to him?"

"Wait here. I'll ask."

She went inside, and a moment later, a small face appeared at the screen door and peered out at them. It was the child who'd been with Powassin on the dock fishing when they'd come the day before. She eyed them wordlessly—suspiciously, Cork thought—then disappeared again into the dark inside the house.

Powassin came to the door, pushed open the screen, and stepped out into the sunlight. He wore a white T-shirt and jeans washed until the blue was practically a memory. His blind eyes didn't blink against the glare of the morning sun. Cherri Allen came with him and stood a little behind him, in deference to his stature.

"What do you want?" he said.

It was a neutral tone, neither inviting nor threatening. Very Ojibwe, Cork thought.

Cork nodded to Stephen.

"Grandfather," Stephen began. "We're trying to find Noah Smalldog."

"Ah, Makadewagosh," the old man said. Although his feelings about the intrusion were unclear at the moment, it was obvious he didn't mind Stephen being there. "I'm afraid I can't help you with that. Nobody here can."

Can? Cork wanted to ask. *Or will?*

"Last night, grandfather, he tried to hurt the baby," Stephen said.

The news obviously disturbed the old man. More lines appeared on his already heavily wrinkled face. "You saw him?"

"We did," Stephen answered.

Though that wasn't technically true, Cork thought. They'd seen someone, and the evidence pointed to Smalldog, but they couldn't actually say with certainty that it had been him. Cork was tempted to clarify his son's remark but held himself back.

The old man thought on this for a long while.

In the way of a lot of white people Cork had known, Bascombe seemed uncomfortable as the silence continued to stretch. He finally blurted, "Looked like a hunting party was leaving when we came up. What are you hunting?"

Powassin didn't answer, didn't show any sign that he'd even heard. Cork thought it might be because the question came from Bascombe and not Stephen. He was a little pissed at the man for butting in, but it was done. He waited with the others. At the old man's back, Cherri Allen watched with interest, as if she had no idea how, or even if, he was going to respond.

Finally the old Ojibwe said, "We're hunting Noah Smalldog."

"Why, grandfather?" Stephen asked.

"I would like to sit down," the old man said.

Cherri fetched a wooden chair from inside the house and brought it to the porch. Powassin sat down with a grateful sigh. In the strong sunlight, his long white hair glowed like electrified filaments. His face was dark, both from his heritage and from decades of life lived mostly outside. He folded his big, gnarled hands across his belly.

"We got called yesterday about Sonny Chickaway," he said.

"That was me," Tom Kretsch said. "I called."

The old Ojibwe continued, "Some of our men went to his place and saw it was all tore up and saw all the blood. They started asking around on the islands, couldn't find Sonny, came up with nothing. That's pretty strange out here."

"What do you think it means, grandfather?"

"I don't know, but it's not good, I can tell you that."

"Grandfather," Cork said, with great respect in his voice, "do you think Noah Smalldog did something to Sonny Chickaway? Is that the reason you're hunting him?"

Before responding, the old man weighed his words for another long period. "In my life, I've tried to understand most of the creatures who call this lake home. Smalldog? He's still a mystery to me. What Noah Smalldog might do, only Noah Smalldog knows. And that probably makes him the most dangerous animal you could run into out here."

The old man squinted, as if the strong sunlight finally bothered him. He leaned forward in his chair and spoke quietly. "My advice is to leave. Leave this lake now. Take the child and go somewhere safe. The safest place you know. But do it careful. Do it real cunning. You're being watched."

"By whom?"

"This is a small community with a lot of eyes and not much to see. Everyone is watching you. And tongues wag. News of what you do is gonna travel across the Angle faster 'n this damn wind."

He sat back, and his mouth formed a line from which wrinkles radiated like stitches on a wound.

"*Migwech*, grandfather," Stephen said.

The old man raised a hand in a gesture of parting, but spoke no more.

Stephen turned away and the others followed.

THIRTY-THREE

Aaron sat on the bench at the end of Bascombe's dock, a rifle across his legs. He faced the cabin, with the lake and the sun at his back. He wore a ball cap that shaded his long, handsome face, so that Rose, as she walked toward him, couldn't clearly see his expression.

"I found blueberries in Seth's kitchen," she said. "I made muffins. I thought you might like one. It's still warm from the oven."

"Thanks." Polite, but without enthusiasm.

She handed him the muffin and sat down beside him. He removed the rifle from his lap and laid it on the boards at his feet. He broke the muffin into two pieces and offered her half. She accepted. While the wind shook the branches of the poplars on the shoreline and the lake washed restlessly around the dock pilings, they ate without speaking.

"Thank you," Rose finally said.

"What for?"

She nodded toward the rifle. "For that. It's uncomfortable, I imagine."

"If this Smalldog actually came, I don't know if I could shoot him."

"I understand. But I think the hope is that, seeing you and the rifle, he'll be prudent and just stay away."

"A man who'd abuse and then torture and kill his own sister?

If we have what he wants, I'm not sure anything can keep him away."

Rose finished her half of the muffin and turned and looked out at the lake. The channel was frothy with whitecaps and brilliant with flashes of blue from the sky and silver from the sun. On the far side rose the deep green of Birch Island, a long, impenetrable wall of trees and underbrush. As she watched, a bald eagle lifted itself on broad wings and curled in a swift arc toward the north.

"It's so beautiful," she said. "I find it hard to think of anything so ugly up here."

"Ugly happens everywhere," he said, as if he were an expert on the subject.

"I've read your poetry. You're very good, but not very optimistic," she told him.

"I'm a realist." He tipped the ball cap back on his head, and when he looked at her, a sliver of sunlight played along his cheek, like a yellow scar. "Frankly, I don't get the O'Connor sunny view of life."

"I don't know that it's sunny," Rose said. "It's just that we've come through a lot of hard times together. We've supported one another. We're a close family, the O'Connors."

"But you're not an O'Connor."

"Not technically. A long time ago, when I was a little lost in what to do with my life, my sister and Cork asked me to help with their first child."

"Jenny."

"Yes. Jo, that was Jenny's mother, was trying to create a law career. Cork was a cop with odd hours. This was in Chicago. I stepped in to fill gaps. Do you know what I found? That the gaps in my own life were filled. I loved helping to raise the children. I never felt like an outsider in this family."

"You and Mal have no children of your own?"

"No. And if you're wondering do we want children, yes. It just hasn't happened."

"Children," he said, as if the word were a hard, heavy stone.

"You don't want children," she said. It wasn't a question.

"Children, in my experience, are an inconvenience. And children, in my experience, are mostly a disappointment to others and are themselves disappointed. Nobody wins."

"I've never looked at it as a competition."

"You understand what I mean."

Rose watched two gulls ride the strong wind over the open water, maneuvering in the difficult air currents with extraordinary grace.

"I do," she said. "And I disagree. But my experience is different from yours."

"And what do we base our choices on but our own experience?" he asked.

"Faith," she offered.

From inside the lodge came the sound of the baby crying. It was quite loud, and easily heard above the rush of the wind. Aaron looked there, and his face, in the shadow of the long brim of his cap, was dark.

"I'm not a religious man," he said coldly.

"Faith in people," she said. "Faith in Jenny. Faith in yourself."

He gave her a sidelong glance, and the coldness seemed to melt for a moment. "You were a cheerleader in high school, I bet."

She laughed. "Hardly." She draped an arm over the back of the bench and faced Aaron directly. "I'll tell you something. My childhood and much of my early adult life was a nightmare of taking care of an alcoholic mother. I prayed sometimes for her to die. When she did, I discovered it wasn't the release I'd thought it would be. My life had been so defined by caregiving that, unless I had someone to help, I didn't know who I was. That was the real reason I agreed to live with Jo and Cork and give a hand with Jenny. I thought it would save me from having to stumble around searching for a life."

"You just went on being a caregiver," he said.

"No. I learned what it was like to nurture. Which is different. That's what the children did for me."

"Semantics," he said, dismissing her.

"I'm not trying to convince you of anything, honestly," she said. "I just believe there's another way to look at life."

The wind gusted with a sudden, unexpected ferocity, and tore Aaron's cap from his head. Rose shot a look toward the southwest, the direction from which the terror of the derecho had come only a couple of days earlier. Although it was filled with speeding clouds, the sky was a soft blue, and nothing threatened on the horizon.

She heard the sound of an outboard and saw Bascombe's launch approaching.

"They're back," she said.

Aaron glanced down at the rifle that lay at his feet. "Finally," he said with clear relief.

Once again, they clustered around the table in the dining area of Bascombe's lodge. The gathering reminded Jenny of a war council.

"Amos Powassin is right," her father said. "It's what I've been saying all along. The safest thing for everyone is if we get the baby away from the Angle altogether, the sooner the better."

"So let's give him over to the authorities. The sheriff or somebody," Aaron suggested. "They'll come for him soon enough anyway."

Jenny shot him a killing look. "I'm not putting him into the hands of someone who doesn't love him. I'm not giving him up until I know that he's absolutely safe."

Aaron opened his hands toward Cork in a gesture of reasonableness and an invitation to agree. "They have the resources to protect him, right?"

Her father didn't answer immediately, and Jenny watched his face closely. She could tell there was a conflict in his thinking, though what exactly it was, she couldn't say.

At last he shook his head and replied with what seemed great reluctance. "Based on the response Tom got when he tried to convince the sheriff that our situation up here was bad, I wouldn't rely on them right now. I'm not sure they'd take our concerns seriously. And even if they did, they've already got their hands pretty full."

"Okay," Kretsch said. "We get him off the lake and take him where?"

A thoughtful silence settled over the table.

Stephen looked up suddenly and offered an answer. "We could take him to Henry Meloux."

"Meloux." Just saying his name gave Jenny an overpowering sense of relief.

"Who's Meloux?" Aaron asked.

"A friend," Stephen answered. "And a really special man. He lives in the safest place I can think of."

"Where's that?" Bascombe asked.

"On the Iron Lake Reservation in Tamarack County."

"Where you're from, right?"

Stephen nodded. "Henry has a cabin in the woods there, and I know he'd help."

"Wait a minute." Aaron put his hand up as if stopping traffic. "This feels to me a lot like kidnapping."

"How can you kidnap a child who has no parents, no home, and no real official existence at all?" Jenny snapped at him.

"You're equivocating," Aaron said.

"And you're an ass," Jenny shot back.

"Hold on a minute," her father said. "Aaron's concern is valid. If things don't work out, we could be in a lot of trouble. Maybe it would be best to take him to Marsha Dross instead."

"Who's that?" Bascombe asked.

"The sheriff of Tamarack County," Jenny's father answered. "And also a good friend."

"Easier to get rid of the baby that way," Bascombe pointed out. "Off your hands quicker, Cork."

Her father appeared uncomfortable, as if he didn't particularly appreciate the light in which Bascombe's words cast him.

The comment made Jenny furious. "I'm taking him to Meloux's." She leveled an icy look at her father. "He'll understand."

"Jenny, I'm just trying to think what's safest for us all."

"No, it's like Seth said. You're just looking for the quickest way to get my baby out of your hair."

"He's not your baby," Cork said.

"And he's no one else's either. Just look at him. Who'd take a child with a face like that?" Now she shot an accusing glare at Aaron.

Silence settled in the room, an uncomfortable waiting. For her part, Jenny felt like a cannon, primed and ready to fire. She watched her father closely.

Finally he shrugged and said, as if in defeat, "Meloux it is, for better or worse." He scanned the room, his gaze settling one after the other on them all. "Are we agreed?"

They all said, "Yes," except for Aaron. He sat back, darkly mum, and although Jenny could see clearly that he disapproved of the idea, he gave, at last, a reluctant nod of assent.

Kretsch offered, "If you really believe the safest place for the child is with this Meloux, you go ahead and take him there. If it causes any legal problems, I'll take the heat."

"How do we get the baby away without anybody seeing?" Bascombe asked. "Powassin was right. A lot of eyes are watching you folks, and we don't know who among them might be in cahoots with Smalldog."

"What makes you think he's not acting alone?" Cork asked.

"He's a smuggler, and in my experience in ATF, smugglers

don't operate alone. He's probably got other Ojibwe helping him. And, hell, maybe even a white man or two. Around here, it's tough to make a living, and throwing in with Smalldog could be a tempting proposition. Besides, there was someone with him when he came for the baby last night."

"We could sneak him out tonight," Anne suggested.

"I don't know that night is the best time," Bascombe replied. "The lake's tricky enough during the day. And if Smalldog's thinking we might do something with the baby, he'll figure night's the best time. It's what I'd figure."

"What if we all go together," Rose said. "Just head over to the Angle and load up in Aaron's truck and drive out. Wouldn't there be safety in numbers?"

Bascombe's face showed that he clearly didn't like the idea.

Apparently, neither did Cork, who said, "I don't know Small-dog. It might be he's crazy enough to do something desperate, and one of us—or several of us—could get hurt."

"The road out from the Angle cuts through a lot of empty, isolated woods," Kretsch added. "If Smalldog knew we were running, there'd be a number of old logging roads he could take to cut us off."

"You think he'd really do that?" Rose asked.

"A man who'd do what he did to his sister, no telling what he's capable of," Bascombe answered.

"So let's take the baby out by water," Stephen said. "Across Lake of the Woods."

"Across the big water?" Kretsch said. "In broad daylight? We'd be sitting ducks for Smalldog and that cigarette boat of his. He'd run us down like a wolf would a rabbit."

"Cunning," Cork said. "That's what Powassin suggested. Somehow we have to take the boy right out from under Small-dog's nose without Smalldog knowing."

"How do you propose we do that?" Kretsch asked.

Jenny saw that her father didn't have an answer. They sat,

staring at one another or out the window, and for a while the only sound came from the rush of the wind in the trees.

Finally Mal said, "Ah," as if he'd just eaten something delicious that Rose had baked, and he grinned broadly.

"What?" Rose said to her husband.

They all fixed their eyes on him.

Mal said slyly, "Have you ever played three-card monte?"

THIRTY-FOUR

As soon as they all understood and had agreed to Mal's plan, Bascombe left with Kretsch, Stephen, and Aaron and headed toward the Angle. The others began their preparations. Anne and Rose helped Jenny get the baby's things ready, while Cork and Mal walked to the end of the dock with rifles in hand to stand sentry. After a long while, Jenny came out with the baby in the basket. She'd put on a red ball cap that her father had given her, and a purple Vikings jersey, and green capris. She stood out like a clown at a wedding. She walked to the bench at the end of the dock, put the basket down, and took the baby out.

Mal said to Cork, "You got this covered?"

"Yeah."

"All right. I'm inside if you need me."

Mal left the dock to Cork and his daughter.

Cork stood looking out at the lake. It was early afternoon, hot and windy. Gulls rose and spun and dove above the channel, as if dodging the silver bullets of sunlight that shot from the waves. Everything appeared normal. The destruction that had been visited on so much of the lake had missed the islands nearest the Angle. Although he knew it wasn't so, Cork felt as if a great deal of time had passed between the storm and this current moment. Changes unforeseen and momentous had occurred. And, once again, he was reminded that life was no more predictable than the flight of a dragonfly.

"Do you think they're watching?" Jenny asked.

"I hope so," Cork said.

She was quiet. Then she turned her face up to him. "Do you think it'll work?"

"It'll work," he said, although the truth was that nothing was certain. "Are you scared?"

"No. Well, yes, but not for me."

He understood what she meant, even though he wasn't comfortable with it. He was a father, and his fear—he could feel the worm of it in his stomach—was for Jenny, not for himself. In her own mind, Jenny was a mother, and her concern was for her child, a concern that put her in terrible danger. And placed the rest of his children in jeopardy as well, though Cork wouldn't say that to her. Decisions had been made, and they'd all agreed, and now they needed to be together in their intent and their actions.

He went back to watching the lake, to looking at the wall of vegetation across the channel on Birch Island for any sign that someone there was keeping them under surveillance. It was probably too much to hope for the flash of sunlight off the lenses of field glasses, but if it was there, he didn't want to miss it.

"Dad?"

"Yeah?"

"I know you think this is crazy."

He glanced down at her as she cradled the baby, and he didn't have to ask what she meant. "Children are important," he said. "That's one of the reasons I took you out to see the pictographs. I sensed that it was an issue between you and Aaron. I haven't had a chance to get to know him. I imagine he's a fine man in a lot of ways, but I get the feeling that being a father isn't big on his agenda. I wanted to let you know that I was on your side. I want you to have children. I just didn't figure it would be this way." He looked at the unsettled surface of the lake and heard himself sigh. "We've all suffered a lot of loss. You especially. It makes a certain sense to me, how you feel about this baby. And who knows? Maybe it would be good to have a strong breath of life come back into our family."

"He's not really family," she said. "I'll have to give him up eventually."

And that, too, had been a part of his objection all along. Even if they all got out of this okay, Jenny, in the end, would be hurt. And her hurt would be his, because that's what it was to be a parent. Still, he had to admit that it felt strangely right, the child there in Jenny's arms. And from the way the baby's dark eyes so often held on her face and his little mouth formed the odd-shaped smile when she spoke to him, it was clear to anyone with half a brain that something powerful bound these two.

She touched his nose with the tip of her finger, and he responded with a sound that seemed to Cork damn near a giggle. "I've been imagining what it would be like if somehow I was able to keep him," she went on.

Cork shifted the rifle, cradling it in his arms in much the way Jenny held the baby in hers. "And how would that work?"

"Aaron wouldn't want to be a part of it," she said.

"Maybe we both underestimate him."

"I don't think so." She glanced up at the sky, where clouds hurried across the immense blue in a race without apparent purpose, then she looked at Cork. "I remember a long time ago, when you and Mom were having that really bad patch in your marriage."

"I wish you didn't remember that," he said.

"No, it's a good thing. What I remember is how, through all that hard time, I never felt that you'd leave us. I knew that, no matter what, you'd always be there. I don't feel that way about Aaron. I don't trust him."

"Okay, if Aaron is out of the picture, what do you imagine with the little guy?"

Her eyes skated away from Cork's face, as if she was a little embarrassed by what she was about to say. "When I imagine raising him, I imagine it in the house in Aurora. I see him growing up on Gooseberry Lane, just like I did."

"It was a good place to grow up. I ought to know. I grew up there, too."

"It's silly," she said. "It's crazy. Impossible."

Cork said, "In my fifty-two years on this earth, the one thing I've learned absolutely is that nothing is impossible, Jenny. Especially where love is involved."

"Maybe so," she said. "But my life has taught me that you should always be prepared to have your heart broken."

Probably wise, Cork thought, though he didn't say so.

Bascombe returned first. Kretsch wasn't far behind him in his own boat, and then Stephen and Aaron, in a rented launch. One after the other, they eased up to the dock and Cork helped them tie up. When they'd all disembarked, they headed with Jenny and the baby to Bascombe's lodge, where Mal and Rose and Anne were waiting.

"Any trouble?" Mal asked.

"Nope," Bascombe said. "And plenty of folks know about the extra boats, so word'll spread quick."

Cork shot a glance at the clock on the wall. It was set into a polished piece of driftwood.

"How long should we wait?" he asked.

Bascombe said, "Give it another hour. If they're watching and keeping their ears to the ground, they'll know by then."

"I wish to God I knew who 'they' was," Kretsch said.

Cork lifted a hand, as if volunteering. "That's something I intend to find out when Jenny and the baby are safe."

"You're not a cop anymore, Dad," Anne reminded him.

Cork replied coldly, "This is personal."

"I'm with you on that," Kretsch said.

"Me, too," Bascombe threw in with a thumbs-up. "I haven't had this much excitement since I left ATF."

Rose looked unhappy at that. "Seth, this isn't a game or some kind of military exercise."

"Sorry," he said, clearly chagrined. "Didn't mean it that way."

"We ought to eat," Rose suggested. "For some of you, it'll be quite a while before your next meal."

"I'll help," Anne volunteered.

"And the rest of us still have things to do," Cork said.

They all stood up, separated, and headed to their duties.

At four o'clock, Mal's plan was set in motion.

They gathered around the table of the lodge. From a back room, Bascombe brought a large, red plastic ice chest. He'd softened the bottom with a pillow and folded blankets. He held it out toward Jenny.

"Think this'll do?" he asked.

Jenny pressed the blankets, felt the softness of the pillow beneath, and smiled. "It's fine, Seth. Thank you."

She'd changed her clothes. She wore jeans and a dark blue T-shirt. Anne was now the one dressed in the purple Vikings jersey and green capris and crowned with the bright red ball cap. She did a little turn for everyone. "How do I look?"

Jenny saw her father nod seriously. "If you keep your back to the lake and the brim of that cap pulled down low over your face, even if they have binoculars, you ought to fool them, kiddo. Good job."

Bascombe said, "I still think we ought to use my boat."

"If they're watching for us to cross the big water," Kretsch said, "they'll be figuring for you to do it, Seth."

"If the wind gets bad out there, that little toothpick you call a boat could be in for a rough ride."

"We'll be fine," Kretsch said.

Jenny was very glad that he sounded absolutely certain.

"Aaron, Stephen, you guys all set?"

"I'd still rather stay here," Stephen said. "I want to help you track down Smalldog."

"I understand," Cork said, and he did. "But, Stephen, I need you at Henry Meloux's to make sure Jenny and the baby are safe there. And you and Henry, well, everybody knows how special you are to him. He won't say no if you're there."

"He wouldn't say no anyway," Stephen countered. "If he did, he wouldn't be Henry."

"I'll feel better about sending the baby if I know you're helping at the other end, okay?" Cork said.

Which was the truth, but not the whole truth. If things got bad on the Angle, Cork wanted as many of his children as possible out of harm's way. For Mal's plan to work, Anne had to stay on Oak Island. Stephen didn't.

"Don't forget," Aaron threw in helpfully. "I've never piloted a boat, Stephen. I need you to get us safely back to the mainland."

Stephen seemed to see the wisdom of that and, although not necessarily happy with it, nodded his agreement.

They shook hands around and the family hugged and bid one another Godspeed and then it was time. Bascombe headed out first, Kretsch next, and finally Aaron and Stephen. Mal and Anne brought up the rear. Mal carried a rifle. Anne carried the basket, inside of which was a rolled-up bath towel swaddled in a blanket. While Mal helped the others cast off, Anne sat down on the bench with her back to the water, lifted the rolled-up towel in its blanket, and held it to her chest in what, from a distance, would certainly appear to be a loving embrace. Aaron and Stephen pulled away in the rental, motored out a short distance, and waited. Kretsch joined them, easing his little Lund Tyee alongside. Bascombe swung away last. As he came abreast of the other two crafts, they all throttled forward, headed into the channel, and curled north.

From inside the cabin, Cork watched until they'd rounded a point of land three-quarters of a mile northwest and disappeared. He knew that as soon as they were out of sight they would split up. Bascombe would head toward Windigo Island. Aaron and Stephen would head toward Young's Bay Landing on the mainland. And Kretsch would follow a circuitous route that would, eventually, bring him to the other side of Oak Island, where Jenny and the baby and Cork would be waiting.

It was Mal's three-card monte—which was the important boat?—but with a twist: Jenny and the baby still appeared to be on the dock.

Cork turned from the window to Jenny, who stood holding the baby. Rose was next to her, and on the floor at their feet sat the ice chest, which Bascombe had stuffed with bedding. "It's time," he said. He saw the apprehension in his daughter's eyes, and he smiled and said, "Everything's going to be fine, Jenny."

She nodded, meaning that she'd heard him and, perhaps, meaning to convey as well that she believed him. But her eyes told a different story.

"Let's get our little guy settled in," Rose suggested.

Jenny laid the child in the soft bedding of the ice chest and covered him with a light blanket. He was awake and stared up at her as she leaned over him. Cork was relieved to see that he didn't seem upset at all with his new carrier. He simply studied Jenny's face with what seemed to be utter fascination.

Cork took up the rifle Bascombe had left for him, then he hefted a pack filled with clean diapers, a canister of formula, and other items for the baby. "This way," he said.

He took them through the kitchen to the rear door of the lodge, which opened onto a small grassy apron between the log structure and the woods that backed the old resort. Hidden from the lake by the body of the lodge, they quickly crossed the grass and stepped onto a path that cut into the woods. Cork led the way, with Jenny in the middle and Rose bringing up the rear. Bascombe had given them a map of the island that showed the walking trails. He'd warned them that the trails could be a little difficult, muddy at times. He'd marked the route to a private cabin and dock owned by a couple from St. Cloud who'd left the Angle a week ago to visit their daughter in Orlando.

In the woods, the bugs were fierce, and the trail, as Bascombe had warned, was often a bed of muck. They made their way quickly, the sounds of their passage masked by the rattle of leaves in the wind. They climbed a modest ridge for a while, then dropped again toward the lake. Half an hour after they started, they emerged at the cabin and walked into the blast of the wind out of the southwest.

Kretsch was there, waiting for them at the dock. His boat rocked on the waves. Cork felt Jenny hesitate.

"It'll be all right," he said.

"Couldn't we just take our chances driving out?" she said.

Cork turned to his daughter and, for an important moment, held her eyes with his own. "We could. But that's not what we've planned, and with good reason. We know that Smalldog's after this kid, and we know the kind of cruelty he's capable of. I think we have a good chance of confusing him, and anyone who's helping him. But it depends on taking your boy out across the big water. Tom says he can do that. I believe him. We'll be fine, Jenny, I give you my word. Okay?"

He believed this or he wouldn't have said it. But he also knew that the foundation of his belief was a matter less of the facts than of faith.

"We should go," Kretsch urged. "Before we're spotted."

Rose said, "You'll call us when you've reached the other shore?"

"Count on it," Cork said. "Just make sure Seth keeps his land line open."

Rose gave them all hugs, even Kretsch, who seemed a little embarrassed at the display of affection. The deputy got aboard and helped Jenny in. Cork handed over the ice chest with the baby inside and then the pack. Kretsch set the ice chest between the two rear seats and put the pack next to a couple of ten-gallon cans of extra fuel he'd secured near the engine. Cork cast off the lines and boarded, too. They donned life jackets, then Kretsch backed away from the dock. The flat stern pushed awkwardly against the roll of the waves until the deputy spun the wheel and put the nose of the bow into the wind. He nudged the throttle ahead, and they started south.

Cork recalled that Bascombe had likened Kretsch's modest Tyee to a toothpick. The comparison seemed to be more than a little apt as they bounced across the chop of waves toward the big water, which at that moment, appeared to be as broad and perilous as an ocean.

THIRTY-FIVE

Rose, Mal, and Anne sat at the table in Bascombe's lodge. Rose had made coffee, and the three of them sipped and listened to the wind and watched the clock set in the driftwood on the wall. Rose thought she'd never known time to pass so slowly. She wasn't sure what the others were thinking, but she was praying.

"I remember once when I was a kid and Dad was sheriff," Anne said eventually. Despite the heat of the day, she had her hands wrapped around her coffee mug as if she were cold. "He had to go out to a cabin where a man was holding his wife hostage."

"Vernon Lucasta," Rose said.

"Right," Anne said.

The clock on the wall ticked away.

"What happened?" Mal finally asked.

"Dad got there and went inside, unarmed. He found Mrs. Lucasta—"

"Bianca," Rose said.

Mal glanced at her.

"She sang with me in the St. Agnes choir," Rose explained.

"Right. Bianca," Anne said. "Anyway, she was tied to a chair in the bedroom, and Lucasta had a rifle and he told Dad he was going to kill her if someone didn't get the damn bugs out of the cabin."

"Insects?" Mal asked.

Anne shook her head. "Listening devices. Lucasta was convinced someone was spying on him, and his wife was somehow involved."

"Delusional?" Mal asked.

"That's what Dad thought," Anne said.

"And with good reason," Rose added, taking up the story. "Vernon was an odd duck."

Anne said, "Remember when he joined the kids in the Christmas pageant and he was dressed like an elephant?"

"An elephant in Bethlehem?"

"He wasn't even supposed to be a part of the pageant, Uncle Mal," Anne said. "He just showed up. I think he might have been drunk."

"He wasn't," Rose said.

"Okay," Mal said. "So he's got his wife tied up and is threatening her. What did your father do?"

"He told Lucasta he'd look for the bugs. He was thinking that, while he did that, he might be able to talk sense into the man or figure a way to surprise and disarm him."

"Did he?"

"No. He found three bugs."

"What?"

"One in the telephone. One in the bedroom, and one in the bathroom."

"Who put them there?"

"Bianca," Rose said. "She sold Tupperware and was convinced that, whenever she was away, Vernon had women there. She wanted proof."

"What did Cork do?"

"He talked Lucasta into giving him the rifle, then talked them both into going into therapy that very day."

"He didn't arrest the guy?"

"No. In the end they divorced, but it was amicable, more or less."

Mal said, "And the point of your story?"

Anne said, "I was just thinking that I'm afraid for Jenny, but if there's any good thing about her situation, it's that Dad's with her."

Rose smiled and put her hand on Anne's arm in a gesture of understanding and agreement. But she didn't say what she herself was thinking. Which was that, even though Cork was a good, reliable man, if bad weather blew in across the big water, everyone in that little boat was in trouble.

They heard the launch coming. Mal went to the window. "It's Seth," he said.

Bascombe arrived and stood in the doorway with his arms crossed, eyeing them sternly. "Well?"

"They got off," Mal said.

"Anyone see them?"

"I'm pretty sure not," Rose said.

Bascombe nodded grimly. "I'll feel better once we get the call that they've made it safe."

He'd given Kretsch the GPS coordinates for a cabin on the south shore of Lake of the Woods, northwest of Zippel Bay. The cabin was empty, he knew, because the man who'd owned it was in prison for smuggling cigarettes into Canada. The land was now forfeited property of the U.S. government, but nothing had been done with it, and the cabin sat abandoned. Bascombe had used the place himself for a weekend fishing rendezvous with a couple of his old pals from ATF. It had a good dock and was isolated and ought to work well for getting the baby onto the mainland without anyone seeing.

The plan was for Aaron to drive his truck to the cabin, along with Stephen, pick up Jenny and the baby, and all of them head to Tamarack County and the safety they hoped Henry Meloux would offer. Kretsch and Cork would return across the big water and begin the hunt for Noah Smalldog.

Bascombe plopped his big body down at the table. "That coffee smells good, Rose. Any left?"

"Let me pour you a cup, then I'll make a fresh pot," she said.

"How's our baby?" Bascombe said, nodding toward the basket where the swaddled towel lay. "Did you show that guy plenty of affection out there on the dock?"

"Don't worry. She played her part well," Mal answered. "Did anybody follow you to Windigo Island?"

"Yep. Had a tail all the way." Bascombe sounded quite pleased. "He kept his boat pretty far back, so I didn't get a good look at him. But Indian I'd say."

"Smalldog?"

Bascombe shook his head. "One of his cohorts, I figure."

Rose put a cup full of coffee down on the table in front of him. "What about Stephen and Aaron?"

"Didn't see anyone take off after them, so I think they're in the clear. I'm guessing I was followed because I've got the best boat. Tom was right about that. I just hope to God he doesn't run into any heavy weather in that little Tyee of his. The open water on that south section of the lake is so huge it generates its own unpredictable weather systems. Squalls can come up out of nowhere."

That put a damper on conversation for a little while. Rose busied herself making another pot of coffee. Mal stood up and limped to the wall where a map of the Lake of the Woods and the Angle hung. He studied it a moment.

"I've been trying to figure out the Northwest Angle," he said. "To get here, you've got to cross the border and drive through sixty miles of Canadian wilderness, or else cut across forty miles of open water on Lake of the Woods. What's a piece of U.S. territory doing this far north?"

"Northernmost point in the forty-eight contiguous states," Bascombe said, with a note of pride. "The result of a misunderstanding during the negotiations for the treaty that set the border between us and Canada."

"What kind of misunderstanding?" Anne asked.

Bascombe slurped his coffee, closed his eyes, and let the good brew trickle down his throat. "Where exactly the headwaters of the Mississippi River lay. Everybody thought they were much farther east than they ended up being. The result was a little northern jut of territory that cut across Lake of the Woods and included the Angle. Up here we call it 'the chimney.' "

Mal hobbled back to join the others at the table. "How long have you been on the Angle, Seth?"

"Been coming here all my life. My aunt and uncle ran this little resort. When they passed, they left the property to me. I was working ATF then, so I couldn't really do anything with it. I'd come here occasionally, try to see to things, but the old place pretty much went downhill. Finally, when I'd had one day too many of wearing a Kevlar vest at work, I retired, and moved here for good to reopen the place, try to make a go of it. Discovered real fast that I didn't have the temperament for that kind of enterprise. I live here alone now. Suits me fine."

Rose finished putting the new pot of coffee together and turned back to the table, where Bascombe sat sprawled, looking worn.

"How long before we hear from them?" she asked.

Bascombe thought it over. "If they don't run afoul of the weather, and if Tom has no engine problems, and if Smalldog didn't somehow get wind of our ruse and is waiting for them out on the big water, I'd say three hours."

"Three hours of waiting," Anne said.

In her niece's tone, Rose heard what they all probably felt: Three hours would seem like forever.

"Mal, Seth," she said, putting all the robustness she could muster into her voice, "you two should get back out on the dock and show a presence here. Annie, let's bake some cookies."

THIRTY-SIX

Cork had never been on water so huge. He was more than uncomfortable. He was seasick.

The big water, as the folks on the Angle called it, was well named. It stretched away to the horizon in every direction, dazzling blue under the vast sky, shot with diamonds of reflected sunlight, alive with swells. Kretsch was intent at the helm, fighting to keep the Tyee on course against the sweep of waves and shove of wind. Jenny sat with the ice chest at her feet, her eyes darting between the baby nestled inside and the vast expanse of water on which they were the only human presence.

Cork understood that it was going to be the longest and most miserable boat ride of his life.

He'd always believed that particular distinction would belong to the dinner excursion he'd made on Lake Michigan the night he proposed to Jo. It should have been romantic but turned out to be comic tragedy. Although they were never out of sight of land, the wind had been strong and the cruise a little rough and Cork hadn't been able to eat much. He'd managed near the end of dinner to pop his question. And then he promptly threw up.

It had been a funny story to tell across the years. He was pretty sure that after this boat trip there would be nothing funny to tell.

He moved to the seat next to the helm and spoke to Kretsch, mostly to take his mind off his rolling stomach.

"How're we doing, Tom?"

Kretsch glanced at the GPS display on the unit attached to the dash. "On target," he said.

Cork eyed the great empty water around them. "No sign of any other boat. That's good."

"Most other boats wouldn't be out here on a day like this."

Cork leaned close to the deputy. "You'll get us there, right?"

Kretsch gave him a look of consummate confidence. "I'll get us there."

Cork sat back, relieved. "You know Lake of the Woods pretty well?"

"There are a lot of folks who know it better, folks who've lived here all their lives. But I know it pretty well."

"How long have you been here?"

"I started coming up to fish walleye with my father and brothers when I was a kid. In college, I spent summers on the Angle, helping with one or another of the resorts. Started guiding eventually. Finally moved up here for good."

"What's your law enforcement background?"

Kretsch shook his head. "Don't have any. I took the job because the sheriff couldn't find anyone else willing. Everything I know is from experience."

The relief that Cork had felt in all of Kretsch's assurances vanished in an instant. "No law enforcement training whatsoever?"

"Ride-alongs with the deputies out of Baudette, and a bunch of seminars over time, but that's about it. Up here, there's not much breach of the law to worry about. It's only a part-time job. The rest of the time I work for a barge company in Angle Inlet, helping deliver big items to the islands."

Jesus Christ, Cork wanted to say. He'd always thought of Tamarack County as a rural operation. This topped everything.

"What if something really big happened?"

"The sheriff comes up himself or sends one of his regular deputies to give a hand. I usually just hold down the fort until they arrive."

The name Barney Fife came to mind, but Cork said nothing. He moved back to the seat next to Jenny.

"How're you doing, kiddo?" he asked.

She looked at his face and said, "Better than you, I think. You're pretty green."

"I'll be all right. And your boyo?"

She smiled down at the baby, who despite the wild rock of the boat and the whip of the wind and the noise of the hull against rough water, was sleeping. "He's doing great," she said.

"This is the most tolerant kid I've ever seen."

A darkness came over Jenny's face. "I wonder about that. I wonder if his ordeal has affected him somehow. Tempered his natural inclinations, maybe. He doesn't cry much, not like the babies I've been around in the nursery down in Iowa City, anyway."

"He's only a few weeks old," Cork said. "He's malleable, right? And resilient. He'll bounce back."

"I hope so," she said.

Cork leaned back and closed his eyes and concentrated on keeping what was kicking inside his stomach corralled there.

The clouds came up fast, black horses galloping wildly out of the west across the sky. Because his eyes had been closed for a long time, Cork didn't see them. It was Jenny who alerted her father to the danger.

"Dad?"

When he heard the urgency in her voice, his eyes popped wide, and he looked where her finger pointed.

"Tom!" he called.

"I see it," Kretsch said. "Nothing we can do now but ride it out. You better cover the baby. Looks like the rain'll be heavy for a bit."

Jenny had brought a windbreaker, and she draped it over the open ice chest, then peeked inside.

"What's the verdict?" Cork called to her above the wind.

She shook her head in amazement. "Dead to the world, thank God."

"Brace yourselves," Kretsch said. "Here it comes."

It was as if a dam had split open and everything held in the reservoir behind spilled out. The wind, already strong, became a rage, and the rain struck Cork's face hard as bullets. Jenny had angled the lid of the ice chest to keep as much water off the windbreaker as possible, and she hunched protectively over the makeshift cradle. Kretsch turned the bow of the boat directly into the storm and held the wheel steady against the full force of all that came at them. The sky above was black and boiling, but Cork could see the edges of the storm system a few miles off. Beyond it was blue sky. They just had to hang tough for a while.

The squall passed, and as quickly as the sky had turned threatening, it cleared again.

Kretsch turned back to them from the helm and patted the dash of his boat. "Tough old girl. Knew she'd get us through."

Jenny pulled the windbreaker from the ice chest, and the sun hit the baby's face. He began to wake and make fussing noises.

"Want me to put together a bottle?" Cork asked.

Jenny had brought a clean bottle and formula. Rose had heated water and put it in a thermos.

Jenny shook her head. "He shouldn't be hungry yet. Just needs a little reassurance, I think."

She picked him up from the bedding in the ice chest, cradled him in her arms, and began talking to him softly. His eyes fastened on her face, and he seemed mesmerized.

Cork returned to the seat beside the deputy.

Kretsch smiled at him, clearly pleased. "I'll have us there in no time."

* * *

And he did. As soon as they came in sight of land, Cork felt the weight of worry lift from him. He could have hugged Tom Kretsch.

It was evening by then. The sun was low in the western sky. The wind had relaxed just a little, and although the lake was still restless, the whitecaps had all but disappeared. Kretsch kept an eye on the GPS display and guided the boat to a tiny cove lined with poplars where a cabin with a small dock stood. The trees looked beaten and ragged; a number of them lay on their sides with the roots torn from the ground, the result of the derecho two days earlier.

"There they are," Jenny said, her voice a song of relief.

At the end of the dock, Stephen and Aaron stood waving. Kretsch motored up, eased back on the throttle, and drifted in. Cork went forward and picked up the bow line. He tossed it to Stephen, who secured the rope to a cleat. Aaron tied off the stern line. Jenny lifted the ice chest with the baby inside and delivered it into his waiting hands.

"You two okay?" he asked.

"He did great," Jenny replied.

Aaron peered inside the chest and said with surprise, "My God, he's smiling."

"Took to it like a duck to water," Cork said. "Where are you parked?"

"In front of the cabin," Aaron replied. "It was a little hairy getting here. Trees still down over the roads everywhere. Looks like a nuclear blast in some places. I understand why the sheriff couldn't spare any help up on the Angle. Major highways are clear, though."

"Good. Let's get you guys gone."

They left the dock and skirted the cabin, a small and unremarkable affair that had lost shingles in the storm and sustained a couple of broken windows. Aaron's truck, a new-looking black Dodge Dakota with a crew cab, was parked on the dirt road in front, which dead-ended at the cove. They put the baby in the rear seat, and before she climbed in beside him, Jenny turned to her father. "You're going back in the dark?"

"Tom says he can navigate by the stars."

Kretsch shook his head and grinned. "GPS, actually. It's much more reliable."

Jenny took the deputy's hand. "Thank you. For everything."

Kretsch looked down, as if embarrassed, and Cork thought he was going to say, "Ah, shucks." Instead, he said, "I'm just glad I could help."

"You get yourself and my father back to Oak Island in one piece," she said seriously.

"We'll be fine, sweetheart," Cork told her. "You just get safely to Henry. I'll feel a lot better when I know you're there. And give a call to Bascombe's place, let everyone know you're safe."

Cork gave her a long hug, then turned to Stephen. "Tell Henry *boozhoo* for me, and thank him. And take care of your sister and the boyo, okay?"

"I'm on it, Dad."

Stephen tolerated Cork's hug, even gave him a quick squeeze of his own in return.

He turned to Aaron and shook his hand earnestly. "When this is all over, we'll sit down with a couple of beers and really get to know each other."

"I'd like that."

Cork nodded toward the truck that held his daughter and the baby. "Thank you."

"I'll make sure we get to your friend's place safely," Aaron promised.

Cork stood back and watched them climb into the cab. Aaron kicked the engine over and turned the truck around. As they headed into the waning light of evening, they gave him a last wave of good-bye.

"They'll be fine," Kretsch said.

"From your mouth to God's ear." Cork turned back toward

the cove. "Let's get ourselves on that lake before I lose my nerve."

"We'll be home before midnight," Kretsch said.

"I don't think so," Cork replied.

"No? Why not?"

"Because we're going to make a stop before we get there."

"Where?"

"I'll tell you on the way," Cork said.

THIRTY-SEVEN

For a good long while, they drove in silence. The baby slept. Aaron had the radio turned low, listening to Minnesota Public Radio broadcast out of Roseau. Stephen stared out the window at the passing landscape, a mosaic of dark evening colors. Jenny was thinking. She thought about all that had happened in only two days, a kind of frenzy that was difficult to put together in a way that felt believable, though she'd been there through it all. She thought about the people she loved whom she'd left behind on the Angle, still in danger, perhaps, and she worried. She thought about the roads ahead: the one that led to Henry Meloux, which she knew well, and the more difficult road she would have to navigate at some point that led through a bureaucratic minefield to a place where the fate of the baby would be decided. Of all the unknowns ahead, that was the one that made her feel most helpless.

They had dinner in International Falls. Jenny left the ice chest in the truck and carried the baby in her arms. She changed his diaper in the restroom and prepared a bottle, which she handed to the waitress and asked her to heat. When the woman saw the baby's cleft lip, she didn't look horrified at all. She was thin, maybe fifty, with hair that was drugstore blond, and too much eye shadow, and ruby-colored nails, and an empty ring finger. She smiled with a genuineness that made Jenny love her instantly.

"I'll have them put a pan of water on the stove and heat it up for you, hon. What's his name?"

Jenny hesitated, awkwardly.

It was Stephen who replied. "Waaboozoons."

"Waaboozoons? Never heard that one before. Is it foreign?"

"It's Ojibwe," Stephen said. "It means 'little rabbit.' We call him Waaboo for short."

"Don't that beat all," she said. "Well, I'll have the little rabbit's bottle for you in two shakes."

"Where'd that come from?" Jenny asked her brother when the waitress had gone.

Stephen stared at his menu and shrugged. "I don't know. It just came to me, and it sounded right."

Jenny could have told him that the term "harelip" came from the resemblance a cleft lip bore to that of a rabbit's divided upper lip, but she didn't. The truth was she liked the name.

It was hard dark when they headed south on U.S. 53 toward Tamarack County. Jenny was exhausted and sat quietly in back, listening to Aaron and Stephen talk up front. They seemed to have warmed to each other as the miles went past.

"How come you're not in school this week?" Aaron asked.

"Most schools in Minnesota don't start until after Labor Day. It's like a law or something. And Labor Day's late this year."

"Do you play any sports? Football or run cross-country?"

"Football in the fall."

"What position?"

"End."

"Offense or defense?"

"Both. What about you? Did you play football in high school?"

Jenny could see Aaron's face, his profile hazy from the glow of the dash lights. It was a handsome face. His voice, when he spoke, had a deep timbre that made her think of some rich, dark wood, like teak or mahogany. He could be extremely gentle, and his poetry was stunning in its sensitivity to relationships in life, especially those between nature and humans. There was so much to like about him. And yet, in the last few weeks, she'd found herself holding back more and more, and the why of it was something she hadn't been able to put her finger on.

"Lacrosse," Aaron said.

"Lacrosse?" Stephen seemed surprised and pleased. "I've never played, but it looks pretty cool. An Indian game, right?"

"Right. Those Indians were pretty creative and competitive."

"We still are," Stephen said.

Aaron glanced at him and gave a serious nod. "Of course."

"Were you any good?"

"We took state my senior year."

Stephen gave a low whistle to show that he was impressed.

They drove through Ray and Ash Lake and Orr, dark little towns surrounded by deep woods and with a few lights in the windows.

"I read a book of your poems." Stephen sounded as though he were making a kind of confession.

"No kidding? Which one?"

"The Heart's Divide."

"Where'd you get it?"

"Bought it off Amazon."

They crossed a bridge that spanned a channel between two lakes. The moon was up, and the channel was a brilliant, iridescent spill between two vats of silver.

"Okay," Aaron said, "the suspense is killing me. Did you like my poems?"

Stephen stared out at the lake, then glanced at Aaron. "I liked the ones where you talked about the land. I could see what you were getting at. Some of the others, well, I didn't understand them."

Aaron nodded. "Fair enough."

At last they turned east and entered Tamarack County. A sense of gratitude overwhelmed Jenny. She'd thought, years ago, when she left for the University of Iowa, that she was leaving

Aurora and the house on Gooseberry Lane behind for good, but now it felt wonderful to be coming home. It felt safe.

"Tell me about this Henry Meloux," Aaron said.

"I'm not sure I can," Stephen replied. "I think you have to meet him. He's . . ." Stephen seemed to be searching for the right word. "Unique." A few moments later, he added, "And important."

"Dad says he's not well," Jenny said from the backseat.

Stephen half-turned. "He told me that, too, when I came home from Texas. He said there's someone staying with Henry. She's like a nurse or something."

"His great-niece. Dad says her name is Rainy Bisonette. She wants to become a Mide, like Henry."

"I'm going to be a Mide someday," Stephen said with certainty.

"What's a Mide?" Aaron asked.

"A member of the Grand Medicine Society," Stephen explained. "A healer. Somebody who understands the harmony of life and how to use nature to restore harmony when it's been lost."

"You seem to know Henry Meloux well."

Stephen hesitated before replying. He glanced back at Jenny, who nodded that it was okay. "Some pretty horrible things happened to me a long time ago, and he helped me heal. He's helped us all at one time or another."

Aaron considered this for a moment, then said quietly, "Maybe if there'd been a Henry Meloux around when I was a kid, my family wouldn't be so screwed up."

It was past midnight when they came into Aurora. The houses were dark, and the streets, too, except where the streetlamps threw down circles of light. Jenny didn't need light to know this town. She could have guided Aaron around every corner with her eyes closed.

"Let's go past the house," she said.

"Why?" Stephen asked.

"I want Aaron to see it."

Stephen shrugged. "Turn right on Walnut," he said to Aaron. "Two more blocks."

In a couple of minutes, they were parked in front of the two-story on Gooseberry Lane. It was white wood with green shutters and a roofed porch that ran along the front. The big elm that had been there even when her father was a boy cast moon shadows across the yard and the house. There was a porch swing, and Jenny remembered how her parents used to sit and talk after she and Anne and Stephen had gone to bed. Her room was just above, and she could often hear them conversing below in the quiet, intimate voices of people who've loved each other for a long time. It had made her feel safe. And now, for some reason, it made her feel lonely.

"Where's Trixie?" she asked Stephen, speaking of the family dog.

"Staying with the O'Loughlins across the street." Stephen turned back to her. "We shouldn't be here. Dad wanted us to go straight to Henry's. Somebody might, I don't know, be watching or something." He peered carefully up and down Gooseberry Lane, which was quite lifeless.

"All right," she said reluctantly. "Let's go."

They drove north out of Aurora, along a county road that paralleled Iron Lake. Occasionally, among the thick growth of evergreens, they could see a light from a cabin or one of the small resorts that sat on the shoreline, but mostly there was just the dark of night and the splash of moonlight between black shadows. They turned onto an unpaved road, and after a couple of miles, Stephen directed Aaron to pull off and stop near a double-trunk birch tree.

"This is where the path to Henry Meloux's cabin begins," he explained.

They got out of the truck and took with them the items they'd need: the ice chest with the baby inside, no longer sleeping but making no sound; two packs, one with all the baby supplies inside and one with a change of clothing for each of them; a flashlight; and three sleeping bags. Aaron and Stephen each shouldered a pack. Jenny took one handle of the ice chest and Aaron took the other. Each of them gripped a sleeping bag. Stephen walked ahead with the flashlight.

"How far is it?" Aaron asked.

"About a mile and a half," Stephen said. "We're in the Superior National Forest right now. In a little while, we cross onto Iron Lake Reservation land. Just beyond that is the cabin. It's an easy hike, you'll see."

Jenny hadn't been to Meloux's cabin in a very long time. Stephen had been a more frequent visitor, a special visitor in many ways. What her father had said about him was true: He had a unique relationship with the old Mide. She was glad he'd agreed to come along.

The way led through deep forest lit by moonlight. Although it was the middle of night, the woods were alive with the chirr of crickets and tree frogs. Occasionally, Jenny heard the crackle of something in the underbrush to the right or left, some small animal startled by their presence and scurrying away in the dark. The path was soft with fallen pine needles, and all around her was the good, fresh scent of evergreen. On the small farm in Iowa where she lived with Aaron, the land had a different smell, heavy and earthy, and she realized how much she missed the cleansing scent of pine pitch.

They crossed a small stream—Stephen said that white people called it Wine Creek; the Ojibwe called it Miskwi, which meant "blood"—and, not far beyond, they broke from the trees and stepped into a meadow that lay white under the moon.

"This is Crow Point," Stephen told Aaron. "Henry's cabin is over there."

He gestured across the meadow to a low structure that was partly illuminated by the moon and lay partly in shadow. Beyond it was the silver shimmer of Iron Lake. As they stood there, Jenny heard a lazy barking come from the direction of the cabin.

"That'll be Walleye," Stephen said.

Aaron asked, "Walleye?"

"Henry's mutt. He's a great old dog, with an emphasis on 'old.' "

A light appeared at the cabin door. Jenny knew that Meloux had no electricity, and she supposed that the light must be from one of his lanterns.

"He's awake," Stephen said. "Let's go."

They followed the path across the meadow, and as they approached the cabin, Jenny saw that it wasn't the old man who was awaiting them. It was a woman in a loose T-shirt and sweatpants. In the lantern light, her face was the color of faded brick. Her long hair was black, except for a streak of gray that ran down it like a vein of graphite. She was pretty, and she was smiling as if their presence was no surprise.

Stephen said, *"Anin,"* offering her the traditional Ojibwe greeting. "Are you Rainy?"

"Yes," she replied. "Uncle Henry told me to expect someone, but he didn't say who or that it would be in the dead of night. Unless I'm mistaken, you're all O'Connors, right?"

From the ice chest came the whimper of the baby.

"Oh, my goodness," Rainy said, peering inside. "What have you got packed in there?"

Without hesitation, Jenny said, "His name is Waaboozoons. We call him Waaboo for short."

A heavy cough issued from the dark in the cabin. They all turned, and Henry Meloux shuffled into the lantern light. He looked surprisingly old and frail to Jenny, gaunt and immeasurably tired. His dark eyes stared at them from a face so deeply lined that there wasn't an inch of smooth left on it. Then he smiled, and despite the pall of illness that clearly hung over him, a gentle and lively spirit seemed to dance in all his aspect.

"You are late," he said. "I have been expecting you forever."

THIRTY-EIGHT

Rainy Bisonette made tea and brought out cold biscuits left over from the dinner she'd made that evening, which had been fish and wild rice stew and which she offered to reheat. They accepted the tea and biscuits but declined the stew, though it was clear to Jenny that Stephen would gladly have eaten a bowl or two. The only room in the cabin was clean and simple. The walls were hung with items that recalled Henry Meloux's long history among the Iron Lake Anishinaabeg: a bearskin, a bow ornamented with feathers, a deer-prong pipe, snowshoes crafted from spruce-wood frames and strips of moose hide, a lacquered rack that cradled an old Winchester rifle. The only furnishing that looked new was the iron cookstove in the center of the room. There were four handmade chairs around the rough-hewn birch table. Aaron insisted on standing, and he leaned against the wall near the door, looking uncomfortable, as if prepared any moment to bolt. Jenny held the baby in her arms. Walleye lay in the corner with his old head cradled on his paws, blinking at the gathering and probably blinking back sleep as well. Henry Meloux sat with a blanket around his bony shoulders and listened as Stephen told their story.

"Waaboozoons," the old Mide said when Stephen had finished. "A little animal who knows how to hide from the wolf." His dark eyes rested on the child, and he seemed pleased with the name.

"*Mishomis*," Stephen said, respectfully using the Ojibwe word for "grandfather," "my father sent us here. He hopes that you'll help us keep the baby safe until he can catch the wolf who hunts Waaboozoons."

"It is a long way to come," the old man said. "Why here?"

"Because on the Angle we don't know for sure who to trust."

"I have an old friend who lives on that great lake," Meloux said. "His name is Amos Powassin."

"We met him," Stephen said.

"And you would not trust him?"

"He pretty much sent us here," Stephen replied. "He was afraid, I think."

A troubled look came over the old man's face, a darkness in every line. Jenny saw that his hands shook with a slight but uncontrollable tremor. "An animal that has made Amos Powassin afraid? Tell me about this wolf who hunts a child."

Stephen said, "I haven't seen him, but Jenny has."

Everyone looked to her. She shook her head. "I've only seen him from a distance, maybe a couple of hundred yards away, when he raised his rifle to shoot at us."

The old man seemed interested in this information, which hadn't been a part of the shortened story Stephen had told. "Two hundred yards? Did he have a scope on his rifle?"

"I think so, yes."

"Did he shoot at you?"

"No."

"Two hundred yards is nothing for a good hunter, but he did not shoot." Meloux seemed puzzled. "Is he not a good hunter?"

Stephen said, "Mr. Powassin seemed to think he was."

"A predator that does not behave as a predator should," the old man noted.

"Mr. Powassin said something to me, *mishomis*. He said that in everything that's good is the possibility of evil, and in everything that's evil, the possibility of good."

The old Mide nodded, and his eyelids drew nearly closed as he considered Stephen's words. To Jenny, he looked immeasurably tired. "I think I will have to sleep on this," he finally said. "Niece, will you make our visitors comfortable?"

"Of course, Uncle Henry."

There was a bunk in the cabin, and that was Meloux's. There was also a cot, where Rainy Bisonette slept. She offered it to Jenny, who refused. "I'd prefer to be outside so that if our little guy gets fussy I can walk him without disturbing anyone. I have a sleeping bag, and he can sleep there with me."

Stephen said, "I've slept in the meadow before. It's pretty comfortable."

"That'll be fine," Jenny said.

"Will he need a bottle in the night?" Rainy asked.

"Probably. I have a thermos if we could heat some water now."

"Of course. I'll stoke the fire in the stove. Uncle Henry, why don't you lie down."

"*Migwech*," he said, thanking his niece. With some difficulty, he stood and returned to his bunk. As soon as he lay down, his eyes closed, and he appeared to go immediately to sleep.

Stephen and Aaron headed outside to arrange things in the meadow. Jenny stayed in the cabin with Rainy, who busied herself adding wood to the embers she'd banked in the stove and blowing a flame to life. There was a sink with a hand pump for water. From the cabinet above the sink, Rainy took out a steel saucepan, filled it, and put it on the stove.

"Uncle Henry and I drink the water straight from the pump," she said. "But to be on the safe side, I think we should boil it for Waaboo."

Waaboo. The moment Stephen had said the name, Jenny had liked it. It fit her little guy. He was becoming fussy, and as she held him, he turned his head to her breast.

Rainy saw and smiled. "Any port in a storm."

"When we were stranded on the island, I let him have my breast," Jenny said, as if it were a confession of some kind. "Just to keep him quiet."

"Did it work?"

"Yes."

"Did you like it?"

It seemed at first an odd question, but the truth was that she had. "Yes," she admitted.

Rainy smiled. "There's nothing at all unnatural in that. Or, for that matter, in a woman breast-feeding a child not her own."

"I've got nothing to offer him."

"Not now maybe."

"What do you mean?"

Rainy leaned against the sink counter with her arms folded across her chest. "I'm a public health nurse. I've seen women adopt a breast-feeding baby and, with time and patience, begin to lactate, though they're not and, in some cases, never have been pregnant. There's a tea I can make."

"That will help me lactate?"

"It may. But it will take some time."

Jenny said, "I don't know how much time I have. Waaboo is mine for only a little while."

Rainy looked at her, and Jenny saw nothing but utter compassion in the other woman's face. "You've stepped onto a difficult road, Jenny."

"I know. But I don't think I had a choice."

"Uncle Henry would say that the choice was made for you by Kitchimanidoo and that there's a reason."

"I felt . . ." Jenny hesitated, realizing she was confessing again.

"Yes?" Rainy encouraged her.

"I felt something from the moment I first saw him all alone in his basket with that horrible devastation everywhere around him. I fell in love with him, Rainy. Another woman's child."

"Do you know what, Jenny? If I were Lily Smalldog, I'd be happy that my child found you."

"He found me?"

"I believe that, where love is involved, we find each other, no matter how random it may seem."

Rainy went to the stove and checked the water. Jenny watched her, this stranger who, in only a few minutes, had begun to seem a good friend.

Aaron opened the door and came in. The moonlit meadow lay at his back, visible through the doorway.

"Everything's set outside," he said. "Whenever you're ready."

"You and Stephen go ahead and lie down. I'll be there in a few minutes."

"Is there anything I can do?"

"No. We're fine."

When he'd gone, Jenny glanced in the direction of the bunk where Meloux's breathing was quiet and regular. "What is it with Henry?"

Rainy put a finger to her lips and said, "We'll talk tomorrow."

The water boiled. Rainy let it cool a bit, then filled the thermos. The baby had gone back to sleep, and Jenny laid him in the bedding inside the ice chest. She faced her new friend, who unasked, took her into her arms and whispered, "You'll come through this, Jenny, and on the other side will be answers to all the questions that trouble you right now."

"Is that a promise?" Jenny asked.

Rainy smiled and laid a warm hand on Jenny's cheek. "It's a fact."

THIRTY-NINE

Stump Island lay black under the hard, white light of the full moon. As they neared it, Cork couldn't help thinking that it very much resembled a huge panther preparing to spring at them.

Kretsch hadn't been excited when Cork told him about the stop he wanted to make on their way back to the Angle.

"Those Seven Trumpets folks greeted us carrying firearms the last time we visited," he'd reminded Cork. "And that was in broad daylight. What are you hoping to find at night?"

"This was the last place anyone admits to seeing Lily Small-dog alive," Cork had said. "When we talked to Hornett, I didn't get a particularly cozy feeling from him. I didn't think he was telling us everything. Couple that with the fact that they've chosen to build their little community in a place way the hell and gone from anywhere, and it makes me wonder what they might be trying to hide."

"You think it might have something to do with Lily Small-dog and the baby?"

"I'm sure there's a lot more to it than that. I'm hoping we'll know more once we've had a chance to look around without a rifle at our backs."

Kretsch had agreed without much argument, and then he'd plotted their landing.

"We should come in from the east," he'd advised. "The Seven

Trumpets camp is on the west end of the island, and if the wind is still up, and I can almost guarantee that it will be, the sound of my old Evinrude'll be carried away from them."

"Is there an easy place to land?"

"Not that I know of. But I haven't spent much time on Stump. It's miles out from everything else, and it's always been owned by religious groups who've been protective of their privacy. The GPS'll keep us from running aground, but as for actually landing, that could be tricky."

Cork had looked up at the moon, which was so brilliant he nearly had to shield his eyes. "We're in luck. We've got good light to see by."

"Means they do, too," Kretsch had pointed out.

Now they were near enough to the island that Kretsch turned off his running lights to be sure they weren't seen. At the far west end of Stump Island lay the bright yard lights in the Seven Trumpets camp, and the big wind turbine like a white dinosaur and the faint spiderweb of the broadcast tower the group was constructing. Kretsch continued to circle to the east until the thick forest that covered most of the island stood between them and the camp.

"Here," he said, handing Cork a pair of field glasses. "Find a likely place to land if you can."

Cork scanned the shoreline, which was well lit by the moon, and finally spotted what appeared to be a small, protected cove.

"Over there," he said and pointed.

Kretsch saw it and nodded and carefully brought the boat toward shore. He eased it forward against waves being kicked up by the westerly wind, keeping his eyes riveted to the screen of the GPS module. A dozen yards out, he cut the engine.

"You'll need to get into the lake and use the bow line to pull us in," he told Cork. "If there are rocks lurking under the surface, I don't want them chewing up my propeller blades. Be quick about it, before that wind shoves us clear over to Canada."

Cork eased himself over the side and slipped into water that reached above his knees. The bottom was littered with rocks, which made his footing uneven and hurt the wounded soles of his feet. Kretsch tossed him the line. Cork caught it and began to haul the boat after him. It took a minute before he stepped onto dry land, where he quickly tied the rope to an aspen sapling. Then he called softly back to Kretsch, "Secured."

The deputy waded ashore, checking the cylinder of his .38 revolver as he came.

"Have you ever actually had to use that?" Cork asked.

"I only fire it on the range," Kretsch admitted.

"Keep it holstered," Cork said. "If we do this right, you won't need to clear leather."

Kretsch seemed relieved to be able to slip the gun back onto his belt.

They turned to the thick wall of forest in front of them, and Cork moved along the shoreline looking for a way in. He'd gone fifty yards when he spotted the narrow opening of a deer trail.

"We're in luck," he said and, with Kretsch at his back, headed in.

The canopy of branches and leaves scattered the moonlight, but there was still sufficient illumination for the two men to see their way. The wind muscled through the treetops, making enough racket to cover the sounds of their passage. Even so, Cork felt all his senses heightened, and he moved with great caution.

They'd gone a few hundred yards when they came upon a large clearing. Cork stopped at the tree line and carefully eyed the open area. Kretsch moved up beside him.

"Hand me the field glasses," Cork said.

Kretsch took them from the case on his belt and handed them over. Cork scanned the clearing. It was roughly rectangular, fifty yards wide by a hundred yards long. Across the far end of the clearing lay a line of what looked to be earthen mounds, spaced a few yards apart from each other, casting small black shadows against the meadow grass.

"What do you make of those?" Cork asked, handing Kretsch the glasses.

Kretsch took a look, then shook his head. "Got me."

Cork crept along the edge of the clearing until he was at the far end. He checked again to be certain that he and Kretsch were alone, then stepped into the open and walked to the first mound. As he approached, he saw glinting on the ground, darts of re-flected moonlight. He bent and picked up something fallen in the tall grass. He held it up to the light and saw that it was brass, maybe four inches long and three-quarters of an inch round.

"What is it?" Kretsch asked.

"A shell casing," Cork said. "From a big-ass weapon. My guess would be fifty-caliber. A machine gun probably."

"Jesus Christ," Kretsch said. "These folks are serious about Armageddon." He glanced down the length of the clear-ing. "They must use this as a firing range." He gave a whistle. "Pretty smart."

Cork turned the shell so that moonlight slivered along the edge. "What do you mean?"

"We're a good five miles from the nearest populated island. And we're pretty much into the big water, so fishermen never come out this far. If they wanted to conduct war games here, hell, they could probably do it without raising any eyebrows at all."

Cork tossed the shell casing to Kretsch and said, "It appears they already have. Let's keep going."

Not far from the mounds, Cork found a wide path more heavily worn than the narrow deer trail, and they followed it.

"Careful," Kretsch whispered at his back. "We're heading for the compound."

"Compound?"

"What did Hornett call it? The Citadel? I'm thinking it's more than just a beautiful spot to spend some time praising the Lord and preparing for the Rapture."

When he saw yard lights through the trees, Cork paused and

whispered to Kretsch, "Most rural folks I know keep the lights at night to a minimum. The beauty of the night itself is something they appreciate. These folks have their area lit up like a prison camp. Makes you wonder what they're afraid might be lurking in the dark."

"Us," Kretsch said and glanced down at his holster, as if to make sure his .38 was still there if he needed it.

There was a sudden lull in the wind, and the trees ceased their restless rattling. All around Cork the woods grew silent. He stopped walking, and Kretsch held up beside him. Cork listened but heard nothing. He signed to the deputy to proceed. The path was strewn with small twigs so that it was impossible to move without the occasional dry-wood snap under their shoes. They continued until they reached a place where the trail led into the cleared area of the camp and its many buildings. Cork took a position behind a tree and signaled to Kretsch for the field glasses. He examined the camp grounds: the boathouse and the dock, the cabins that housed the residents, a large shed with a gas pump outside that probably housed vehicles and equipment, the communal shower, the laundry building, the wind turbine, the metal web of the broadcast tower under construction, and the great hall, the largest of the finished buildings, which served as church, community center, and dining room. There was a light on in the great hall, the only building lit from the inside.

Through the field glasses, Cork saw a match flare in the shadow of the recessed front entryway. A moment later, the match was waved out, leaving only the red glow from the tip of a cigarette. He continued to study the shadow and the ember, which fell and rose and blossomed and fell again with the act of smoking. After a couple of minutes, a man stepped into the wash of the yard light, and Cork saw that he carried a rifle slung over his shoulder.

Cork handed the field glasses to Kretsch and indicated the great hall and the man who stood before it. Kretsch spent a moment looking, lowered the glasses, leaned close to Cork's ear, and whispered, "Is that an assault rifle he's carrying?"

Cork nodded. Bright lights and armed guards. What was this group protecting?

The door of the great hall opened, illuminating the shadowed entryway, and several people emerged. They spoke for a moment with the man who shouldered the assault rifle. Their voices carried but so low that Cork couldn't make out the actual words. Their backs were turned, and even with the field glasses, he couldn't make out who they were. They moved quickly on, leaving the man with the assault rifle stationed where he'd been, and headed toward the dock. Cork followed them with the glasses and watched them enter the boathouse. A light came on there, and a minute later he heard a deep roar in the windless night, the sound of big engines. A boat backed out onto the lake, then shot south across the big water, running without lights.

"A cigarette boat," he whispered to Kretsch.

"Smalldog?" the deputy asked.

Cork hadn't seen enough to answer that question.

Two figures reemerged from the boathouse and returned to the great hall. A short while later, the light inside went out. The guard had finished his cigarette by then, and he began to patrol the perimeter of the building. He disappeared in back, and Cork swung the field glasses to the compound yard, because he'd spotted something there. Near the broadcast tower was another figure, this one draped in white and moving slowly, drifting like mist.

"Who does that look like to you?" He handed the glasses to Kretsch.

Kretsch studied the ghostly figure. "It's Hornett's wife. The woman who thinks she's the Virgin Mary."

Cork took the glasses from Kretsch and watched as Mary Hornett, who wore a white shawl though it was a warm night, went to the dock and stood at the very end, staring out across the big water. Cork thought that she might be looking where the powerful engines could still be heard from the south, then real-ized she wasn't paying any attention to the cigarette boat. Her face was turned toward the night sky.

In the silence that had descended with the cease of the wind, Cork's ears caught something surprising.

"Hear that?" he asked.

"Yeah," Kretsch said. "Is she singing?"

"She's singing," Cork confirmed.

"I can't quite make it out."

Cork said, "Twinkle, twinkle, little star."

The song died abruptly, and a different sound came to Cork, a deep and prolonged wail. He understood that in its own way this was also a song. The heartbreaking song of grief.

"I think we've seen enough," he said. "Let's get out of here before someone spots us."

FORTY

Aaron's call had come near sunset, telling them that Kretsch had brought the boat safely to the south shore of the big water, and that Jenny and the baby and Stephen and he were on their way to Meloux's cabin. Even so, no one could sleep. Rose and Anne made cookies and coffee, and Mal and Bascombe played cribbage, and they waited deep into the night to hear the sound of Kretsch's small boat motoring up to the dock. They watched the clock on the wall, and nearly an hour after the stroke of midnight, Bascombe said to no one in particular, "They should have been here by now."

"Can you raise them on the radio in your boat?" Rose asked.

Bascombe shook his burly head. "Tom wanted to run silent. He didn't want to take a chance on anyone picking up anything over the air. No telling who might be monitoring transmissions."

"And there's no cell phone reception out there?"

Again, Bascombe's answer was a dour shake of his head.

"The wind's died down," Anne noted. "Isn't that a good thing?"

"Not necessarily," Bascombe replied. "Means the sound of Tom's engine'll carry pretty far in all directions. If someone's watching for him, he'll be easier to spot."

"Who'd be watching for him?" Mal asked.

Bascombe laughed, not a funny sound. "Besides Smalldog?

Could be half the Angle for all I know. This whole business has me looking at all my neighbors in a different way. And frankly, I don't like it."

Rose said, "They grope in darkness with no light; he makes them stagger like drunkards."

"What's that?" Bascombe said.

"From the Book of Job," Mal replied. "A book about trust in God and patience in the face of adversity."

Bascombe cast them both a cold eye. "Religion," he said, as if spitting.

Anne brought the coffeepot around to refill cups. "What do you have against religion, Seth?" she asked.

Bascombe lifted his cup to his thick lips. Before sipping, he replied, "Seen way too much bad to believe there's anybody up there trying to do any good. Or if there is, they don't know their ass from applesauce." He paused, and a modestly contrite look came over his face. "I know you folks are religious, but that's the way I feel."

"No need to apologize," Mal said.

Bascombe drank his coffee and fell into a brooding silence.

Rose picked up her mug and walked to the window of the lodge. Outside, the lake was calm at last and so white under the moon that she thought it resembled a great meadow after a snowfall. In the room at her back, she felt an uncomfortable tension that came from Bascombe. She understood the big man's despair of religion and his doubt of God, and she thought that maybe she ought to say something to take the thorns out of his thinking, but honestly, she had her own doubts.

Then she heard the sound of an engine, and across the lake appeared a long, dark trail of disturbed water, which Rose discerned was the wake of a boat. Running lights came on, and she turned back to the others. With a clear note of relief, she said, "They're here."

* * *

"These folks are deadly serious about End Times," Mal said after Cork and Kretsch had told their story.

"I don't understand why Smalldog would be there," Anne said. "What does he have to do with their beliefs? Is he one of them?"

Cork said, "I've been thinking about that." He had his hands wrapped around a mug of freshly brewed coffee, and on the table in front of him sat a couple of Rose's good sugar cookies. "Judging from the casings Tom and I found on that firing range, I'm guessing they have some kind of arsenal out there. They had to get the hardware from someone, and from what I understand about Smalldog, he might be just the ticket. A man with a military background, already involved in smuggling."

"Match made in hell, you ask me," Bascombe said.

"Is there anything you can do about all those weapons?" Rose asked, directing her question toward Deputy Tom Kretsch.

Kretsch looked uncomfortable. "We didn't find anything solid, really, and what we did find was because we were trespassing. I don't imagine any judge would look kindly on that in considering a search warrant. And for all I know, they may have a license for all those firearms."

A look of incredulity leapt to Rose's face. "A license for a fifty-caliber machine gun?"

Bascombe said, "The sale of machine guns among private individuals is regulated by ATF, but not banned, provided the weapon in question was manufactured prior to 1986. The process is complicated, but not particularly difficult. So Tom's right. It's entirely possible that what they're shooting out there is completely legal."

Rose gave a snort of disapproval, to which Bascombe responded, "I understand your personal feelings here, but there's a constitutional amendment that gives those folks the perfect right to bear arms. I believe strongly in that amendment myself."

"Surely a fifty-caliber machine gun in the hands of a civilian wasn't our founding fathers' intent," Rose shot back.

"Ma'am, with all due respect, there's a lot of case law says otherwise."

Cork broke in on an argument he knew was pointless at the moment. "Tom's right. We can't approach a judge with what we have, but I'd sure like another opportunity to talk with the faithful of the Seven Trumpets. See what I might be able to shake loose."

"How about in daylight this time," Kretsch suggested. "First thing in the morning?"

"That'll do," Cork said. "I don't know about you guys, but I'm bushed."

"You'll be able to sleep?" Anne asked, nodding toward the coffee mug that Cork cradled.

"Sweetheart, a stampede of wild horses couldn't keep me awake."

"We ought to keep somebody on guard," Bascombe suggested. "In case Smalldog comes sniffing around again. Maybe switch off at hour intervals. I'll be happy to take first watch."

"And I'll take second," Mal said.

"I'll relieve you," Kretsch volunteered.

"Then I'll stand the last watch," Cork said, "which should take us to dawn."

"I'll give a hand in any way I can," Rose offered. "But I won't carry a firearm."

"Same here," Anne chimed in.

"How about you fix us a hearty breakfast in the morning," Mal suggested. "And keep the bed warm for me."

Anne said, with a note of disparagement, "Women's work."

Rose put her hand on her niece's arm and smiled. "We asked."

Despite what he'd told Anne, Cork couldn't sleep. It wasn't the caffeine. He just couldn't get his brain to shut down. He went over the events of the last couple of days in his head again and again, and no matter how he juggled things, nothing made sense. He couldn't wrap his thinking around a man like Smalldog, a man who may well have abused and then tortured and killed his own sister. A man who hated white people yet smuggled arms to a group of white religious zealots. A man who'd been raised by a father whom the Ojibwe of Windigo Island admired but had, nonetheless, turned into hate on two legs. What caused a man's soul to be so misshapen? He wished Henry Meloux were there so he could ask his old friend that very question. If anyone could understand Noah Smalldog, it would be Meloux. And if anyone could tell Cork what he ought to be doing about Smalldog, that was also Meloux. But Henry was in his cabin on Crow Point, which was a good thing, because Jenny and Stephen and the baby were there with him, and as long as that was the case, Cork knew they were safe.

He finally got up from his bunk and pulled on his clothes and walked outside. It was Mal's turn on watch, and Cork spotted his brother-in-law sitting on the bench at the end of Bascombe's dock. Mal wasn't alone. Rose was with him, her head laid against his shoulder. In the quiet that had come that night with the end of the wind, he could hear them talking, though so softly that he couldn't make out words. It was a scene of intimacy, of two people whose separate lives were braided together into a single strand. Cork was happy for them. And at the same time, the sight of them made him feel empty and alone. He stood in the shadow of the cabin cast by the moon and let himself, as he sometimes did, remember his wife fully. He could see her face, which had been beautiful, her eyes, which had been deep blue and sharp with intelligence, her hair the color of corn silk. He could hear her voice murmuring his name in the way she'd sometimes done after they made love, which had been like the whisper of a secret. And he felt her body shaped perfectly to his, as it had often been when he held her in the cool quiet after the heat of their passion.

The truth, he knew in his rational thinking, was that his marriage had not always been so perfect, but at that moment it didn't matter. What mattered was that he was happy for Mal and Rose, and that he hoped, if Jenny and Aaron chose to work things out, they would find a way to braid their two lives together with love, and that, although he was himself alone now and lonely, he hadn't always been.

He turned and went back into his cabin and lay down thinking that if he, a man who'd known great love, felt lonely, what must a man like Noah Smalldog feel? Was there any limit to how alone a human being could be?

FORTY-ONE

The child woke at first light. Jenny lifted him from the bedding inside the ice chest that had cradled him all night and walked away from where Aaron and Stephen still lay in their sleeping bags, dead to the world. From the stovepipe atop Meloux's cabin, smoke rose white against the faint blue of the dawn sky, and Jenny could smell biscuits baking. She saw light through an open window, heard the whisper of quiet conversation inside, and thought about joining Rainy and Henry, who were clearly awake. For a little while, however, she wanted to be alone with Waaboo.

There was a path that led away from the cabin, across the meadow, and through an outcropping of tall rocks. On the other side was a fire ring full of the ash of many fires and surrounded by sections of tree trunk cut to serve as stools. Jenny had been there on many occasions with her father and Stephen, while Henry Meloux fed sage and cedar to the fire in the ring. It was a place sacred to the old Mide. She sat on one of the makeshift stools, and stared at the water of Iron Lake not more than a dozen feet away, smooth and gray as smoked glass. Somewhere on the lake a loon cried and another answered.

"Waaboozoons," she said aloud. She brushed his fine black hair with her fingertips and stared down into his dark eyes, which stared right back at her. "What are you thinking, Little Rabbit?"

"Not much," came the reply, but it didn't come from Little Rabbit. It was Henry Meloux who'd spoken.

Jenny looked up as the old man walked slowly toward her from the opening in the rocks. He wore overalls and a long-sleeved flannel shirt, though the day was warm already and promised to be hot. He wore no hat, and his long white hair hung down and framed his face, which was like sandstone fractured by time and the elements. His old dog, Walleye, came with him, padding softly at his heels. Meloux seated himself on a sawed section of tree trunk next to Jenny. Waaboo's eyes swung toward him briefly, then back to Jenny's face.

"He does not think," Meloux said. "He only feels. And what he feels is comfort and love. What every child should feel, but some do not. This one is lucky."

"His mother was killed, Henry. How lucky is that?"

"But he is alive. And he found you, and you found him."

Walleye had taken an interest in the child. He put his wet, black nose near Waaboo and sniffed, and his tail thumped the ground. Then he walked in a circle twice and lay down near Meloux.

The old Mide watched the baby in Jenny's arms, his eyes warm with affection. "I don't claim to understand the Great Mystery that is Kitchimanidoo, but I believe that nothing happens without purpose. This child has been given to you for a reason."

"He's not mine, Henry. I'm sure the authorities will find someone else they'll say he belongs to."

"Belongs." Meloux seemed to consider the word. "I believe no one belongs to anyone else. You, me, Waaboozoons, we are all dust borrowed for a little while from Grandmother Earth. And even that dust does not belong to her. She has borrowed it from all creation, which is the Great Mystery, which is Kitchimanidoo. And if you ask this old man, I would say that another way to think about Kitchimanidoo is as a great gift. Kitchimanidoo is not about keeping. Nothing belongs to anyone. All of creation is meant as a giving."

"I'm not sure that a white court would see it that way, Henry."

The old man smiled. "Think big."

Rainy appeared between the rocks and came toward them. In one hand she held a bottle prepared for the baby, in the other, a steaming mug. She brought them both to Jenny.

"What's this?" Jenny asked, taking the mug.

"An old Ojibwe brew," Rainy replied with a sly smile. "Henry taught me how to make it."

The old man nodded. "I have seen it help a woman make milk. If you are going to be mother to this child, it would be a good thing to be a mother in all ways."

"What's in it?"

Rainy said, "It's safe, Jenny. Don't worry. And it's really rather good."

Jenny sipped and found that Rainy was right. It tasted of blackberry and honey and something that she couldn't identify but that wasn't at all unpleasant.

"It may help," Meloux said. "But I believe there is something powerful at work here that will help you more."

"What, Henry?"

"I will let you think about that," he said. "I am going back to the cabin. Come on, old dog. You are probably hungry. I know I am."

Walleye eased himself to his feet.

Rainy said, "I'll be there in a minute, Uncle Henry."

"I can butter and jam my own biscuit, Niece," he replied, a bit churlish.

He walked away slowly, and Walleye followed at a pace that kept him easily at the old man's side.

When he'd gone, Rainy explained, "He's generally okay with me being here, but he sometimes gets resentful of my nursing."

"What do you do for him?"

"Mostly the heavy work. His washing and the cooking and the cleaning. I go into Allouette for groceries," she said, speaking of the larger of the two communities on the Iron Lake Reservation. "I charge my cell phone while I'm there."

"You walk?"

"My Jeep's parked on a logging road a couple of miles from here. Henry, if he could, would walk the whole way into town and back. He's done it all his life. Until now."

"He has to be well over ninety," Jenny said. "Isn't it about time he slowed down?"

"Try telling that to Uncle Henry."

The baby pulled away from Jenny and began to fuss in a way that she had learned was all about his empty stomach. Rainy handed her the bottle. Jenny tested the warmth of the formula with a few drops against her wrist. Satisfied, she offered it to Waaboo, who took it immediately. Jenny gently sealed the cleft in his lip with her index finger. She looked up and saw Rainy watching, her almond eyes warm with what Jenny read as approval.

"You told me last night we'd talk more about Henry this morning," she said. "What's going on with him?"

"I don't know," Rainy said. "And for all his wisdom in the art of healing, he doesn't either. He believes it has nothing to do with his age, and he may well be right. I've known Anishinaabe men and women who've lived a good life and worked hard well past a hundred. There's no reason that Uncle Henry, who's taken good care of himself all his life, shouldn't be among them. But something's threatening him, it's clear. What that threat is, we just don't know, either of us."

"The hand trembling, could it be Parkinson's?"

"It could be, but with Parkinson's I'd expect to see more symptoms—the tremors spreading beyond his hands, a shuffling gait, a stoop, compulsive behavior, orthostatic hypotension—which I don't. It could be a dozen other diseases, although the symptoms don't really fit very well with any diagnosis I've tried on my own so far."

"He won't see a doctor?"

Rainy shook her head. "And I'll respect his wish."

"Though it may kill him?"

"There are so many things in life we have no control over. Dying ought to be one that we do. If it's what Uncle Henry wants, that's the way it will be."

Jenny said, "This can't be easy for you."

The first bit of dawn sun finally inched above the treetops, a sliver of fire that made Iron Lake burn. Rainy stared out across the still, brilliant water and breathed deeply the clean morning air.

"I love this place. I came thinking I could help Uncle Henry. I've found that being here has helped me as well." She smiled at Jenny. "My children are grown and gone. For a long time, I haven't had a clear direction in my life. Being here, though it's not always easy, has been a blessing. The one demand I made was that we get a new woodstove so I could cook decently," she said with a pleasant laugh.

"Stephen said you want to become a member of the Grand Medicine Society."

"Uncle Henry has been teaching me. If I become a Mide as a result, that would be good. But it's his knowledge, his wisdom I'm after." She laughed. "In this, there are no diplomas."

Waaboo finished his bottle. Jenny laid him against her shoulder and patted him until he'd burped. Then both women stood and turned toward the cabin.

"*Migwech,*" Jenny said.

"For what?"

"For helping Henry. And for helping me."

Rainy hugged her and said, "Love is the only river I know whose current flows both ways."

FORTY-TWO

Standing the last watch alone, Cork saw the sun rise over Lake of the Woods. Only the third dawn since the storm, but it seemed to Cork that in that brief period there'd been a whole lifetime of occurrence. The day came bathed in the color of blood, and he thought of the old rhyme: "Red sky at morning, sailors take warning." He didn't need the sky to make him vigilant. He'd been tingling all night, as if some radar in his nature was on high alert.

He stood at the end of Bascombe's dock and heard the door of the lodge slap shut. He turned and saw Rose approaching, a mug of steaming coffee in her hand.

"Thought maybe you could use this."

"God bless you," he said.

She studied his face. "Did you sleep at all?"

"No." He could smell bacon on her clothing. "Working on breakfast?"

"That was the bargain, wasn't it? You men stand guard, and Annie and I feed you. She's scrambling eggs even as we speak. Everything should be ready in a few minutes. So what kept you awake? General worry?"

"That," Cork said.

"And?"

He was tempted to shrug off her question, reluctant to

confess. But he needed to unburden himself to someone, and he knew that, if Jo were still alive and with him, he would have told her the truth.

He said, "I blew it, Rose."

"Blew what?"

"This." He opened his arms to the lake. "All I wanted was for us to be happy. And what did I do? Brought us to a place so far from everything even God's forgotten it's here. And when Jenny needs me most, what do I do? I turn my back on her."

"You didn't turn your back, Cork."

"I didn't exactly open my arms to her either."

"You mean to the child."

"I'm afraid she's going be hurt again."

"And if she's hurt, you'll be hurt again, too."

Which was the truth at the bottom of it all, he had to admit.

"She's strong, Cork. She'll survive. And so will you."

She looked nothing like her sister, but in Rose's advice, Cork heard Jo speaking. He nodded, and then he leaned to her and kissed her cheek in gratitude.

"I'm going to do my best to make sure we all survive," he said.

The morning was still and warm. Even so, Rose hugged herself as if she were chilled. "So what do we do now?"

"I think today we flush out a snake or two."

"Noah Smalldog?"

"And maybe some of his cohorts."

"The Church of the Seven Trumpets?" She shook her head in a deeply troubled way. "If they're involved in this, what a sad thing for Christian folks."

"Anyone can call themselves Christian, Rose. Doesn't make it so. A wolf in sheep's clothing. Probably every religion has its crazies."

"To invoke God's name in such cruelty," she said. "It's enough to break your heart."

"Or make you really pissed." Cork glanced down at Bascombe's Marlin gripped in his left hand.

Rose saw his look. "Answering violence with violence, Cork? You told me a couple of years ago that you'd never lift a firearm against another human being again."

"Any person who'd do what was done to Lily Smalldog or condone that kind of cruelty isn't, in my book, a human being, Rose. Any person who might do that to a child of mine, I would kill without remorse. I'm funny that way."

She reached out, and her hand was cool against his cheek. "I'm praying it won't come to that."

From the lodge door, Anne called out, "Come and get it."

"So," Bascombe said with a bit of egg caught in his beard, "we make an assault on Stump Island today?" He sounded eager.

"No assault, Seth," Cork replied. "Just a lawful inquiry. And it'll be only Tom and me going to Stump."

"Whoa." Bascombe lifted his head abruptly from where it had hovered over his plate as he shoveled his food in. "Wait a minute. I want a piece of this action."

"I need you to do something else."

"Yeah? What?" He didn't sound happy.

"Your computer doesn't work, right?"

"That's right."

"Is there somewhere on the Angle that you can get access to the Internet?"

"I guess lots of folks would let me use their computers if I asked."

"Good. I'd like you to head to the mainland this morning while Tom and I are at Stump Island. Get onto the Internet and find out anything you can about the Church of the Seven Trumpets and the Hornetts."

"Hell, that doesn't sound like much fun."

"It's important. I'd like to know everything I can about these folks. Where they came from, if they've been in trouble before. It's exactly the kind of thing you probably used to do in your work for ATF."

"Yeah, but I always preferred being out in the field. And how is that going to get us to Smalldog?"

"That's the second part of what I want you to do," Cork said. "I want you to go over to Windigo Island and talk to Cherri Allen and Amos Powassin. See if any of the Ojibwe who went out yesterday found anything that might help us track down Smalldog."

Bascombe's eyes lit up at that. "Okay. But if we go hunting him, I'm not sitting that one out."

"It's a deal," Cork said. "Mal, are you okay sporting a rifle on the home front here?"

"Like I did last night, I'll hold the thing and make sure anyone who might be watching knows that I've got it. But, Cork, if it comes to having to shoot, I won't promise."

"I can't imagine Smalldog would try anything in broad daylight. But I don't know the man, so I can't say for sure."

Mal said, "I'll do what I can."

Near the end of the meal, Kretsch excused himself and went to his cabin. He came back dressed in the khaki uniform of a Lake of the Woods County sheriff's deputy—badge, duty belt, and all.

"I don't often wear it," he admitted, "but I kind of like the feel of authority it lends."

"You look magnificent," Rose said.

When they'd finished breakfast, they headed to the dock. Cork and Kretsch got into the deputy's boat, and Bascombe got into his launch.

"Be careful, Dad," Anne said.

"I'll be the picture of diplomacy," Cork told her, and he hugged her for good measure.

Kretsch and Cork headed off first, then Bascombe. When

Cork looked back, his daughter and Mal and Rose were still on the dock, huddled together, shielding their eyes against the strong morning sun as they watched the boats grow distant.

They rode out mostly in silence. As Stump Island loomed on the horizon, Kretsch turned to Cork and said, "I've never had to carry out any kind of real investigation on the Angle. Mostly I break up fights and arrest drunks and give out parking tickets. I know you were a county sheriff for a long time. Would you mind taking the lead on this?"

"I think you should ask the questions, Tom. It's your jurisdiction. But tell you what, if there's something I think you've missed, I'll toss in a question or two of my own. Okay?"

Kretsch didn't seem entirely comfortable with the arrangement, but he said, "Okay."

Because Cork wanted a good look at the whole island before they landed, he asked Kretsch to circle Stump. What he saw was a wall of forest that could have hidden an army. With enough men and arms to defend it, that island, so isolated in the vast expanse of Lake of the Woods, would be a bitch to storm, whether by the forces of Satan or by the men and women of law enforcement.

It was nearing noon, and the sun was almost directly overhead. By the time they approached the dock on Stump Island, the day had turned hot. Two men came from the Seven Trumpets camp to meet them. Both carried rifles. Kretsch motored close, and Cork leaped from the boat with the bow line and tied up to a cleat. Kretsch killed the engine, tossed the stern line, and when Cork had finished securing the boat, joined him on the dock. They turned to meet their welcome committee.

"Good morning," Kretsch said and introduced himself and Cork.

The two men were big and broad and wore army green ball

caps that shaded square faces. One had longish blond hair; the other appeared to be completely bald.

The bald man said, "Morning," in a way that suggested more a threat than a greeting.

"I'm looking for Gabriel Hornett," Kretsch said, still chipper.

"Not here," the man said.

"You mean he's not on the island?"

"That's what I mean."

"Could we speak with Abigail, then?"

"She's not around either."

"Both of them are gone?"

"I just said that, didn't I?"

"Is there someone we could talk to, someone in charge? Joshua Hornett, maybe?"

"He's not here either, and if he was, he wouldn't be in charge. That'd be me."

"And you are?"

"Darrow."

"Is that a first or a last name?"

"First name's Patrick."

"And you are?" Kretsch said, addressing the blond-haired man, who'd stood like a fence post with eyes.

"Billings," the man said. "Chester A."

Kretsch nodded and looked past them toward the camp buildings. "Could you tell me where the Hornetts have gone?"

"Away," Darrow replied.

"You don't know where?"

"No idea."

"You?" Kretsch asked Billings, Chester A.

Billings said nothing, only gave his head the faintest ghost of a shake.

"Mind if we look around a little?" Kretsch asked.

"Got a warrant?" Darrow challenged.

"No. Not looking for anything special. Why? You have something to hide?"

"Not a thing, Deputy."

"Then there's no reason we couldn't just have a stroll, right? When we talked to Hornett day before yesterday, he was pretty hospitable."

The two men exchanged a look, then Darrow gave a nod. "We'll walk with you."

In the absence of a wind, the day was still, and Cork heard metallic hammering ahead. When they cleared the first of the buildings and came in sight of the base of the broadcast tower, Cork saw several men at work there. At the moment, it appeared that getting the tower up was the primary business of Seven Trumpets. The story of the Tower of Babel came easily to Cork's mind.

He said, "Two days ago, Hornett told us you folks'll be broadcasting scripture and the like pretty soon."

Darrow didn't appear to think that required a reply.

"It'll have to be a pretty strong signal to reach anyone from here."

"It'll be strong," Darrow said.

"And what will your message be?"

"Don't fuck with us," Billings said.

Cork scratched his unshaved jaw, making a sound like rubbing sandpaper. "I don't recall that line from scripture."

"He means," Darrow interjected, "that we're about the Lord's work up here, and in a Godless world the righteous will stand firm."

"Yeah," Billings said. "What I meant."

"A mighty fortress, is that it?" With a sweep of his hand, Cork indicated the camp.

"Do you believe in the End of Days?" Darrow asked him seriously.

"I have to admit, I have my doubts."

"Then you'll perish, brother. And the last words you hear will be coming from us, broadcast over our tower there."

Kretsch said, "Telling the rest of us that you told us so?"

Darrow gave the deputy a dark look. "It's all God's word, all laid out in the Bible, if you ever took the time to read it."

Cork could have argued, but he'd learned a long time ago that, when confronting men with big rifles and little minds, discretion was best.

The community hall sat on a slight rise ahead, and Cork saw that, like the night before, an armed guard stood at the entrance.

Kretsch said, "Mind if we have a look inside your community hall?"

Which was exactly what Cork was thinking.

"I don't think so," Darrow said.

"Hornett took us in the other day."

"That was Gabriel and that was then."

"You have your church sanctuary inside, right?" Cork said.

"Yes."

"Suffer the little children to come unto me, and forbid them not," Cork said.

Darrow gave him a blank look.

Cork said, "Gospel according to Luke. If you ever took the time to read it."

"You want in, come back when Gabriel is here."

"When would that be?"

"Don't know."

Kretsch said, "We've had some reports of the sound of heavy gunfire on Stump Island. Automatic weapons, machine guns, that kind of thing. Know anything about that?"

"Don't have a clue," Darrow said.

Kretsch nodded toward the firearms the two men sported. "You ever fire those rifles, do some practice shooting?"

"We practice."

"Got a firing range?"

"Nothing formal."

"Not much of a fortress here if you can't defend it," Kretsch said.

"Oh, we can defend it," Billings said. "Just try us."

"You got some ID?" Kretsch asked the man.

"What for?"

"You don't sound Minnesotan. Just wondering where you're from."

"Mississippi, not that it's any business of yours."

"What about you?" Kretsch asked Darrow.

"Idaho."

"Folks here from all over?"

"All over," Darrow replied.

"Gathering because you really believe the final days are upon us."

"You got to be blind to miss the signs," Billings said.

Kretsch looked to Cork. "Seen enough?"

"There's one more thing I'd like to have a look at," Cork said.

"Yeah? What's that?" Darrow was growing surlier by the minute.

"The boathouse."

Darrow thought it over, gave a shrug, and turned back toward the lake. He led them to the boathouse, from which, the night before, Cork and Kretsch had seen Smalldog's cigarette boat depart. He opened the door and let them have a look inside. The slip was empty.

"Where's the boat you keep in here?" Kretsch asked.

"We don't keep nothing in here. All our boats we keep at the dock."

"We saw two boats tied up at the dock day before yesterday," Cork said. "They're both still there. What did the Hornetts use to go wherever it is that they went?"

Darrow hesitated a moment too long, then said, "Someone picked them up."

"Who?" Kretsch asked.

"Didn't see. Let's go." With the barrel of his rifle, Darrow waved them back outside.

On the dock, Kretsch pulled out his wallet, took a business card from inside, and handed it to Darrow. "Have Gabriel give me a call when he returns."

"Whatever," Darrow said, and Cork had the feeling that, as

soon as they were gone, the man would tear the card into little pieces. Or maybe eat it.

They cast off and motored away slowly.

"What do you think?" Kretsch said.

"An island of really scary loonies," Cork answered.

"They're hiding something, and my guess is that it's in the community hall."

Cork thought the same thing. "Their arsenal, maybe?"

Kretsch said, "Big structure, huge foundation. If there's a sublevel to that place, you could park a battalion of tanks down there." He shook his head. "Still got nothing for a search warrant, though."

"Maybe Bascombe will have found something," Cork said.

Kretsch turned the boat north toward Oak Island, far beyond the empty horizon. Just as he eased the throttle forward, Cork said, "Wait!"

Along the shoreline of Stump Island, among the trees a good two hundred yards outside the camp buildings, he spotted a figure waving to them wildly. He took the field glasses he'd brought and put them to his eyes.

"Who is it?" Kretsch asked.

"Joshua Hornett's wife."

"Mary, right? Believes she's the mother of Christ?"

"Whatever she believes, it's pretty clear she wants us to come to her." Cork swung the field glasses back toward the camp and saw that the men who'd escorted them were no longer on the dock. "Let's see what she wants. Can you get in close?"

Kretsch checked the GPS display. "It'll be tricky, but we can make it."

He swung the boat east and came carefully at the shoreline. The woman waited for them, pacing like a tiger, glancing nervously in the direction of the compound. As soon as the boat was near enough, she called out, "Please take me away from here!" She looked prepared to leap into the water and swim to them.

"Easy," Cork called back. "We're almost there."

He went to the bow, watched the water for rocks, and waved at Kretsch to cut the motor when they were still a few yards out. He eased himself over the side and waded to the woman.

"You'll have to get into the water, ma'am," he said gently. "That's as close as we can get."

She nodded her assent and let him help her to the boat, where Kretsch lifted her over the gunwale. Cork followed her up.

"Are you all right?" Kretsch asked her.

She looked up at him with startled green eyes. "They killed my son," she said. Which was exactly what she'd said to them a couple of days before in the community hall.

"I understand," Kretsch said and shot Cork a look that told him they were dealing with another loony.

"No," the woman said. "You don't. They killed my son." She wore a simple dress the color of old butter and with a faint check-ered pattern across it. There was a pocket sewn to the front of the skirt. She reached into the pocket, brought out a photograph, and handed it to Kretsch. Cork moved to look over the deputy's shoulder. It was a color Polaroid, worn and clearly much-handled. It showed the woman, a good deal younger, with a baby cradled in her arms. The baby looked to Cork to be only a few weeks old. His face was wide and his eyes oddly angled. Down syndrome, Cork thought. There were mountains in the background. The woman looked happy.

"This is your son?" Cork asked.

"Was my son," she said. "I named him Adam."

Kretsch handed the photograph back and asked gently, "What happened to Adam?"

"They killed him," she said, and a moment later, she began to cry.

"Who killed him, Mary?" Cork asked.

"My name's not Mary," she shot back, wiping at her eyes. "They tell everyone that so you'll think I'm crazy. My name's Sarah."

"Why didn't you say anything the last time we were here?"

"Because they'd kill me, too."

"You said they killed Adam? The Hornetts killed him?"

"They're brutal, heartless murderers," she said.

"Why did they kill your son?"

She glanced fearfully back at the island and said, "Please get me away from here. If they realize I'm gone, they'll come and shoot us all."

FORTY-THREE

They sat in the lodge until it felt like a prison and they the prisoners. Anne finally stood and said, "I have to go outside, just for a little while, just for a little sun."

Mal said, "I'll go with you."

Rose stayed, using the excuse that she wanted to figure out what to prepare for dinner that evening. In truth, she wanted time to herself for some deep thinking and some desperate prayer.

In her brief sleep during the night before, she'd had a dream. It had been so terrible that she didn't even share it with Mal, but it had jarred her awake and left her fearful of closing her eyes again.

In the nightmare, Rose had seen them all—every one of the O'Connors and her and Mal—standing in a clearing surrounded by bodies. None of the bodies was whole. They'd all been torn into bloody pieces. Rose and the people she loved most in the world huddled together and fearfully eyed the edges of the clearing, where amid the dark, unfathomable shadows of the trees, things moved. She couldn't make out what lurked there, human or beast, but whatever it was, it was preparing to come at them and tear them apart in exactly the way it had torn apart all those bodies around them. Rose was not just afraid, she was terrified. And worst of all, she had the sense that they were absolutely alone in that clearing, that God had abandoned them completely. It was this that scared her most. That somehow she—they—had done something that had made even God turn his back on them.

As soon as Mal and Anne left, she went to the kitchen, but rather than rummage through the refrigerator and cupboards, she stood awhile with her eyes closed. She prayed silently that, in whatever lay ahead, God would be with them and would stay their hands from doing anything that might, in his eyes, be unforgivable. Was there such a thing, she wondered, even as she prayed, something so terrible that even God could not offer pardon?

Her eyes were still closed and her mind focused on prayer when she felt a strong arm wrap around her chest and the blade of a knife press against her neck, and the coldest voice she'd ever heard whispered, "One sound and I'll slit your throat."

Rose stood paralyzed, and the feel of the nightmare, of being alone in the clearing abandoned by God, overwhelmed her.

"Who are you?" the cold voice asked.

She barely managed to speak. "Rose," she said. "Thorne."

"I don't care about your name. I want to know who you are. Are you one of them?"

One of whom? she wanted to ask.

Before she could reply, the whisperer from behind demanded, "Where's the baby?"

This she would not answer.

"Tell me where the baby is, or I'll kill you now."

Her heart beat so hard and fast she could feel the pound of it in her throat beneath the blade of the knife. Somehow, she found words and stammered, "Now or later, you'll kill me anyway."

"Maybe not, if you give me the baby."

"So you can kill him like you killed his mother? No."

The man stayed at her back, his body pressed so tightly to hers that she could feel the iron of every muscle. "Move," he said and forced her from the kitchen to the front door of the lodge. "Call them in."

She made no effort to comply. She felt the knife cut into her flesh and blood trickle down her neck.

"Call them in."

"If I call them in," she said, nearly breathless, "you'll kill them, too."

"Maybe not," he whispered. "Or maybe I'll do it whether you call them or not."

She didn't reply, nor did she call out to Mal and Anne.

"Be afraid, woman. You will die."

"We all die eventually."

He was quiet, his breath hot against her ear. "You're not afraid?"

"Yes."

"All I want is the baby."

"I'll die before I give you that child."

"He's not yours to give." It was said with anger as sharp as the blade he held.

At that moment, Mal and Anne stood up and started for the lodge. Rose thought of crying out, of sacrificing herself for them, but before she could speak, the man at her back released the arm he'd wrapped around her chest, brought it up and clamped his hand over her mouth, and drew her forcefully back into the kitchen, where they stood together.

All Rose could do was pray, which she did with her whole being. She heard the door open and two voices and a little laughter from Anne.

"Rose?" Mal called.

The man moved her to the kitchen doorway. Rose saw her husband's face, stunned as if a horse had kicked him. The rifle was held in his right hand, but he did nothing to bring it to the ready. Whether this was a conscious choice or simply that Mal had never used a firearm and his mind didn't naturally leap in that direction, Rose couldn't say. Nor could she say whether or not she was relieved by her husband's inaction.

"Noah Smalldog," Mal said.

"Tell me where the baby is, and I'll let her go."

"We know what you did to your sister," Mal said quietly, reasonably. "Even if I could tell you where that baby is, I wouldn't. None of us would."

"*What I did to my sister?*" The man sounded at the edge of mania, and Rose felt his body begin to shake with rage. "I've seen your boats coming and going from Stump Island. Are you part of them?"

"No," Mal said. "We have nothing to do with those people, except insofar as they can answer the questions we have about your sister and her baby."

"Why do you care?"

Before anyone could speak further, the sound of a boat engine came from the lake. Through the windows behind Mal and Anne, Rose saw Kretsch's boat arrive at the dock. They tied up, and Cork and Kretsch and a woman walked toward the lodge. No one inside moved an inch.

The woman stepped in first. She stopped so abruptly that Cork nearly ran into her. He looked past Mal and Anne, who stood statue still; his eyes took in the situation, and he came forward slowly. Kretsch entered last. As soon as he saw Smalldog, he cleared his handgun from its holster and brought it up. He wavered, uncertain, and Rose understood that it was because he couldn't fire without being sure that she would not be hit. For what seemed like forever, they faced one another in that standoff, and no one said a word.

"I know you."

It was Smalldog speaking to Cork.

"No," Cork said. "You've only seen me. You don't know me."

"You threw rocks at me."

"I didn't have anything else."

"Still got the bruise on my rib. David and Goliath," Smalldog said.

"That's pretty much the same thought I had out there," Cork said. "I was kind of desperate."

Something in Smalldog's voice had changed, and Rose felt the rage ebbing from his body. She wasn't sure what was happening, but for some reason, the man had responded positively to Cork.

"The woman who was with you?" Smalldog asked.

"My daughter."

Smalldog was quiet a moment, putting things together. "She took the baby, trying to get to safety, and you stayed back to throw rocks and give them both a fighting chance."

"That's the size of it," Cork said.

"Why?"

"Why what?"

"Why risk your lives for a child not even yours?"

"We saw what was done to your sister."

"And you thought it was me and that I'd do something like that to her baby?" Smalldog sounded as if all the pieces were falling into place for him.

"I didn't know who you were, only that you were hunting us."

"And when you found out who I was, you still believed I could have done it." Anger had returned to his voice and tension to his body. "You thought because I'm Indian I would do a thing like that to my own sister? *Chimook.*" He spat out the unkind Ojibwe word for a white man.

"*Anishinaabe indaaw,*" Cork said. I am Anishinaabe.

"You're Shinnob?"

"My grandmother was true-blood Iron Lake Ojibwe."

"You don't look Shinnob."

"And you look like a man who might have killed his own sister. How can either of us be sure?" Cork waited a moment. "It's clear to me now that you thought we were the ones who killed Lily. Why would we do that?"

"I didn't know. I only knew she was dead, and there were two strangers out there with her baby. You tell me what you would have thought."

The tone of the conversation had become more reasonable, Rose believed, but the man still held the knife to her throat.

"Did you think that we were part of the Seven Trumpets people?" Cork asked.

"Or sent by them. You've been out to their island a lot the last couple of days."

"Put that knife down and we'll talk," Cork said. "I think we all want the same thing here, the safety of the child, and there's a great deal we need to know."

The man didn't move. Rose continued to feel the trickle of her blood. The room was deathly quiet, and she could hear the pound of her heart in her ears. She prayed silently, *Dear Lord, please let this end well.*

At last, the blade came away. She felt the jerk of Smalldog's body as he threw the knife. She watched it somersault in the air, and the blade sank deeply into the floorboard at Cork's feet. The knife, frightfully large, quivered a moment, then was still.

In the instant that followed, Rose heard the sound of boots fast at her back, and the grunt of Smalldog, and the man dropped beside her. Rose turned. Seth Bascombe stood behind her, his rifle poised in a way that made it clear he'd used the butt to take down the Ojibwe.

"Spotted his boat in a cove the other side of the island," Bascombe said. "Found his tracks on the trail there, headed this way. Figured he'd try something like this, sneak up and slit your throats. The son of a bitch." The big man spat. He glared down where Smalldog lay on the floor, unmoving. "Hope I killed him."

FORTY-FOUR

Smalldog lay unconscious across the cushions of the sofa Bascombe kept in the small open area of the lodge. Anne, who'd received some nursing training during her stay with the Sisters of Notre Dame de Namur in El Salvador, cleaned his wound and said, "We should get him to a hospital and have his head X-rayed. He's got substantial swelling back there."

"Ice'll take care of that," Bascombe said without sympathy. "I think we should tie him up before he comes to."

Cork said, "I know your heart was in the right place, Seth, but you may have killed any hope we had of getting through to this man."

"We don't need to get through to him," Bascombe said. "We got him right where we want him. Now all we need to do is call the sheriff and have this piece of crap hauled away. Except I can't do that."

"Why?" Mal asked.

"I came in the back way, same as Smalldog. I saw that he cut my phone line. Tom, maybe you better get to the Angle, give your boss a holler."

Kretsch nodded. "If nothing else, we've got Smalldog on assault."

"He didn't hurt me," Rose threw in quickly. "I think he was only concerned about the safety of the child, same as us."

Cork held up the knife that Smalldog had pressed against Rose's throat. "He let her go, Tom. He threw this away. To me, that says we need to talk to him and listen to what he has to say."

Bascombe looked astounded, stared at them all as if he were dealing with a group of imbeciles. "You may be Ojibwe, Cork, but you're also former law enforcement. Can't you tell a manipulative, psychopathic liar when you meet one? I say Tom and me haul him to the mainland, call the sheriff, and turn him over."

"He's injured," Anne said.

"Let the sheriff worry about that," Bascombe shot back. "We need to cuff him and transport him before he wakes up. When he opens his eyes, he'll be plenty mad and not easy to control."

"Before we move him, we should let him wake up," Anne argued. "We should make sure he's in shape to travel."

"What if he doesn't wake up?" Bascombe spoke as if the idea appealed to him.

Cork said, "Tom, maybe you should head to the Angle and bring Lynn Belgea back so she can take a good look at Smalldog. You could call the sheriff while you're at it."

"Cuff him first," Bascombe said.

"Probably a good idea," Kretsch agreed. He took the handcuffs from his duty belt and clamped them over the Ojibwe's wrists. He handed the key to Cork. "Until we have a chance to talk to him, we ought to assume the worst, so keep a good eye on him, okay?"

"Will do," Cork said.

"I'll go with you," Bascombe offered.

"No need," Kretsch told him.

"I want to get someone out here to fix my phone ASAP," Bascombe replied. "And we're getting low on food. I'll pick up a few necessities while I'm there."

Kretsch shrugged. "All right."

Sarah stood quietly in a corner, as if trying to be as inconspicuous as possible. Cork had briefly introduced her but hadn't had time to fill the others in on the reason for her presence.

Bascombe nodded in her direction. "Maybe we should bring her along. Get her safely to the Angle and out of reach of those religious zealots."

"No," the woman said. "I want to stay here."

"Suit yourself," Bascombe said. "Ready, Tom?"

"We'll be back as soon as we can," Kretsch promised.

The two men headed out, and Cork watched them pull away in Kretsch's boat. At his back, he heard Rose ask, "Would you like some coffee?" He turned and saw that she'd approached Sarah and was smiling gently at the woman.

Sarah looked Rose over carefully and finally said in a soft voice, "Yes."

Rose went to fetch the pot from the kitchen.

Cork said, "Sarah, why don't you sit down and tell the others your story, if you're willing."

She moved like a ghost, silently and as if she had no substance. She seemed to Cork a woman used to being invisible. She sat in one of the chairs at the table, and Rose set a mug in front of her and filled it from the pot. She picked it up, closed her eyes, and sipped, then drank greedily.

"I haven't tasted coffee in years," she said. "Those people, they believe it's an evil."

"Those people?" Rose said. "Isn't one of them your husband?"

Cork said, "Why don't you tell them everything, Sarah?"

And he listened as she told again the story he'd first heard on Kretsch's boat. She stared down at her hands and began hesitantly, in a way that made Cork think she was unused to speaking to so many people at once.

"My father, see, he was a pretty hard man, real disappointed in life. My mother died when I was a kid, and my father and me, we just kind of drifted around. He was a drunk. He'd earn a little, drink a lot, get mad at the world, beat me up. He blamed me and everyone and everything else for what he called his misfortune."

She risked a look up, as if to gauge some criticism she

thought might be leveled at her for being that kind of victim. Cork hoped what she saw in their faces would only comfort her.

"Go on, Sarah," he said gently.

"Well, when I was sixteen, we found ourselves in Spokane, Washington, listening to a man named Reverend Jerusalem Hornett talk about the end of the world, which he believed was right around the corner. He said it was the responsibility of the righteous to be prepared to fight the armies of Satan. In his mind, that was the government and the Jews and the liberals and pretty much anybody who wasn't a member of his church. For a preacher, he didn't say hardly nothing about love. Everything he read from the Bible was all about killing and vengeance. My father, he just ate that up. Before you could snap your fingers, we were signed up with Reverend Hornett's church."

She stopped and drank the last of the coffee in her mug and asked timidly, "Could I have some more?"

Rose obliged, and Sarah watched the coffee pour as if it were gold.

"So you joined the church," Cork said.

She nodded. "The Reverend had three sons. Joshua, he was youngest, was real good-looking and quiet and sweet, not like the other Hornetts, and if I didn't particularly like the kind of people Reverend Hornett's sermons drew to his church, I sure liked the look of his son. And he liked me, I could tell. The Reverend was married to a woman just as hate-filled as him, sharp-eyed and sharp-tongued and sharp-witted like some kind of, I don't know, vicious hunting animal. I'm telling you, she had a razor blade for a soul. It was like somebody broke a chunk off the hard rock that was her husband and used it to make her, too."

"Any idea why they were like that?" Cork asked.

"The Reverend, he spent time in prison early on, which is where he claimed he had his vision of the End Times and was tapped by God to be some kind of general in the holy army. Abigail, hell, I believe she was born purely evil. Some people are like that."

"I don't believe that's true," Rose said quietly but firmly.

"Well, maybe she had a rough childhood then or something, I don't know. By the time I met her, her heart was dead to anything except the Reverend and bringing about his vision of Armageddon."

"You and Joshua fell in love?" Cork said, encouraging her to continue her story.

She shook her head. "More like we fell in lust. He was pretty ripe for picking. But Abigail was dead set against it. She had another girl chose for Josh, homely as tree bark but real strong and real set in her belief in all the crap the Reverend slung around. Long and short of it, I got pregnant, and Josh and me had to get married, and Abigail, I swear, hated my guts."

"That must have been uncomfortable," Rose offered.

"I thought I could handle her," Sarah said. "I didn't understand how heartless that woman could be."

"Tell them what happened that summer," Cork said.

Sarah drank from her mug and wiped the corner of her mouth with the back of her hand.

"The Reverend moved a bunch of the church folks up to a wilderness area real near the border with Canada, where he had a kind of compound. It was real basic. No running water. No indoor toilets. No electricity. I don't think it was ever meant to be a permanent place, just somewhere safe and isolated where he could make plans for another place he called the Citadel, which was supposed to be some sort of fortress for Christian soldiers to gather and ride out Armageddon. He had pretty elaborate ideas."

"How was he going to pay for it?" Cork asked. This part was of particular interest to him.

She shrugged. "I don't know. I mean, most of his followers weren't much better off than me and my dad."

"Okay, go on," Cork said.

"Once we were there, we stayed. It became like a prison, real hard to leave. I didn't ever once see a nurse or doctor. Abigail tended me, if tending you could call it. When the baby came, I delivered on a bunk in a log cabin by the light of a kerosene lamp. Me and Josh, we'd already picked out names for the baby. Eve if it was a girl, Adam for a boy. Well, it was a boy. But the minute I saw his face, I knew he was different. I understood about Down syndrome. I'd seen those folks on television and in magazines. When I looked at little Adam, I knew. So did Josh. He didn't want nothing to do with his son. He blamed me. Told me I hadn't taken care of myself right. The Reverend, he said it was some kind of judgment from God. My father, he just stayed out of it."

She seemed on the verge of tears. Rose put her arm around the woman's shoulders, and Sarah looked up at her gratefully.

"I didn't care my baby was different," she said to Rose. "I loved him every bit as much as if he'd come out perfect. In a way, I was glad he wasn't perfect. I thought here is a person who will need me and love me his whole life, which was something I never had before."

"I understand," Rose said.

"Then one morning, a few weeks after Adam was born, when I woke up and went to get him out of the little dresser drawer I was using as a crib, he was gone. I screamed bloody murder, but everyone claimed they had no idea what had become of my baby. I tore around that church compound, pulling out my hair and crying like I don't know what. Joshua, he couldn't look me in the eye. But Abigail, she stared me down and said, and God help me these were her exact words, 'Satan must have come to claim his own.' If I'd've had a gun at that moment, I'd've shot that evil woman dead."

Her green eyes were, at that moment, like jade knives.

"What happened after that?" Cork said.

She collapsed a little in her chair. "I went kind of crazy. There's quite a spell where I don't remember much. When I finally came around, I gathered that I'd been ranting about being the Virgin Mary and losing my son. I pretended to still be crazy, because I figured if I told them exactly what I thought of them, they'd kill me like they killed my baby boy. I thought about running away, but we were so far out in the middle of nowhere, I didn't have no idea which way to go."

"How long ago was this?" Cork asked.

She thought a moment, calculating. "Five, six years. I been biding my time since, waiting for my chance. When you folks showed up, I decided it was now or never."

Cork asked, "Why didn't you say something when Tom Kretsch and I were there the first time?"

"They'd've killed you for sure. They done it before and got away with it. They think they're God's special people and don't believe in any law except what they say comes straight from the Bible to them."

"Where's Jerusalem Hornett now?"

"Died just before we came out here. One of his sons stayed back in Washington State to head up the church there while Abigail and Gabriel and Josh came out here with some of the faithful to start building the Citadel."

"Those folks bought Stump Island with hard cash," Cork said. "And all the construction they're doing can't be cheap. Do you have any idea where their money comes from?"

"Things go on at night. Boats come and go. It's got something to do with that, I expect, but I don't know exactly what."

Cork looked down at Smalldog, still unconscious, and said, "Maybe when he comes to he can enlighten us."

FORTY-FIVE

In the late morning, Rainy Bisonette took heated water from the stove reservoir and poured it into a big washtub, and she and Jenny washed little Waaboo. Earlier, Henry Meloux had left the cabin and gone with Stephen and Aaron to gather mushrooms and tubers and herbs. Aaron wasn't particularly enthusiastic, but he'd gamely agreed. Walleye, who would normally have trailed along behind the old Mide, seemed interested in the baby, and he stayed, lying in the meadow grass nearby, and watched with interest as the women went about their work.

"Part of it," Rainy said, continuing the discussion they'd begun earlier that day, "is that he's clearly sick, and he can't figure out what's at the heart of his illness. I've never seen him so tense, so anxious."

"Is it possible he's afraid of dying?"

"Uncle Henry's the last person I would suspect of being afraid to make the passage and walk the Path of Souls." She handed Jenny a bar of soap. "But maybe."

Waaboo squealed with delight at the feel of the warm water and Jenny's gentle, slippery palms. His little arms flailed, and water splashed, and the air above the tub was filled with droplets that sparkled in the sun.

"You told me you have children," Jenny said.

"Three, all grown. My oldest, Alex, died in Iraq two years ago."

"I'm sorry."

"Kari is a first-grade teacher in Eau Claire. She has a won-derful voice and sings with a couple of bands. She'd love to make her living that way. My youngest, Peter, is struggling. Issues with substance abuse. He's clean at the moment and working as a mechanic in Rice Lake."

"You're not married?"

"My husband died a few months after Peter was born. A brain aneurysm."

"You never remarried?"

"Too busy raising my children and supporting us all. And, I suppose, I never met a man I really thought I could live with." She laughed. "Or maybe the issue was a man who thought he could live with me."

Jenny finished with the child, and Rainy handed her the towel she'd brought from the cabin. "You're very good with Waaboo. You've clearly had experience with babies."

Jenny told her about working in the day care and nursery in Iowa City. And then, because she felt a deep comfort in her connection with the other woman, she told Rainy about her pregnancy at eighteen and her miscarriage and the feeling of emptiness that had sometimes overwhelmed her since.

"Have you ever talked with Aaron about how you feel?"

"Not really. He's a good man in a lot of ways, but this isn't something he would understand."

Walleye, who'd been lying quietly in the soft bed of the wild grass, raised his head suddenly and looked toward the woods that edged the meadow. He lifted his nose and sniffed the wind. He stood quickly, and a low growl crept from his throat. He held rigid, watching the shadows among the trees.

Rainy shielded her eyes against the sun and peered toward the trees that had captured the dog's interest.

Jenny had wrapped little Waaboo in the towel, and she held him to her breast. "What is it?" she asked, trying to decide if she should be concerned.

"A bear, maybe, or a wolf. We get them sometimes. They

never bother us, but why don't we take the baby inside, just to be safe."

They gathered their things and walked to the cabin. Walleye hesitated, still focused on the woods, then finally relaxed and followed. Inside, he turned back, and just before Rainy closed the door against the view of the bright meadow and the dark woods beyond, he gave a low woof that wasn't friendly in the least.

FORTY-SIX

Nearly an hour had passed since Kretsch and Bascombe had headed to the Angle. Cork sat watching Smalldog for any sign that the man was regaining consciousness, but the Shinnob lay completely still. Cork was beginning to be more than a little concerned that Bascombe had done serious damage. In a chair near a front window, Mal leafed through an old *National Geographic*. Bascombe's rifle lay propped against the wall next to him. Rose and Anne sat at the dining table, sharing coffee with Sarah and listening as the woman continued to piece together life with the Church of the Seven Trumpets.

"Lily," Sarah said, sounding immeasurably sad. "She was such a lonely girl. She had her mama mostly, and when Vivian was gone, she didn't have nobody. I wanted to help her, honest, but if I did anything to give myself away, Lord only knows what they'd've done to me. I heard some talk about her getting visits in the night from Indian men. Joshua, he seemed real interested in that."

Cork glanced her way and saw that the woman was staring down into her coffee and seemed disinclined to look Rose or Anne in the eye. She was quiet for a long while.

"I think he might've started using her," Sarah finally said. "For sex, I mean. The great lust Satan had put in us early on he still had. Part of why I played crazy was so he wouldn't be bothering me that way. I didn't want nothing to do with that coward anymore."

"Did Abigail or Gabriel know about him and Lily?"

"I can't imagine they didn't. They must have just decided to look the other way."

"Does Joshua believe all the religious dogma?"

"I think the truth is that he's afraid of Abigail, and he'd never say anything contrary to her. But deep down, I think he doesn't believe it any more than I do. It's just the way his life's played out. The church is all he knows."

"So when Joshua couldn't use you, he used Lily instead?" Rose asked gently.

Sarah lifted her face, as if seeking understanding. "I feel real bad about it, but what could I do? If I tried anything, I'd've probably got us both killed. Then she was gone, just up and gone. Truth is I figured she threw herself in that lake out there. God knows I been tempted myself." She let out a deep, exhausted sigh. "Now I find out she went away and hid somewhere and had herself a baby. Lord, but it's a strange world."

"It gets stranger, girl."

The voice was Bascombe's, and it came from the kitchen doorway. When Cork looked there, he saw Kretsch in front of the big man, the deputy's hands bound with silver duct tape. A strip of duct tape sealed his mouth as well.

Bascombe shoved Kretsch into the room with the others. He held Kretsch's rifle and slowly arced the room with the barrel, so that at one point or another it was aimed at them all.

"Let's get this straight. Anyone tries anything, they're dead. Mal, stand up real slow and move away from that rifle next to you."

Mal did as he was told and joined the women at the table.

Kretsch mumbled something behind the duct tape over his mouth. Keeping a wary eye on Bascombe, Rose reached out and pulled the tape away.

"Sorry," Kretsch said to the others. "He jumped me. I just

didn't expect . . ." He didn't finish. He didn't need to. None of them had expected this from Bascombe.

Cork said, "What's going on, Seth?"

The big man eased his way around the dining area until his back was to the front windows and he stood between everyone else and the second rifle. "I tried to get Smalldog away from you the easy way, but you wouldn't have it. So now we got to do it the hard way." He spoke as if he was disappointed and they were the reason.

"And the hard way would be?"

"We wait. The Seven Trumpets folks should be along shortly."

Cork said, "You and them." It wasn't a question. It was a statement of understanding. "Then what?"

"That's up to Seven Trumpets."

"I don't get it," Kretsch said.

Things were falling into place quickly, details Cork should have noted but, in the chaos of all that had occurred, did not.

"I think I do," he said. "The Seven Trumpets folks needed armaments. A former ATF agent would be someone who knows how to get them. They pay you pretty well, Seth?"

"As a matter of fact, I've got a lot more money in the bank than I'd have if I worked a hundred years for the damn government."

To Cork, Bascombe sounded like a man trying to convince himself that the responsibility for all the wrong that had been done was not on his shoulders.

Cork nodded, continuing to think it through. "You told us you worked ATF in the Pacific Northwest. I'm guessing your investigations there brought you into contact with the Seven Trumpets people. I thought you didn't believe in all their religious crap."

"I don't. In my book, those folks are crazy as loons," Bascombe said. "But loons with money."

"It must have been you who suggested Stump Island to them for the Citadel," Cork said.

"When I heard that the Baptists out there were putting it up for sale, I knew it was exactly what the Reverend had been searching for."

"And took an early retirement from the government and came out here to help them in the same way you did back in Washington State, I imagine," Cork speculated.

"More or less," Bascombe said.

"What do they want with Smalldog?"

"Right now, he's got a lot of their money."

"Stole it?"

Bascombe laughed. "You think they'd just hand it over?"

"That's why they tortured Lily?" Cork said. "They were trying to get to Smalldog through her?"

At the mention of the murdered girl, Bascombe seemed to grow sullen. He leveled the rifle directly at Cork. "Enough talking. Just shut up and wait."

Like flesh electrified, Smalldog moved. He shot from the sofa and, in one long stride, reached Bascombe. His cuffed hands grasped the rifle barrel and swung it toward the ceiling. He used the momentum of his body to drive Bascombe into the wall. The big man's head flew back and shattered the window. Cork was sure that would end him, but Bascombe let out a roar, and his big, strong body, pumped with rage and adrenaline, seemed to grow even more powerful. He threw his weight on Smalldog, and both men tumbled.

The rifle clattered across the floor. Cork was on it in an instant. "That's enough!" he shouted. When the fighting didn't end, he lifted the barrel toward the ceiling and pulled off a round. The sound in that close room was like cannon fire, and the two men froze.

"Seth, you stay on the floor. Smalldog, you stand up."

Each man did as instructed.

"Mal, get the other rifle." When the second firearm was secure, Cork said, "How long have you been awake?"

"A while," Smalldog said. "I couldn't quite remember what

happened. Seemed best to play dead till I had things figured. You don't need to point that rifle at me. It's not you I'm after."

"The baby?"

"Yeah."

"Why?"

"To keep those religious sons of bitches from getting him."

"What do they want with him?"

"It's just like you told Bascombe there. They want to use him to get at me."

"All because of money?"

"There's a hell of a lot more to it than money."

"Tell us about it," Cork said.

And Smalldog did.

It was Bascombe who'd made the initial approach. The big man tracked him down in Kenora and laid out a sweet deal. He wanted Smalldog to bring shipments of B.C. Bud—marijuana grown in British Columbia and famed for its purity and potency—across Lake of the Woods. Transport, that was all. Nothing particularly dangerous for a man with Smalldog's reputation, a man who knew the lake so intimately that he could run at night without lights or GPS, a man who'd smuggled before and had a stomach for trouble. Smalldog had agreed. For a couple of years, the arrangement had been fine. It paid better than the cigarettes and Cuban cigars and alcohol and even the human cargo that Smalldog had, on occasion, transported.

It hadn't been difficult for Smalldog to find out what Bascombe was up to: selling the potent marijuana to contacts on the U.S. side of the border at a good profit.

"He paid fifteen hundred dollars for every pound of B.C. Bud, and I'm betting he got two, maybe three times that when he sold it to his contacts," Smalldog said. "Most shipments ran a couple hundred pounds. He used some of that money to buy weapons. The rest went back to Seven Trumpets, where it had come from in the first place. Weapons and money, that's what those people were after, and he was the middleman, making himself a fine profit."

"And the Seven Trumpets people have all the money they need to build their mighty fortress?"

"Not anymore," he said.

"Because you stole it? Why? To keep them from buying weapons and building the Citadel?"

Smalldog's face turned hard. "What do I care if *chimooks* kill each other? They wipe themselves out, it's fine with me. Hell, in Afghanistan, I saw plenty of what white people call 'helping.' Slaughtered a hell of a lot more innocent people than they ever did the Taliban. Most of the time it made me sick and ashamed to be there. No, I did it to get back at those Seven Trumpets bastards for letting Lily get used like a whore."

"You took Lily from Stump Island?"

"Sonny and me."

"We found something carved into the wood above her bed. *Gizaagin.* I love you."

Smalldog looked disgusted. "That was for the Hornett kid. He's an oily, coward son of a bitch."

Sarah said, "All good looks and no heart."

"Lily thought he loved her," Smalldog said. "When Sonny and me figured out what was going on, we took her away from there. Until she started showing—and that wasn't till toward the end—we didn't know she was pregnant."

Cork said, "You're sure Sonny couldn't have been the father?"

"He never touched her that way. She was like a sister to him. The Seven Trumpets people, they put out all that dirt."

"You set her up in that old hunting camp. Why?"

"I was afraid that, if she knew exactly where she was, she'd try to get back to Hornett. And Hornett, if he knew where she was, would try to get to her, so it was best to put her where she couldn't get away easy and she'd stay hid. Me and Sonny visited her all the time, brought her supplies. I threw one of her sweaters in the lake near Stump Island so the Seven Trumpets people would figure she was dead.

"I wanted to get back at them for letting her get used the way they did, but I bided my time. A couple of weeks ago, Bascombe had me pick up the biggest shipment of bud yet. Five, six hundred pounds. Worth close to three million dollars to them. Instead of making the usual drop, I stashed it where nobody'll ever find it. Figured that would put a big fat hole in all their plans. That's when they started hunting me."

"How'd they know about Lily on the island?"

"Lily's baby developed some kind of allergy to her milk. Made him break out in terrible hives. I told Lily she needed to start bottle-feeding him. Near broke her heart, but she understood. I sent Sonny to get some formula and bottles and nipples and stuff, and he wasn't careful about who saw him. Word must've got back to Hornett, and he got to Sonny. I figure they did to him pretty much what they did to Lily. Probably forced him to show them the way to the island, then finished the job and dumped his body in the lake. After that, they started in on Lily."

Smalldog had the darkened skin of the Anishinaabeg people, but Cork saw it grow darker as the Shinnob spoke. The man's voice became taut as he fought to control his rage. "She couldn't tell them where I was. I've got a place no one knows about. I don't know how she kept the baby from falling into their hands."

"She hid him," Cork said. "And my daughter found him."

"She died without giving him away." Smalldog's eyes, like hot stones, fell on Bascombe. "Now everyone who had a hand in that butchery dies."

"I had nothing to do with what happened to Chickaway or your sister, I swear," Bascombe said. "I didn't know those people were capable of that kind of thing. Christ, they're nuts, but they call themselves Christians, don't they?"

Anne asked, "Did you ever study the Inquisition, Seth?"

"Not all of them could do that kind of thing," Sarah said. "I don't believe Josh could. He doesn't have the guts. But Abigail does."

"Why do you say that?" Cork asked.

"Because she's just like the Reverend. Obsessed. She absolutely believes everything they stand for. End Times and Satan's armies and that anything done in the name of the Second Coming is justified. If you're not one of them, you're on the side of Satan. Black and white. Good and evil. Right and wrong. She can't see it any other way. Even Gabriel's not so bad. He delivers the fiery sermons these days, but she's the power behind the church. Whatever was done to Lily, if Abigail didn't do it herself, she was there making sure it was done right. She's pure hate in human form."

Cork looked to Bascombe. "You said they're on their way here?"

Bascombe shrugged. "I radioed them from Kretsch's boat."

"It's me they want," Smalldog said. "I'll be happy to greet 'em."

"They're coming prepared for all-out war," Bascombe said. "God's on their side. They won't stop with killing just you. They'll kill everybody here. There's more to this than you know."

"What do you mean?" Cork said.

"If I tell you everything, will you let me go?"

"Go where?" Cork said. "We have enough to hang you no matter where you go."

"Let me take him out back," Smalldog said. "In five minutes, he'll tell me everything he knows, I guarantee it."

"No!" Rose and Anne spoke together.

"Tell you what," Cork said. "Give us everything you've got, and we'll speak on your behalf to the authorities when this is over."

"Gee, thanks," Bascombe said.

"Or, maybe I will let Smalldog here take you out back. Or better yet, I'll just put you out in front of us as a human shield when those Seven Trumpets folks arrive. I'll give you odds they won't hesitate a minute to cut you down to get to us."

Bascombe thought it over quickly. "Is that a promise, that you'll speak up for me if we get out of this alive?"

"I give you my word," Cork replied solemnly.

"Okay. They got huge debts because of all those projects on Stump Island. The Citadel," Bascombe said derisively. "They need the money from the bud Smalldog stole. But they know that, even if they have him in their hands, he won't give them a thing. So Abigail wants the baby. She'll be willing to skin that child alive if that's what it takes to get Smalldog to talk."

"She'll never find him," Rose said.

Bascombe swung his gaze to her, and everyone in the room could see the dismal truth even before he said a word.

"You told them," Cork said. "You told them about Meloux."

"That doesn't matter, does it?" Anne threw in. "They don't have the slightest idea how to get to Henry's cabin. And nobody on the rez is going to tell them."

Bascombe took a deep breath, the kind Cork had sometimes heard coming from the confessional in St. Agnes while he waited his turn.

"The ice chest I filled with bedding?" Bascombe finally said. "I cut a little chamber in the bottom and put in a long-range GPS tracker. Wherever that ice chest goes, they'll follow. It'll lead them right to the kid."

For a long moment, it was as if they'd all become stone. No one spoke or moved or even breathed. Then Cork said, "How many?"

"Abigail and her two sons headed out in their boat last night."

"The fast boat?" Cork asked.

"Yeah. You thought it was Smalldog. Christ, you think his is the only cigarette boat on this lake?"

Cork realized he'd been so narrowly focused on Smalldog that he'd never considered another possibility. He kicked himself for it, but what was done was done.

"Anyone else?" he asked.

"Two more took a boat to the Angle and drove to the south end of the big water to meet them."

"Five," Cork said. "Heavily armed, I'm sure."

"You got that right," Bascombe said.

"We have to get word to them," Kretsch said. "Was that true, Seth, what you told us about your phone line being cut?"

Bascombe nodded.

"Use the radio on your boat to contact the mainland," Cork suggested.

Kretsch gave Bascombe a killing look. "After he radioed Seven Trumpets, he smashed the unit."

"Then we use the one on Seth's boat."

Bascombe shook his head. "I took the battery out of my boat this afternoon. Didn't want anyone leaving the island. The Seven Trumpets people'll be here before we get it back in and hooked up."

"Then we have to get to the Angle," Cork said.

"No time," Bascombe said. "They'll be here any minute."

Kretsch said, "With the men and firepower they'll bring, we won't stand a chance. Maybe we could make it over to the Angle Inn Lodge."

"That's a good half mile away. And even if we made it there, these Seven Trumpets people are willing to kill all of us," Cork said. "Do you think they'd hesitate to mow down your neighbors, too?"

"Overturf," Smalldog said.

Cork shot him a questioning look.

"Jim Overturf," Kretsch said, and it was clear he understood.

"Who's this Overturf?"

"A mixed blood. Lives on Windigo Island," Smalldog replied. "He has a floatplane he uses to take fishermen to remote sites. If you can get to him, he can fly you off the lake."

"Heck, he could fly you all the way to this Henry Meloux you talk about," Kretsch said.

"Okay," Smalldog said. "This is how it goes. You all head out the back way and across the island and take the deputy's boat. They won't be looking for you there."

"What about you?" Anne said.

"I'll give the Seven Trumpets people plenty to think about here, keep them occupied while you make it to Windigo."

"We can't just leave you," Rose said.

"I'm not staying alone," Smalldog told her. He looked toward Bascombe. "This son of a bitch is staying with me."

"Wait a minute," Bascombe objected. "What do you need me for?"

"You're going to go out on your dock and greet your Seven Trumpets friends and do whatever song and dance you can to delay them while these folks make it to the deputy's boat."

"Yeah, says who?"

Smalldog held out his hands to Cork. "Take these cuffs off me."

Cork drew the key from his pocket and freed the Shinnob.

"Give me your rifle."

Cork hesitated.

"You have to decide who's on your side," Smalldog told him. "And you don't have much time."

"Give it to him, Cork," Rose said. "I believe him."

"She's right," Mal said.

Cork handed the Marlin to Smalldog, who took the weapon and leveled the barrel at Bascombe. "Want to argue with me now?"

"Christ, they'll shoot me down like a dog," Bascombe said.

"Maybe they will and maybe they won't. You're pretty good at putting yourself in the middle of things. Let's see how good you are at getting yourself out."

"I'm staying, too," Tom Kretsch said.

Smalldog shook his head. "Overturf knows you. You've got to convince him to help these folks."

"They can go to Amos Powassin. He'll help them."

"I'm not leaving you men here," Cork said. He hated the thought of deserting them. He was pretty sure that, if they stayed behind, there wasn't much hope they'd come out of their encounter with Seven Trumpets in one piece.

"Go," the deputy ordered, with all the authority of the law. "There's no time to argue."

"I can't just run out on you," Cork insisted.

Smalldog looked at him, for the first time with something resembling affection. "The man who threw rocks at me and wouldn't back down, that's the man I want standing between the Hornetts and my sister's baby. And you got a daughter to think about, too. I'll feel a whole lot more comfortable sticking here if you go."

"Goes for me, too," Kretsch said.

Every instinct in Cork cried out to argue with them, but he knew they were right. His duty lay elsewhere now. As much as he hated leaving these two good men to their uncertain fate, he hated more the thought of what might happen at Henry Meloux's cabin on Crow Point if he couldn't find a way to intervene.

"Bascombe." Smalldog eyed the big man. "You do your best to help get these folks away from Lake of the Woods, and I'll do my best to cover your back while you're out on the dock. You do anything to screw it up, though, and you're dead, I promise you that."

"Someone cut me loose," Kretsch said.

He held out his duct-taped wrists.

Cork used Smalldog's knife to free the deputy, who grabbed the second rifle.

"Thank you," Cork said.

He wanted to take a precious moment to shake their hands, but from the lake outside came the engine rumble of boats approaching.

"Go," Kretsch said. "Get the hell out of here."

And they did—Rose and Anne and Sarah and Mal and Cork—hurried out the back door of the cabin, across the apron of grass, and into the woods. They hit the trail at a lope, Mal grunting every time he put weight on his injured ankle, but he kept up, and the trees quickly swallowed them.

They were almost to the little cove where Kretsch's boat lay anchored when they heard the first of the shots far behind them. A moment later came the rattle of automatic weapons fire.

Rose whispered, loud enough for Cork to hear, "God be with them." Then he heard her add, "God be with them all."

FORTY-SEVEN

It was late afternoon in Tamarack County, Minnesota. On Crow Point, the shadow of the rock outcropping that walled Meloux's fire ring stretched across the green meadow grass. The forest that edged the clearing had become murky as the daylight grew pale in the elongated slant of the sun. There was not a breath of wind. The water of Iron Lake was so perfect a mirror that, whenever Jenny looked there, it was as if she saw two skies.

She and Rainy had spent the past couple of hours preparing dinner, a savory stew made of herbs and venison and vegetables, which filled the cabin with a delectable aroma. Rainy had baked bread as well, something the new stove facilitated. Waaboo lay in the ice chest on the floor, and Jenny made certain that when he was awake he could see her. He seemed perfectly content watching.

Walleye seemed restless, occasionally rising from the floor to pad around the cabin and sniff the air. In that room, Jenny thought it would be impossible to pick up any scent except the wonderful smell of the stew.

"They're coming," Rainy said.

She was looking out the east window toward a stand of aspen that ran along the shoreline of Crow Point. Jenny stood next to her and saw them returning, Aaron in the lead, with Stephen and Henry Meloux many paces back. Stephen carried the old Mide's beaded bandolier bag. In his right hand, Meloux held a long walking stick, and he seemed to lean on it significantly as he made his way across the meadow to the cabin. Jenny went out to greet them, and Walleye tagged along.

"You were gone a long time," she said to Aaron.

"I think we walked every inch of the Superior National Forest." He smiled as if he'd actually enjoyed it.

"How was Henry?" she asked in a quiet voice.

"One tired old man," he said. "But he kept pushing himself. A lot to admire there. And, Christ, I've never met anyone who knows so much about everything around him, and I'm not just talking about the woods. I swear, the minute I think something, he looks at me as if I spoke it out loud. Spooky."

"My dad says that Meloux reads people, everything about them. Their eyes and faces and hands, how they hold themselves and walk and speak. He says even the silence of people tells Henry a lot."

They stood together, waiting, and in a few moments, Stephen and Meloux caught up, with Walleye beside them.

"We got some great mushrooms," Stephen said. "A ton of morels. I figured they'd all be gone by now, but Henry knows where to look."

"And now you do, too," the old man said.

"*Migwech, mishomis,*" Stephen said.

"I have been thinking about that mattress on my bunk for the last two miles," Henry said.

He nodded to Jenny and went ahead with Stephen, and they both entered the cabin. Walleye started inside, then stopped and turned back and stared at the woods on the far side of the meadow, sniffing the air.

Aaron stood looking at the grass beneath his feet. "I think it's true. Silence says a lot. I've been tight-lipped lately, I know. This whole thing with Waaboo has had me pretty confused."

Jenny was pleased to hear him use the name, pleased that

the baby was someone to him now, not just an inconvenient circumstance.

He lifted his eyes and looked at her with sad determination. "Jenny, I've been doing a lot of thinking, and there are some things I need to say."

"I'm listening."

He took a deep breath and spoke somberly. "My parents never wanted me. They never wanted a child. Their lives were all about them, and mostly I was an inconvenience. That was a sad truth. But the sadder truth is that I've grown up to be just like them. My life's all about me. I could never look at Waaboo the way you do. The kinds of sacrifices you make without thinking twice I could never make." He stopped and took her hands, and she could feel him trembling. "I can't be what you want me to be, Jenny. I'd be a selfish husband and such a bad father that I don't even want to try. Whatever you decide about Waaboo, you need to decide it without me in the picture. I love you, but I can't do this. Do you understand?"

They stood together a moment, the quiet between them uncomfortable and weighty.

"I hope you get your baby," he finished.

She thought maybe she should feel as if she'd fallen off a cliff, but she didn't. She felt strangely free and wasn't quite sure what she should say. What came to her was simply this: "Thank you, Aaron." And delicately she kissed his cheek.

At the cabin doorway, Walleye let out a low woof and started barking again, wildly this time, coming up off his front paws as he snapped. In a minute, Meloux stepped from the cabin. Stephen and Rainy were right behind him.

"What is it?" Jenny asked.

"I don't know," the old man said. He peered toward the woods. "It's been a long time since my eyes saw what they ought to. Stephen, do you see anything?"

Stephen stepped forward and studied the trees. "There," he said and pointed.

Jenny followed the line his finger indicated across the

meadow. In the pallid, late afternoon light, the grass was tall and yellow-green. Where the meadow met the pine woods, a dark, sharp line of shade lay. The forest beyond that line was deep and brooding, and the shadows there were thick and almost impenetrable. Then she saw what Stephen saw.

"It's a woman," she said.

"What is she doing?" Meloux asked.

"Just standing there," Stephen replied. "Looking at us."

Walleye's barking had grown furious. He charged forward and came back and charged again. He was an old dog, but in his fierce and protective fury, he had become young again.

"There is more in those woods than a woman," Meloux said. "Walleye may not see much better than me, but his nose is still good. Into the cabin, everyone."

They quickly retreated inside. Meloux crossed to the wall where a rifle lay cradled in a rack. He took the rifle down and said to Rainy, "The box in the cupboard. There are cartridges."

She opened a door and pulled out a small, beautifully carved wooden box. She lifted the lid and spilled the contents into the palm of her hand: six cartridges. She looked down at them, then up at Meloux, and asked, "Uncle Henry, when was the last time you fired that old Winchester?"

He worked the lever and pulled the trigger and said, "It will fire just fine."

"It's not the rifle I'm worried about," she said and held out her hand to him. "These rounds look pretty old."

"They will have to do," he said. One by one, he took the cartridges from her palm and fed them into the rifle's magazine.

"Now wait a minute," Aaron said. "Before we go off half-cocked and shoot an innocent someone, I think we should talk to this woman. Maybe she's Ojibwe and is coming to you for advice? Or maybe she's just a lost hiker or something. Hell, maybe she's not even there anymore."

"She's there," Stephen said from the window. "And she gives me the creeps."

Meloux started toward the window. In the middle of the

room, however, he stopped and stood dead still as if paralyzed. Jenny was afraid that he might be suffering a stroke. But a kind of light had come into his face, and she saw his body change, straighten, draw erect. She watched a new spirit enter him. What had been a thin construct of flesh and quivering muscle and brittle bone became sturdy and strong. As if it were an actual stream of substance, vitality filled Henry Meloux.

"Ah," he said.

"What is it, Uncle Henry?" Rainy asked.

He put out his right hand, and it held steady in the air. "No trembling."

"I don't understand," Rainy said.

"Neither did I, Niece. But it is clear to me now."

"What are you talking about?"

"The problem and its answer are out there in the woods," he said.

"I don't understand what you mean, Uncle Henry?"

"I believe that you will, Niece," he said. "Very soon."

"This is crazy," Aaron said. "I'm going out to talk to her."

"She will not talk," the old man said. "She is here for one purpose. To bring death." He looked down at the ice chest, where the baby lay watching Jenny with quiet intent.

"Is it Noah Smalldog?" Jenny said. "He's found us?"

"That's not Smalldog. It's a woman, for God sake," Aaron said. "Henry, you point that rifle at anyone, and there will be hell to pay. Look, you all just wait here. I'll go talk to her and clear this whole thing up."

"No, Aaron. Please don't go." Jenny grabbed his arm.

"It's all right. Really. You'll see."

"Henry," Jenny pleaded.

"It is a mistake to go," the old Mide said to Aaron. "But if it is to be done, then I will do it."

"It's my idea," Aaron said stubbornly. "I'll go. You stay here with the others. If you're right, they'll need someone who knows how to shoot that thing." He smiled indulgently, gave Jenny a kiss on the cheek, opened the door, and walked out.

"What do we do, Henry?" Jenny asked desperately.

"We honor his wish." The old man knelt at the open, screen-less window and laid the rifle across the sill. "And we cover his back."

They gathered behind Meloux and watched Aaron cross the meadow toward the woman, who stood just inside the shadow of the trees.

"He's right, Henry," Jenny said, trying to convince herself. "I'm sure she's just a lost hiker, like he said."

The old man didn't reply. He gripped the rifle, laid his wrinkled cheek against the stock, and sighted.

FORTY-EIGHT

Overturf flew a legendary bush plane, a De Havilland Beaver. Rigged as a floatplane, it had a maximum airspeed of 155 miles per hour. The distance from Windigo Island to Iron Lake was almost two hundred air miles. Under normal circumstances, it would have been a beautiful flight over lovely wilderness scenery and would have seemed relatively brief. But to Cork, every mile felt like ten, and every minute like an eternity.

They'd done as Kretsch suggested, gone to Amos Powassin for help. He'd listened, then had called Overturf and said what he needed. He'd told them where on Windigo Island they would find Overturf's place. They'd found it without any problem; the De Havilland on the water was a dead giveaway. They'd docked, and as they approached, a young collie who'd been drowsing in the porch shade of the little yellow house had scrambled to his feet and began a furious racket.

"Ojibwe burglar alarm," Cork had said, and they'd waited in the yard until the front door opened and a man stepped out. He was big and wore a ball cap and wrinkled khakis held up by red suspenders. He had on a green T-shirt with a NASCAR logo across the front, faded but unmistakable. He'd stood very still, studying them. Finally he'd said something to the dog, who'd ceased barking and sat on his haunches. The man had lifted his arm and beckoned and hollered, "You the folks Amos called about?"

He had already gassed the De Havilland, and they'd flown out immediately. He'd taken them high over Oak Island. There were four boats still at the dock, Bascombe's launch and three others, but of the men who'd stayed behind—Tom Kretsch and Noah Smalldog and Seth Bascombe—or of those who'd come from Stump Island, nothing could be seen. And if there was yet gunfire, it couldn't be heard over the sound of the De Havilland's engine.

"Look there," Overturf had said.

He'd pointed toward half a dozen boats speeding across the lake from the direction of Windigo and Little Windigo. In the blue water, all had left wakes that fanned out behind them like the white tail feathers of eagles flying in formation.

"Amos Powassin spread the word," he'd told them. "Bunch of our guys are heading over to Oak Island to give Smalldog and that deputy a hand."

"If they're still alive," Anne had said.

"Listen," Overturf had offered. "If I could choose any man to have at my side in a firefight, it'd be Noah Smalldog. And Tom Kretsch, he's got heart. The Seven Trumpets people'll have their hands full, believe me."

Cork wasn't himself much inclined toward hope, but he appreciated the man's sentiment, and the effect his words seemed to have on Anne and the others.

Now they were nearing the south end of the big water. Overturf radioed the Lake of the Woods County Sheriff's Department. He was told that, in response to a frantic 911 call from Young's Bay Landing, units had been dispatched to the Angle. Cork got on the radio and explained the danger in Tamarack County. He asked that the sheriff's office there be notified; it was imperative that armed officers be sent to Crow Point on the Iron Lake Ojibwe Reservation. The dispatcher gave him over to a deputy named Spicer, who listened as Cork once more told the bare-bones facts. Spicer, God bless him, gave a ten-four and promised to make the call to Aurora. He came back on the radio a few minutes later and confirmed for Cork that the Tamarack County's Critical Incident Response Team was being mobilized. Then he said, "They tried the cell phone number you gave me for Rainy Bisonette. No answer. They'll keep trying. And listen, O'Connor, you've got friends down there. Sheriff Dross personally asked me to let you know she's got every available officer headed to Crow Point."

Cork signed off and sat back in the seat next to Overturf.

The pilot leaned to him and said, "I'll get you there as fast as I can. Believe me, even if all I've got to land on at the other end is a puddle of rainwater, by God, I can do that."

"Thanks," Cork said. "Guess there's nothing more we can do except wait." He tried to sound calm, but the helplessness of his situation nearly killed him.

Anne put a hand on his shoulder. "That's not true, Dad."

Rose, as if she'd read her niece's mind, said, "We can pray."

Cork wanted to be with them in the way they held to prayer and believed in its power. But he was remembering the death of his wife and how hard he'd prayed for her safety and the uselessness, finally, of invoking the divine. Better, he thought, to believe in the wisdom and cunning of Meloux and the desperate ingenuity of Jenny and Rainy and Stephen and even the clumsy love of Aaron.

Best, he thought, would have been to be there with them at that very moment, holding a rifle.

FORTY-NINE

They watched from the cabin as Aaron crossed the two hundred yards of meadow. The sun was low in the sky, the late afternoon windless and still. Crow Point was silent, as if all the birds had fled. Jenny forced herself to breathe.

"He'll be all right," she whispered. But her words felt heavy and useless.

Meloux kept his cheek to the rifle stock. Jenny was grateful to see how steadily he held the weapon.

Aaron reached the woman, and they appeared to talk for a minute. Then he made a gesture toward the cabin and turned, and they began to walk back together. Jenny saw Meloux shift the barrel of the rifle a bit and realized he'd been aiming directly at the woman but was now scanning the woods at her back. It wasn't until they were within fifty yards that the old man drew the rifle out of the window. He stood, went to the cabin door, and opened it. He didn't go out, nor did he set the rifle aside.

Aaron smiled as he came up to the cabin, just ahead of the woman. He stepped inside, and she followed. "Folks, meet Abigail. She's a little lost."

Jenny judged the woman to be in her late fifties, with short hair gone gray. She was lean and muscular, as if from hard work or working out regularly. Her face was thin and plain, the bone beneath sharply defined. She had eyes that were glacier blue, and those eyes were clearly appraising her hosts. It could have been simply a stranger attempting wisely to take the measure of the group before trusting herself to them, but Jenny sensed something terribly unsettling in their intensity.

"I was out hiking with my husband," the woman explained. "He went off looking for mushrooms, and we got separated. Now I don't have the slightest idea where he is, or where I am, for that matter. Frankly, I'm a little worried."

Jenny said, "You're not from around here."

"No." The woman's eyes froze on her. "From Michigan. My sister lives in Duluth. We're visiting." Her icy gaze left Jenny and took in the cabin, settling at last on little Waaboo lying quietly in the cooler. "I wonder if anybody has a cell phone I could use to call my husband."

"I would have given her mine," Aaron said, "but I'm not getting any signal out here."

"Mine works," Rainy said. She went to a crocheted bag hanging on the wall and dug inside. She pulled out a cell phone, powered it on, and handed it to the woman. "It can be hit and miss, but I usually get a bar, even this far out."

"Do you mind if I take it outside and make the call?"

"No, go right ahead."

The woman stepped from the cabin and walked a few yards into the meadow.

"You see?" Aaron said. "A perfectly normal explanation. Henry, I think you can put that rifle down now."

Meloux made no move to comply.

The forgotten stew bubbled over and sizzled on the hot stove top. The sound caught them all by surprise, and they turned for a moment from the door.

"Where's my head?" Rainy said and hurried to move the pot to a cooler place at the edge of the stove.

The woman returned and stood just outside the cabin. "Thank you. He's on his way." She held out the cell phone toward Rainy. "There's a creek back in the woods. He's coming from there."

"Wine Creek," Rainy said, taking back her cell phone.

"The Anishinaabeg call it *Miskwi*," Stephen threw in, "which means 'blood.' "

That brought an arch to the woman's eyebrows. "Interesting," she said.

Stephen looked beyond her and pointed. "There he is."

A man stood at the edge of the woods on the path that Jenny and the others had taken the night before. He lifted an arm to signal his presence, and the woman said, "Thanks so much for your help. I was afraid I might wander these woods forever."

"The path will take you back to the county road," Stephen said. "It's less than two miles."

The woman looked inside the cabin, eyed the cooler where Waaboo lay, and her voice, which had been generally pleasant, suddenly took on a razor edge. "In old times, children with cleft lips were believed to be the spawn of Satan."

Jenny went rigid and replied, none too hospitably, "Fortunately, we live in a more enlightened age."

"Yes," the woman said. "Fortunately." She turned and walked across the meadow toward the waiting man.

For Jenny, the woman had left a sourness behind, and she asked Rainy, "Who did she call? Can you tell?"

"Her husband," Rainy said, without looking.

"Could you check the number?"

Rainy clearly believed it was unnecessary, but she tapped her phone to power it on, then tapped again. "It's dead," she said with surprise. "But I charged it just two days ago and that's the first call that's been made on it since."

"Let me see." Aaron took the phone, tapped a few keys, then slipped the battery cover off. "The battery's gone," he said. "But she left this." From the compartment, he pulled a piece of paper folded several times. He carefully opened it and read, "Give us the baby or you all die. Middle of the meadow. Fifteen minutes."

He glanced out the door at the figure of the woman retreating across the clearing and seemed stunned. "Who is she?"

"Whoever she is, she's not getting Waaboo," Jenny said.

As soon as the woman joined the man on the far side of the clearing, two more figures stepped from the woods. They all held large rifles.

"Over there," Stephen said, indicating the rock outcropping that walled the fire ring. "Somebody's there, too."

Jenny saw him, standing atop the rocks, cradling a big firearm.

Meloux said firmly, "You will all go out the back window. Take the canoe, Niece. *Bimaadiziwin.*"

"What about you, Uncle Henry?"

The old man stood tall and shook his head. "This is the moment I have been preparing for, Niece. The trembling, the resistance. My body and my spirit understood long ago. My brain has been slow to catch up, but I understand now."

"What is it, Henry?" Jenny asked.

"Great death is in those woods," he said calmly. "My death, I think, is coming."

"No, Henry!" Stephen said.

The old man smiled. "It is no great thing, Stephen. We all walk the Path of Souls someday. I am ready. And if, before I make this journey, I can do a last good thing, that would please me greatly. Go, and I will keep them here until you are safe."

"Henry—" Stephen began.

"Go now," the old man said, sternly this time. "Take the child and go. *Bimaadiziwin,* Niece. You know the way."

Jenny hated the thought of leaving Meloux alone. She had no idea who these people were or why they wanted her child, but she understood absolutely they were the ones who had tortured and killed Waaboo's mother. They wouldn't hesitate to do the same to an old Indian. But Waaboo was her concern, and Meloux had offered the exchange of his life for the safety of the child and them all, and she would honor that gift and be grateful. She lifted the ice chest.

"This is crazy," Aaron said.

"Don't argue, damn it," Jenny said.

Rainy had lifted the pane of the back window, which overlooked the tip of Crow Point. The shore, no more than twenty yards distant, was lined with aspens.

"Wait," the old Mide said. He moved to the west window that looked toward the fire ring. He knelt and laid the rifle barrel on the sill. Carefully, he took aim at the man on the rocks. He breathed quietly and squeezed the trigger. The hammer fell with a click, but the round did not fire.

In the wake of the failed shot, Jenny felt dread fill the silence of that small room.

Meloux worked the lever, ejecting the bad round and sliding another into the breech. He took careful aim, breathed again, and drew his trigger finger back. The crack of the rifle startled Jenny, startled them all, including Waaboo, who began to wail.

"Now," Meloux said fiercely. "Go now."

They went through the window quickly. At their backs, the crackle of rifle fire broke out, and Jenny heard the shatter of window glass and the chunk of bullets embedded in the thick logs of the cabin's front wall. The noise of the gunfire was a good thing because it covered the sound of Waaboo's cries.

They ran single file down a path worn between the aspens to the shoreline of Iron Lake, where a wooden canoe lay tipped. Two wooden paddles leaned against the hull. Rainy grabbed the stern and Stephen took the bow. They waded into the water and, together, righted the canoe, settled it on the lake, and steadied it for the others. Jenny put the ice chest and Waaboo in the center between the two thwarts, then climbed in behind. Aaron took his place in front of the ice chest. Paddle in hand, Stephen clambered into the bow, while Rainy did the same in the stern.

"We'll keep close to the shoreline," Rainy called to Stephen. "The trees will give us cover. We're going about a mile east." She dipped her paddle and stroked hard, and Stephen followed her lead.

Under a sky that was a brooding blue with the approach of evening, they left Crow Point and cut over the glassy surface of the lake, leaving the gunfire behind and headed, Jenny dearly hoped, for safety.

FIFTY

Bimaadiziwin. It was an Ojibwe word, Jenny knew, but she had no idea of its meaning. Whatever it was, this was where Rainy was guiding their canoe.

In the bow, Stephen stroked powerfully, and Jenny marveled at his strength. She'd always thought of him as just her little brother, but in this terrible business, he'd conducted himself with courage and resolve, and now, to a degree, her life and the life of Waaboo were in his hands. In that moment, she loved him more than she ever had.

At her back, she could hear the dip and occasional splash of Rainy's paddle, and feel the glide of the blade whenever the older woman ruddered to bring the canoe to a new heading. This was a woman who, until last night, had been only a name to her. Now she was friend, ally, savior, meeting Stephen's every stroke with her own, speeding the canoe away from the gunfire on Crow Point, doing her damndest to save Waaboo, to save them all.

The baby had grown quiet, soothed, Jenny guessed, by the motion of the canoe. Her father had once told her that, in the old days of the Anishinaabeg, when a baby could not be calmed, a canoe ride was a well-known cure.

"There it is," Rainy said.

Jenny looked where Rainy pointed, toward a gray wall of rock on the shoreline. The cliff rose a hundred feet above the lake. A quarter of the way up, across its face, grew thick black-berry bramble.

"I don't see anything," Stephen called back.

"A cave, behind the blackberry bushes. We'll pull up to the right. There's a kind of landing and some natural stairs in the rock."

Rainy guided the canoe to the south end of the cliff, and just as she'd said, there was a narrow shelf above the waterline. Rugged, natural stair steps led up toward the blackberry brambles. None of this was obvious, and if you didn't know it was there, you'd have easily missed it. Stephen stepped out of the canoe and held the bow while the others disembarked. Last of all, Jenny lifted out the ice chest.

"Listen," Stephen said.

Aaron cocked his head. "I don't hear anything."

"Exactly," Stephen said darkly. "No more gunfire."

They all exchanged glances, but no one said a word of what they were thinking.

"I'll hide the canoe," Aaron volunteered. "In that inlet over there. Then I'll join you."

"Do you know how to paddle?" Stephen asked.

"I spent five summers at Camp Winn-eh-bego. I can braid a lanyard, too."

"Just follow the stairs behind the brambles," Rainy told him. "You'll find us."

Aaron stepped back into the stern of the canoe, wrapped his hands around the paddle, and took off for the small inlet, which lay a hundred yards south.

By the time Rainy led the way up the cliff, the sun was low in the sky. Its rays glanced off Iron Lake and lit the face of the rock with intense brilliance. They brushed against their own shadows as they climbed, and it seemed to Jenny that they were being paced by a column of specters, of the dark and the doomed, and she tried to thrust that thought from her. At the brambles, they had to press themselves hard against the cliff and edge their way carefully in order to avoid the thorns. Then Rainy bent and disappeared. A moment later, Jenny came abreast of the opening. She laid the ice chest on the floor of the cave mouth, and Rainy grabbed hold and pulled it inside. Jenny crawled in after, and Stephen followed.

Except for the sunlight that lay at the opening, the cave was dark, and it took a few moments for Jenny's eyes to adjust. The floor sloped down toward the entrance, so that any water that might have found its way in would have quickly drained. The chamber was small, fifteen feet in diameter, and edged with rock shelves. On the shelves lay many items, some that appeared to be quite old. Jenny could see no rhyme or reason to what had been placed there: a bow made of hard maple with a deer-hide quiver full of arrow shafts whose featherings had long ago turned to dust; a colorfully beaded bandolier bag; a rag doll; a muzzle-loader with a rotted stock and beside it a powder horn, still in good condition; a woven blanket; a coil of rope. There were knives and a tomahawk and what looked to be a collection of human scalps. There was, however, one item she recognized: a rolled bearskin. It had belonged to her father, but a few years ago had disappeared from the house.

"What is this place?" she asked.

"*Bimaadiziwin*. It means 'healthy living.' A healthy way of life."

"What are all these things?"

"Symptoms of sickness," Rainy said.

"What do you mean?" Stephen said.

"These are the symptoms of illness in some people," Rainy said. "These are symbols of the burdens that they could no longer bear and that made them sick, in body and in spirit. Hate. Anger. Revenge. Jealousy. Even love, I suppose. These things, these are reminders of what they hoped to leave behind in this place. They wanted to lead a different kind of life, an unburdened life, a life of wholeness and spiritual health."

"Hoped to leave?" Stephen said.

"There's powerful energy here," Rainy replied. "But even

that power can't work unless the desire to be healed and whole is sincere. That's what Uncle Henry has told me anyway."

Jenny wondered what sickness it was that her father, in leaving the rolled bearskin, was trying to heal.

"Henry," Stephen said, and his voice was only a wisp of a whisper and full of sadness. "Do you think he's really . . ."

Jenny thought that her brother could not finish.

But Stephen drew himself up and said, "Do you think he's on the Path of Souls now?"

"I don't know," Rainy said. "But if so, he was prepared to make that journey."

Waaboo began to fuss, and Jenny picked him up from the bedding in the ice chest. "He's hungry," she said. "I wish I had a bottle."

They heard a rustling from outside and froze. All except Waaboo, who'd begun to flail his arms and legs and emit unhappy little squeals. A moment later, the sunlight that filled the cave opening was eclipsed.

"You in there?" Aaron asked.

"Come in," Rainy said. "It's a little tight, but we'll fit."

Aaron crawled in, dripping wet.

"There's no way to get to that little landing except by canoe or swimming," he explained. "The lake's pretty chilly. I hope we don't have to hide out here for long."

Stephen shot his hand up, signaling them to be quiet. Again, they all held still, except Waaboo, who was becoming more vocal in his insistence on being fed. From outside the cave and somewhere above them came voices. Angry men.

"I don't know, but the signal was coming from somewhere around here. Then it was gone," one of the voices said.

"There's nothing here, Josh. Unless they jumped off the cliff."

Waaboo fussed, and the sound seemed huge in the small cave and in its consequences. Jenny offered him her little finger as a pacifier, and she was thankful when he took it.

Please, God, she prayed, *let him be quiet.*

"They're here somewhere," the first voice said. "We'll find them."

In the cave, they barely breathed.

"How did they follow us?" Stephen whispered.

A question to which no one had an answer.

Waaboo pulled away, maybe sensing all the tension, and let out a cry.

God, please, Jenny prayed and slipped the tip of her little finger back into his mouth.

Stephen leaned near the opening of the cave. "They're still above us," he whispered.

Aaron went to his hands and knees and crawled toward the opening. "I'm going out there."

"No," Jenny said.

"I'll try to lead them away."

"Aaron, don't."

"I'll be okay. Never told you this, but I was a champion hurdler in high school." He kissed the top of her head, then crept into the cave mouth and slipped outside.

A moment later, Jenny heard a splash in the water.

"There! See him?"

"Yeah, come on."

For several minutes, everything was quiet. Waaboo had settled, and Jenny hoped desperately that Aaron was successful and safe.

Then the evening stillness outside was shattered by gunshots. Several of them. Rainy took Jenny's hand. Stephen put his head into the cave mouth and listened. They held that way for several minutes more.

Stephen drew back suddenly, and Jenny understood immediately why. She heard the scrape of boots on the rock face outside and the rustle of blackberry brambles.

Let it be Aaron, she prayed.

"All right, you have a choice," came a voice from the mouth of the cave. "You can come out, or we'll just spray the inside of this place with bullets. You have ten seconds to decide."

They exchanged looks, and Jenny saw in the eyes of the others exactly what she felt, too: sudden and complete despair at the inevitability of what lay ahead.

"Wait," Rainy said, in a tired voice. "We're coming."

One by one, they crawled out, Stephen first, then Jenny with Waaboo, and finally Rainy. Two men stood outside, one on either side of the cave opening, each holding a powerful-looking rifle.

"All right, Josh is going to lead the way," said the man to Jenny's right. It was his voice she'd heard before. He was tall, with a sharp jaw, long nose, and eyes as blue as a cold winter sky. "You folks just follow him. And if you try anything, I'll put a bullet through you as surely as I'm standing here."

"Aaron?" Jenny asked.

"Your boyfriend?" said the man with the cold blue eyes. He shrugged. "Like shooting fish in a barrel."

FIFTY-ONE

Just before sunset, the De Havilland approached Iron Lake. From above, the expanse of water appeared smooth and shiny in the late afternoon light, and the irregular shoreline gave it the look of a ragged piece of gold lamé torn from a dress. Cork saw the jut of Crow Point far ahead, and as they approached, Overturf put his hand to his headset, then lifted the radio mike and spoke into it.

"I read you, Deputy."

He turned to Cork. "Says there's a hostage situation in progress down there. He wants us to land on the northwest side of the point, well away from where the cabin sits. He'll have somebody there to meet us."

"A hostage situation?" Rose said at Cork's back. "What does that mean?"

"I don't know," Cork replied. But it wasn't good.

Overturf brought the Beaver down smoothly onto the lake. A uniformed officer waved from the shore, and the pilot motored the plane to where he stood. Cork climbed out, and the others followed.

Overturf slid back the cockpit window and called, "I'll stay here with the plane, Deputy. You figure you need me in some way, just let me know."

"Ten-four, sir, and thank you." The deputy was George

Azevedo, a man Cork knew well. They shook hands, and Azevedo said, "This way."

"What's the situation, George?"

Azevedo spoke as they walked. "A standoff at the moment. As nearly as we can tell, your daughter and son and the baby are inside the cabin. We think that Meloux and his niece are inside as well, but that's unclear. How many of the bad guys are in there is also unclear. We've got the cabin surrounded, so no one's going anywhere. The sheriff and Captain Larson are trying to figure how to handle this. They'll be glad to see you, I expect."

They walked through the woods that edged the clearing until they came to the path that connected Crow Point with the county road. There they found Sheriff Marsha Dross and Captain Ed Larson, two of Cork's old friends. They'd been his subordinates when he was sheriff of Tamarack County years before. Dross was in her early forties, Cork's height, with a strong-boned look to her body. Like Azevedo and all the other officers present, she wore a blue Kevlar vest with TCSD stenciled on the back. In the cool evening light, he could see how drawn her face looked. The sheriff got immediately down to business.

"We have them contained, Cork, but that's about it at the moment. We're trying to get some communication established. So far, I've had no response with my bullhorn. I'd love to get an open line into that cabin."

"George told me you're sure that Stephen and Jenny and the baby are inside. True?" Cork asked.

"Deputy Pender was first on the scene," she explained. "He had instructions to wait before approaching the cabin and to observe and assess the situation until the rest of us arrived. He spotted several people coming along the eastern shoreline. He ID'd Stephen and Jenny. Hell, we all know them. A woman was part of the group—Rainy Bisonette, we believe, but haven't confirmed. Two armed men escorted them. The group entered the cabin before we had a chance to intercept.

"We were able to get two of our people into those rocks." She pointed through the trees toward the outcropping around

Meloux's fire ring. "My guys found a body there, a male shot through the right eye. Driver's license says his name is Able Denning. We're assuming he's one of the Seven Trumpets people. There's another body lying on the path through the meadow grass about fifty yards out from the tree line. Male and there's an assault rifle next to the body, so we believe it's also one of the Seven Trumpets group. After I gave them the first call with the bullhorn, one of them attempted to make it to the rocks where my guys are positioned. They let him come and tried to subdue him when he got there. He resisted and they took him out. According to his driver's license, he's one of the Hornetts. Gabriel. If what you told us is accurate and there were five people who came from Stump Island, then there are only two left. We've got them penned in, and they know it, but they won't respond to my attempts to communicate."

A man shot through the right eye. Cork knew that, before Meloux's hands began to tremble, the old Mide might still have been able to make such a difficult shot. But now?

"Any gunfire from the cabin?" he asked.

"No. Nothing but silence. Oh, by the way, we've got an update from the Northwest Angle. Before the Lake of the Woods sheriff's people arrived, there'd been a significant exchange of gunfire on Oak Island between the Seven Trumpets people and some locals. There were casualties, but the situation's under control."

"Any ID on the casualties?"

"Not yet."

Cork, of necessity, put aside his concern over those they'd left behind on Oak Island, closed his eyes, and thought out loud. "Three men down. That means Abigail Hornett is still alive and inside, along with the last man from Seven Trumpets. Did Pender get a look at the two guys with Jenny and Stephen?"

"Yeah. Black hair, lanky, maybe six feet. Once we ID'd Gabriel Hornett, Pender confirmed that he'd been one of the men. Pender also said the other guy looked a lot like him."

"Joshua Hornett, his brother."

"Real soldiers of God," Ed Larson said. The first words he'd spoken, and it was as ·if he'd spit. He was a man nearing sixty, slender and with grayed temples. He wore wire rims. Although he headed up major crimes investigation for the Tamarack County Sheriff's Department, he looked as if he'd be more at home in a college classroom. "True believers. The worst kind."

"Gabriel Hornett, for sure," Cork said. "But from what I understand, not so much his brother, right, Sarah?"

Sarah Hornett stood by herself. Among the gathering of law officers, she'd looked helpless and a little dazed. When Cork spoke to her, she seemed grateful to be able to offer something.

"Joshua's not like the others," she told them. "He doesn't really believe all that crap. He's just weak and won't stand up to them. He scares pretty easy."

Anne and Rose and Mal stood near Cork. The two women held hands. Cork glanced at them, wanting to offer assurance, but at the moment, he had none.

"You have a plan?" he asked Dross, and then shot a look at Larson. Their too long delay in replying told him everything he needed to know.

"We've got a call into Bemidji BCA for a hostage negotiator," Larson said.

"It'll take hours for him to get here," Cork said. "And that'll only work if you can get those Seven Trumpets people talking."

What he was afraid of but didn't say because of the proximity of Anne and Rose was that in a situation like this, with Abigail Hornett, the truest of the believers, inside, she might well choose the road of martyrdom over negotiation, go out in a flame of religious fervor and a hail of bullets and take the hostages with her. She was the person probably responsible for the torture and murder of Lily Smalldog. God alone knew the full horror of her capabilities.

"Who's in the rocks?" he asked.

"Morgan and Pender."

That was good. Aside from Meloux when he'd been a young

man, Cork didn't know anyone who was better with a rifle than Howard Morgan.

"What did you issue Morgan?"

"The Remington M-Twenty-four."

"All right," Cork said, thinking fast. "Meloux's cabin has a window in the west wall. It looks out at the rocks where you've got Morgan and Pender. If we can get Abigail Hornett to the center of that room, Morgan'll have a good chance of taking her out."

"How do we do that?" Larson said. "If those two Seven Trumpets people have half a brain, they're not going to do anything that'll give us a clear shot."

"We leave that up to Meloux," Cork told him.

"If he's still alive," Larson said.

Which was a possibility Cork hadn't considered. And decided not to.

He explained what he had in mind and ended with "If it doesn't work, they won't be any worse off in that cabin than they are now."

But if they were lucky, he thought to himself, if God or Kitchimanidoo or simple luck were on their side, Jenny and Stephen and the others might have a chance.

"If Morgan is able to take out the woman, that still leaves one of the Seven Trumpets inside," Larson said.

"Cut off a snake's head and the body dies," Cork said. "It's Joshua Hornett with her. If what Sarah says is true, he's different from his mother. She's the head; he just follows."

"It's true," Sarah insisted.

Dross shook her head faintly, not convinced.

"Look, Marsha, those are my children in there, my friends," Cork argued. "And Abigail Hornett, she's already tortured and killed a young girl and was more than willing to skin that baby alive if it got her what she wanted. To her, they're all doomed anyway, all part of the army of Satan. And in her deranged thinking, she's the good guy. I believe she wouldn't hesitate to kill them all, negotiator or no. The sooner we get her out of the picture, the better chance we have of getting everyone else out of there alive. Believe me, Marsha."

He knew this was one of the most difficult decisions she'd ever had to make, but he was determined she would.

"Make the call," he said.

She looked toward the cabin and said mostly to herself, "If it doesn't work, they're no worse off."

"That's right," Cork agreed quietly, as if he were the voice of her conscience.

She turned to Larson. "Call Morgan," she said. "Explain it to him. Tell him to be ready to take the shot when the opportunity comes. Don't wait for our okay."

"There are two other women in there," Cork reminded Larson. "You tell Morgan to make absolutely certain of his target before he fires."

"He knows that," Larson said. He put a reassuring hand on Cork's shoulder, then moved away to make radio contact with Morgan.

The bullhorn sat on the ground at Dross's feet. She opened her hand toward it. "Your show, Cork."

FIFTY-TWO

As if prisoners of war, they'd been marched to the cabin, an armed man leading and another bringing up the rear. Jenny and Stephen held the ice chest between them with Waaboo cradled inside. He was quiet, which because of all the activity and tension, Jenny thought was odd. But she knew him well enough now to understand that he was a child who, more often than not, was perfectly content to observe.

They came to the clearing on Crow Point, and as they crossed the meadow, Jenny saw an outline of flattened wild grass and then saw the body that lay there.

"Keep moving," the man at her back ordered.

They approached the cabin, and everything inside her screamed not to enter. When they'd fled, Meloux had been alive. There'd been gunfire behind them, a lot of it, and then silence. Because these men had come for them despite Meloux's intervention, Jenny believed the fine old man was dead. And his bullet-riddled body was something she did not want to see.

The door opened at their approach, and the woman Aaron had introduced as Abigail stepped out. She held a military-looking rifle, and seemed quite comfortable with it in her callused hands. She said to the man in the lead, "There was one more. Where is he?"

"Fish food," came the reply.

The woman nodded and looked directly at Jenny, as if to gauge the effect of this exchange, and Jenny made her face stone. She was determined to give this woman nothing. As if she'd erected a shield, she wouldn't even allow herself to think about Aaron now. For Waaboo, she held herself together. She had to be there, in each moment, be vigilant and alert. She had to watch for any opportunity to act, because if she didn't find a way to change the direction everything was headed, they would, all of them—she and Waaboo and Stephen and Rainy—end up as outlines in the wild grass.

As to the why of it, she had no idea, and it didn't matter. Someone was going to die, that was the only truth important at the moment. She would do her best to make sure that no one else she cared about was among them, even if it meant sacrificing her own life. She was fully prepared to act and to die.

"Bring them in." The woman turned and disappeared inside.

Stephen hesitated. Jenny glanced at his face and saw his fear of what lay inside the cabin, a dread even greater than her own. Her brother's love of Meloux ran deep and possessed mysterious qualities that Jenny sensed but couldn't exactly give a name to. She understood only too well that the loss of the old man would be devastating to him. Rainy was ahead of them, and although Jenny couldn't see her face, she could read in the body language of Meloux's great-niece—the slump of her shoulders, the bow of her head, the deep breath she took before entering—that she, too, dreaded what she was about to see.

The tall man who'd led them stepped aside and ushered them in. He was about to follow when the woman turned back to him and said, "You stay outside, Gabriel. I want Joshua in here to see this."

The willowy, brooding young man who'd brought up the rear looked at Abigail, as if confused and reluctant, but at last he obeyed. He stepped inside and stood beside the woman. The other man, the one the woman had called Gabriel, remained outside, as if to stand watch.

Jenny was surprised and overjoyed by what she discovered in the cabin: Meloux, still alive. He sat in one of his handmade birch-wood chairs, facing them but with his eyes on the woman, Abigail. Jenny could see, along his left cheekbone and jawline, the darkening from subcutaneous bleeding. Not exactly a bruise yet, but it promised to become one, huge and ugly. His hands were bound with duct tape.

"Henry!" Stephen cried with relief.

The old Mide glanced their way, and although he didn't smile, there was a light in his brown eyes, evidence of his pleasure in seeing them all.

A little whine came from the other side of the room. Jenny saw a trail of blood across the floor. In the shadow under Meloux's bunk lay Walleye, licking what looked like a long bullet graze across his haunch.

"Who are you?" Rainy demanded.

"Abigail Hornett," the woman replied. "This is my son Joshua. My other son, Gabriel, is outside."

"Church of the Seven Trumpets," Stephen said.

"We almost met once," she said to him with mock pleasantry, "but you were using the commode, as I recall."

"What do you want with us?" Jenny asked.

"Nothing with you. I just want the baby."

Waaboo began to cry, perhaps in response to the arctic chill in the woman's voice but also, perhaps, because he was hungry.

"Shut him up," the woman said.

Jenny lifted Waaboo from the ice chest.

"Take a look at your spawn," the woman said to her son. "Another disgusting, misshapen creature from your loins."

Joshua Hornett glanced at the child, then looked away, as if ashamed.

"I said shut him up," the woman lashed at Jenny.

Jenny held Waaboo against her breast and rocked him and cooed to him, but he wouldn't be calmed. She could see the Hornett woman's growing irritation and was afraid of what she might do to Waaboo. She was about to try offering him her breast when Meloux spoke for the first time since they'd entered the cabin. He began to sing, an Ojibwe chant whose words Jenny didn't understand. In a few moments, Waaboo had quieted.

"What were you singing?" the Hornett woman asked.

"I told him that he is a gift to us from the Great Mystery, and that he is loved, and that there is nothing he has to be afraid of."

"The Great Mystery?" the woman responded coldly. "You mean God."

"I have heard it called that name," Meloux replied.

"How did you find us?" Stephen broke in. His tone was angry, threatening. Which was dangerous, Jenny thought. They all needed to be clearheaded.

"Maybe it was God that led us to you," Joshua Hornett said in a mocking tone.

Abigail shot her son a killing glare, and he lost his smirk and looked away.

"Are you all right, Uncle Henry?" Rainy asked.

"It was only a pistol whipping," the woman said dismissively.

Jenny saw Meloux's old Winchester leaning against the wall. On the floor around it, she spotted three cartridges that were still whole and the brass from three spent cartridges. Half the rounds had fired. And, apparently, two of those had found their targets. Meloux had done a remarkable job in covering their backs.

"You want the child," Rainy said. "Why?"

With a brooding look, Joshua Hornett said, "For the same reason she killed Lily. Our little freak there is the key to something Noah Smalldog stole from us."

"That's enough," Abigail snapped. "We have what we came for. It's time to end this and be gone. Call your brother in, Joshua."

Before Joshua could move, the cabin door opened, and Gabriel Hornett stepped quickly in.

"Abigail?"

"What is it?"

"Someone in the trees out there. Have a look." He handed her a pair of field glasses. "On the trail back to the county road."

The Hornett woman stepped into the doorway and directed the field glasses across the meadow.

"What is it?" Joshua asked.

"A cop," she said.

"Just one?"

"Where there's one, there are others," she replied. "Joshua, take a position in those rocks to the west. We'll give them a cross fire, if it comes to that."

The youngest Hornett studied the shadowy woods on the far side of the meadow. "If they're already in position out there, they'll cut me down before I get halfway to those rocks."

"Then go out the back window, like these people did, and stay in the trees along the shoreline."

"And then what?"

"Open fire if you have to," his mother replied.

"And when they fire back?"

"Die, if that's what God asks of you. Are you afraid to die? Is your soul unprepared?" She gave him a stern look. "Jesus knows your heart. If there's doubt, he sees it. Do you doubt, Joshua?"

"You, inside the cabin! This is the Tamarack County sheriff. You are surrounded. Put down your weapons and come outside with your hands up."

The words, amplified by a bullhorn, came from the woods across the meadow. Jenny recognized the voice of Sheriff Marsha Dross, and her heart leaped at this glimmer of hope.

The woman didn't take her eyes off the son she'd ordered into the rocks around Meloux's fire ring. "Do you doubt, Joshua?" she demanded.

His face glistened with sweat. He stared into her unblinking blue eyes. "Hell, yes, I doubt. And I'm not going out there."

"I'll go, Abigail," the other son said.

The woman lifted the rifle that she held, fitted the butt against her shoulder, and aimed the barrel at her son's heart. "Either you do as I've told you, Joshua, or I'll send you to hell myself."

"Abigail," Gabriel Hornett said softly but firmly. "We need to be together in this. We need Josh right now. I'll go to the rocks. It'll be all right. If shooting begins, I'll keep the police occupied, and you two take the baby and go out the back way."

Abigail didn't respond to her elder son, and Jenny thought she would surely blow Joshua's heart right out of his chest. Finally the woman lowered her rifle. "You're right, Gabriel." She lifted her hand, palm open, in a kind of benediction. "Go with God's blessing and God's strength."

Gabriel Hornett slipped through the back window. He dashed to the cover of the aspens that lined the shore of Crow Point and disappeared among the foliage there.

The woman turned back to the others in the cabin. Jenny had expected to see a look of regret or, at the very least, deep concern for the safety of her son. Instead, what she saw was a passionate fire that seemed to light every feature of her hard, sharp face.

"And so it begins," Abigail Hornett said.

She spoke as if this was not at all an unexpected turn of events, or one that frightened her in the least.

FIFTY-THREE

Bullhorn in hand, Cork walked to the edge of the trees. In the shadow of the forest, beneath a fiery sunset sky, he took a position behind the trunk of a large red pine. Flanking him on either side were deputies who'd found their own protected positions and had their firearms trained on the cabin. Cork leaned enough to one side of the pine so that he could see Meloux's place without presenting a good target to anyone who might be sighting a rifle from there. He put the bullhorn to his lips. Before he spoke, he said a silent prayer: *Please, God, let this work. Please, God, let Meloux understand.*

He took a breath.

"Meloux!" he called into the bullhorn. *"Ishkode! Baashkiz!"*

He waited a moment, then spoke again.

"Ishkode! Baashkiz! Do you hear, Meloux? *Ishkode! Baashkiz!"*

He lowered the bullhorn, and there was nothing to do then but wait.

"What's he saying?" the woman demanded of Meloux. "What's this 'ish co-day' stuff?"

There were high clouds in the west. The sunset sky was a

brilliant red-orange blaze, and the clouds were on fire. The light of that conflagration poured into the cabin, burned across the floor, and lit Meloux as if he were a torch.

"It means 'fire,' " the old man replied.

"Fire? What's he talking about?"

Meloux looked calmly into her intense face. "Do you know the name our people are sometimes called by? Ojibwe. It means 'to pucker.' I have heard it said that the name was given to us by our enemies, because when we captured them and roasted their flesh, it puckered. That may be what he is talking about. He may be saying that, before this is finished, he will be roasting your flesh over a fire."

She gave him a frigid look of disbelief and impatience.

"Or," the old Mide went on, "it could be he is reminding me that inside each of us is a fire, which we call spirit or soul, that is a small spark of the fire that burns at the heart of the Great Mystery."

"The fire that is the wrath of God," the woman said, as if correcting him.

Meloux shook his head gently. "The Great Mystery or the Creator or Kitchimanidoo or God, or whatever name it is known by, is not a fire of anger or a fire that consumes. It is the fire of life. It is the heart whose burning sends out every spark that becomes the possibility of a living thing, great or small, good or evil."

The woman spoke, and each word was one hard stone laid against the next. "There is only one God, and he is not the God of heathens like you. He is a vengeful God, make no mistake. It's you, and all those like you, whose flesh will pucker in the fires of hell."

The old man appeared to think this over, then he shrugged. "There is another possibility. It may be that Corcoran O'Connor is simply speaking of the warrior's trial by fire."

"What's that?"

"A test of a warrior's spirit. A test of the strength given him by Kitchimanidoo." The old man smiled. "It would be a good test, the strength of your God against mine."

"What is this test?"

"Untie me, and I will show you."

She studied him and made no move to comply.

"Untie me, and we will test the strength of your faith against the strength of mine. Unless you are afraid that the spirit at the center of this old, beat-up body may be stronger than the spirit at the center of yours."

"It's a trick, Abigail," Joshua Hornett said.

"You have the rifles," Meloux pointed out. "If you believe it is a trick, you can shoot me any time you want."

Still the woman didn't move.

"You have killed in the name of what you call God," Meloux said. "Is it possible that the reason for your killing had nothing to do with God but simply a hatred that burns inside of you? Is that why you are afraid to test the strength of your spirit and of your belief? Is it possible that inside of you there is only ash and no spirit fire?"

The woman's face moved as if something under her skin was alive. Her eyebrows twitched, and her temples pulsed, and her jaw clenched and unclenched. Finally she said, "Cut him loose, Joshua." She leaned toward Meloux, and when she spoke, it was pure poison. "When this is finished, I will, myself, cut out your heart."

"We need to think about this, Abigail," her son pleaded.

"I said cut him loose, Joshua. Do it! I'll keep the others covered."

Reluctantly, Hornett set his rifle against the door, snapped open the pouch on his belt, and brought out a folded knife. He opened the blade and crossed to where Meloux sat. The old man held up his hands, and Hornett cut the tape that bound the wrists. He stepped back quickly, as if afraid Meloux might spring at him. He put his knife away, returned to the door, and again took up his rifle.

"Watch the others," the woman told him. She set her own firearm against the cabin wall and said to Meloux, "What now?"

Meloux rose slowly. He walked to the stove in the middle of the room, where the light through the western window was strongest. He stood on one side and nodded for the woman to stand on the other. Rainy's pot of stew still simmered where it sat near the edge of the hot stove top.

Meloux said, "In the old days, in order to test the strength of their spirits, two warriors would face off over the glowing coals of a great fire. Each would hold a hand over the coals until one of them could no longer stand the heat. The last to take his hand away was the stronger spirit. And the longer his hand remained over the coals even after the other had withdrawn, the greater that spirit and the greater his name."

The woman looked down at the hot stove top, then up at Meloux. Without hesitation, she said, "Any time you're ready."

Meloux put out his hand and held it over the center of the stove, a quarter of an inch above the searing metal. The woman did the same.

It seemed to Jenny as if the cabin became a vacuum. There was no air, no movement, no sound, not even from little Waaboo. Her eyes were riveted to the stove and to the two people on either side of it, illuminated in the fiery glow of sunset. She saw that the woman trembled and her jaw was drawn taut, but her eyes were locked on the face of the old Mide, and her hand didn't waver from the place she held it. Jenny was surprised that the woman's belief, dark and angry and vengeful though it was, seemed to be the equal of Meloux's. They both stood with open palms above the stove, immobile, as if they were forged from the same insensate iron.

Then a smell assaulted Jenny's nose. The alarming and sweet aroma of scorched flesh.

In that same moment, the glass of the window in the western wall of the cabin shattered, and the woman collapsed where she stood. From beneath her on the cabin floor spread a glistening crimson pool fed by the dark red lake of her heart.

Waaboo began to wail.

Meloux lifted his hand from the stove top.

Joshua Hornett stood frozen, staring in horror and disbelief at his mother's body.

Stephen and Rainy, acting with a single mind, leaped on this last reluctant soldier from the Church of the Seven Trumpets. They tumbled onto the floor in a squirming heap. Hornett struggled to throw them off, but they fought against him fiercely.

Then Meloux was standing above them, the woman's rifle in his hands. He spoke in a voice of such clear authority that all motion stopped instantly.

"Enough. It is finished. Be still." When he saw that his words had been heeded, Meloux said, "Take his rifle, Stephen, and hand it to me."

Stephen, who already had a firm grip on the firearm, yanked it from Hornett's grasp and delivered it to Meloux. The old man opened the cabin door and stood at the threshold. He flung first one rifle then the other far out into the meadow grass. After that, he lifted his arms and crossed and uncrossed them several times above his head in a sign that all was now safe.

Through the doorway, Jenny saw figures in blue Kevlar emerge from the woods and begin to cross the meadow. Waaboo screamed, and she held him against her and spoke to him quietly. "Don't cry, little rabbit. Don't cry. It's all over. We're safe now."

Stephen stood poised above Hornett, prepared to battle him again should he rise. It wasn't necessary. The man lay on the floor and stared upward, dazed and dumb in defeat.

"Uncle Henry, let me see your hand," Rainy said. She went to Meloux and looked at the palm he'd held over the stove.

"We need to get you to a hospital," she said firmly.

"Niece," Meloux replied, "have I taught you nothing about healing?" Then he smiled. "Two hours ago, I thought I was dead. Yet here I am alive. What is a little puckered flesh to me?"

"*Mishomis*," Stephen said. "I never heard of that warrior's test."

"Until the words came from my mouth," the old man said, "neither had I."

Jenny heard her father call from outside. A moment later, he was in the doorway, standing next to Henry and Rainy, with the sheriff's officers pressing in at his back.

"Thank God you knew what I meant, Henry," he said.

"What *did* you mean, Dad?" Stephen asked.

First his father gave him a powerful hug, then explained. "*Ishkode*, one kind of fire, the kind that burns in Henry's fire ring. *Baashkiz*, another kind of fire. To fire a gun."

"Your Ojibwe needs work, Corcoran O'Connor," Meloux said. "But I understood." He lowered his eyes to the woman dead on his floor. "It is good for us that she did not."

Her father came at last to where Jenny sat with Waaboo crying in her arms.

"You and our little guy, you're both okay?"

"*Our* little guy?" she said.

"Whatever it takes, Jenny, we'll give this child a home, I promise." He looked the cabin over, then asked, "Aaron?"

"He tried to lead them away from us. He didn't have to, but he did." She shook her head and said at last the words that, because of the circumstances and her own need to stay focused, she hadn't even allowed herself to think. "He's dead. They killed him, Dad."

Tears spilled from her eyes so suddenly that she was caught by surprise. She couldn't tell if it was grief for Aaron. Or relief at being saved. Or her deep fear, despite her father's assurance, that now that the danger was past, she might very soon have to give up this child whom she loved as if he were her own.

She cried so hard that she couldn't speak. She held so tightly to her baby that no one could have taken him from her.

EPILOGUE

November arrived, and there was not yet snow in Tamarack County or in any part of northern Minnesota or across the border in southern Manitoba and Ontario. This was unusual, though not unheard of, and it greatly simplified the travel of those who'd come from Lake of the Woods for the Naming Ceremony.

Crow Point that afternoon lay under a sky completely covered by low clouds the color of an old nickel. There was no precipitation in the forecast, however, and hardly a breath of wind. Although the temperature hovered just below fifty degrees, there was a festive feel among those gathered in the meadow in front of Meloux's cabin. The air was redolent with the aromas of fry bread and savory meats and hot dish made from wild rice. Rose and Rainy had been cooking on the woodstove all morning, and many of the guests had brought food to share as well. Tables had been set in the meadow and were already filled with casserole dishes and salads and desserts waiting to be served onto paper plates.

Smoke drifted up from beyond the outcropping of rock near the end of the point, and at a given signal everyone who milled about the meadow made their way in that direction. Rose walked with Mal and Rainy and Tom Kretsch, who was still recovering from a bullet wound to his right leg and used a cane. Stephen and Jenny and Anne and Cork were already at the fire, along with Henry Meloux. Amos Powassin was with them, standing next to his old friend, smiling blindly.

For nearly two months, Jenny and Cork had dealt with the bureaucracies on both sides of the border. Because it was impossible to prove the baby's true birthplace, and because the mother's last known residence had been Stump Island, the Canadian authorities finally agreed that they had no authority over or responsibility for Lily Smalldog's child. At which point, it fell to the Tamarack County social services to deal fully with the disposition of the baby. At first, there'd been some question whether things would be complicated by the Indian Child Welfare Act. But Lily Smalldog's tribal affiliation would have been with the Reserve 37 Ojibwe, where she'd never actually been an enrolled member, and so the court chose to treat her case as a routine adoption. The baby's father, Joshua Hornett, was sitting in the maximum security facility at St. Cloud awaiting trial on a number of federal charges. He'd been more than cooperative in signing the consent to adoption, in which he gave up all parental rights. A dozen members of the Church of the Seven Trumpets were there with him, also awaiting trial. Seth Bascombe was being held separately, locked away in the correctional facility in Oak Park Heights, mostly for his own safety, because in exchange for leniency, he'd agreed to testify against his former cohorts.

Most fortunate was that, from the beginning, Tamarack County Judge Randalyn Nickelsen had overseen Waaboo's welfare. She'd known Cork and his family forever, and when she understood the whole story of what they'd all risked for the child, she'd done her best to expedite the adoption process. She'd signed the county's petition for protective services for Waaboo and had placed him temporarily in Jenny's care. She saw to it that the requisite home study was completed with due haste and, in the end, had been the one to grant Jenny's petition for adoption. Within two months of her return to Tamarack County, Jenny had, legally, become a mother.

The Sunday before the gathering on Crow Point, the child had been baptized at St. Agnes in Aurora. In the christening, Father Green had used the boy's legal name, Aaron Smalldog O'Connor. The Naming Ceremony on Crow Point was an important Ojibwe ritual, one that would complete the process of bringing the baby into a family that embraced and celebrated its mixed heritage.

The only egregious absence at the gathering was that of Noah Smalldog, who'd been killed in the exchange of gunfire on Oak Island. The O'Connors and Rose and Mal had been present at his burial on Windigo Island and had watched as the Ojibwe there put tobacco between his fingers and placed a spirit dish in the coffin and closed the lid and lowered it into the earth. Now, on this overcast November day, as she gathered with the others around Meloux's fire ring, Rose couldn't help thinking about the observation Amos Powassin had made weeks earlier amid all the destruction on Lake of the Woods. He'd said that in everything good was the potential for evil, and in everything evil the potential for good. She had known Noah Smalldog for only a very short time. He'd held a knife to her throat and drawn her blood, and she'd been certain that he would have killed her without hesitation if doing so would have served his purpose. He was a man filled with anger, who had no use for *chimooks*, yet he'd willingly sacrificed himself for her and the others. And she thought about the terrible storm that had begun it all, the derecho. It had been a great destroyer, but it had also, in the end, been responsible for beautiful little Waaboo entering their lives. And last, she thought about Abigail Hornett and the Church of the Seven Trumpets, who'd taken the words of a man of peace and found in them justification for horrible violence.

It was just as Amos Powassin had said: Kitchimanidoo, the Great Creator, God—they were all different names for the same thing, which was creation in all its aspects and all its possibility.

The smoke from Meloux's fire smelled of sage and cedar. A hush fell over those gathered on Crow Point, and the old Mide began the ceremony, offering tobacco to the four corners of the sky, speaking in each direction the Ojibwe name of Jenny's boy: Waaboozoons.

In a whisper, Rainy explained to Rose and Mal and Tom Kretsch that the Naming Ceremony honored First Man, who'd named everything in this world. Speaking the child's name in the four directions allowed the spirit world to recognize this new person and accept him.

When that was done, Meloux addressed the gathering. His words were Ojibwe, and Rainy gave her companions a rough translation of what he said:

"I am an old man. In my life, I have been asked to name many children. The names have always come to me after fasting and dreaming, which is the old way. This child's name came in another way. A strange way. Maybe it is the new way. It was delivered to Silver Fox, Stephen O'Connor, in a diner in Koochiching"—which Rainy explained was the Ojibwe name for International Falls—"and he has told me that there was, most definitely, no fasting involved." Meloux grinned at Stephen, and those gathered around the fire laughed.

Meloux grew solemn again. "In the beginning of the journey of this child, or any child, is the understanding that each foot will fall into a different track. Happiness on one side, sadness on the other. Pleasure and pain. Wisdom and folly. With each step, this child will learn that there is in him the possibility of great good and also great evil. It is a serious matter, guiding this child along the path of right living.

"Jennifer O'Connor." Meloux now spoke in English. "Will you instruct Waaboozoons in *ninoododadiwin*, which is the way of harmony, the path between the two worlds of possibility—good and evil—created by the Great Mystery?"

"I will do my best," Jenny promised.

"Have you chosen *we-ehs* for Waaboozoons?"

We-ehs, Rainy explained, were like godparents, responsible for the child's upbringing in many ways.

"I have," Jenny said. "Anne O'Connor and Stephen O'Connor."

Meloux nodded, as if satisfied.

Jenny handed her baby to Anne, who kissed the child and said, "Waaboozoons." She handed the baby to Stephen, who did the same and then returned Waaboo to his mother.

"This child," Meloux said to the whole gathering, "this little rabbit, came into the world and survives because of the great sacrifice of others. But he owes them no debt. In his time, in his turn, he, too, will be asked to sacrifice. We live by the grace of Kitchimanidoo and the goodness of one human being toward another. That is all I have to say."

Under the old-nickel sky, they filed through the rocks and returned to the meadow, and the feasting began.

Rose lingered near Meloux's cabin, watching her family and the guests celebrate. Jenny stood in the meadow holding Waaboo, with Anne and Stephen beside her, all of them beaming. Cork and Rainy Bisonette walked together, involved in a lively conversation, and Cork was smiling, as if the happiest of men. Rose knew Jo would have been fine with all of this. The Great Empty that had come with her sister's death would never quite be filled, but all around it lay the possibility of peace for those she'd left behind.

Mal came to her with a filled plate in his hand.

"Happy?" he asked.

"Immensely," she answered.

He scanned the gathering. "You've got a great family, Rose, wonderful children."

"I know."

He smiled and looked up at the thick clouds and said, as if caught by surprise, "A beautiful day."

"A beautiful life," she replied.

And she kissed him, boundless in her appreciation and her love.